BOOKS BY BARRY MATHIAS

THE ANCIENT BLOODLINES TRILOGY

BOOK ONE
THE POWER IN THE DARK

BOOK TWO
SHADOW OF THE SWORDS

BOOK THREE
KEEPER OF THE GRAIL

THE CELTIC DREAMS TRILOGY

BOOK ONE
CELTIC DREAMS OF GLORY

BOOK TWO
IN THE ASHES OF A DREAM

BOOK THREE
THE FINAL DREAM

EBB TIDE
COLLECTION OF POETRY

WOLF HOWL
A COLLECTION OF SHORT STORIES

PUBLISHING HOUSE

Canada V0R 1X4

For information and bulk orders, please go to
www.agiopublishing.com
Visit this book's website at www.barrymathias.net

ISBN 978-1-927755-88-4 (paperback)
ISBN 978-1-927755-89-1 (ebook)

Cataloguing information available from Library and
Archives Canada.

10 9 8 7 6 5 4 3

THE FINAL DREAM

BOOK THREE OF **THE CELTIC DREAMS TRILOGY**

BARRY MATHIAS

Agio
PUBLISHING HOUSE

DEDICATION

To Clare

LIST OF CHARACTERS
(as they appear in the story)

Earl Reginal de Braose – Norman Marcher Lord of Hereford

Earl William Fitzosbern – Second most powerful man in England, cousin to King William I

King William the First – known as William the Conqueror of England

Lord Gwriad ap Griffith – Welsh Lord at Aberteifi, husband to the presumed deceased Lady Angharad

Lord Dafydd ap Griffith – husband to the late Lady Teifryn; younger brother to Lord Gwriad

Lord Jon – Lord Gwriad's adopted son

Prince Anarwd ap Tewdwr – Prince of Morgannwg and protector of Gwent

Derryth – Local Wise Woman and Lord Dafydd's lover

Davis – Soldier in the Castle at Aberteifi

Megan – Young kitchen servant, friend of Lord Jon

Tegwen – Daughter of Lord Dafydd and the late Lady Teifryn

Megan senior – Cook in charge of the Castle's kitchens

Gavin – Older soldier in the Castle who becomes Sergeant

Owen – Young soldier

Penn – Sergeant, senior soldier in the Castle

Father Williams – Priest for Llanduduch, friend of the Griffith family

Deri and Anwen – Young adults from Llanduduch

Iago – Elder son of Pritchard the Miller

Efan – Younger brother to Iago

Uncle David – Inn keeper and brother of Pritchard

Aunt Edith – Wife of David

Alys – Nurse and friend to Tegwen

Gomer ap Griffith – Former Lord of Aberteifi and father of Jon

Evan and Morris – Fishermen from Llanduduch

Lord Edwin ap Tewdwr – Cousin to Prince Anarwd and Lord of Gwent

Prince Alun – Only son of Prince Anarwd

Bethan – Weaver, engaged to Idris

Gwenllian – Bethan's daughter

Osian – Peasant

Idris – Blacksmith, engaged to Bethan

Angwen – Mute friend of Bethan (the original Angharad)

Sir Maelgwn ap Owen – General and friend of Prince Anarwd

Hywel, Rhodri and Gwynn – Soldiers in the Castle

Emrys – Steward

Emlyn – Young soldier

Adeliza de Tosny – Wife of Earl Fitzosbern

Jennin – Lady companion to Adeliza

Bishop Odo – Brother of King William

Prince Maredudd – Ruler of Deheubarth

Rees – Jon's second-in-command

Madog – Women molester

Michel – Young Norman Officer

Henri – Norman Officer

Sir Medwin – Prince Anarwd's aide-de-camp

Prince Eoin – First cousin of Prince Maredudd of Deheubarth

Brin and Morgan – Medics

Gwynn – Prosperous sheep farmer

Morgana – Wife of Gwynn

Wynny – Iago's girlfriend who becomes his wife, daughter to Gwynn
and Morgana

Eadric the Wild – Saxon Lord

Lord Iestyn ap Llywarch – Replacement for Lord Edwin

Clovis – in charge of intelligence for Earl de Braose

Marged – peasant woman who believes Angwen is a witch

Afanen – urchin child

WELSH PATRONYMIC NAMING

In early times, the Welsh family name changed through the male line with each generation. A son was given a first name and linked to his father. Hence *Gruffydd ap Llywelyn* was *Gruffydd son of Llywelyn*, and his son *Cydweli* became *Cydweli ap Gruffydd*. The word *ap* is a contraction of the Welsh word *mab*, which means *son*. Occasionally, some women were given their full family name: *Angharad* might be known as *Angharad ferch Cadell ap Bleddyn*, or *Angharad daughter of Cadell son of Bleddyn*.

Over the years, and for reasons including outside pressures, the Welsh took on continuing family names such as Jenkins, Jones, etc.

In this novel, a woman is known generally by her first name and occasionally by her skill or job, as in *Derryth the Wise Woman*.

I have used the traditional patronymic naming for people of rank, and a first name only for peasants and slaves. In some cases, characters have two names, such as *Prince Anarwd ap Tewdwr*, when introduced for the first time.

ANCIENT WELSH PLACE NAMES USED IN THIS STORY
WITH MODERN NAMES WHERE APPROPRIATE

ABERTEIFI: now known as Cardigan

BRECON: Small town on the River Usk. A natural gathering place

CAERDYDD: Cardiff, now capital of Wales

CAERFYRDDIN: ancient name for Carmarthen

CEREDIGION: kingdom in mid-west Wales, including the village of Aberteifi

CWM: Small Welsh village near the border

DEHEUBARTH: ancient name for region of south-west Wales

GWENT: important kingdom in south-east Wales, adjoining Morgannwg

GWYNETH: the most important of the Welsh kingdoms, situated in the north-west, including modern Snowdonia

HEREFORD: Important Saxon/Norman town within a day's ride of the Welsh border

LLANDUDUCH: also called St. Dogmaels. Village on the Teifi River

MORGANNWG: kingdom in south Wales

NGHENARTH FALLS: Important crossing of the River Teifi

OFFA'S DYKE: ancient earth barrier constructed by Offa, Saxon King of Mercia, approximately 770–790 AD. Stretched from estuary of River Dee in the north to River Wye in the south. Separated Wales from Saxon lands.

POWYS: powerful kingdom, second to Gwyneth in mid-eastern Wales

RHYD-Y-GROES: site of famous battle near the border with Saxon England

SAINT DAVIDS: Cathedral in south-west Wales

YNYS MON: Anglesey. Large island off north-west Wales. Ancient Druid centre. Teifryn's birth place.

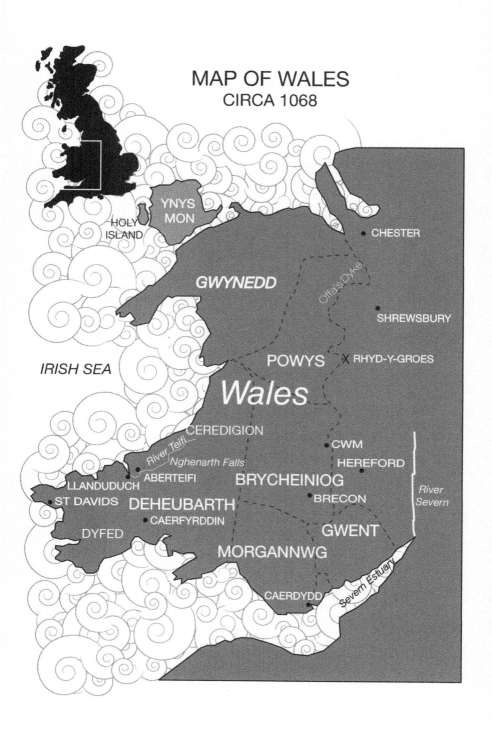

MAP OF WALES
CIRCA 1068

YNYS MON

HOLY ISLAND

CHESTER

GWYNEDD

Offa's Dyke

SHREWSBURY

POWYS   X RHYD-Y-GROES

Wales

IRISH SEA

CEREDIGION

River Teifi

CWM

Nghenarth Falls

HEREFORD

ABERTEIFI

BRYCHEINIOG

River Severn

LLANDUDUCH

ST DAVIDS   DEHEUBARTH

BRECON

CAERFYRDDIN

DYFED

GWENT

MORGANNWG

CAERDYDD

Severn Estuary

PROLOGUE 1067

A t dawn an elderly shepherd, walking across a low hill in the Welsh border country, observed a small army of armoured horsemen galloping down the narrow path that meandered through the bare valley below. He stared. "Normans?" he gasped, and began to run to raise the alarm.

For as long as the locals on the border could remember, their enemy had been the Saxons, but recently new dangers had been mentioned and these soldiers might be them. "Normans! God help us."

The Normans were well armed, with chainmail hauberks, iron helmets and long swords or maces, and each carried a short, decorated shield. They had come to kill, plunder and rape with the encouragement and blessing of Reginal de Braose, the recently appointed Earl of Hereford. Earl Reginal was subservient to Earl William Fitzosbern, the second most powerful man in England, and cousin to King William the First, known as the Conqueror. In the King's absence, Fitzosbern ruled the country. Fitzosbern had sub-divided the security along the Welsh-English border to a number of Norman nobles known as the Marcher Lords. They wanted to impress their Earl, and this was why Reginal de Braose, Marcher Lord for the area of Hereford and Gloucester, had ordered his men on a punitive raid to establish his clear authority in the area.

Although new to the border country, these men were hardened mercenaries who, since the Battle of Hastings nearly two years before, had helped to quash the various uprisings that had occurred around England. They had fought in the boggy lands north-east of London, in the dense forests around York and the lush pastures of the west, but this was the first time these men had invaded Welsh territory.

A scout had reported a small village ahead that was celebrating a market, making it an ideal time for a raid, and their officer promised them loot. When he could see the smoke from the village's fires, he pointed to a small track that appeared to circle the village to the left. Without breaking pace, a large soldier riding a black horse peeled off from the main body of cavalry and, followed by a dozen others, raced off to prevent any of the Welsh from escaping from the back of their doomed village.

"Keep together! Kill everyone!" the officer yelled as they charged towards the unsuspecting villagers. "Burn the place down!"

With blood pounding in their ears, they bared their teeth as their war horses thundered over the recently drying ground. The Welsh were their enemy, and they would show no mercy.

Ahead of them was a motley collection of hovels with a few stronger wooden buildings jumbled around a wide green where the villagers had set up stalls, makeshift fenced spaces for animals, and some improvised tables. There was a lively dance taking place in the centre of the market with string instruments and drums providing the music, and many villagers and young people from distant farms were enjoying the festivity. In this pleasant atmosphere few of them carried weapons other than small knives and sheep poles, and their concentration was on the dancing and the beat of the drums.

There had been reports from travelling merchants that the Normans, the new invaders of England, might try to capture Welsh lands to add to their conquest. "We have to be prepared," some villagers had argued, and others suggested: "We should train the young men, have a rota of sentries and build a look-out tower." But the council of the village of Cwm, while giving nodding agreement to these suggestions, had done nothing, preferring to leave it to others. Everyone knew that life as a farmer was hard, and taking young men away from their work for something that might just be fear-mongering was not to be encouraged.

The horsemen had almost reached the small, bunched crowd of Welsh peasants before a warning was yelled. People panicked and ran screaming in all directions, seeking protection behind their flimsy stalls as the foreign soldiers rode into their midst killing indiscriminately. Their war horses were trained to crush people under their heavy, iron-capped hooves, and this increased the terror of the attack and added to the confusion.

The village centre, a scene of joy only moments before, was suddenly a nightmare of deadly confusion, with the peasants pushing and shoving each other as they tried to escape the implacable Normans who cut down anyone who came within their reach, no matter what their age or sex. Some Welshmen managed to arm themselves, while others used poles and pieces of their stalls to fight back. But their bravery was soon extinguished, and the soldiers began to force their way into the small buildings, looking for loot and women and setting light to the thatch roofs.

Earl Reginal had stopped his horse on a piece of higher ground, from where he could watch and control the attack. If there had been any real fighting, he might have stayed engaged, but he was not prepared to involve himself in the slaughter of peasants. That was what he paid the soldiers for.

"Check the end of the village and get the job done," he ordered an officer. "I don't want to waste time on this place."

The cavalry officer yelled for others to join him as he rode towards the smithy and small pub. Their unexpected attack had resulted in a bloodbath in the market, and he was both pleased but also disappointed: it had been too easy. Now, as he led a group of his men towards the biggest buildings in this meager village, he hoped for some opposition worthy of his attention. But here too, when they burst into the pub, there was little resistance as most of the drinkers were still unaware of the attack occurring in the market, and a few of the peasants were already well into their cups. Although some Welsh fought back with surprising vigour, the unprotected men with only knives and poles were no match for the well-armed and armoured soldiers.

Unlike most of the surrounding hovels, the pub had two doors, and while his customers died bravely, the rotund landlord and his wife and baby were able to escape out of the back of the building and hide in the surrounding forest.

The attack on the forge next door was the only place where the Normans were offered any real resistance. The blacksmith possessed swords that he had made some years ago when he had joined the Welsh attack on the Saxon town of Shrewsbury, and he and his adult son were able to fight back. But although they managed, with skill and bravery, to kill and injure a few surprised Normans, their lack of armour and the overwhelming numbers against them proved deadly.

Soon, the whole village was in flames. The soldiers ensured there were no survivors, having previously taken their lust out on the women. Finally, they rounded up any animals worth taking and slaughtered the rest. They loaded their horses with any meager loot they could find, and moved slowly back to where Earl Reginal de Braose waited impatiently. The Earl was annoyed by their unexpected losses; peasants were not supposed to be any threat to his experienced, well-armed soldiers.

Meanwhile, other Norman attacks were occurring nearby, directed against isolated farms and settlements, with the aim of increasing the fear of future attacks. Earl Reginal was keen to order a regrouping and a return across the border, for although it had been a useful day in spite of a few losses, he sensed he would come to regret his adventure.

CHAPTER ONE

As he stared down from his battlements at the turbulent river below, Lord Gwriad looked a picture of gloom and despondency. It had rained incessantly for the past few days, filling the River Teifi, turning the local roads and tracks into quagmires, and preventing him from his promised visits to the local hamlets of Ceredigion to collect the yearly taxes. It was not the delay in receiving the money and produce that depressed him, but simply the missing of a chance to travel with a purpose, rather than wandering aimlessly around the castle, annoying the kitchen staff and interfering with the smooth organization of the guards.

Since their return nearly a year ago, he and his younger brother Lord Dafydd had reacted in different ways. Dafydd had immediately immersed himself in the monetary aspects of the running of the castle, and although Jon, Gwriad's adopted son, had efficiently managed the castle in their absence, it gave Dafydd great pleasure to check everything minutely. Also, unlike Gwriad, Dafydd had a woman to return to.

Everyone in the castle knew the story of how the two Lords had lost their wives two years before, when the Saxon Harold Godwinson, later to become the short-lived King of England, had unexpectedly invaded South Wales and as he retreated had encouraged his men to kill any Welsh people they encountered. Unaware of this mini-invasion, Gwriad and Dafydd were on a visit to Prince Anarwd ap Tewdwr, ruler of Morgannwg. They became separated from their wives and it was hours later that Dafydd had discovered the body of his murdered wife, Teifryn. However, in spite of an intense search, the body of Angharad, Gwriad's wife, had never been found. After months of mourning, the brothers had decided to dedicate their lives to getting revenge on Harold, especially after he became King of England, and had journeyed to London pretending to be on a pilgrimage. Their unlikely plan failed, but when the Normans defeated the Saxon King at the Battle of Hastings, the brothers had returned to Wales with a sense of elation.

The heady sense of their revenge, albeit without their involvement, lasted for only a few months after their return to their castle at Aberteifi in South-West Wales, and slowly a sense of emptiness and futility had begun to consume Gwriad, especially when he remembered his volatile earlier life. He was the elder brother, and had always been the hunter, the fighter and the womanizer. His former wife, Angharad, had often commented that he was never happier than when he was fighting or hunting, and both had a reputation for being sexually outrageous. In contrast, his younger brother avoided hunting and womanizing, and was never drunk or violent. Although a man of learning and intellectual pursuits, Dafydd had always supported his older brother, and when fighting was unavoidable had demonstrated a quiet heroism and a ferocity that was surprising to both of them.

Hunting was still Gwriad's main passion, and he also enjoyed getting out and visiting the communities within his territories, the lands he had inherited from his uncle. But during the winter and early spring months few landowners came to visit and his brother was a poor drinking companion. He was also aware that he had lost the urge to bed any of the local women, although many would have been willing. His wife, Angharad, had never seemed to notice his fleeting passions, although as far as he knew she had never been attracted to other men. Best not to think about her, it was too painful.

Gwriad, absent-mindedly, examined the mortar between the stones of the parapet above the main gate, and wondered how long it would be before the castle needed refurbishing. He blew out his lips; his adopted son, Jon, could take care of that when the time came, probably with Dafydd's help. He began to pace along the battlements, and noticed a horseman approaching the gate who cantered up to the guards on a tired horse and exchanged some banter. He did not appear to be in a hurry and Gwriad assumed he was visiting on a local matter. Jon could sort that out.

He began to pace aimlessly around the walls, ignoring a young soldier on duty who was anxious to avoid attention when his Lord was in one of his dark moods. Some days the Lord could be friendly and amiable, but when he was silent and grim-faced it was best to keep out of his way.

From the corner of his eye, Gwriad was aware of a woman approaching the castle up the steep slope to the gate. She walked with an easy, swaying action that was like a magnet to male eyes. She saw him on the wall and waved, her smile friendly and seductive. A sexual woman, who exuded confidence and charm.

"Derryth!" he called, a smile instantly replacing his former scowl.

"My Lord Gwriad!" she called back and waved joyfully. "The weather will be lovely from now on."

If another woman had said that, it would have been interpreted as small talk, but from Derryth, the local Wise Woman, it was taken as a prophecy. The soldiers rushed to open the small gate into the castle; she was a popular visitor as well as being Lord Dafydd's mistress; an open secret among the soldiers and servants.

Gwriad watched as she crossed the inner bailey, skillfully avoiding the muck and horse droppings on her way to the keep. The soldier on duty outside the thick, oak doorway gave her a small bow and was keen to open the door. As she passed inside, the guard was smiling.

"What a woman," Gwriad muttered. He reflected on the fact that he did not envy his brother having such a woman as his mistress, it was more a feeling of admiration. In his younger days he would have called out some suggestive invitation, but since the loss of his wife, two years ago, he sensed he had lost the sexual desire that had been a cornerstone of his personality. Although, when he thought carefully, his libido had lessened following his serious head injury in a battle with the Saxons three years ago.

"Do you have a girlfriend, Davis?" he said, smiling in a man-to-man fashion.

"Oh, yes, m'Lord," the soldier responded noting the Lord's change of mood; it was like the sun had broken through a dark cloud.

"From Aberteifi?"

"Oh no, m'Lord, from Llanduduch," Davis laughed. "All the good-looking girls in Aberteifi have been taken."

"All the good-looking older women have been taken as well," Gwriad observed as he glanced towards the keep.

"Yes, m'Lord," he said respectfully. He knew the Lord was referring to Derryth, the Wise Woman, and did not want to say anything that might be misinterpreted. "Llanduduch might be just a small fishing village, but it turns out some pretty girls." As he finished the sentence, he realized he might have gone too far.

"You mean like Megan, the girlfriend of my son, Lord Jon?" Gwriad asked, his voice cold and threatening.

There were times when Davis wished he could sink into a hole. "Well... um..." his voice trailed away.

Gwriad suddenly guffawed. "Don't worry, Davis, I won't tell Lord Jon you fancy his girlfriend!" He began to descend to the courtyard, shaking his head with mirth and leaving the relieved soldier to shuffle uncomfortably on the battlements. As he walked across the courtyard, Gwriad was interested to see Jon marching towards him from the direction of the stables with a very purposeful gait.

"My Lord!" he called out, as he was expected to do in the public areas of the castle, "I have news."

It was like a breath of fresh air; perhaps something he could focus his mind on. Gwriad paused as his tall, adopted son approached. "Well?"

"We've had a message from Prince Anarwd: there has been a recent attack by Normans on a village near the border in lower Powys, and earlier a number of villages in the north-east of Brycheiniog have been destroyed and many Welsh families have been murdered." Jon spoke with a clear unemotional voice, but Gwriad could sense his anger. "Prince Anarwd has blamed a Norman Earl called Reginal de Braose, he's one of the new Marcher Lords."

"What do you think, Jon?"

"I think it's outrageous! They must be punished, or they will continue to attack us."

Gwriad nodded thoughtfully. "We don't have a standing army. What do you suggest?"

Jon knew his adopted father was testing him. "Prince Anarwd has an army. You and Lord Dafydd joined forces with him three years ago, and you raised an army that destroyed Shrewsbury and Earl Harold's palace. You defeated the Saxons in battle. They respected us after that. You and

Lord Dafydd must rally the country again and fight back! And I want to fight alongside you!"

Gwriad felt suddenly old. "Fighting is never without a price. You remember I was badly injured in that last battle? I took more than a year to recover." He rubbed his forehead, surprised that after all this time he still felt emotional. "Then, when we were making a visit to Prince Anarwd, Earl Harold made a revenge attack on Caerdydd and I and Lord Dafydd lost our wives...." He paused, took a deep breath and stared miserably at the ground. "I still don't know where my wife is buried." He spoke softly as though to himself.

Jon licked his lips and turned away to glare at Davis who was staring down from the battlements, showing obvious interest in the lively exchange. "Carry on, soldier!" he bellowed, causing David to quickly turn away and continue his patrol along the walls.

"Sorry," Jon said. "I didn't mean to criticize." He punched a fist into the palm of the other hand. "I just want to take a part in the defence of Wales. I know you have been involved in a number of battles with the Saxons and the Picts, so you must know how I feel?" He took a deep breath. "I need to get away from here for a while." He looked ill at ease. "I need to travel a bit and see some of the world."

Gwriad placed his hand on Jon's shoulder. "I do understand. I remember how I felt when I was your age. All young men feel the need to travel and to prove themselves on the battlefield, and defeat the enemy. But if you are lucky to survive, you come to realize that there is very little heroism and glory, just mud, boredom and life-altering injury. Very few men survive a war unscathed." He looked into Jon's animated face, "You know how I suffered."

"At that time, it was Saxons, now it's Normans. Things change, and each generation must defend itself." Jon straightened his shoulders and faced the man he revered. "Men of my age have little if any experience of how to fight. We rely on men like you and Lord Dafydd to lead us. If we don't defend our borders, the Normans will soon be besieging our castle. I want the chance to fight them!"

He took a deep breath, and on a less emotional note finished his message: "Prince Anarwd wants to retaliate this summer, and thinks we should mount an attack in force to show we are capable of fighting back.

He wants you and Lord Dafydd to contact him, once you have discussed it." He stuck out his jaw. "I know you'll support him, and I want to come with you."

There was a short pause as Gwriad chewed his lower lip reflectively. "You may be right, Jon. I'll consider what you've said." He looked carefully at the young man he had adopted, although if he were honest it was his wife Angharad who had really seen Jon's possibilities. This adopted son had come to them as the lowest servant in the kitchen, a boy who had grown up as little more than a slave to a cold-hearted old crone who had lived in his uncaring step-father's poor shack. On the death of his father he had been forced to find work at the castle. It was only later, and thanks to Angharad, that they had discovered that Jon was the illegitimate son of their late uncle, Lord Gomer ap Griffith, from whom they had inherited the castle.

"I still remember you as the thin, apologizing youth who knew nothing when you came to work in our kitchens." Gwriad smiled, "You've come a long way, Jon."

"I will always be grateful to you and Lady Angharad, and also to Father Williams." The animation faded from his face. "I've heard he's not in the best of health." He cleared his throat self-consciously. "I've been busy around the castle. I haven't visited him recently."

"I've arranged for the Wise Woman to keep an eye on him, and you are free to visit him whenever you like."

"Yes. Thank you, father," he paused. "I'll ride to Llanduduch this afternoon." He bowed and marched off to the stables, leaving Lord Gwriad staring contentedly after him. "Maybe that's what I need," he mused, "Jon's right, we must fight back. I'll talk it over with Dafydd," he chuckled, "when he's available." He glanced towards the stables, and placed a finger on his nose, deep in thought.

He strode across the yard with a bounce in his tread and bounded up the steps, causing the sentry to snap to attention and quickly open the door. Once inside, the cool of the Great Hall enveloped him. He stood in the shadows and gazed around; his eyes pausing on the weapons and flags that decorated the wall above the cavernous fireplace. A small fire smouldered in the ashes, as was the custom in the warmer months. In the winter it would be a roaring blaze around which people would choose to gather, but today the hall was empty and the servants were working elsewhere. A large hunting dog slept peacefully near the fire, another creature who could do with some exercise, he reflected.

By the side of the fireplace were two spinning wheels that neither he nor Dafydd had seen fit to move. When their wives had been alive, the hall was always full of life: the wives spinning, the wet nurse caring for Teifryn's daughter, Tegwen, and women coming and going. Now their castle lacked the softness and colour that women provided. It was true there was the wet nurse who had become Tegwen's personal guardian and friend, and Jon's supposed girlfriend, Megan, who worked in the kitchen. But, apart from old Megan, the chief cook, there were no other women of importance in the castle.

It was at this moment that the outline of a woman suddenly appeared at the top of the stairs leading to the rooms above. He straightened up with a start and for a brief moment he thought it was a ghost. He relaxed when he recognized Derryth the Wise Woman, his brother's acknowledged mistress, descending rapidly. From the shadows, he could see her face as it was illuminated from the light of a brazier on the wall. She was scowling, a most unusual expression for someone noted for her cheerful and confident disposition, and she appeared to be talking to herself. Derryth reached the bottom of the staircase, paused to glance back upstairs, swore loudly, and charged towards the door.

"Ah! Derryth. How good to see you," Gwriad said quickly, worried that she might collide with him.

She came to an immediate stop, having seen him at that very moment. "Oh, my Lord, I'm sorry. I was in a hurry." She smiled, her face changing to one of warmth and animation.

"I'm sorry to see you leaving. You've only just arrived." Although he did not have sexual desires for her, he enjoyed her presence and especially her buoyant disposition. He had never seen her angry.

"I'm sorry I can't stay," her tongue passed quickly over her lips. "Meg Thomas is expecting at any moment."

"Another Thomas!" Gwriad laughed. "I think Dai wants to create his own army!"

"Yes, m'Lord. I've brought seven of her boys into the world and it's about time Meg had a girl."

They both laughed as he opened the door for her. She gave him a quick curtsy and fled across the courtyard. He watched her disappear through the castle's small door with the help of a smiling soldier, and wondered what her real reason had been for the abrupt exit. He remembered that on arriving she had appeared relaxed and seemed happy, without any apparent concern for the state of the fecund Meg Thomas.

As he turned to go back into the hall, he heard a horse moving swiftly across the courtyard, making towards the main gate. He saw it was Jon, and waved. Jon ignored him, and with some abrupt words to the guards, raced off down the slope to the bridge. He shrugged his shoulders, "What's bitten him, I wonder?"

He slowly climbed the steep stairs to where he and his brother had spacious bedrooms that seemed larger without their wives. At the far end of the corridor was a small room that Dafydd used as his office. It was where he kept the records of the castle and its estate, and where he wrote his long letters to men of equal education, including Abbots, Welsh nobility and even Saxon prelates.

The door to Dafydd's bedroom was open and after a quick glance to confirm it was empty, Gwriad approached the closed door of the small office. He gave a perfunctory knock and opened the door with a flourish. Dafydd was sitting on a wooden stool with his head resting on his desk, his arms hanging down on either side. He sat up with a start, as though he had been stung by a bee. His clean-shaven face was flushed, and his normally groomed hair was dishevelled. "You could have knocked," he growled.

"I did. Were you asleep?"

"No." Dafydd stood up and stretched. "Did you want something?"

"I wondered what had happened between you and Derryth. Did you have a tiff?" Gwriad poked his younger brother with his index finger. "She left in a bit of a fury, man. I've never seen her like that before."

"It's none of your damn business!" Dafydd looked down angrily at his shorter brother. "I don't ask you about the women you associate with."

"Chance would be a fine thing," Gwriad quipped. He turned towards the door. "I'll leave you to fester, then. I'll be in the Great Hall enjoying some wine." He left the door open as he walked off, and was on his way down the stone steps as it banged shut. "Oh? How unusual," he mused. "It sounds like a rejection to me."

He opened the door to the courtyard and nodded to the guard. "I don't think we are going to be attacked tonight, do you, Gavin?"

"No, m'Lord." The soldier was one of the older soldiers in the castle, and was known for his skill in hunting and trapping. He gave Gwriad a broad smile. "I'd be prepared to bet on it."

"Indeed. I hear there may be a bear in the area?"

"I think there's more likely to be a unicorn, m'Lord," Gavin laughed. "However, the wolves are back."

"Yes, I heard them last night." He raised his thick brows. "Do you think, perhaps, they might stay?"

"It depends, m'Lord, if the alpha female is in whelp. If she is, they might decide to stay, especially if they can take a sheep or a horse." The guard relaxed his stance. "Would ye be thinking of hunting them, m'Lord?" His voice betrayed his enthusiasm.

"Never fear, Gavin. If I decide to hunt them, you will be the first to hear about it." He turned back into the hall and closed the door. After pouring himself some wine, he threw a log on the fire and sat facing the stairs. The dog awoke and came to nuzzle his hand.

Outside, the guard grinned; he liked Lord Gwriad, even though he could be unpredictable when he became angry. He did not dislike Lord Dafydd either, although the younger brother was often distracted and would move around the castle with a very purposeful gait as though in a world of his own. Those who worked in the castle respected Lord Dafydd, but his obvious intelligence and learning prevented the cheerful interactions that it was possible to have with the older brother. Dafydd was usually calm and polite but also firm, and none of the soldiers or servants wished to cross him. This was especially so since the murder of his wife.

Upstairs, Dafydd had moved to his bedroom where he paced back and forth like a caged animal. After a while he stopped and with a grunt of irritation marched to the door. He paused, snatched up his sword and belt and pounded down the steps into the main hall.

"You need a drink!" his brother called out as Dafydd stalked towards the door. "Have some wine and take a deep breath."

9

"Leave me alone!" he yelled as he burst through the door, startling Gavin who was unused to seeing the normally placid Lord Dafydd exhibiting anger. He jumped to attention with unusual haste and watched as the younger Lord rushed towards the stables as though pursued by hornets.

A short while later, Dafydd trotted across the yard and yelled at the soldiers to open the main gate. Once he had passed through, the soldiers watched him ride down the hill.

"I bet he rides to the village," Owen jested. "I know I would!" He raised his fist in a sexual gesture.

"Wrong again, ye dumb-wit," Sergeant Penn hissed. As the senior soldier he enjoyed dominating the younger soldiers. They watched as Lord Dafydd galloped over the stone bridge crossing the river. "He's off to Llanduduch. I wonder if he's wanting to catch up with Lord Jon?"

CHAPTER TWO

O n the hill above the fishing village of Llanduduch, Father Williams, the elderly priest for the area, dozed in his favourite chair from which, in the distance, he could see the River Teifi's flood plain before its narrow exit into the broad bay. He loved to watch the effect of the full tide when the tidal plain was transformed from a brown muddy landscape of intersecting channels to a blue inland lake rich in small fish and the birds that fed on them. High sand dunes separated the tidal plain from the wind-flecked sea enclosed in a wide bay. To the left was a long sandy beach where some of the fishermen caught shrimp and crabs and where their small fishing boats were pulled up above the high tide mark. To the right were high imposing cliffs that endured the crashing waves that thundered relentlessly against their dark rocks. Way in the distance the cliffs ended and beyond them was a small uninhabited, wind-swept island in a sea of hidden rocks. This was where many small boats had floundered, including those of the dreaded Picts with their long, multi-oared ships.

The priest's small, comfortable house was positioned behind a modest stone church that looked down on the impoverished cluster of homes over which Father Williams had maintained a benevolent religious control for decades. In his earlier life, he had even helped defend the mostly fishing families from attacks by Pictish raiders.

Those days were passed. A combination of age, good wine and a propensity for large meals had taken their toll. His rotund body and his red-veined nose were clear evidence of the effects of the compensations he gave himself for the lack of intellectual and social stimulation that had increased as he became older and less physically active.

As a younger priest he had made daily trips down the steep hill to check on his village flock, and insisted that all would attend his Sunday services. He had been an excellent horseman, and would visit isolated farms, and make frequent visits to the castle at Aberteifi. But after one particularly hard winter when travel was impossible for some weeks, he had started to drink to banish his loneliness. With the bad weather, the villagers made excuses for their lack of attendance at his services in the cold church up the steep hill, and he felt physically unable to climb down to call on them. Initially, it depressed him how soon they seemed to have forgotten his teachings and the fact that he had saved their lives and their homes when the Picts had attacked. But on reflection he realized he had expected too much of them.

In earlier times, Lord Dafydd had been a regular visitor, and they had spent many stimulating hours together discussing philosophy, history, and religious beliefs. However, the sudden Saxon attacks on the Welsh border and the Celtic counterattacks had involved both of the young Lords, and had ended these welcome visits, throwing him back on his own company. When Lady Angharad arranged for Jon to be taught, Father Williams had a revival of his previous enthusiasm for scholarly activity, preparing for hours before each lesson and being constantly amazed at the rapid progress of a young man who was desperate to learn.

With the warmer weather he saw more of his flock, and his lively and sometimes amusing sermons elicited a positive response from the uneducated peasants who continued, in secret, to follow the Druid beliefs of their elders, and who found Christianity confusing. He was aware that their daily concerns for food, drink and sex were more important than the future damnation of their souls; they believed in luck, both good and bad, and in the appeasement of their Sea God and the various ghosts and spirits that inhabited the forests, the caves, the river and the night.

When the priest blessed the fishing and the boats came back full of fish, they were happy to celebrate the power of his God. But, when someone drowned they knew that the Sea God was angry with them. The burial service in the little church yard was a meaningless ceremony. It was conducted by the priest in a language they did not understand, but was, they were told, the only way to speak to the one God, who only listened to the priest. Their weeping and the sorrow felt by those who knew and loved the dead person were as sincere as if the service had been conducted by a Druid priest. In the end it was the gathering together and the solemnity of the occasion that was important, enabling them to move on with their brief and often brutal lives.

In the summer the priest would arrange a celebration at a time when the fishing was good and when the homemade beer and wines were fresh and tasty. It was at that time, and for a brief moment, they would join him in a genuine outpouring of thanks, but whether it was to his God, or the Sea God of the fishermen, or to the Moon Goddess that many women secretly worshipped, was always unclear.

When the wives of the two Lords were murdered, he had persuaded the two brothers to move beyond their grief and to accept their wider responsibilities. He had been pleased and surprised when they left for Canterbury on a journey they named a pilgrimage, but was saddened when their long absence resulted in Jon having to take on the running of the castle and having little time to visit him. Since their return, Lord Dafydd rarely visited, and Father Williams was certain he knew why.

There were the occasional weddings and baptisms and the more frequent burials, but often these only occurred because he insisted they should. Given the opportunity, the villagers would have been happier to have simpler ceremonies, conducted in the old ways, when they understood the words, and where music, song and feasting were the central themes.

He suddenly awoke, and stared angrily around in all directions, his eyes flashing in his usually amiable face. He was expecting a young couple to visit him for the preparation for their marriage tomorrow, and he did not want them to discover him asleep. "It won't do," he muttered to himself as he struggled out of his chair. There was nobody in sight, so he breathed out, straightened his shoulders, adjusted the belt around his habit and walked purposefully, though slowly, towards the church. He liked weddings, but sometimes felt he was failing the ones he married if they were clearly unsuitable. In his earlier days he had raised the matter with the previous Bishop, who had severely chastised him for failing to see God's plan. Father Williams had realized why he would never become a bishop.

He checked the candles which he lit only during ceremonies, brushed off the dust on the alter and bowed briefly towards the large wooden cross. It was more ritual than a belief that God was impressed. Finally, he arranged a chair in front of the alter and sat down with a sigh of contentment. At that moment the two young peasants he was expecting entered diffidently through the door.

"Welcome, Deri and Anwen." He raised his arms in salutation. "Come and stand in front of me, my children." He had always thought this religious terminology to be unsuitable for priests, who in theory, were celibate.

They stood awkwardly before him, their eyes fixed on his face like rabbits before a stoat.

"And you're going to love each other throughout your lives?" he said, smiling encouragingly at the embarrassed couple. They seemed so young.

"Yes, Father," they chanted together.

The young fisherman had been noticeably present at his recent services, and it seemed only yesterday that the nervous young woman had been a constant giggler in the back of the church.

'You understand that you, Deri, and you, Anwen, will, tomorrow, be promising in front of God, and all your relatives, that you will be true to each other and not share your love with anyone else?"

"Yes, Father," they both responded. Deri had suddenly blushed.

"This means that you will love each other, and only each other, throughout your lives. You understand what you are committing to?"

"Yes, Father." They both grinned sheepishly.

Over the years, he had come to know every person in the small village, from their births, to their marriages, and in some cases, their deaths. He knew Deri had a reputation with other girls and that Anwen was a pretty but silly youngster. She had, somehow, ensnared Deri, which would have been seen as an important conquest among the other girls of her age. The priest wondered as he studied them, if she had told Deri she was with child? Whether she was or not, the next few months could prove difficult for both of them. It would not be the first time that a girl of the village had forced a young, carefree man into marriage, and it had nearly always resulted in an unhappy union.

He decided to take it one step further. "You understand that you are young and have little experience of life?"

They both nodded. Deri was sweating and Anwen chewed her lip and looked anxiously at the tall, muscular young man beside her.

"After tomorrow, your previous boyfriends and girlfriends will

14

never be your closest friends again. You will have each other, and you must always put each other first. It's a big change in your lives. Do you understand that?"

They nodded and replaced their nervous grins with a strained seriousness. Both seemed uncomfortable.

"Well then, Anwen, and you, Deri," he smiled, "you will be married at midday tomorrow. Then, there will be a feast and a big celebration, and everyone will know you are pledged to each other." He paused, rose slowly from his chair and turned to face the cross on the altar. They stared at his shaved head. "But, I have known young people, who even at this stage, have decided to wait. In some cases they married a year later, and others married someone else. If you have any doubts as to whether you want to live the rest of your life with the person next to you, you still have time to change your minds." He paused, turned slowly to face them, made the sign of the Cross and in the singsong ritual of the Church declared: "In the name of the Father, the Son and the Holy Ghost, Amen."

He smiled at them. "I will see you tomorrow. You have a lot to think about."

"Thank you, Father," Anwen gave a quick curtsy her face crimson and close to tears, and Deri nodded his head earnestly, a look of relief on his deeply tanned face. "Thank you. Thank you, Father." They both fled down the short aisle.

"Um," he murmured happily, "perhaps there won't be a wedding tomorrow after all." It was an occasion he would miss having, but he was certain he had done the right thing.

.   .   .

EARLIER IN THE DAY, JON had been in fine fettle and, after talking to his father, it had seemed likely that Lord Gwriad would raise an army to help the Prince and that he would get his first taste of battle. As he approached the stables Megan beckoned to him from behind a storage hut.

"Ah, Megan my love," he said as he advanced confidently towards her. She looked both ways and backed back into the shadows.

"I've got some exciting news. I might be going to fight the Normans!" he exclaimed as he approached her, failing to notice her drawn, pale face.

"Shut up and listen!" she said abruptly, clenching her fists. Her greeting was so unusual that he was tempted to remind her he was a Lord.

"You've given me a baby! You idiot!"

"What?"

"You promised me you'd seen the Wise Woman, and that everything would be alright." She began to cry, her body shaking with violent tremors.

"Yes, I did," he was unsure what to say. "But, but it doesn't matter. Um… I'll look after you." He felt a sense of panic. "It'll be alright. I'll look after you. We'll be happy."

"Don't you understand?" she gasped. "I'm ruined. My life is over." She began to wail inconsolably.

"No, no. I'll marry you. You'll be my wife. I want you to want this baby. Our baby." A sense of overwhelming inadequacy seized him, and he was suddenly uncertain of what to say.

"You know nothing. You're just a stupid boy!" She beat her fists on his chest, and raised her anguished face to stare wildly up at him.

"I can sort this, Megan. Everything will be alright." He tried to take her hands, but she pushed him away. He glanced over his shoulder, afraid someone would see them arguing. "I will marry you, I won't let you down!"

"You understand nothing. My life is over. You can't marry me. Don't you understand?" she was shouting hysterically.

"Megan. Please calm down. I—", he gasped as she slapped him across the mouth and ran off towards the kitchen.

He stood, rubbing his lower lip and staring wide-eyed after her. A servant stopped in the courtyard and stared at the distraught girl. As she turned to follow Megan, she saw Jon and immediately dropped him a curtsy, her face red with embarrassment.

Jon turned away, pretending he had not seen her, and hurried towards the stables.

"Saddle up!" he yelled, pacing backwards and forwards outside. "Hurry!" He had only one thought: to ride away from the castle and seek the advice of Father Williams.

CHAPTER THREE

M ay is a favoured month in Wales, when the hardwood trees burst into full leaf, grey skies gave way to blue and the world seems a better, kinder place. Everything burgeons with life: birds are busy feeding their ever-hungry chicks, animals are raising their noisy off-spring, and young men speculate on their chances with girls, who up to now have been kept warm and dry within the confines of their parents' homes. Without warning, like the colourful spring flowers in the fields, the women of marriageable age would suddenly and magically appear, with their bright eyes and warm, welcoming smiles. No longer clad in the dark, heavy shawls and warm sheepskins necessary to survive the wet and cold of winter, they emerge in lighter more revealing smocks and skirts and with thoughts of future husbands and motherhood firmly in their minds.

Iago, the elder son of Pritchard the Miller, was enjoying himself. He had managed to persuade his bullying father to allow him to take their lumbering wagon to a market at a nearby village to sell a load of sacks containing last year's milled flour and wheat seeds. He had agreed to take his younger brother Efan, amid loud protests from his three envious younger sisters who were left to do the heavy work around their house and the mill. He was particularly pleased as it might allow him the chance to renew his acquaintance with a pretty girl named Rhiannon, whose father owned a prosperous farm.

It had been a long, seemingly interminable winter, and the heavy snow had forced Iago's family to remain in close proximity to one another inside their cramped house. The boredom had led to angry exchanges, especially when his father had been drinking his home-made beer, which was a frequent occurrence during the dark cold evenings when time hung heavy for a man with little imagination. But once the days began to get longer, with the increased hours of daylight, Pritchard made sure that everyone in his family was kept busy from sun rise until sun set. "The devil makes work for idle hands!" he roared. "And we'll have no idle hands in my house, see!"

"Lucky isn't it that Pa had that landowner to meet?" Efan said contentedly as the old horse moved slowly along the rutted lane. He felt important sitting with Iago on the high wagon. He was only two years younger than his seventeen-year-old brother, but had none of Iago's muscular frame, having inherited his mother's slim body and her artistic gifts.

"Lucky for you, you mean. I would've gone anyway, boy." He gave his brother a playful shove. "Let's hope you're strong enough to lift those sacks. You're only a little runt really."

They indulged in a friendly tussle while the experienced horse continued to amble along the familiar pathway. "Muscles of a young girl, you have," Iago teased. "I might have to get one of your sisters to replace you, boy!" He tried to squeeze Efan's thin arm.

"Going to replace me with Rhiannon more like?" Efan let out a roar of derision. "I don't think it's sacks you're hoping to lift, Brother. I think it's a certain girl's dress!"

Iago gave a roar and was just about to force Efan off the wagon, when he saw the smoke. "That doesn't look good, does it?"

"You're not fooling me!" Efan tried to grab hold of his brother, oblivious to his sudden change of voice.

"Look! You half-wit. Look for God's sake! The village is on fire!"

Efan was suddenly aware of the dark smoke. "Oh no. That's where Cwm is. What d'ye think is happening?" he wailed. In the distance, behind a row of tall trees, thick black smoke was belching up into the still, blue sky, and it was clear it was not a single fire.

"If I knew I'd be much happier." Iago bit on his lower lip. "They wouldn't have fires that big in the village, and they wouldn't be burning stubble in the fields at this time of the year." He pulled the horse to a stop, stood up on his seat and looked in all directions. Then, he jumped off the wagon and grabbing the horse's bridle led the animal and wagon into the cover of a nearby wood on their left.

"Where are we going?" Efan bent low to avoid the branches. "What're we doing?" He sounded frightened.

"I reckon there's only one thing that could cause that amount of smoke," he replied and took a deep breath. "The village is being attacked and we need to hide."

"Normans?"

"Who else?

"Should we race home and warn them?"

"Race? With this old horse?" He pulled the wagon to a halt behind some bushes. "Quickly, Efan. Get back to the path and cover the wagon tracks. I'll join you when I've settled the old girl."

Efan ran back the way they had come, and saw that there were clear impressions in the soft earth where the heavy wagon had turned into the forest. He sighed, he would not have thought of this, and immediately began collecting last year's oak, elm and horse chestnut leaves that lay thick and soggy along the ground. He spread them over the ruts and had mainly obscured their wagon's telltale trail by the time his brother joined him.

"Good work, boy," Iago said encouragingly. He stood in the middle of the path and stared anxiously towards Cwm. It was where his mother's family and some of their friends lived and was less than an hour's walk from their mill that had been built beside a fast-flowing stream. Their house was perched on higher ground nearby, with a handful of other houses that all belonged to small farmers. It was just a collection of houses, unlike Cwm, which was a farming village and large enough to have a weaver, a smithy and a leather worker, along with a small ale house. It was the largest place the boys had ever been to, and on market days they enjoyed the excitement and bustle of the crowd, with the chance of meeting strangers from distant farms and seeing new things.

"Now, what do we do?" Efan stared towards the forest beyond which dense, dark clouds were reaching high into the windless sky. "Do you think they'll see the smoke from our mill?"

"Yes," Iago said with a conviction he did not feel. "Oh, yes. They'll see it from there." He knew he had to be positive, as Efan was prone to be a worrier. "The big problem is what do we do now?"

Efan nodded furiously. He expected Iago to have the answer.

"Well, let's think about this. We're not far from Cwm; closer than to our mill. We could take a short cut through the forest and see what's really happening. Then we'll know what to do. Alright?" In the bright sunlight, Iago looked tall and strong; his black hair hung past his shoulders and his bright blue eyes flashed with excitement. He was in, Efan's eyes, a natural leader.

"I've got my knife," Efan said bravely.

"Right. I've got mine too. Pop back to the wagon and get our sheep poles." In spite of the possible danger, he smiled at his younger brother's enthusiasm as he rushed back into the forest. Iago checked both ways and listened carefully for any human sounds, but could hear only the birds.

He looked up as Efan reappeared with the two sheep poles, and noticed how he was having a growth spurt. "You're growing, boy, you'll soon be as tall as me."

Efan smiled. He glowed in his brother's approval. "You lead, Iago. I'll follow."

They crossed the track and entered a forest of old trees and dim light. Iago led the way in the direction of the village, and occasional gaps in the thick canopy allowed him to see the columns of black smoke that confirmed his sense of direction. The forest was strangely quiet, missing the bird song and the usual small animal sounds, as though everything was holding its breath. Then, like unexpected thunder, they heard a loud crashing ahead as if people or large animals were rushing towards them.

"Get down," Iago hissed. He grabbed Efan and forced him behind a wide oak. "Draw your knife, and keep silent."

The sounds increased, and in moments a short, thickset man with a full beard raced past their hiding place carrying a long knife. He was accompanied by a younger woman carrying a baby. They were both panting heavily. Iago stood up as though stung by a horse fly. "Uncle David! Aunt Edith!" he exclaimed.

The adults stopped and stared back at them wide eyed, as though they were seeing ghosts.

"What you doing here, boys?" the man asked gruffly. He advanced slowly towards them, his stern face breaking into a smile. He embraced them both, and their aunt kissed them on their cheeks. She was a strong, likeable woman and her baby gurgled happily in her arms.

"We were coming to the market and saw the smoke. What's happening?"

"Bloody Normans!" The man stared back the way they had come.

"Hush, David," his wife gasped. She turned to Iago, her face was hot and sweaty and she was breathing loudly. "The market was busy you see, and without any warning Norman horsemen galloped down the road from the border and began attacking everyone, even women and children. It was terrible." She took a few breaths. "Some of our men tried to fight back, but the Normans were well armed. Our men had no chance. We had to run for our lives."

"They may come after us," David growled. "We should get back to your mill to warn them."

"Our horse and wagon are hidden on the other side of the path, but back a bit," Efan said. He was desperate to be noticed.

"Right, take us there, but don't cross the path until we've checked. The Normans may be using the main pathways to quickly attack more homes." He wiped his brow. "Or they may retreat back over the border, now they've stolen our goods and our animals."

"And murdered our people," Edith added as she made the most of their short break to nurse her baby.

"Our old horse, Sampson, would be useless if we were pursued by Norman cavalry," Iago said.

"We've got a load of flour and wheat seeds," Efan said, as though it would help. He saw the others were not impressed. "If the Normans destroy everything, this could be a useful load, don't you think, Uncle?"

"Oh yes, well done, Efan," David said encouragingly, "you've thought ahead. We must make sure the Normans don't find that wagon."

"Are we going to go back to the mill, Uncle, or should we see what has happened at the village?" Iago murmured.

David looked anxiously at his wife. "Everything we own is back there, but I can't risk the Normans finding us." He cleared his throat, he was not used to making decisions. "I think we best... um... we'll go to the wagon, and watch the road to see if the Normans pass in the next while. If they don't, we'll know they've probably left Cwm, and retreated back across the border."

He added some choice words and his wife tutted disapprovingly. "For shame, David, not in front of the boys."

"For goodness sake, woman, with my brother as their father there's nothing they haven't heard before."

Edith sniffed and turned to Iago. "You'd better lead us to your wagon. By then, your Uncle will have decided what we should do."

A while later, they reached the path. David slowly checked both ways and then, like an experienced soldier, he beckoned them across, although he would have been the first to admit he had never been involved in any fighting, and apart from the long knife, which he used for cutting cooked meat, and a cudgel that he kept behind the counter of his small ale house, he had no other weapons.

They soon found the horse and wagon, and Edith expressed her relief as she sank down on the ground against a front wheel. "I can't believe the baby has been so quiet," she gasped. Iago passed her his flask of water and climbed up on the wagon. "The smoke is not so thick; perhaps they've retreated?"

"In a while, you and I will go back to the road and see if there's any sign of those murdering Normans," David panted. He was not used to vigorous activity. He gestured to the two boys to sit. "This is the first time they've attacked us since a new Norman Lord took over across the border," he tried to sound authoritative. He sat down by his wife and waggled his fingers at the baby. "We had a merchant come through the village last month. He said that the Norman King William has given this land, our land, to some Norman Lord who had fought for him at the big battle when the Saxons were defeated. Not that I've ever had much love for the Saxons either." He spat on the ground.

"Uncle David," Iago said as he climbed down, "would it be best if we left Aunt Edith and the baby with the wagon," he glanced at his younger brother, "and left Efan to guard them. Then, you and I can creep back to the village to see what's happened?"

David took a deep breath, he was feeling his age and his lack of recent physical activity. "I think that's a good suggestion." He smiled at Efan, who was about to protest. "Do you think you can look after your aunt and my son, and the wagon? It's a big responsibility, boy."

Efan swallowed his pride. "Yes, Uncle." He took his aunt's hand. "You and little Gwyn will be safe with me, Aunt Edith."

His aunt squeezed his hand. "Thank you, Efan." She gave a sideways nod to her husband. "Will you take the horse, David? If you're sure the Normans have gone it would be easier for you to get to the village and back, and I'm sure Iago is happy to walk, aren't you, my big nephew?"

Iago beamed. "Oh, yes indeed." He would have done anything for his favourite aunt.

They unhitched Sampson and made their way slowly back to the path, where David insisted they wait and listen for any sound of riders. Iago stepped onto the path and stared up at the clear sky.

"No smoke. Shall we risk it, Uncle?"

David rubbed his beard thoughtfully, and blew out his cheeks. "Well then, um, I suppose we can't stand here all day." He flashed a brave smile at Iago. "If you'll help me up on this old horse of yours, I'll try to remember how to ride. It's been a few years."

"Oh, don't worry, Uncle, he's very gentle, and he's used to us riding him bareback." Iago stood by the side of the horse as David placed an uncertain foot on his nephew's cupped hands and tried to force his heavy body up on the horse's back. Eventually, after much cursing and gasping, David finally lay like a beached seal on the broad back of the horse, which had stood quietly throughout the antics.

"Well done, boy," David said as he sat up, gasping for breath. He tried to balance with his short, stocky legs sticking out uncomfortably on either side. As the owner of a small ale house, he enjoyed drinking with his customers, and apart from making ale and keeping the building clean he rarely took any exercise. "I must get out more," he said apologetically, "I'm not as fit as I used to be."

Iago walked by the side of the horse, holding its bridle, and walking as fast as he could get the animal to move. He mused that the animal and the human were both in the same state of advancing age and immobility. When they were close to the village and could see a smoke haze in the sky, they turned off the path. David slid off the side of the horse, and if it had been a less stressful occasion, the nephew might have laughed as he crashed to the ground, and lay there muttering, "I'm fine. I'm fine. Just getting my breath back."

They moved slowly through the trees, until they could see a part of the village in the distance. Iago moved forward. "Best if I went first, Uncle.

I'll let you know what's happening." David nodded earnestly. It was not something he wanted to do.

Iago walked cautiously towards the smell of burning and the increasing sounds of distraught women. From behind a large elm he stared at the carnage that had struck the small village. Most of the houses were reduced to blackened, shells, their thatched roofs and wooden walls having been easily destroyed in the attack. The few peasants stood in a small group, lamenting the human losses and trying to explain how they had survived. The soldiers had looted the village before torching it and had taken the livestock, killing what they were unable to take away, and leaving these few survivors destitute.

He could not draw his eyes away from the gruesome sight of people he had known and liked lying lifeless around the ruins of their village. His Uncle's ale house was destroyed, as was the house of the leatherworker and many of the less substantial buildings. Even the blacksmith's sturdy house and smithy had been reduced to a smoking hulk. There were corpses lying everywhere, and if he had not known otherwise he would have assumed his uncle and aunt to be among the dead. He returned silently through the trees to where his uncle was hiding with the horse. David jumped up from the ground as Iago approached. "What news, boy?"

"The Normans have gone, Uncle, but it's bad. There are only a very few survivors. Your pub's been burnt to the ground. Everything, including the smithy, is destroyed," he swallowed to contain his emotion.

"Even my ale house?" David turned away and stuck his fist in his mouth. "I suppose if anyone was to be burnt out, it would be me." He raised his eyebrows and nodded his head as though having a conversation with himself. "Yes, it's the problem with beer, everyone wants it." He stared ahead, "What will I do now? I mean, I have a wife and babe to support, don't I?" He jumped when Iago placed a hand on his shoulder.

"Don't worry, Uncle David, you can all stay at our house. We'll look after you."

David blew out his lips. "Thank you, boy. But I can take care of my own family." He stuck out his chest in what he imagined was a defiant posture.

"'Course you can, Uncle. Shall we get back to the wagon?"

David nodded. He could not conceal his anxiety. Getting him on the horse was as difficult as before, but eventually they completed the return journey.

"What news?" Edith demanded, rising to her feet. Iago briefly explained as David struggled his way off the horse, took a deep breath and tried to look as though he was in charge.

Edith hugged him. "We'll be alright, David. At least we're all alive."

He nodded and took a deep breath. "I think we should travel by the main path, and you be alert now, boys, the Normans might still be around." He patted his wife's arm and, trying not to show any fear, helped Iago hitch up the horse and wagon, then led the way back to the path. Iago helped Edith to climb up with her baby that was, unbelievably, still asleep.

Once on the path David climbed onto the wagon beside his wife, and Efan sat in the back. It was a silent journey with each person straining to hear any sound that might indicate the approach of Norman cavalry. There was an unnatural quiet in the woods on both sides of them, and Edith and David gazed wide-eyed on opposite sides while Iago stared ahead and Efan checked the back. The old horse plodded along at the only speed he was capable of maintaining, and Iago knew better than to urge him on.

After a while they began to climb up a slight slope, and once they reached the summit the boys knew they would be looking down on their mill by the stream and close by it was their old house with the small collection of other less prosperous homes on a nearby rise.

"I smell smoke!" Edith cried.

A moment later they reached the top of the hill and were staring down at an horrific sight. The hamlet was under attack, and many of the houses were already alight, their dry thatch bursting into individual infernos, while Norman horsemen, like nightmares from hell, were murdering the unarmed peasants as they rushed for safety. Smoke was billowing out of the mill, and unidentifiable bodies were scattered around the ground as the soldiers gave vent to their blood lust.

"Merciful heaven!" David gasped. He stared in disbelief, unable to react.

"Look after your wife and baby, Uncle!" Iago yelled as he vaulted off the wagon. "I'm going to help my Pa. I know he'll fight them off."

"Iago, I'll come with you," Efan said bravely.

"No, it's better if I go by myself. Uncle David will need you to help protect Aunt Edith and her baby."

"It's our family being attacked. I want to help!" His voice hit a high note.

"The best help you could be, Efan, is to protect me and your uncle," his aunt said quietly. "Iago, you go down and see if anyone is alive in the mill. Your house is on fire. The best hope is the mill." She stared into his blue eyes. "Take care now, and don't do anything silly. Promise?"

Iago nodded his head and quickly disappeared into the forest on their left. David drove the horse and cart into the cover of some nearby trees and he and Efan crept back towards the edge of the hill until they could see the awful carnage below. All of the small cottages were now in flames and the bodies of the peasants lay scattered around, innocent victims of a war they knew nothing about. Smoke was erupting from the mill, but as yet there was no sign of flames. Their attention was drawn to a woman with a baby in her arms who was running towards the river, screaming in terror, and pursued by two mounted soldiers. "That's Dylis!" Efan gasped. "Oh no!"

They stared, numbed, like rabbits staring into the eyes of a stoat, as they saw her cut down by one soldier, and as she fell, the other soldier made a low sweeping movement, killing her child before the small body hit the ground. The soldiers walked their horses around her corpse and raised their swords in triumph as though they had fought a dangerous opponent.

"My God, they're killing us like sheep," David muttered. His wife had crept up behind them, and after a brief glance turned away; Efan's face had changed to a sickly grey. "Let's go back to the wagon and stay hidden now. There's nothing we can do." David took his wife's arm, and nodding to Efan, led the way back into the trees. In the back of his mind was the fear that his brother and all his family might be dead.

CHAPTER FOUR

J on arrived at Llanduduch shortly after the young couple had left the church. He steered his horse up a side path to the priest's house, where he found Father Williams enjoying a goblet of wine in the comfort of his warm room.

"Welcome, my son, you are just in time to join me."

Jon smiled and gladly accepted the wine. "I had heard you were unwell?"

"Nonsense," he protested. "Just old age and boredom."

"Boredom?" Jon frowned. "Yes. I'm sorry I've not been a frequent visitor during the winter months. Even with the return of the Lords, I've still tended to run the daily life of the castle."

"I imagine Lord Dafydd has been happy to take over the accounts?"

"Oh yes, and he has also begun to write the history of the castle, and this has resulted in long correspondences with the few literate landowners from this area, but mainly with our Bishop and some distant Abbots. My father," he smiled self-consciously, even after two years he still felt awkward using this term, "has no real interest in how the castle runs, and never has. His enthusiasm is still for hunting and travelling around his lands. Strangely, the Norman troubles on the border don't seem to excite him. I think he also gets bored during the winter months."

"I understand he drinks less these days, but how about food? He always had a monumental appetite."

"No. He shows no great interest in big meals, unless he's entertaining some visiting Lord, which is not often," he sipped his wine, "but he still enjoys eating the meat he has hunted. The recent wet weather has resulted in him pacing the castle like a caged animal."

"Ah, yes," the priest said and drank deeply. "So, there is no new woman in his life?"

"No, Father. Lord Gwriad remains in private mourning for Lady Angharad. As do we all."

"Yes, indeed." He finished his wine and poured another goblet for himself. "For you?"

"No, Father Williams. Thank you. I need a clear head." He paused and seemed to be searching for the right words.

The old priest watched him contentedly. Jon had become a fine young man, well suited to the title of Lord, and a worthy adopted son to Lord Gwriad. It was hard to remember him as the thin, uncertain waif who had been living in abject poverty; he had become tall, muscular and a fine horseman. He was said to be the best swordsman in the castle, and thanks to the many lessons they had shared and those he had received from Lady Angharad and Lord Daffyd, he was both literate and erudite.

"You've come to talk to me about Megan?"

"Megan?" He tried to drink from his empty goblet. "Yes, you're quite right."

After a short silence. Father Williams added: "I understand that in spite of my warning, you have taken up a relationship with this young woman?"

"I love her, and I want to marry her. I want you to marry us." He stared at the priest with a frightening intensity.

"That is a ridiculous thought. You can't marry a fisherman's daughter."

"She's not just a fisherman's daughter anymore, Father." He spoke quickly, as though desperate to get the subject over with. "She's become a qualified cook and can run the kitchen now, when the older Megan is unable to cope. There are many different demands on her."

"Can she read and write?"

"She's learning to."

"Does she know how to speak English?"

"No. But she can sing."

"Can she spin? Dance? Ride a horse? Could she hold a conversation with noble women? Does she know how to dress for different occasions? Her family have never had her baptised. How can she possibly be considered as the wife of the future Lord of Aberteifi?"

Jon's face had gone pale with anger. "No, but like me she can learn."

"But you are the bastard son of Lord Gomer ap Griffith. You are part of their bloodline. You have a right to be the next Lord, especially since Lord Gwriad made you his adopted son. Megan is the daughter of an uneducated fisherman. She can never be accepted as a Lord's wife, no matter how much you may wish it."

Jon helped himself to more wine, and sat staring at the floor. Finally, he said: "She's expecting my baby."

There was a long pause as Father Williams composed himself. "Your mother was a village girl and mistress to Lord Gomer. He had no scruples in disowning her, not because he was a wholly bad man, but because there was no way he could have acknowledged her and taken her as his wife. That is why he persuaded that fisherman, your father, to pretend to be the father of the unborn child. He paid some money, and dismissed you from his mind. Lords do this, because they have the power, and therefore the right to take mistresses and when they get pregnant they discard them, because they can. I warned you to keep away from her. You came to see me when she was taken on in the kitchen, and I gave you the right advice."

"I can't destroy her life!"

"You have no choice. She will return to her parents, and after the birth of the baby you will give her enough money to get a post with another landed family. You may even be able to find her a willing husband in the village, especially if she has some money to bring to the marriage." He spoke forcefully, but not in anger.

"I can't do that. We love each other."

Father Williams nodded and took a swig of his wine. He had feared this might happen, and when Megan had first moved to the castle, he had spoken to Derryth and asked her to ensure that Jon knew about the way children were conceived. His Bishop would have been outraged, and those at the castle would have been surprised to know, that he respected the Wise Woman and that they had often shared information concerning the welfare of people whom they wished to help. In his early days before becoming a priest he had fought in foreign lands and was well aware of human desires and weaknesses. His distant friendship with Derryth was, from his enlightened viewpoint, an acceptance of the local beliefs and traditions. It was the way the common people lived, and to pretend he could change their behaviour was a delusion. He saw himself as a guide not a tyrant, but he also knew there were differences between the rich and the poor that it was impossible for any single person to change in a lifetime.

"Start with an acceptance of the facts, Jon. By sheer luck, you were discovered to be related, albeit somewhat distantly, to the heirs of the castle. You were intensely lucky that Lady Angharad took an interest in you and that she and her husband even discovered who you were. Your final piece of incredible luck was that Lord Gwriad accepted you as kin." He shook his head. "You could have led a life as an underfed kitchen urchin. You might never have lived to be an adult. That is an amazingly fortunate series of events, from which you have benefitted beyond your wildest dreams. It is only your foolishness that has caused you to make a serious error." There was a silence disturbed by the sinking of a log in the hot fire. "Do you agree?"

"You are right in everything you say, but it changes nothing. Megan is going to have my baby and I want to marry her."

"Are you prepared to return to being a peasant? If you insist on acknowledging that you are the father and you want to be married to her, you will have to leave the castle. There is no way the Lords will accept a lowly servant as their equal, and there is no way the other servants and soldiers will accept Megan as being their mistress of the castle, let alone their Lady. I will not marry you, and you will be unable to stay in this area where you are both known as being at opposite ends of the social scale. You and Megan will be outsiders. You will have banished yourselves."

The priest stood up. "I want you to go back to the castle, think about what I have said, and have a long careful discussion with Megan. When you are decided, and there is only one decision you can make, come back and see me, and bring Megan with you. I will help you to plan her future." Without looking at the miserable Jon, he swept out of the door and walked with unusual agility towards his church.

CHAPTER FIVE

"Stupid! Stupid! Stupid!" Derryth muttered as she strode towards her small house. She had maintained the same fast walk down the steep hill from the castle, across the small valley and up the sharp slope towards the edge of the village, without breaking her stride and unaware of some villagers further up the path. She lived on the edge of the village and close to the river, which some might have thought made the house vulnerable to attack, but which she had chosen for its relative isolation.

She was a free spirit, who feared no man or woman and was widely respected as a healer and a font of knowledge. Known as the Wise Woman, she was an expert in the use of wild plants and herbal remedies; she was also gifted in identifying the various maladies that afflicted her patients, and was a popular midwife. When she was unable to cure a person, she was always able to help them cope with their pain and ease their short journey at the end of their life.

She was approaching her forth decade, and showed no signs of aging or any loss of vitality, and being good looking, she was admired by many local men whose unwanted advances were always stalled by Emyr, her large, long-haired hound, that guarded the house and was her constant friend.

Another reason why local men had stopped hoping she might become available was that it was widely rumoured that she had become Lord Dafydd's mistress. This piece of hot gossip had first come from the castle, and was received with quiet satisfaction by the women of the village, both the single ones and the married. They all agreed that Derryth was a very attractive and sexual woman who turned men's heads, but as almost all of them had benefitted from her skills when they were ill or in childbirth, there were few who dared criticize her.

She barged through her unlocked door, catching Emyr dozing in front of the unlit fire. The large animal leapt to his feet, snarling and barring his teeth, the fur on his back standing on end. As he prepared to launch himself across the room, Derryth faced him, her hands on her hips. "Don't be silly, Emyr, it's me!"

The dog immediately became transformed into a tail-wagging, fawning creature with a stupid toothy grin and a welcoming series of whining noises.

"Oh enough, you big baby, I've only been gone a short while." She wrestled playfully with the dog, and then pointed to the door. "Out now, Emyr, and find yourself something to eat." The dog bounded out towards the river, barking joyfully.

She took in a deep breath, shook her arms allowing her fingers to move freely, while she stretched her jaw muscles. "What would I do without a dog?" she murmured as she concentrated on flexing her stomach muscles. "Well, that feels better. Yes, indeed." She lit her fire, poured herself a mug of her homemade cider and relaxed in her only chair as she reflected on what had caused her unusual outburst of anger. "Men are stupid."

She had noticed that recently Lord Dafydd was acting strangely, as though he was building himself up to say something, and she had also been aware that the joyful abandonment of their occasional lovemaking had been replaced with a more mannered approach, as though he was trying to organize it.

Dafydd was certainly not her first lover, and she knew that most women did not enjoy the freedom she took for granted. As a girl she learned from her mother the way to avoid becoming pregnant, and with this knowledge she had approached sex in a liberated way, enjoying the act and avoiding the consequences of unwanted babies which befell most women.

She was not a loose woman, although most priests would have called her a Jezebel, and her choice of men had always been highly selective. Most of her partners had rarely lasted more than a brief few encounters, as they seemed always to want to control her, which she would never allow.

Her recent visit to the castle had started so well. The weather was glorious, people were happy, and she had wanted to share this optimism with the man she cared for. Even Gwriad had beamed with genuine delight at her visit, and had not shown a hint of envy. She knew he desperately missed Angharad, whereas Dafydd had had a different relationship with his wife, Teifryn. Derryth had made a mental note to see his young daughter Tegwen, whom she rarely saw. Alys her nurse acted as a surrogate mother, keeping her away from her preoccupied father for most of the day.

She had asked Dafydd why he spent so little time with his daughter, and he had appeared awkward and uncomfortable, saying she was still young and was better with Alys. He referred to the demands of his work and the need to have her constantly supervised in the castle.

"If you had a son, would you see more of him?" she had asked.

"Yes, I suppose so," he said. "Boys are more suited to castle life. Tegwen needs the company of women, and there are few suitable women in Aberteifi."

She realized now, as she sat in her chair, that she should have listened more carefully. It was clear, on reflection, that Dafydd had been hinting at the way his mind was working. She nodded to herself, he was not the most subtle of men. She continued to relive the afternoon at the castle.

The guard had smiled at her, when he opened the door, and she entered the Great Hall with gathering excitement. The hall was empty as she expected it to be, and she raced up the steps and along the landing to the small office. She tapped on the door, always subconsciously aware that this was not her home, and waited impatiently for Dafydd to open it.

"You don't have to knock," he said, almost bowled over by her as she threw herself into his arms. She was not a short woman, but Dafydd towered above her.

"Are you pleased to see me then?" She clamped her arms around his neck and kissed him with a passion that left him gasping.

"I'm always pleased to see you. You know that. I would like to see much more of you, and I—."

"Stop talking, Dafydd, my love," she giggled as she pushed him towards the open door of his bedroom. Once in the room, she kicked the door shut and, catching Dafydd off balance, fell on top of him on the bed, covering his mouth with hers.

"Derryth," he gasped, trying half-heartedly to push her away. "Stop. I want to ask you—."

"Dafydd! Do stop talking. Can't you see I'm wanting you." She sat astride him and slipped off her blouse, revealing her ample breasts. As she started to undo his shirt, he grabbed her hands.

"Derryth, I must speak to you. Now!" He stared into her confused face, and after trying unsuccessfully to move himself into a more equal position, he blurted out: "I want you to become my wife."

"What?" she looked at him as though he had said something utterly stupid. "That's impossible. You know it is."

"No. It's not impossible. It's what I want. I need you in the castle, and Tegwen needs a mother who can teach her what girls need to know. Gwriad won't mind, I'm sure he likes you. You're the ideal woman!"

She slowly removed herself from the bed and replaced her blouse. Dafydd stared at her angry face in alarm, and stood up beside her. "What's the matter, Derryth? I am asking you to be my wife. I want you."

"You don't understand, do you? We were having fun. We were enjoying ourselves. For a short while you stopped being the Lord, the serious intellectual, the unemotional Dafydd. For our brief moments of love making you became a real man. But it wasn't enough, was it? You had to start to organize everything. You no longer want me as a woman, you want a wife, a lady of the castle, a step-mother for your daughter, someone you can control."

"No, it's not like that. I love you and I want you to become my wife."

"Don't be stupid, Dafydd! You love order, and you love your view of the world. But what about me?

"But, I love you, Derryth."

"And what about my life? You only see this as your life. The way I can fit into your organized world. What about my life?"

"I can make you happy."

"I'm already happy. I love my life. I don't want to marry you. I don't want to be the Lady of the Castle, and I am not suitable to be the mother of your daughter. Why couldn't you let things be?"

"We can make this work, Derryth. We love each other."

"No!" she yelled at him, her face flushed with emotion. "You don't understand the meaning of love! You can't let go. You can't let life be. I had hoped you could, but I was wrong."

Dafydd tried to take her in his arms, but she pushed him aside with a strength that surprised him. "We're finished! It's over. Find yourself a perfect wife. It's not me!"

As she turned to leave he tried to stop her. "Don't go, Derryth! I need you." He grabbed her right arm moments before her left fist landed on his jaw. It was not a hard blow, but it was so unexpected that he fell back on the bed as she stormed out of his room.

Now in the quiet of her home she sipped her cider and smiled, but her eyes were sad. "Stupid man," she murmured. "Well meaning, but stupid."

.   .   .

DAFYDD WALKED AIMLESSLY ALONG THE seashore, watching the incoming sea rippling gently on the wide, empty beach. Behind him, his horse grazed safely on the windblown grasses that grew above the reach of the highest tide. This was one of his favourite places that he had known since his earliest childhood memories. He did not remember his mother, who had died when he was very young, just a succession of servants whom his father, the famous General Cydweli ap Griffith, had employed to act as nurses and surrogate mothers to him and his elder brother Gwriad. But he remembered this beach, which ended with a host of deep rocky pools that gradually gave way to high granite cliffs. It had been the playground for the two boys, where they had risked their lives swimming far out into the bay, and catching huge conga eels that always fought back with murderous intensity. Finally, after the death of their father, when they became the wards of Lord Gomer ap Griffiths, they had learned to gallop their horses across the hard, flat sands, preparing for the futures their uncle had predicted for them, and which Dafydd knew he had only partially embraced.

He realized it had been a long time since he had come back to this special place, and it seemed somehow appropriate that he had chosen to return when his life had suddenly lost its focus. He sat on a rock and stared out to sea, vaguely aware of the two small row boats bobbing in the gentle swell; each held four fishermen from the small village of Llanduduch. They had come downriver with the outgoing tide and would soon be using the incoming tide to aid their return.

On his right, far down the beach, the River Teifi emptied itself into the waiting sea. He could hear the soft lament of a large flock of sandpipers that had settled on the flat sand, waiting for the tide to gradually cover it and bring in a host of shrimp, tiny crabs and small fish. There was the occasional rasping sound of the fishing herons, and overhead a multitude of seagulls squabbled as they cruised the line of the advancing sea. This place was a symbol of unchanging rhythms and certainty. People had died here, victims to the anger of the sea and the cruelty of men, but for him it was a place of peace and beauty; a spot to remember and reflect.

He glanced into a nearby pool where a large crab caught his eye as it scuttled sideways in search of food. It was waiting for the incoming tide to release it from its confinement, or was it? The predictable coming of the sea would once again allow it to travel out into the world, or it might choose to remain in its confined pool, existing on the uncertain bounty of chance.

Was he like the crab? Dafydd stood up and began to walk slowly back towards his horse. Was it guilt that made him feel so empty and insecure, so locked in, hiding away in his room? He knew he had gradually stopped loving Teifryn, and their daughter was a constant reminder of his failure as a husband, and as a father. It was unfair to blame Derryth, as her passionate association with him had been based on his agreement to take more interest in his wife and her needs. Since Teifryn's death, Derryth had helped him recover from the sense of loss that still plagued Gwriad, and she had tried to show him that love was a free spirit, not something that had to be fettered and enclosed.

He shook his head. He was not like that. He believed in structure and organization, and in the God-given rites of marriage. He groaned. It was humbug: he had broken his vows, proving that marriage had not worked for him, and although he attended the occasional religious service, he knew he did not believe in the God that Father Williams preached, or the vows he had taken when he married.

Perhaps he should have spoken to the old priest before he proposed to Derryth? But then he would have been forced to admit to his infidelity, and he was unsure of how the priest viewed the Wise Woman, or whether he would have supported the continuation of an adulterous liaison. What Dafydd did know with certainty was that she was unlikely to have a quick change of mind, and that it was possible she might never agree to resume their relationship.

He reached his horse, mounted and sat staring out at the incoming tide. In spite of himself, the wild splendour had rejuvenated him, and he cantered the obedient animal towards the mouth of the river. "Good girl," he murmured. "Well done, Duwies." He smiled to himself; whether Father Williams would have agreed that 'Goddess' was a suitable name for a supposed Christian Lord's horse was questionable. Duwies was a large animal, bred for battle, and bought in Caerdydd. He and his brother had needed horses when they returned to Wales after a long voyage in a small ship, and Duwies would always be a reminder of their return to Wales following their escape from England after the Battle of Hastings, and the problems of the Norman invaders.

He approached the end of the beach, and watched as two fishermen in their one-man circular coracles paddled out into the river, pulling a long net between them. They had secured one end firmly in the bank with a wooden spike and, holding tightly to the other end of the net, they allowed the incoming tide to curve them round, and when the net was extended, they paddled hard with one hand until they almost reached the shore. The man on the outside of the net let go and brought his small craft onto the shore, about twenty paces from where they had first started. He jumped out, grabbed the other coracle, and pulled it up onto the sandy beach. Then, both men began to pull in the net, and when it was almost in, one man moved the coracles back up the shore out of the way, while the other held the net steady. Already Dafydd could see large shapes thrashing in the net's restricted space.

Both men pulled the wet net over their shoulders and moved slowly back towards the wooden spike, pulling the heavy netting up on the sand. With cries of encouragement, they dropped it and, pulling out small wooden clubs attached to their belts, they began to crush the heads of the large salmon caught in the web. Once there was no further movement, they unfolded the net and laid out the salmon on the beach. One giant fish was almost the length of the shorter man.

The men stood and stared at their monster catch, and were vigorously congratulating each other when Dafydd walked his horse over to them. "Well done, Evan, and you, Morris. I've never seen such a fine catch!" he said from the height of his raised saddle.

The two men straightened up, squinting into the sun and gave a quick bow. "You're quite right, my Lord. You're quite right," Evan replied enthusiastically.

"That's the largest fish I've ever seen," Dafydd said, shaking his head in wonder.

"You're quite right, my Lord. You're quite right," Evan beamed from ear to ear. Morris kept his head bent and said nothing.

"That was very skillful. You judged the tide exactly right."

"You're quite right, my Lord. You're quite right."

"Would you want to take one, my Lord?" Morris asked. There was a hint of resentment in his voice.

"Thank you, Morris. I'm not here to take your fish," Dafydd said firmly. He turned to Evan, "If you have any for sale, Evan, bring them up to the castle and I will ensure you get a good price for them."

Evan beamed. "You're quite right, my Lord. We'll bring some to the castle. Yes, indeed."

Dafydd nodded and trotted off, barely concealing his mirth. Evan's nickname: 'Quite right Evan' was well earned. Although a cheerful, simple-minded man, Evan was one of the most skillful fishermen in Llanduduch.

He would have thought it "quite right" to give a fish to his Lord, and although Dafydd was entitled by tradition to take one fish, it had never been his practice to accept gifts from the poor. Gwriad had no such scruples. He would have taken a large fish, and have had the truculent Morris laughing at his jokes and happy to part with his hard-earned catch.

On his way home, he galloped past Llanduduch, passing the path that led up to the Church and Father Williams' house, failing to see Jon walking his horse miserably down the steep hill. After arriving back at the castle, Dafydd dropped in at the kitchens, where preparations for the evening meal were well under way. The older Megan was outside bullying two kitchen servants in the outer yard as they plucked a pile of geese and hens, and inside he could see the younger Megan rolling dough. She looked pale and unhappy.

"Megan!" he called to the older woman, breaking into her tirade of insults that she was bellowing at two sullen girls.

"Oh, my Lord Dafydd!" she gave him a perfunctory curtsy. "What can I do for you?"

"I have arranged for some large salmon to arrive for tomorrow."

"Thank you, my Lord." It was always difficult to tell if she was pleased, as she rarely smiled.

"What's up with young Megan?" He indicated with a nod at the girl who was usually bubbling with good humour.

"I don't think it's my business, my Lord." She took in a deep breath and her mountainous bosom raised as if for an attack. "I think it best you ask Lord Jon." She sniffed, turned and stalked into the kitchen.

Dafydd decided it was best not to investigate further, and turned to lead his horse to the stables. He handed the sweating animal to the stable boys, and sat on a straw bale in a corner of the spacious building to watch as they removed the heavy saddle and tackle, forked some straw into its feeding bin and began to wipe and brush the animal's glossy coat. He could hear them talking quietly to Duwies as they worked away, unaware of his presence. He was pleased to see they liked his horse.

He leaned back against other bales, and was content to be in the shadows as he reviewed the events of the day. It was a time of change, and he felt a strange feeling of unexpected contentment. He was aware of the occasional sound of the chatter of the kitchen workers and the gruff challenge of the guards as they patrolled the walls. It was something Jon had insisted on when he and Gwriad had been away for so many months. It was an indication of how seriously Jon had taken his responsibility.

After brushing the straw off his jerkin, Dafydd crossed the courtyard, made a joke with the uncertain guard and, entering the hall, was surprised to see Gwriad asleep in a chair, an empty wine jug by his feet. He realized his brother must have been there for a few hours, and cautiously walked over to the recumbent body with increasing alarm.

"I'm not dead, in case you wondered," Gwriad announced with evident satisfaction, sitting up suddenly and stifling a yawn. "But the way you, Jon and Derryth have behaved today, I might as well be. Even young Megan burst into tears when she saw me. Have I developed two heads or what? Oh, don't try and answer. Just get me another jug of wine, and get yourself a cup. I'm starved for company."

Dafydd went to a side door and yelled for a servant. In a short while a jug of wine, cups and a plate with slices of cold meat appeared. He dismissed the servant and sat down opposite Gwriad, filled their cups and in an unusually bibulous display, drained his cup in a single series of loud gulps.

"Bloody hell!" Gwriad exclaimed. "Have you got something serious to tell me?" He sipped cautiously at his wine, and watched, fascinated, as Dafydd quickly refilled his cup.

"Derryth and I have parted company." He took a deep breath and drank deeply.

"Oh? Well, I… um," Gwriad took a slurp from his wine. "I'm sad to hear it, boy. Yes," he was lost for words, "…that's a great shame, isn't it?"

Dafydd filled his mouth with meat and sat silently chewing. Gwriad refilled his own cup.

"No chance of sorting it out?"

"None."

Both men sat silently chewing and drinking until the meat was finished and the jug was empty. Without discussion, Gwriad walked to the side door and yelled for more wine. While he waited he relieved himself in the small anti-room, conscious that the receptacle had not been emptied. It was Jon's job to chase the servants.

When they had refilled their cups, Gwriad said, "Well now, as you no longer have a reason for staying around the castle at this moment, and I notice that you are leaving the welfare of your daughter to Alys, you may be interested in my proposal."

"Oh?" Dafydd lowered his cup.

"I think it's time we raised an army and marched to support Prince Anarwd."

Dafydd's jaw dropped. He had expected his brother to suggest a noble hunt, or a visit to some local Lord, but raising an army and going to fight was a shock. The second major attack on his ordered life in one day.

"Why? Why now? I know that we're getting to the time of the year that armies march, but has something happened that I don't know about?"

"There's been a Norman attack on the village of Cwm in lower Powys. The village has been destroyed with serious loss of life and the local area devastated. This has to stop!" Gwriad banged a clenched fist on his right knee. "Prince Anarwd has asked for our help, and I think we are duty bound to support him."

Dafydd took a long sip of his wine. "Also, if they continued to attack that area, it might occur to them that they could claim it as part of England. If that happened they would be within marching distance of Ceredigion. Who knows where they might attack?" He stared thoughtfully at the red ashes, then slowly stood up and added some wood.

Gwriad's eyes opened wide, and he gazed at his brother in amazement; he had been certain it would take a lot to persuade Dafydd to give up his ordered life. "Good point," he muttered. He had thought of the expedition as a welcome bit of excitement, and a chance to renew his friendship with the Prince. He envisioned ambushing the predatory Normans, and giving them an unexpected defeat, and returning in triumph with little loss of life. Was his brother thinking of something bigger? "What would you suggest?"

"I think we should urge the local men to get planting, and plan to march in late June or early July. By then, we should have been able to persuade the local Lords and landowners to contribute men and horses, arrange for provisions, and make plans to produce weapons and try to make soldiers out of farmers and fishermen. We need to be organized."

"So, you're in favour?"

"Yes. It's necessary, and it's what we both need."

"Indeed," Gwriad reflected briefly on the fact that he should never underestimate his brother. "I think Jon might be interested in coming."

Dafydd nodded. "Definitely." He took a long sip of his wine. "I think he might have fallen out with Megan."

"I noticed she's not happy."

"I tried to raise it with the elder Megan and she referred me to Jon. I understand he left the castle in a in a foul mood."

"There must be something in the air," Gwriad grinned. "So, you'll take care of the planning, and I'll contact the local Lords and landowners. I'll talk to Jon. Earlier today he was keen to get involved. He can take on the local training of the farm lads: he's a natural with the sword. I'll appoint Sergeant Penn to train the castle soldiers, who are worse than useless as fighting men. Penn's getting old, and I might well decide to leave him in charge of the castle when we depart." He was speaking quickly, and his eyes flashed with enthusiasm.

Dafydd sat forward on his chair and poured more wine for them both. His face was flushed and he felt an excitement he had not felt since their dangerous encounters in England, just before the great battle between the Normans and the Saxons. "We need horses and wagons. Leave that to me, and I'll start to work out the food supplies and the baggage train. We'll need an officer corps."

"There are a lot of good lads around here who were part of my Central Army under King Gruffydd, and many of them were involved in our attack on Shrewsbury and on Harold's so-called palace." He shook his head. "That's more than three years ago, boy. We're all a bit older."

"But wiser as well," Dafydd began to laugh. "This is going to be so good, Gwriad. The two of us, fighting together with Jon to cover our backs!" He stood up impulsively and raised his cup. "To Wales!"

"To Wales!" Gwriad stood up and touched cups, which they both emptied and sat down. At least Gwriad sat back in his chair. Dafydd flopped down, missed his chair, and collapsed on the old hound who yelped in fright, and ran off barking.

"You could never hold your drink, there's a twpsyn," he jested as he dragged his brother to his feet.

"I'm not a stupid person," Dafydd slurred. "You couldn't cope without me."

"How true, Brother. How true." He called for a servant who manhandled the mildly protesting Lord up the stairs to his room. "What a very interesting day it's turned out to be. What do you think, Ifan?" he said as he patted the old hound. "Shall we go to war?

CHAPTER SIX

Hours later, as Jon approached the main gates of the castle with the words of the priest echoing in his ears, he realized he had no choice but to speak to his father. The light had faded, but the soldiers on the wall recognized him and ordered the main gate to be opened. He passed through, ignoring their cheerful greetings. The braziers had been lit and the shadows in the courtyard seemed like a warning, as he made his way towards the stables. He felt nervous and jittery.

"Here! Damn you! Wake up in there!" He was surprised to hear the sound of authority in his voice that caused the stable boys to rush out to take his horse. He knew it was unusual for him to abuse the servants, even when they failed in their duties, but he could think of nothing other than the forthcoming interview. He stormed up the stairs into the Great Hall, passing the guard and slamming the door behind him.

"Ah, it's you again!" Gwriad called out from his chair near the fire. "I hope you're not intending to slam all the doors in this castle?"

"My Lord," Jon bowed. "I didn't see you there." He bowed again and rushed across the hall and made for his small room.

He sat on his bed for a short while, preparing himself for a return to the hall, and the uncomfortable meeting that he knew he had to have with Gwriad. He tried different approaches, but all led to the fact that he was going to be the father of Megan's child, and that Lord Gwriad would be furious.

Jon groaned, rubbed his eyes and began to pace about the cramped space. He half hoped that Dafydd might be there, but on second thoughts he feared that his adopted uncle, with his high moral attitudes, might be even more difficult to reason with. The single candle in his room began to gutter and he went outside where a wall brazier provided enough light to reach the door to the hall.

When he entered, Gwriad was sitting in the same place as before, although the chair on the other side of the fire was on its side. The braziers gave the hall a friendly atmosphere, and Jon hoped it was a good sign. He hesitated.

"Oh, just come in and make yourself at home, my boy!" Gwriad bellowed. "And for God's sake stop calling me 'my Lord' when we're alone."

"Yes, Sir." Jon always had difficulty calling Gwriad 'Father'. He noticed his flushed face and the jug of wine and wondered whether it was a good time to talk to him. "I have something on my mind."

"Yes. I noticed." He leaned forward and poured wine into a cup, refilled his own and indicated to Jon to come over and sit near him. "Tell me about Megan."

Jon looked alarmed. "You know?" He picked up the chair and sat down.

"Only what I've observed... as has Dafydd." He raised his cup. "Well, get on with it, or I'll soon have finished another jug."

Jon quickly finished his cup of wine and placed it firmly on the table with a flourish. "Megan is expecting a baby. My baby."

Gwriad looked into the fire. He had thought this was the reason for Jon's anger and Megan's unhappiness. "What are you going to do about it?"

"I want to marry her."

Gwriad gently rubbed Ifan's head in a thoughtful way, as he reflected on his earlier life. He had explored the delights of sex with many young women by the time he had reached Jon's age, and had never given any thought to the possible consequences. The fact that none of them had become pregnant was more luck than judgement as far as he was concerned. Even when married to Angharad, he had occasionally had brief affairs with older women who were keen to please him and themselves. With them, he had also escaped any repercussions, and had always thought that Angharad was the one who was unable to have children during their passionate marriage, especially as he had been certain she was not a virgin when he married her. Only recently had he faced up to the fact that he might be the infertile one.

"You can't marry her," he said bluntly. "When you confessed to Father Williams, what did he say?"

"He said he would not marry us." Jon reached out and poured himself another cup.

Gwriad raised his eyebrows, and silently held out his own cup, which Jon refilled. Nothing was said while they both sipped their wine. "He said it was impossible for a Lord to marry a fisherman's daughter," Jon tried not to sound upset.

"That's true. I imagine he explained why it's impossible?"

"But I love her."

"Of course you do. But it's as impossible to marry her as it is to swim up the Cenarth Falls. You might be the strongest swimmer in the River Teifi, but it would still be impossible. Now, there is nothing wrong with walking around those treacherous falls, just like there is nothing wrong with accepting your responsibilities. Father Williams could help Megan chose an ambitious young farmer from another area who would, for a price, take her on as his wife. She would lose touch with the local people for a while, have her child and come back into her social level as the happy wife of a rich farmer. I would provide the money."

Jon stared in horror at his father. "But I love her."

"Which shows you have feelings. All young men fall in love, usually many times. You've been unlucky." He paused, "She might think she's been unlucky, but if it had not been you, she would have to have married a local fisherman by now, and live in poverty." In a decisive gesture he finished his wine, stood up and staggered slightly. "I'm off to bed. Think carefully." He glared at Jon, "Tomorrow, I want to quickly agree the details with you, and then you can help me plan our future war on the Normans." Without another word, he walked determinedly towards the hall, yelled for a servant, and with his help slowly climbed the stairs.

Jon sat miserably staring into the fire. He wondered if he might rouse Megan from her straw pallet in the big kitchen. But he rejected the idea. A host of servants slept there and he would be noticed. He started to pace around the hall, muttering to himself and causing the old hound to raise its head anxiously, and watched him for a moment before returning to sleep.

He knew now he could not hope to continue as the future Lord Jon ap Gwriad and marry Megan. It might mean going back to the poverty of his childhood and leaving the area, but he was certain he could not desert Megan. He must face up to his responsibilities as a father. With that firmly in mind he went off to his room.

.   .   .

IN THE MORNING HE MET Megan behind a storage hut, having instructed a servant to tell her. When she approached, he noticed she was looking composed and strangely calm, in complete contrast to the day before.

"You're not to worry, Megan," he said, forcing a smile. "I'll look after you." He held out his arms to embrace her.

She stopped a few paces away. There was no smile on her face. "I know. Megan told me."

"Megan? The cook? What does she have to do with it?"

"Lord Gwriad gave her a message, before he went out riding. She has explained it all to me, "It makes sense. There's no other way."

"What did he say?"

"You know what he said," Megan face hardened. "I'm going to marry a farmer that I don't know. He's going to marry me for money, and I'm going to leave this area, at least for a while. I'm going to be looked after, and my baby will not live in poverty as I did." She dropped her head. "It's for the best. You know that."

"But I'm the father, and I want you to be my wife. I love you."

"Don't be so bloody stupid!" she yelled. He had never heard her swear, and it hit him like blow. "Stop living in your world of make-believe, for God's sake. You're a grown man now, so act like it!" She wiped tears from her eyes. "We have no choice. You should have thought about this. You gave me your word. I'm just lucky that Lord Gwriad will help me. This is no longer your baby! Don't try to speak to me again!" She ran off towards the kitchens, leaving Jon wide-eyed and confused.

As she helped prepare food, she told the old cook what she had said, and how Jon had taken it. "He kept saying it was his baby and how he wants to marry me. He's just a boy."

"Most men are," the older woman said. "Men like him always assume the baby is theirs, the others are convinced it's someone else's." She laughed, "Women have the children, and take the responsibility. You need to speak to Father Williams. He'll know who to approach, and Lord Gwriad will pay the money and make your prospective husband look after you well. I know the priest will marry you." She turned to get on with her work. "I wouldn't tell your family that you're expecting a baby. Just tell them you're getting married to a farmer. They've had little to do with you since you came to the castle, and they'll be delighted that you have married into money." She laughed, "You might end up with a better husband!"

Megan nodded slowly, deep in thought. "I know it's for the best. I knew I could never be a Lord's wife. It was exciting at first, and Jon had told me he had seen the Wise Woman and that he knew how to prevent a child." She sniffed, "I believed him."

"You should have talked it over with me."

"Yes," she put her arms around the older woman's shoulders. "It was just… it was unreal, and I didn't want anyone to know."

"Ha! It was the talk of the castle, m'dear. But we all thought it was just some sort of innocent fun. After all, with him becoming a Lord and all the learning he was given, we just thought he and you were playing about." She turned, rubbed her hands on a rag, and embraced the girl. "But Jon's not like his step-father. Oh no! Lord Gwriad was a great man for the women and knew how to have fun as well. Jon's too serious, like Lord Dafydd. He doesn't really want to marry you, he just feels he should do," she laughed. "He'd make an awful father!" She paused. "Do you love him?"

"No. I thought I did, but it was just exciting, that was all. I never imagined marriage or becoming a mother." She frowned, "And when I found out, I just wanted him to feel responsible. I never wanted to marry him."

"Well, you're going to be lucky, young Megan. I happen to know Lord Gwriad has sent a message to Father Williams, and soon you'll be told who your husband's going to be, and in a year or so, nobody will remember or care if he's the father."

"Thank you," she bit her lower lip. "I'm going to miss working here, with you."

The older woman placed her hands on her hips and adopted her usual stern expression. "It's going to be a big change for you, young Megan, and you're going to have to work hard being a farmer's wife. But you've been so lucky. You could have had to return to your village, pregnant and unwanted. Your family would have treated you as a slut, and you would have suffered, although it was his fault, and no one would have cared. Don't you waste this opportunity now."

"No, I won't. I promise," she stepped back.

"Well, don't stand around, young Megan, there's some big salmon to be dealt with."

CHAPTER SEVEN

Iago ran downhill through familiar woodland, until he reached the fast-flowing stream, and cautiously made his way past thick willow trees whose branches hung like supplicants over the water. The smell of burning became intense, and in the distance he could see flames and thick smoke erupting from the mill. As he crept closer, he could hear the shouts of the foreign soldiers, some were cheering. He moved nearer, unsure what he could do, but determined to somehow protect any surviving members of his family.

The Normans had dismounted and left their horses out of range of any danger from the burning mill. The door into the structure had been smashed open, and a group of soldiers stood in a half circle around it and watched intently with their swords drawn as the fire spread around the building.

It was the time of the year when his father cleaned up the place, made the necessary repairs and prepared for the autumn influx of wheat to crush and turn into flour. Many years ago, when the miller was a young man, he had constructed his mill with the help of local friends, but it had reached the stage of needing constant annual repair. The door, like many small jobs, had always wanted attention and its repair had never been seen as necessary. It would have been easy to force open, assuming it had been closed when they attacked.

Iago crept closer, moving into some dense bushes away from the water and trying to see if any of the bodies near the mill were those of his family. He was about thirty paces behind the soldiers, when his father burst through the broken door wielding a wood axe. Pritchard was a big man, and given to violent anger, and he attacked the Normans as though he was the well-armed leader of an avenging army, not a poorly clothed peasant with an old axe.

He swung at the nearest soldier, and would have decapitated the man had the soldier not instinctively jumped back. The axe narrowly missed, and the miller was unbalanced for a moment. The soldiers took advantage of this and rushed him, attacking from all sides. In a short, vicious fight he injured two of them, before being cut down and stabbed repeatedly, even when he had stopped moving.

The whole awful event was over so quickly, that Iago found himself standing like a statue unable to believe that his all-powerful father had been murdered in mere moments. He swallowed hard, trying to control the wave of emotions that surged through him, and was unaware that he was clearly visible to the soldiers once they looked his way. A cry went up as one of them pointed at Iago, and with a roar of excitement the blood-crazed soldiers ran towards him. Suddenly alert, he turned into the woods and ran like a rabbit with a pack of hounds behind.

He had played and hunted in these woods since childhood and his knowledge of the area enabled him to quickly shake them off. His belief that the weight of their armour would slow them down proved correct, but he had not thought that they would return to their horses and continue the hunt. His first knowledge of the danger was when he heard men shouting in the distance, their voices getting closer, like hunters trying to flush out game.

He knew he was close to the river, and ran towards it, weaving through the willows as he sought the small path that led to a ford known only to the local people. The recent rains had turned the normally placid stream into a raging torrent, and as he entered the water he wondered if he would be dragged away by the current. The water was colder than he expected and if it had not been for the approaching shouts of the soldiers he would have returned to the bank.

Shaking with a combination of cold and fear, he gradually moved out into the stream, slowly forcing himself across, his feet following the unseen stony ridge that enabled a safe crossing for most of the year. When the water was over his waist, he sensed he was half-way across, and at that moment, he heard the dreaded calls of the hunters getting closer. In spite of his trembling, he forced himself forward until he reached the other side, and climbed out, thankful to have survived. Normally, there was clear evidence on both sides of the stream that horses and wagons had crossed, but the recent heavy rains had washed away any such telltale signs, and after quickly checking that he had covered his exit. He looked around for a safe place to hide.

Iago was exhausted, a combination of physical effort and mental shock. He staggered into a small copse of willows just back from the water and collapsed on his stomach watching to see if the soldiers would find the ford and, even if they did, would they believe it worth crossing when they were uncertain he had come this way. He lay still and listened as the sounds of his enemy faded away. Slowly he stopped trembling and as his body warmed he relaxed in his hiding place amid the curtain of willow fronds.

He stared resentfully at the opposite bank, trying to come to terms with the loss of his family. He was certain his mother and sisters had been murdered even though he had been unable to recognize their bodies among the corpses scattered around in front of the mill. A shudder wracked him as he relived the horror of his father's violent death.

Up until the coming of the Normans, Iago's life had been predictable and uneventful, and even the occasional beating from his father had been part of the family life of a rural peasant. He had never seen a dead body, nor had he been involved with events outside the immediate neighbourhood. Now, without warning, his world had been torn apart. His eyes closed as he was lulled by the soporific timbre of the water.

It was approaching sunset when he awoke with a start, unable to believe he had slept for so long. He jumped to his feet, and tried to decide what he should do. There was no sound of the soldiers and he realized his brother and the remainder of his family would be worried about him. If they had continued to hide in the trees, they would be unaware that he had been forced to flee, and might fear that he had been caught and murdered. He returned to the ford, took a deep breath and waded into the cold water.

He was certain the soldiers would have soon given up looking for him as he was of no importance to them. Reaching the other bank, he struggled out of the grip of the water and quickly rubbed himself down with his strong hands. He had to discover whether any members of his family had survived, and with that thought he ran back towards the site of the mill.

Soon he could smell the burning and by keeping to the edge of the stream he was able to approach from the back of the mill. It had been utterly destroyed, and only some burned planks remained. The heavy stone grinder lay on its side and the once impressive wooden water wheel had been hacked off its spindle and was lying half-sunk in the river. He had known this mill all his life, and as a child had often spent happy hours watching the water wheel turn and the water cascade down from the top of the paddles to splash in the river below. As he grew older he had helped his father pour the sacks of wheat onto the path of the great mill stone, and refill the same sacks with the resulting flour. Now it was all gone, destroyed by an enemy he did not know and whose motives he did not understand.

He crept forward, his eyes stinging with the acrid smoke and checked the immediate area. The soldiers had gone, and corpses lay in unnatural positions on the flat ground in front of the smouldering embers of the mill. He hesitated, not wanting to get too near. He knew his father had been killed, and he did not wish to see his father's mangled corpse. He had seen him die. It was enough. Yet, he had to know if his mother and his sisters were among the cluster of broken bodies.

It took only moments to find them. His mother and his two youngest sisters were lying face down in the churned soil, and Iago stared at them in mute grief, trying to resist the emotion that threatened to overwhelm him.

But when he found his elder sister lying on her back, her eyes staring at the sky, her dress above her waist, he collapsed to his knees and retched uncontrollably.

Later, having adjusted his sister's dress and closed her eyes, he sat beside her, his arms round his knees and rocked backwards and forwards as he tried to stop the spasms that wracked his body. Gwen had been his favourite sister, noted for her kindness and her smiling eyes.

"I should have been here," he moaned as hot tears rolled down his cheeks. "I could have helped. I could have saved them." But even as he spoke he relived his powerful father being cut down by the men in armour as though he had been a defenceless child. Common sense had prevailed, and Iago knew he could not have saved them.

He stared around, unsure what to do with his dead relatives: he had nothing to bury them with, and he wasn't too sure if he had to have a priest to bless them before their burial. He looked up the hill, and suddenly remembered that his uncle and aunt and his younger brother were hiding up there among the trees. His uncle would know what to do, or at least his aunt would.

He checked around for any sign of movement and seeing there was none, he stood up and gazed briefly at his sister, trying to imprint her face on his memory, then tramped towards the hill. He was breathing heavily when he reached the top, unaware that he had been rushing as fast as his legs would move.

Iago strode into the wood and pushed his way through the bushes, until he came to the place where he clearly remembered he had left the wagon. There was no sign of it, and he was afraid to call out to his brother in case the soldiers were still around. "They'll have moved to get better cover," he said to himself. "That's what I'd do." Even as he spoke, he felt a nagging doubt.

The soil was damp in places, and he was able to follow the ruts of the wagon as it had weaved its way through the trees. He felt increasing optimism until he reached a place where the wagon had reached a small path and had turned to the left, travelling only a few paces before the soil had become a quagmire of iron-shoed hoof prints. He stopped and examined the ground. Away from the muddy mess of the interaction of numerous horse imprints and the wagon ruts, he could see clear evidence of the wagon having been turned and heading back in the opposite direction with horse prints going in the same direction.

To the left, Iago found the place where the wagon had turned back and before that only the horse prints. He went back to the quagmire where the wagon appeared to have encountered the horses; there was blood on the ground. "Oh no!" he yelled. "No!" He looked frantically around and began to search the undergrowth. On the other side of the path, partially hidden by bushes and in a small ditch, he found all four of his relatives. They had been brutally murdered.

Iago was unable to respond. He stood in the one spot staring at the blood-covered bodies, trying to convince himself that this was just a bad dream and he would awake and everything would be fine. He checked his small brother for any sign of life, but his wounds had stopped bleeding and his body was cold. When darkness fell, he finally gave way to grief and sat next to the remains of his family, leaning against a small oak with his knife in his hand.

He awoke at first light, and in a numbed state began to follow after the horsemen and his family's wagon. His only thoughts were of revenge.

CHAPTER EIGHT

Earl Fitzosbern was aged forty-seven when he was created Earl of Hereford in 1067. King William considered him his most important supporter, for not only was he a cousin who had fought bravely at the Battle of Hastings, but he had proved to be the most loyal and successful of William's close coterie of proven knights.

Shortly after the great battle with the Saxons, the newly-crowned king had appointed his cousin to take control of the Isle of Wight, and in a short campaign Fitzosbern destroyed all elements of opposition on the Isle, and thereby established a safe fall-back position if the Saxons ever managed a successful comeback on the mainland. To emphasise his control, Fitzosbern began construction of Carisbrooke Castle, which stamped the Norman authority on this strategically important island.

"Cousin, welcome to London!" King William used both arms to raise up the knight who knelt before him. It was late in the evening, but Fitzosbern had just arrived. "You must be tired?"

The Earl shook his head, he rarely felt tired, even after a battle. "It was an easy voyage, my Lord: calm seas, a good wind and a fast horse."

With the necessary social niceties over, the King went straight to the important issues. "I'm grateful to you for your speedy success on the Isle of Wight, and for your building of the castle. That was a masterful stroke." He turned and indicated an ornately carved chair for Fitzosbern then sat opposite him, nodding at a servant who immediately served a fine Burgundy wine in silver chalices.

They smiled at each other and tasted the wine. "As always, my Lord, a distinguished choice." William was noted for his love of wines and fine living, and the two men had known each other since childhood.

"When we're alone you call me Wil as you've always done. I get bored

with the obsequious performances of the sycophants who surround me."
He sipped his wine. "One of the trials of kingship."

"Are your plans working out as you hoped, Wil?" Fitzosbern relaxed in
his chair, and helped himself to an array of cold meats that silent servants
had placed on a small inlaid table.

"The Saxons are proving obdurate. I had hoped to have more control
by now," the King stared discontentedly into a blazing fire, in front of
which slept his favourite hound. William sat up suddenly in his chair, the
constant man of action, and leaned towards his cousin. "I'm appointing
you Earl of Gloucester, Worcester and Oxfordshire, and with your
previous appointment as Earl of Hereford, you will take charge of the
eventual subjugation of the West."

Fitzosbern nodded. He knew his cousin never wasted time and that
all social events were to solidify his ongoing plans; it was a trait that ran
in the family, it was how he himself worked. "I'm honoured, Wil, and I
won't let you down." Fitzosbern raised his challis. "To you, King William
the First of England and Duke of Normandy."

They both drank deeply and a servant quickly refilled the wine.
Anyone looking at these two men would immediately notice the family
resemblance: the aesthetic face, their shared love of detail and artistic
achievement, and their unflagging energy. Both were lean, tough men
who valued courage and were utterly fearless.

"That makes you my most important man in England." William sat
back, and stared at the fire. Fitzosbern could see he was selecting the
discussion of his plans in order. "I must soon return to Normandy, and
I want you and my half-brother Bishop Odo of Bayeux to rule England
while I am away."

"Trouble?"

"There's always trouble when a ruler appears to have deserted his
realm," he laughed. "I just have to bang a few heads." He chewed slowly
on a leg of chicken. "I know this is a lot to ask, but I'm sure Odo can keep
control of London, leaving you free to lead an army against anyone who
sticks his head up."

Fitzosbern nodded. "I intend to allow some of the lesser knights in
my army to be responsible for certain unruly areas. It gives them some
experience of leadership, and keeps the men busy. It's a problem with

battle-hardy soldiers: they have a problem settling into normal life." He finished his wine and waved off a servant with more. "You can be assured the country will be in good hands and awaiting your return."

They both stood up and embraced each other. "You are my most trusted friend. I'll be leaving for Normandy as soon as the winds are agreeable." The King walked towards the door with his arm over Fitzosbern's shoulder. "Odo has already arrived and is organizing his priests like an army! You can leave the politics to him."

At the door William appeared to remember that people have lives beyond politics and war. "Remember me to your wife."

"I will, my Lord." Fitzosbern bowed, accepted his cloak and sword belt from an anxious servant and with dignified style descended the wide staircase with a small army of servants in attendance. From above, the King nodded contentedly and returned to his map table, where he began to familiarize himself with the northern parts of England. "Send in the messengers!" he ordered. "And any of the courtiers who are still up." He felt excited, it would be a long night.

.   .   .

PRINCE ANARWD, THE RULER OF Morgannwg and the protector of Gwent, was pacing around his roomy, but unattractive, stronghold like a caged lion. Unlike other Welsh Princes, he did not spend his wealth on comfort or impressive buildings. He was a practical man who preferred to invest in a small standing army, new weapons and fine horses. As he was constantly aware, he lived in a dangerous area where warfare between the Welsh and those on the other side of the border, be they Saxon or Norman, was a never-ending, on-ongoing occurrence.

The Prince was not only an experienced fighter, but also a diplomat who employed people across the border to keep him informed about what the recent invaders were up to. He had already taken note of Earl Fitzosbern, the new Earl of Hereford, and had learned some of his brief history since the invasion: most importantly, that he was the second most powerful man in England. It gave him food for thought when he learned that King William had departed for Normandy and that this same Earl was now the acting ruler of England. He realized that this could be a vital time in the defence of Wales.

"I must discuss this with the local Princes, and with the Lords of Aberteifi," he muttered.

The next day he sent off a cohort of his cavalry under the command of his friend General Maelgwn, to ride to the brothers' castle in Ceredigion. He felt it was vital to ensure that his message reached them and that they knew of its importance. He also sent for his long-time friend Lord Edwin ap Tewdwr, ruler of nearby Gwent, who had reacted immediately.

The two men were standing looking out over the fast-moving river below Prince Anarwd's rugged stronghold watching the fading sun disappearing behind the nearby mountains.

"You think the new king in England will be a problem?" Lord Edwin said. He had just arrived, and after supervising the needs of his small detachment of cavalry, he had followed Anarwd up into the main hall and was already in tactical discussions, when all Edwin wanted at that moment was a cup of wine or even a flagon of beer.

"Don't you?" Anarwd was a driven man, constantly aware that he seemed to be the only leader who took the changing situation seriously. "In Gwent you must know of the growing threat?"

"There's always been a threat." Edwin glanced around the large, cold room with its limited furnishings. "Do you have anything to drink, my friend?"

"Oh? Drink? Yes, of course. I'm a poor host." He called for a servant, and soon the two of them were sitting in large, deep chairs enjoying mugs of beer around a hot fire, while servants lit the braziers and brought in plates of cold meats and warm bread that they placed on a low table. It was the only space in the room that could be said to be comfortable. In front of them a large animal, more wolf than hound, lay motionless, its dark eyes staring, unblinking at Edwin.

"I see Blaidd still doesn't trust me."

"His stare is worse than his bite," Anarwd leaned over and rubbed the thick hair of its head. "It's alright, Blaidd. You know Edwin."

The dog looked reluctantly away and with a muted growl of protest, stood up and rested its huge head on its owner's lap. "He's good in battle. Best war dog I've ever had: he can bring down an armoured horseman." Anarwd's ruddy face creased into a broad smile. "Foot soldiers are terrified of him!"

"I've never used a war dog," Edwin frowned. "To be honest, I'm not comfortable with large dogs." He gave the animal a quick glance, not wanting to lock in to that ferocious stare. "Good God, man, he's as big a small pony."

"A good war dog is only loyal to its master. This dog would die for me. If I was to be knocked down, he would guard me against all comers until they killed him. You can't say that about most people."

Edwin nodded silently and drank deeply. "Anyway, what's your problem? I was sitting with Carys this morning, planning our daughter's betrothal to some drip from Caerdydd, when your messenger arrived," he paused and cleared his throat. "Well, that's not true. He's not a bad choice."

"But not one you would have chosen for your eldest daughter's husband."

They both laughed, and Anarwd refilled their flagons. They were cousins who known each other since childhood. Both had married at much the same time, but Anarwd's wife had died giving birth to his only son, and since then he had directed his immense energy into the defence of his beloved Morgannwg. There were many local women of noble birth who would have welcomed his attentions, but as his bloodline was secure, he had no incentive to take another wife. He was a short, stocky, muscular man with thick black hair, and penetrating blue eyes, who was constantly on military maneuvers or negotiating with his neighbours. He was always the last to get to bed, and the first to rise, and his friends joked that he would never have time for another wife.

His son, Alun, was also a warrior, and at the age of eighteen commanded a platoon of older men. In many ways he was the spitting image of his father, and to the Prince's intense pride had perfected his ability with a long bow. His popularity was such that all the younger men in the area had worked hard with the long bow to make themselves worthy of his praise. Anarwd had immediately seen the military possibilities of having a strong pool of archers who practised frequently while still farming. What had earlier been a hunting weapon had, when used in a large formation, become the deadliest of weapons on the battlefield.

Edwin was an equally energetic man. Slimmer and taller than his friend, and with a receding hair line that made him look much older than Anarwd, he was a family man who loved and supported his three daughters and adored Carys, his spirited wife. He had the reputation as a brave fighter, who led from the front and whose soldiers gave him their unstinting support.

As he often said to his wife, "My job is to lead. My men follow me not because I pay them, but because they would fight, even without a leader, but mostly they fight because I do, and they don't want to let me down."

Carys would always laugh. "You'd fight on even if they all ran away. You can't help yourself!" And they would both laugh.

"Tell me about this sudden worry that you have," Edwin asked.

Anarwd's face changed from mirth to a serious intensity. "You've heard about the destruction of the village of Cwm?

Edwin nodded. "In Brycheiniog?

"Yes. Norman soldiers massacred the peasants and laid waste to the area. It was a slaughter. Then they retreated back over the border with some animals. It was a poor community and the people were not attacked for their wealth or as punishment for raiding English farms. I believe they were murdered as part of a long-term plan to occupy that area." He stared into the fire. "I believe that over the next few years these Normans want to conquer the whole of Wales."

"The Saxons tried that, and we always gave them a bloody nose. We can do the same to the Normans."

"The Normans are different. They're better armed, they have more horses and when they win a battle, they don't go home, they build castles."

"Castles?" Edwin held his cup out for more wine. "Stone castles?"

"Yes. That's how they are gradually conquering the whole of England."

"I hadn't heard that."

"There's this Earl called Fitzosbern. I understand he's related to the Norman King William. He was responsible for putting down the Saxon opposition on the Isle of Wight. He's the one that builds castles."

"I see," said Edwin. He was not much interested in what happened in parts of England of which he had no knowledge. As someone who had never left Wales until the time when he had helped to attack Earl Harold's palace, he was happy to leave the information-gathering to Anarwd.

"After the attack on Cwm, I contacted the Griffith Lords, Gwriad and Dafydd, and asked them to help me plan a large retaliatory attack on the

Normans this summer. I was thinking of something on the lines of the army we raised to attack Earl Harold's lands."

"Indeed. A good idea. However, that was nearly three years ago. June fourteenth in fact." He leaned forward to refill his mug, and Blaidd gave a threatening growl from the other side of his master's lap. Edwin pretended not to notice and refilled both mugs.

"I've changed my mind about a summer attack." Anarwd stared into the fire, absent-mindedly stroking the head of his huge hound. "I'll tell you why. I had some news today which I think changes everything." He turned to Edwin. "This Earl Fitzosbern has recently been made Earl of most of the South-West of England. He's now Earl of Chester, Earl of Hereford and Earl of Shrewsbury. He's the most powerful Norman in England other than the King." He raised his mug, "And listen, man, the King has just returned to Normandy, and has left this knight in charge of the country's security. He's left the legal and the religious side to Bishop Odo of Bayeux."

"Who?"

"Bishop Odo. He's the King's half-brother."

"How does that affect us?"

"It's obvious, man," Anarwd spoke with unrestrained enthusiasm. "If Fitzosbern has the whole country to govern, he won't have the time to protect his border with us. Now is the time for us to get our revenge for their unprovoked attack on Cwm, and make him think twice before he lets his soldiers attack our villages."

Edwin nodded slowly and tried to ignore the unblinking stare that Blaidd was fixing on him. "There are a few problems, you know. It will be difficult to raise a large army at this moment: it's planting time. Also, while I agree that it might seem the right time to attack their farms and villages, the Normans have a large standing army they can use at any time. Unfortunately, we have very few Lords who have more than a handful of professional soldiers, and any farmers and peasants who are willing to join our army will disband as soon as they return to Welsh soil."

"I know all that," there was a trace of irritation in Anarwd's tone. "Whenever we attack our enemy we will face the possibility of retaliation, and I know we must somehow find the means to afford a standing army." He stared into the fire. "King Gruffydd ap Llywelyn built up trade with

Ireland, and raided the Saxon shipping in the Severn Estuary. We had the money for two major armies in those days, although the Northern Army was the best funded."

Edwin nodded thoughtfully. "Every winter we would stand down the majority of our forces, which is how Gruffydd was caught unprepared by Earl Harold. Nobody ever thought the Saxons would attack when snow was on the ground."

"Exactly. Harold did the unexpected and, although he lost most of his army, he won the decisive battle, and caused our King to flee." Anarwd shook his head. "But, as we know, it was really only decisive because Gruffydd was murdered by those northern scum as he came through the Llanberis Pass to rally the Central Army. However, we must not forget that Lord Gwriad is a fine General. He controlled the Central Army, and his brother was the great organizer who made things happen. They did well when we attacked Harold's palace, and I believe they can do it again."

He rose to his feet and, ignoring the rumbling complaints of Blaidd, began to pace around the empty room, where the flickering light from the few wall braziers cast his shadow as he passed.

"If we attack early in the season, when the Normans aren't expecting us, and when the local Earl is tied up with uprisings elsewhere, we should be able to strike them hard before they can organize themselves." He stopped to take a quick drink and then continued his pacing. Edwin sat back in his chair and watched him. "How many troops do you think you can afford to retain after a quick raid? One hundred? Two hundred?"

"I've got about fifty at the moment. They have free board and lodging, and I don't have to pay them much, but if we launch a successful attack, we could use the prospect of pillage as the way to build up the numbers."

"Most men like the idea of stealing stuff from the enemy," Anarwd agreed. "They never think they might die, or that they could be injured. It's all to do with the chance of getting rich, in their terms. Also, it's a chance for them to break out of their usual humdrum lives."

"The younger ones think of being heroes and having their way with the enemy's women." Edwin gave a humourless laugh.

Anarwd frowned. "Not just the younger ones either. I've never been in favour of rape, but it's impossible to prevent it happening after a battle. I know King Gruffyd always said he would hang any of his soldiers who attacked women and children. I don't think it had much effect," he paused, "but it made him feel better."

"So, supposing we managed to get Gwriad and Dafydd involved, and we raised a sizeable army, what happens when we return? How do we maintain a viable force to oppose the expected Norman counterattack? I've heard they are constantly in the field, and their armies move around the country ready to quell Saxon opposition. They're experienced and battle-hardy and they're a different enemy to the Saxons we used to have to fight, who also had to use local peasants to bolster their trained soldiers."

"Their counterattack is always a consideration whenever we fight them. If we leave the attack to mid-summer, it is likely that King William will have returned and the notable Earl Fitzosbern will be ready for us. If we attack in the next few weeks, we should be able to catch him off guard and make a deadly impact on the Hereford area. We have no choice, we have to fight or Wales will lose its lands, perhaps for ever."

There was a long pause as both men recharged their mugs and sat staring at the fire. "I know you're right," Edwin said. "I also know we're inviting a reaction. So, our main concern is how to be prepared for on-going war that will last until the Normans realize it's not worth their bother."

"Indeed. So how to raise the money and reorganize our defences is the problem we have to solve. We managed under Gruffydd, and we can do it again."

"But we don't have an unending supply of soldiers anymore. Under Gruffydd we had the major populations of Gwyneth and Powys. That was when we were united. I believe Gwyneth is still ruled by Cynan ap Iago, the bastard who murdered our King?

"That's true. Also, the self-appointed Prince of Powys, Bleddyn ap Cynfya, whom we forced to help us when we marched through his lands on our way to attack Harold's palace, is still in charge, although I am informed he's useless. He spends his time feasting and womanizing, and worse still he's been trying to ingratiate himself with the Normans. I think we could have trouble getting either of those important areas to help us."

"I would never trust Cynan, and he'd never trust us." He sniffed. "You say you've contacted the Griffith brothers?"

"Yes, indeed." He grabbed some meat, and indicated that Edwin should do the same. "Originally, I asked them to take part in a summer assault and I heard back immediately from Dafydd. They seemed very keen to be involved. He said they could be prepared by early July, and soldiers, wagons and weapons did not seem to be a problem. But when I heard that William was back in Normandy, I knew we had to advance our plans. That's why I have sent my return message with General Maelgwn. He understands my reasons. I hope he's successful."

"So, we wait to hear what they have to say?"

"Yes. I always seem to be waiting, when there's so much to do."

Edwin finished his mug, and his eyes began to close. "Oh yes!" he sat up. "I heard a story about how Gwriad and Dafydd travelled to London to kill King Harold?" He laughed. "Did that really happen?"

"It did. Furthermore, I heard they were pressed into fighting alongside the Saxons in the big battle against the Normans! Imagine that – Welsh Lords fighting for the damn Saxons! Luckily, they escaped before the battle ended. We must get them to give us the real story when they travel here."

"Did Gwriad ever find his wife's body?"

Anarwd looked grim. "No, unlike that of Dafydd's wife, Lady Teifryn, Lady Angharad's body was never found."

The fire sank down and the two men shared the dregs of the jug in silence.

Presently, the Prince called for his servants and had them light the way to the sleeping quarters. "You're having my wife's old room," he said sleepily. "It's the one you always have."

Edwin nodded. He would have been content to sleep in front of the fire. "We'll sort it out tomorrow," he murmured and staggered into the bare room. Just a large bed with a quilted duvet, a table and a chair; nothing ever changed.

CHAPTER NINE

A t dawn, thin plumes of smoke began to rise above the hamlet, as the women blew on the hot ashes of their fires and added the kindling in preparation for heating the porridge. Men stepped out and relieved themselves in the trees behind their huts, while the young women carried out the night waste and moved further into the forest to attend to their own needs. Some homes had dogs that had spent the night chained outside the single doors to alert the owners to robbers or wild animals, and they began barking loudly, anxious to be let free. Young boys, yawning and protesting, released the frantic creatures and tried to make plans with their friends before their fathers called them in to do their chores.

Outside one of the larger structures, a tall woman with long black hair tending towards grey was carrying a selection of colourful weavings. She had arranged a rope along the side of the house on which she pegged her bolts of woven wool to air in the emerging sun.

"Lovely day, Bethan," a neighbour called out. "You taking those beauties to market?"

She smiled, "I am, Osian. Are you going to sell your chickens?"

"I might. Yes, indeed. Would you like a lift in my cart?" There was a hopeful lilt to his voice.

"No, thank you, Osian. I'm going with Idris."

"Oh, yes. Well, um, perhaps next time, then?" He bustled back into his hovel.

An attractive girl, with a strong resemblance to the older woman, appeared from the house carrying another weaving. "Osian never gives up, does he? He must know that you and Idris are a couple."

"Don't be unkind to Osian, he's just a lonely man. He's trying to be neighbourly, that's all." Bethan smiled; she liked being admired. Her husband had died more than three years ago and for some time she had been sharing the bed of Idris the blacksmith. She was waiting for her daughter to marry a farmer's son from a nearby hamlet, and then Idris could leave his hovel connected to the smithy and move in with her.

"Oh, Mother!" the girl exclaimed. "He's got the hots for you. If Idris found out, there wouldn't be much left of Osian."

"Gwenllian, for shame, you've got a vivid imagination." She stepped back and admired the weavings she hoped to sell at a weekly market. Although more than two hour's journey away, it was still worth the effort. "Have you seen Angwen?"

"Yes, Ma, she was out collecting wood. You know how she's always up early."

At that moment an unusual woman appeared. Many would have considered her beautiful if it were not for the livid and unsightly scar around the front of her neck. She walked with poise and authority, and her piercing eyes and high cheek bones marked her out as being different to the local peasants. Her worn dress showed signs of repair, but the material, the design and the faded colours were distinct from the shapeless skirts and blouses of the other women, which were mostly black or in shades of brown.

If asked a question she would be unable to answer, as she had lost her ability to speak, and her memory also had vanished, leaving her with some dim, and not always pleasant, recollections of a time in a small nunnery, or priory, before arriving at the hamlet. She was also unable to remember her name, and had accepted the suggestion that she be called Angwen. Her friend Bethan had helped her reveal the fact that she was a competent spinner, and had taught her how to weave, which had enabled her to maintain her independence in this poor community.

She had been lucky to be given a small hovel that had belonged to an old woman who had died shortly before she had unexpectedly arrived, and she had tried since then to repay the kindness of her new friends. But these were simple people who were unable to read or write, and most hated the priests and friars whom they considered were leeches, always wanting money and threatening eternal damnation for those who opposed them.

In the deep forest, where few people travelled beyond the nearest market, and where strangers were unwelcome, it was natural to be superstitious and to believe in witches and devils. It was easier still to think that a strange woman who had no memory and was unable to speak was a witch, especially when she was a good-looking female with a strange mutilation. Some of the married women wanted Angwen to be driven from the hamlet, as they saw her as a constant temptation for their menfolk, but the combination of Bethan and Idris, who liked and respected the strange woman, kept the opposition at bay, although the word witch was still whispered by some.

"Hello, Angwen," Bethan said and gave her a hug. "Your weavings look good, don't they?"

"Almost as good as my Ma's," Gwenllian grinned. "Certainly, better than mine."

Angwen put an arm around her shoulders, and did a mime involving the weavings and pointing along the path out of the hamlet.

"No, I'm not going to the market," Gwenllian said happily. "I'm off to see my future husband. Since you came, I don't have to go with Ma to stand behind a stall all day. You've no idea how much I hated it."

"Don't listen to a word she says!" Bethan pretended to look angry. "She couldn't wait to get to market to meet some boys. Of course, once she met Arthur then it was a different matter, and since you started coming with me, I have released her." She turned away and muttered to Angwen, "I can't wait for Arthur's family to fix a date for the wedding. She keeps telling me it will be after the planting is finished." Bethan frowned. "I might have to travel to meet this young man and his family. He's never come here."

Gwenllian had moved away to talk to a young woman who was breast-feeding a baby.

Angwen drew a happy face and a sad face in the dust and raised her eyebrows.

Bethan nodded. "I am worried. They've only known each other since the snow disappeared, but she has no doubts that Arthur will marry her. She's a lovely girl, although I say it myself, but if my husband had been alive he would have kept a tighter rein on her." She looked sadly down the path where her daughter was laughing loudly in a small group of girls. "I worry about her. She's so trusting."

Angwen nodded and patted her gently on the arm. At that moment Idris pulled up beside them on his wagon which was pulled by an old plough horse. The wagon was a remarkable creation in this primitive and lonely place because of the care and decoration that had been lavished on it. Most carts and wagons were created purely for transporting wood, dung, crops and animals. They were built to be functional, not works of art. But this vehicle would have been a welcome transportation for a queen.

Idris was a powerful, good-looking man approaching his fourth decade who was an on-going puzzle for the local men: he would spend long hours perfecting his work, be it a plough or a horseshoe, and never over-charged anyone. He made axes, knives and wood-saws, and it was believed he made swords, although nobody had ever seen him make one. His most requested items were spades and garden forks, while his woodworking tools including hammers, planes and chisels were rarely required and he made them mainly for his own use.

The women were equally puzzled: he had arrived more than seven years ago, a tall man with a fine head of hair. He had been immediately welcomed by the peasants who quickly recognized his skills, and it was true to say that he had made life easier and more enjoyable for anyone who chose to ask him. His tools had improved the way the men farmed and the women managed their small gardens, and he had introduced weekly musical evenings that had been a welcome pleasure in their drab lives. The women noticed that although he could create metal wonders and was able to build in wood, he lived in a very basic hovel where he lived frugally.

"You're early, Idris," Bethan observed.

"I'm always early, woman, you know that."

They both burst into raucous laughter, which Angwen understood had a sexual meaning. She had quickly come to realize that the two of them were deeply in love and were quite open about their carnal relationship. She wondered what it must be like to make love to a man; she thought she would like it. It was at times like this that she was saddened by the thought that she may have had a lover, maybe more than one, but she could remember nothing about them, or what the experience might have been like.

She admired Idris. He was a shy, gentle man with a dry sense of humour whose association with Bethan was the envy of the older women and the cause of many knowing smiles among the men. Angwen discovered that when he first established himself as a valuable member of the community, he had ignored the advances of a number of single women, and it was not until after Bethan's husband had died that he had taken any notice of her.

They loaded the weavings into the back of the clean wagon, and Idris helped Bethan and Angwen up onto the front bench, an action other men never thought about, and then climbed up beside Bethan. They were the first of the hamlet to leave for the market, but as this was always the case it failed to be a subject of comment. Most only went to the market when they had something to sell, as few had money to spend.

Idris was silent as they travelled at walking pace along the narrow, deserted trail, leaving Bethan to keep up a steady flow of comments about the weavings and the different colours she was trying and the quality of the wool from different farmers.

"'Course, the main reason we have so much to sell is because of Angwen." She placed an arm around her friend. "I don't know how I managed before you arrived."

Angwen pulled a face and gave Bethan a friendly nudge. "No, seriously, Angwen, with your help I am getting to be a wealthy woman!" She leaned the other way, and rested her head on Idris's shoulder. "Who knows I might soon be able to attract a wealthy young landowner."

"Should I start to make his coffin?" Idris replied innocently.

"Only if I'm going to kill him off. If I left it to you, my proposed lovers would live to a great age."

The friendly banter continued until Idris suddenly stopped the horse. "What do you hear?

"Nothing, my love, what should I hear?"

Angwen leaned forward and did a mime of listening. She turned towards Idris with a worried frown, and held her nose.

"You're right, Angwen, it is worrying. Normally, we would hear the noise of the market by now, and there is a smell as though there's been a fire nearby."

"What shall we do, Idris?" Bethan whispered, turning to look in all directions.

"I'm going to leave the wagon over there," he said quietly, pointing to a small opening in the forest. "I want you both to hide together in the bushes and wait for me while I find out what has happened."

"Now, you take care," Bethan said, her eyes wide with fear. "If there is any danger, you come straight back. Agreed?"

"Agreed." Idris parked the wagon forty paces into the trees. He helped both women to climb down and pointed to the bushes where he would expect to find them when he returned. Nobody spoke as he raced into the trees, following a game trail towards the nearby village of Cwm. He knew that this close should be able to hear the music, the laughter and the murmur of voices, and he felt a fear he had not experienced in years.

As the smell increased so did his apprehension. He never carried more than a knife, and had always avoided fighting. He hated violence, and it was because Bethan's husband, whom he had barely come to know, had died that he had become concerned for her welfare and that of her daughter; he had never expected her to find him attractive. He took a deep breath and gritting his teeth, moved carefully through the trees.

Suddenly, the devastated village came into view, and the sight was overwhelming. Not a structure remained standing, and he could see dead bodies scattered around as though they were of no importance. His throat tightened and he fought back the need to give way to his emotions. These were people with whom he had become friends over recent years. His eyes filled with tears as he saw that even children and babies had not escaped the horror.

He moved slowly forward like a man in a dream and stood outside the burnt remains of the blacksmith's forge. Amid the charred beams and some barely smouldering embers he could see the indestructible iron anvil, and beside it an unrecognizable charred corpse, and similar shapes behind. Idris screwed up his eyes; this man and his family had been his close friends. He staggered away towards what had been the centre of the village, and tried not to look at the burnt and dismembered bodies, but stared about hoping to see some sign of life, some evidence of survivors.

A small pack of dogs barked at him, but ran off when he threw an accurate stone. A murder of crows hovered overhead, making raucous cries, and there was evidence that they had been removing the eyes of both animals and humans. He did not wish to think about what the dogs had been doing.

Idris moved aimlessly around, unable to take in the sadness of it all. He realized it must have been a large band of attackers to cause such carnage, and the pathetic remains of tables and stalls indicated it had happened during a market. It was almost impossible to believe that such a massacre had occurred a full week ago and they had not heard about it.

He did not know what to do, the magnitude of the tragedy overwhelmed him. "I must get the other men to help. We must give these poor people a decent burial," he muttered to himself, "and the women don't need to see it.

A short while later he returned to his wagon and after giving the women a brief report, drove home. He was too upset to give any more than the barest details as they travelled along the quiet trail to their hamlet, and after a few tries, Bethan gave up asking.

They had been travelling for more than an hour when a ragged figure burst from a clump of trees. The sudden appearance made Idris reach for his knife as Bethan let out a cry of alarm. The figure stopped in front of the horse and they could see he was young man who was crying. "Help me!" he sobbed piteously, "Please, help me." He staggered and looked as though he might collapse; he was certainly not a murderous robber.

Idris jumped from the wagon and rushed to help, as the women climbed carefully down. By the time they reached the stranger, he was lying unconscious on the ground and Idris was holding his head. "Bring some water," he ordered.

"You get the water. We'll deal with him," Bethan replied. "You're better at climbing into the wagon than we are."

Angwen smiled. In her recent memory, few women she knew were so assertive. What interested her was that Idris did not seem to mind.

Later, when the young man had been revived, they discovered he was called Iago, and that all his family had been murdered by the Normans. He was starving and seemed to have lived on small birds' eggs and stream water.

Angwen chose to sit with the weak young man in the back of the wagon. Iago had faded again into unconsciousness, and she placed his head on her lap and softly stroked his face.

"Don't get too attached to him." Bethan quipped. "He's too young for you!"

Raising her face, Angwen pointed to her vivid scar, and indicated that she and the young man had both shared awful things happening to them. Bethan nodded and wished she hadn't tried to make a joke of it.

When they arrived, unexpectedly early, back at their hamlet, everyone wanted to know what had happened. While Idris explained and described the state of the village of Cwm to the men, Angwen arranged for the unconscious Iago to be carried into her modest dwelling. Bethan was relieved it did not have to be in her house, and was happy to loan a blanket. Another peasant, whose son had recently left home, was willing to loan a straw paillasse, and some young women offered to help with caring for him.

"If a young woman had been in his state," Idris observed, "you wouldn't have allowed a group of men to look after her."

"That's quite different, as you well know." Bethan narrowed her eyes. "When did you last nurse a woman?"

"You still have a lot to learn about me," Idris cuddled her. "How much longer before that lovely daughter of yours gets married?"

Over the next few days, Idris organized the men and arranged a mass burial service just outside Cwm, and insisted that everyone pay something towards the brief attendance of a reluctant priest. Meanwhile, Iago was fed warm honeyed drinks, and as he began to recover his strength he was given a thick gruel and Welsh cakes. Angwen was grateful to have the young women willing to help look after him as she was uncertain as to what to do regarding his bodily needs. It was as though she had never had to be involved with the basic things of life, yet knew how to spin and was a competent and imaginative cook.

Although Iago was still weak, he was soon able to move about, and they would talk, often sitting on a bench outside when the weather was good. She explained to him through mimes and drawings in the dust that she was unable to speak or remember anything before her time in a nunnery. He, in turn, was willing to talk about the Norman attack on his house and family, but gave up trying to explain that his father was a miller and had owned a mill. She seemed at times almost child-like in her grasp of the things he assumed everyone knew, yet at other times she demonstrated a fearless approach to life, and was not in awe of men or anything that might come in the night. He, in contrast, had grown up constantly afraid of his father's violence and had shared his mother's fear of the spirits that she claimed came out when darkness descended.

When Iago suggested Angwen might have been attacked by Normans and how terrible they were, it did not frighten her, nor did she seem concerned about another attack. "They attacked Cwm, and this hamlet could be next," he said. "You could all be killed."

She shrugged her shoulders and did a mime that indicated that she and the others would fight back. Iago found her confidence unsettling; she seemed to think the enemy was different to those he had experienced: the murdering, iron-clad, mounted soldiers with their superior weapons and their complete lack of mercy towards anyone of any age.

After a week, Idris suggested that the lad, now he had his strength back, might work in his forge. Although Iago had no experience with a smithy, he was good with horses and was able to carry the heaviest iron bars. On Idris's final visit to the abandoned village of Cwm, he took Iago with him, and they collected the iron stock from the site of the ruined forge.

"This was a good family," Idris said. "He was my best friend. We shared some of our knowledge of iron and helped each other at times. He would have wanted me to take this metal." He stood, unmoving, in front of the tangled, wreckage of burnt wood and bowed his head.

Iago remained silent, thinking of his Uncle and especially his Aunt Edith, and was unable to speak, even if he had wanted to.

"How are you, boy?" Idris asked as the huge plough horse plodded home.

"Alright," Iago muttered. He was still feeling emotional.

"What are you going to do with yourself? Do you have any other relatives you can go to?"

"No," he felt as though a safety rope had broken and he was falling. "I haven't thought about it," he lied. It had been the one thought that had kept him awake at nights.

"Do you want to work for me?"

"Oh, yes!" The safety rope had not broken. "I really would, Idris." He turned to face him. "I'll work hard for you, I promise."

Idris smiled, and held out his hand. "I can't pay much, but you can be sure of a roof over your head at the smithy, and we'll eat well." They shook hands and both grinned. There had been some good to this day after all.

Later, when they had both eaten, and Idris was sharing a mug of his homemade beer, he began to explain how he thought things were going to develop. "The Normans will continue to raid our small communities, but eventually our local Lords and Princes will hit back. These raids will have a bad effect on the area beyond the death of our friends: people will stop spending their money and will put off having a new plough, or other implements for their farming. Fewer folk will bring their horses to have them shoed."

"Why?"

"Because when people are scared, they don't plan ahead. That is something they do when they feel safe." Idris sipped his beer and stared into the fire. "So, this will affect my normal trade, but may help another side of my craft that I have not used for some years."

"What will you do?" Iago was fascinated. His father had never spoken to him in this way.

"I will get back to making swords and spears. I might even have requests for armour," he sounded excited.

"Who will buy these weapons?"

"The local Lords and Princes. They're the only ones who have the money to pay for weapons. They'll be searching the area for smiths like me. Just this week, I've had a farmer offering me meat, flour or animals in exchange for a weapon." Idris was clearly animated and finished his beer with a gulp. He stood up from his stool, and patted Iago on the shoulder. "Get some sleep. We'll start at first light."

.   .   .

ANGWEN RETURNED TO HER HUMBLE abode as the sun set, and the temperature began to fall. She did not worry about the quality of her temporary house, for that was what she knew it to be. She had no rights to this old building, and it was hers only until some young couple claimed to have some distant connection to the old woman who had lived there. Bethan had said it was available until she established herself, and could afford for some local men to build her a home of her own. Bethan had been vague about where it could be built, and Idris had said nobody would object if she built at the end of the village. The ownership of the land was not something that the local peasants were concerned with.

She stoked up her fire, made herself a hot drink and warmed up some broth she had left over from breakfast. She had spent the day with Bethan, spinning while her friend concentrated on weaving. Angwen usually ate her midday meal with Bethan, and at such times they would talk, which meant that the weaver would talk and Angwen would nod or shake her head. When she wished to give a reason or suggest another way to do things, she would mime and draw pictures in the dusty earth.

Today's subject for discussion had been what to do now that the nearest weekly market had been destroyed, and where they might sell the weavings. Bethan had suggested a village further south that was the nearest, one that held a large weekly market. "It will take us at least two hours, maybe more, to get there, and while it might be alright in the summer with the bright mornings and light evenings, it will not be safe in the winter."

Angwen had listened carefully, and after a while had proposed that they should try to get orders from other hamlets and from isolated farms.

Her idea would be that one day of the week they would call and try to sell their weavings or take orders.

"Most of these people don't have much ready coin," Bethan had explained, "so they would want to barter, and we would be left with a surplus of hens' eggs, hams and milk. It wouldn't work."

A short time later, as Angwen began to weave, she suddenly became very excited and explained to Bethan that they could sell the barter by having a market here the day following their travels around the area. Now that there would be no competition from Cwm, it was the best time to start a new market.

"Oh, you are an unusual woman, Angwen! That's a fine idea." Bethan paused. "It will be a lot of hard work, but I like the idea. I'll speak to Idris tomorrow. I know he will help build the stalls, and Iago will help." She embraced Angwen, and they parted in a state of excitement.

Now that she was back in her empty building, Angwen realized how much she had enjoyed having Iago sharing the small space. There had been nothing sexual in their relationship. It had been the simple pleasure of having someone to share her food with, and once Iago had become used to the fact that he was the one who spoke, their ways of communication had been both amusing and thoughtful. But Angwen had known that once he recovered Iago would have to live elsewhere, or she would have offended the community's sensibilities continuing to share her home with a virile young man who was young enough to be her child. Bethan had spoken to Idris about the situation, and he had been pleased to offer Iago lodging in his home.

Angwen was lonely. She had been lonely in the nunnery too, even though surrounded by other women, and she realized it was not just the fact that she was unable to speak to others – it was the memory loss of her early life that had created a deep well of emptiness within her. She had no idea of her real name or even where she might have lived, and her lurid scar was a constant reminder that something terrible had happened to her.

Sitting by her fire, Angwen began to examine those things about her life that she had come to understand. It was Bethan who had said that the quality of Angwen's dress showed she must have been a rich person, though Angwen had no memory of how rich women dressed. She remembered that the nunnery had her two rings, and she knew no woman she had met in recent times had worn such rings. Even her behaviour was different to the women in the village: they saw themselves as inferior to men, and if any of them had been ordered by a Bishop to take off their clothes, they would have done so, with the exception of Bethan. However, none, not even the confident Bethan, would have done what she did and punish such a powerful man.

She was different, not only in the way she thought but in the things she felt confident in doing. She could spin, and had taken to weaving with a skill and understanding that had amazed Bethan. Most local women were unable to weave: they had neither the money nor the time to spend on such skills, and any spinning was usually done by grandmothers while they kept an eye on their grandchildren, allowing the mothers to work in the fields. She could organize and see the wider picture outside of the simple hamlet and, in particular, was not attracted to the local men, who never washed, whose breath stank and who mostly treated their wives with patient indifference.

Angwen had quickly discovered that basic living was not something she was familiar with: how to maintain a fire overnight; how to cook with very few implements; how to make candles; and the necessity of how to find food in the local forests and streams. Bethan had teased her over her lack of basic knowledge, but had been surprised when she had demonstrated her ability to write in the dust. Although Bethan was unable to read, she had seen religious men writing records for wealthy merchants in a market some years ago, and recognized the shape of some letters.

"Can you read as well?"

She nodded and drew a sketch of the nunnery. She wrote some words in the sand and then, pointing to the nunnery, wrote different words underneath. She pointed to the top line and pointed to Bethan and then drew a cross and indicated that the bottom line was words of the church.

"Oh," Bethan replied, "Latin?" She had no understanding of what that meant, but she knew the priests spoke in Latin. "Not in Welsh then?"

She shook her head.

"Why?"

Angwen shrugged her shoulders. She pointed to the cross and the bottom line and pointed at the sky.

"They speak to God in Latin? Do you believe that?" Bethan stuck out her chin. "I don't. I think the priests are all rubbish. They charge for everything. They tell us to go to church and then they speak in a language we don't understand, and they are always asking for money. My father always thought they were no good. He preferred the old gods; they made sense."

As she settled down on her pallet near the small fire, Angwen wondered if she would ever discover who she had been and whether she had any family. Perhaps, she should return to the nunnery and speak with Ceri, the mother superior, who had always been kind to her? She remembered her name there had been Ellen, but that was a name that the nuns had given her.

As she began to rehearse what she wanted to know, she suddenly realized she could write her requests on paper. There was ink and paper at the nunnery, and she would not have to mime and draw in the dust. It all seemed so obvious, that she relaxed and was asleep in moments.

CHAPTER TEN

It was a perfect day: the sun beat down from a cloudless, dark blue sky, there was a slight breeze bringing with it the aroma of the distant sea. The river had lost its ominous spring flood roar and everyone in the castle was in a relaxed mood. Most were watching Lord Jon's graceful movements as he glided around a group of clumsy peasants he was attempting to train in the use of the long sword. Sergeant Penn looked grimly on: he knew he could no longer match Jon's ability and it pained him. Davis and the older Gavin were on guard, and although the gates were open, they had become transfixed by the demonstration and were drowsy in the bright light and the warmth of a gentle day.

"Hard to believe our Lord Jon was an ignorant kitchen boy a few years ago," Davis said.

"You're about his age, Davis. If you'd spent the hours he's spent on training you'd be as good. He's all flat muscle, whereas you're starting to look as if you might be pregnant." Gavin yawned and glanced back casually towards the bridge. At that moment a trumpet sounded, its blare disrupting the tranquillity of the afternoon. "Bloody hell! We're being attacked!" He lunged for the warning bell as Davis rushed down to close the gates.

By the time the riders had reached the castle, the gates were bolted and Jon was standing on the battlements staring down at them. He was uncomfortably aware that gasping and bare-chested, with his sword resting on his left shoulder and perspiration pouring off him was not the way he would like to have presented himself as the Lord of the castle.

In contrast, the riders were disconcertingly impressive. They wore bright body armour, identical helmets with nose guards that accentuated their threatening appearance. They carried swords, spears and round shields, and a few had bows. The large horses they rode were well groomed and powerful, and Jon had no doubt that these were elite soldiers. As he had never encountered Normans, he assumed these must be the vanguard of an invading army. At the same time, he noted they were not appearing to be hostile, nor did they possess any way of attacking the castle. He prepared for the start of negotiations.

It took a few moments for the riders to calm their horses, and eventually a short, powerfully-built man rode forward on a white horse. He removed his helmet revealing a shock of grey hair. "I am Sir Maelgwn ap Owen, General of the forces of Prince Anarwd ap Tewdwr. I have come on urgent business with Lord Gwriad ap Griffith and his brother Lord Dafydd." He spoke in a strong, vibrant voice.

"I am Lord Jon ap Griffith, son of Lord Gwriad. My father and my uncle are away rounding up soldiers as agreed with Prince Anarwd." Jon tried to keep his voice as authoritative as the man below. "Welcome to Aberteifi, my Lord."

Sergeant Penn and the relieved soldiers of the castle quickly arranged a warm welcome for the visiting riders and Megan transformed her quiet kitchen into a hive of industry. Jon, having chased up some servants, showed Sir Maelgwn to a room where he could discard his armour, wash and borrow a robe. In the meantime, Jon ordered a reluctant Penn to send out some of his men in search of the Lords Gwriad and Dafydd. It was rare for Penn and the castle soldiers to meet other soldiers, especially those who served in the war zone, and Penn knew he would not be popular sending his men out on what might be a pointless mission.

"Don't argue with me, damn you! Just find the Lords as soon as possible!" Penn bellowed. "It's not my bloody idea." At least, he consoled himself, he didn't have to go: his orders were to be in charge of guarding the castle. "Hywel! Rhodri! Get a move on."

Sir Maelgwn used a servant to help him remove his armour, then dismissed the man before stripping off his damp clothes. It had taken nearly three days of hard riding, and even though there had been no problems on the journey, he realized that he was a different man to the one who had first visited Aberteifi nearly five years ago. While he still had the strength to fight, he lacked the stamina that his younger soldiers took for granted. He knew he had been like them when he was their age, but it was a hard fact to accept.

He washed slowly, enjoying the cool water and soaped himself all over. Unlike some Lords, he was scrupulous in his hygiene. When he was refreshed he lay on the narrow bed and was instantly asleep, not waking until a servant knocked on his door.

Jon had also washed and put on a fresh robe, and had given Emrys, the new steward, precise orders as to how to cope with the unexpected influx of so many soldiers and their Lord. As a result, a semblance of order had been established: a large, crackling fire was driving out the chill and dampness from the hall, and long trestle tables had been erected in the main space, with a raised platform in front of the staircase on which a traditional high table had been placed. As the servants rushed around, Jon had retired to a quiet space near the fire, where a jug of wine and cups were placed on a small table close by. Ceri, the old hound that usually slept there, had been taken to the kitchen, and Emrys was darting around, making every effort to please his demanding young Lord.

Jon was determined to act the host in a way that his father would have done. He had arranged for Emrys to serve smoked salmon slices and bread while he and Sir Maelgwn drank wine before the meal. He suspected this was a rare delicacy in the border lands, and he was determined to make the visitor welcome, especially as Dafydd had frequently mentioned General Maelgwn when talking about the defence of the border country. He was mindful that it was late afternoon, and it was possible that the Lords might not return until tomorrow.

"Lord Jon! I hope I haven't kept you waiting?" Maelgwn said as he came down the stone steps, his voice filling the hall.

"Not at all, Sir Maelgwn. I'm delighted to meet you." Jon stood up and gave the Lord a short bow before offering the usual embrace between men of standing. He was conscious that he was a head and shoulders taller, but considerably slimmer than this famous soldier.

They made small talk for a while as they sat on either side of the fire. Emrys refilled their cups, and handed round the tray of smoked salmon which proved to be a great success.

"I didn't meet you when I came here with Lord Edwin?" Maelgwn queried.

"No, my Lord. My blood link to this family was unknown to my father at the time. He has adopted me as his son."

"Ah," Maelgwn nodded. "He's lucky to have an heir such as yourself."

Jon felt his face redden and was thankful for the dim light. "My wife died in childbirth. It was to be my first child," he chewed meditatively on a slice of salmon. The wine had relaxed him, and he was pleased to talk to this engaging young man. "I married again, and have two daughters," he drank deeply, "but my second wife died of plague six years ago. I rarely see my girls who are growing up in a village near Caerdydd. They're with my sister and her daughter." He gave a sad laugh. "We're a family of daughters."

Jon did not know what to say and, after indicating to Emrys to bring more wine, he turned the conversation towards what really interested him.

"How are things on the border? We heard about the attack on Cwm. It's the reason my father and uncle are away raising an army. They hope to march just after St Dogmaels Day, the middle of June. But I think it will be nearer the end of June if they want to raise a large army." He smiled at the craggy face in front of him. "I'm in charge of trying to knock our small gang of soldiers into a fighting force. There's no doubt that trained men like yours are each worth ten farmers, no matter how bravely they fight.

"That is true." Maelgwn took more salmon. "However, battles are rarely won by a handful of trained soldiers. Having a large army, no matter how inexperienced, is a major factor in how well the opposing forces fight. A large army, especially if it appears to be determined, will cause the opposing men to run away as soon as the first people die. Most soldiers are not brave. They have little interest in serious fighting, they just want to pillage and rape the enemy's women and get back to their homes alive and to be acclaimed as heroes."

"You were with my father and uncle when they attacked Earl Harold's palace and burned Shrewsbury, what was that like?"

Maelgwn rubbed a hand down his bearded chin. "It was wet, horrible conditions, and the experienced soldiers spent their time trying to prevent the peasants from deserting. When we took Shrewsbury, it was dark by the time the main resistance had been defeated and our army was under strict orders to leave the Saxon women alone. Anyone who was caught attacking a woman would be put to death, and nobody was to set fire to any building."

"What happened?"

"The experienced soldiers under good officers fought bravely, while the peasants got drunk, raped the women and set fire to the town. Lord Gwriad and Lord Dafydd were outraged, and the sergeants did their best to force the drunken soldiers out of the town and into some semblance of an army. Luckily, when we reached Harold's fortified palace, the size of our army persuaded the defenders that they had better give in. The men, women and children were given a promise of safe conduct, as long as they left their weapons behind and left immediately. Fortunately, they didn't realize that many of our soldiers were in no condition to fight."

"So, having a large army worked?"

"In that case. But if it had only been a smaller army of trained soldiers when we attacked Shrewsbury..." he made a face, "who knows?" He settled back in his chair. "The winning of battles and what happens after are two quite different things. As a General of an army, I have watched how my men behave. Some are people I have known for years, yet they become murderous devils when the fighting is over. They will kill injured enemy soldiers who have surrendered, attack local peasants who have had nothing to do with the fighting, and rampage around local farms looking for something to steal or women to attack." He looked at Jon's alarmed face. "Remember, there is no glory in war, only horror, suffering and a desire to get back to your quiet life, if you still have one."

"Why do you continue to fight?"

"Because I love Wales. I avoid fighting my own people, which is why I refuse to seek vengeance on Cynan ap Iago, the self-appointed King of Gwynedd, for his treachery towards King Gruffydd. However, I might try to remove Prince Bleddyn ap Cynfa of Powys: he's a traitor who wants to have a treaty with the Marcher Lords." The scowl quickly left his face and he beamed, "But I will fight Saxons and Normans and any foreign power who wish to conquer us and make us slaves. That's why I fight."

"I want to fight for the same reason," Jon said earnestly. "I want to support my father and my uncle. This is their land, and I want to fight to protect it, and fight for Wales."

"Good for you, boy," Maelgwn nodded approvingly. He yawned and finished his wine. "I hope the Lords get back soon, or I'll be asleep."

Jon stood up quickly. "I'll just check to see if there is any news, my Lord." He moved quickly to the door, indicated that Emrys should bring more wine, and realized as he left the hall that the General had not answered his question about the threat on the border, which Jon had hoped would have led to Maelgwn revealing the reason for his unexpected arrival.

As he walked across the courtyard he wondered where Megan had gone. He knew she had been hurried away to some farm up north near the village of Ystrad. Although he was grateful to his father for arranging everything, he felt, deep down, that he should have been more involved. He knew he had let everyone down, not least Megan, but one moment he had been ready to marry her, and the next he was no longer involved. Dafydd had explained that it was best if he did not know who her husband was going to be, and then he would never have the temptation of trying to see his child. "You must move on, Jon," his uncle had said forcefully, "as Megan is having to do." Jon took a deep breath; he would have liked to have known that she was being well-treated, and the sex of the child when it was born. If a male, it might even someday become his heir, just as he himself had been raised up into nobility.

From the direction of the barracks he could hear singing as the soldiers celebrated together, and in front Sergeant Penn was slowly climbing the stairs to the battlements. Jon called to him, and Penn stopped.

"My Lord?" he turned swaying slightly and began to return to the yard, his left hand resting on the wall for support.

"What news of the Lords?"

The sergeant shuffled forward, and squinted up at Jon, who was aware that he was now the taller of the two. He remembered how Penn had bullied him when he first arrived; then, he had been a thin, underfed waif and Penn had seemed to tower over him. Over the years the balance of power had shifted, and with age, Penn had started to shrink in size. He stood uncertainly in front of Jon and mumbled something incomprehensible.

"Have you been drinking, Sergeant?"

"No, m'Lord. I'm on duty." His words were barely audible.

Jon moved closer but was unable to detect the smell of beer. "Are you feeling unwell, Sergeant?"

As he spoke, the older man sank slowly to the ground like a portly doll. His eyes closed and he went down into a kneeling position, made a low groan and fell forward, his arms by his side, and lay motionless, his face partly in the muck of the yard.

"Guards!" Jon yelled, and within moments soldiers arrived. "The Sergeant is unwell. Carry him to the barracks and make him comfortable. Someone is to stay with him until he recovers. Report to me if he remains unconscious."

Two soldiers dragged him off, and Jon prevented a third from following. "Gwynn, do you know anything about Sergeant Penn? Is he ill?"

"Well, he fell off his horse yesterday, m'Lord."

"Why? What happened?"

"It were odd, m'Lord. He were just trying out a new mare we got recently, and he just fell off the horse. It weren't even moving." The soldier shrugged and raised his eyebrows.

"Then what happened?"

"It were as though he'd just gone to sleep. After a moment, he wakes up and seems a bit confused. He never speaks to any of us, just walks away as though nothing has happened."

"Has he done this before?"

Gwynn looked uncomfortable. "Well, um, I'm not sure, m'Lord. Sergeant Penn's not the easiest man to talk to. Most of us just keeps out of his way like."

"Tell the others I want you all to keep an eye on him. Report to me if there's any change."

As Jon continued to the main gate he decided he would call in the Wise Woman in the morning.

"Riders approaching!" a guard yelled.

The warning bell began to toll. As soldiers raced from the barracks and the kitchens, Jon ran up the narrow steps to the battlements overlooking the main gate. In the dim light of a fading sunset he recognized the two Lords and their small retinue approaching. "Thank God," he muttered and returned to the main hall, where he found General Maelgwn asleep in his chair.

Later, over a fine meal of salmon, lamb and venison Maelgwn and his soldiers were welcomed and entertained with local music and stories of courage and valour delivered by a travelling bard, whose sonorous voice vibrated in the stone hall, and held everyone's attention. The servants were kept busy refilling the jugs of ale while those at the high table drank wine. There was loud joking and raucous laughter around the hall, and up at the high table Dafydd reflected that when Angharad and Teifryn, their murdered wives, had been present everyone had observed a more reserved behaviour. The castle was not the same without women.

"Maelgwn, my friend, we will move upstairs to my room to discuss the details of your message from Prince Anarwd," Gwriad announced grandly. He stifled a yawn and stood up. Everyone in the hall immediately rose to their feet in recognition of a meal that few of them ever experienced.

In his spacious room, Gwriad had installed some Welsh banners. Emrys, glorying in his new role as steward, had added tapestries that Angharad had woven when she had been the Lady of the Castle. The large bed to the left of the door had new blankets and coverings, and he had arranged four chairs around a small table in front of the open window. There were candles burning and on the table a jug of wine and four cups.

The General paused at the door and surveyed the room. He noticed the attempt to soften the effect of the cold stone, and reflected on the last time he had been here. Then, the presence of a wife had been evident in many subtle ways, and he recognized the loss that Lord Gwriad had suffered.

"I hope everything is to your satisfaction, my Lord?" Emrys said, an expectant smile on his face.

"Yes," Gwriad nodded. "You may go. I'll call for you if I need you."

"Well done, Emrys," Dafydd said good humouredly. He understood that the man was desperate to please, and watched as a big smile enveloped Emrys's face as he bowed out of the room. The occasional kind word was all that such a man required, and he would work from dawn to dusk and never complain.

He also stifled a yawn. It had been a long day negotiating with a varied collection of local landowners and members of the minor nobility. They had covered a large circular area of Ceredigion starting to the east at the village of Lampeter and moving north and finally back via a number of hamlets along the coast. Most of the time they had been on their horses, often delivering their message from their saddles before travelling on. He enjoyed riding, but their expected rest at the house of a local Lord had been interrupted by the news of Maelgwn's arrival. While they returned at a fast pace, he had reflected on their task and the possible reason for the General's unexpected visit.

He kept notes on the constant changes in the country's ruling Princes, who were forever squabbling over their presumed importance, and the amount of land they owned. Thanks to their uncle, Lord Gomer ap Griffith, Gwriad and he had inherited most of Ceredigion, which was, in theory, under the control of Maredudd ap Owain, Prince of Deheubarth. In practice though, the Prince was old, had no male heir and was content to remain out of the continuous bickering of local nobility. He had always been friendly towards Lord Gomer and his brother the famous General Cydweli, and on their deaths had continued to allow the Lords Gwriad and Dafydd to control most of Ceredigion, while his benevolent reign covered the lands south of Aberteifi, including Dyfed and the church lands of Saint Davids.

Dafydd knew that if they were to create a sizeable army, he and Gwriad would have to approach Prince Maredudd, and negotiate with his subordinate Lords, who would likely use the opportunity to take advantage of the Prince's increasing age and attempt to promote themselves as future rulers. It was an occasion he did not look forward to. They hoped, in the next few days, to meet the Prince in the ancient town of Caerfyddin, south of their castle at Aberteifi. Dafydd had learned that Caerfyddin was the oldest town in Wales, and still remained one of the few such centres of population that could be called a town. It boasted the remains of a Roman fort that church historians claimed was built in AD 75, when it was called Meridunum. It was information like this that made his careful letters to Welsh scholars and church leaders so worthwhile, and formed the basis of much of his personal writing.

Dafydd walked over to the table and took his seat opposite Jon, with Maelgwn on his left and Gwriad on his right. As he sat down, he glanced out of the unshuttered window at the calm night and the warm flickering of the braziers below, and felt a deep feeling of contentment: it had been a good day. He tried not to think of Derryth; it was over, and he had to follow the advice he had given Jon.

.   .   .

"I WAS SURPRISED YOU WERE SO enthusiastic," Gwriad said dryly. He and Dafydd were sitting around the remains of the fire in Gwriad's room, as even on a warm evening the castle retained its stony chill. Jon had shown the tired Maelgwn to his room, and had decided to check on Sergeant Penn, leaving the two brothers to ponder on Prince Anarwd's new plan.

"His request is logical and I believe will help to re-establish our sovereignty in that area. The Normans are testing us, and we have no alternative but to fight back."

"I agree, but if we leave in the next few days, we will have only a fraction of the soldiers we could have if we waited another month. I think the Prince's idea to attack while Earl Fitzosbern is away with his army fighting the Scots is a good strategy, but I'm worried that we may not have enough men."

"If we attack immediately, the Normans will not be expecting us to retaliate so soon, and we could win a few small victories, then be back over the border before they can put up any real resistance." Dafydd's enthusiasm had been much in evidence at the meeting, and Maelgwn had been visibly surprised at the ease with which he had managed to get agreement on Prince Anarwd's plan.

"They'll come after us for sure, then what? Do we retreat into the mountains and leave them free to scour our lands?" Gwriad had gone along with the idea, but still had his reservations.

"By the time that happens, we should have our main army in position. When they cross our border, we will be waiting for them." It was as though Dafydd had taken on the military enthusiasm that Gwriad had formally exhibited. He eyes flashed with excitement. "We could help to arrange the initial attacks, and Jon could bring up the local men. Our main army will meet up with us as we withdraw."

"He can't lead an army. Jon's got no experience," Gwriad said decisively.

"Remember, we've already arranged for the Ceredigion nobility to lead their own forces until they reach Prince Anarwd. I've told Jon that you have agreed that he will lead our local forces. He will share the authority with the others, when they meet up. Don't forget, he took on the running of this castle when we went to Caerdydd." His voice faded as the memory of the abortive journey and their personal losses hit him like a sudden toothache, and he glanced awkwardly at his brother.

Gwriad seemed not have noticed. "You might be right." He rubbed his face; he needed to sleep. "I suggest I travel down to Caerfyddin to see Prince Maredudd, and arrange for him to send some of his annoying nobles to lead an army that would meet up with Jon and our main forces at the end of June and reach the border at the beginning of July. He might be glad to offload some of his quarreling relatives." He turned to Dafydd. "How old would he be now? I haven't seen him for years."

"I received a letter from the Bishop of Saint Davids a few weeks ago. He was saying that although the Prince is well into his sixth decade, he's still as shrewd as ever."

"That's a comfort. He's been a good friend to this family," Gwriad nodded thoughtfully, "as we have been to him. During Gruffydd's reign we took all the pressure off him. He's one of the few nobles in Wales who is content with his life, and has rarely traveled beyond his lands."

"Unless he wants to see some strange creature that has been discovered."

Gwriad raised his eyebrows. "Really? What do you mean?"

"I understand from the Bishop that Prince Maredudd spends much of his time watching birds and wild animals. He keeps records of them and makes drawings. Last year he travelled down to a small fishing village near St Davids, where there had been reports that a huge whale had been washed up on the beach. The Prince was very excited, and spent two days there and even paid the fisherman for their report."

"Well, how strange." It seemed incomprehensible to Gwriad that a grown man, especially a Prince, would waste his time in such childish pleasures. "Anyway," he said forcibly as he got to his feet, "you take charge of the organization, and take Maelgwn with you, and especially his men. Their appearance should encourage the locals to enlist." He stretched and rubbed the back of his neck. "I'm going to bed."

Dafydd grinned. "Good luck with the Prince. Tell him about how Jon killed that mighty wild boar, it might make him like you." He walked to the door and felt a thrill of excitement: things, unusual things, were beginning to happen.

In the meantime, Jon was deep in thought in front of the red embers of the fire in the main hall. The servants had removed the tables and benches, and all evidence of the feast had been cleared up. Since the end of his relationship with Megan, he had paid particular attention to the behaviour of the servants, particularly when Gwriad had found fault with his duties. The appointment of Emrys as the steward had been his idea, and had relieved him of his more tedious responsibilities. It allowed him to focus on important matters... military matters.

He had sent a guard to the barracks to report on the state of Sergeant Penn. Jon decided that once the man returned he would try to sleep in spite of the stimulating news that set his heart racing: he was going to war! While he would have preferred to travel with the two Lords on their initial attack across the border, he was over-joyed to be given the responsibility of leading the main portion of their local army to the border, and then to have his chance to fight the Normans when they launched their almost-certain counterattack.

His initial role was to march the local men, led by a section of Maelgwn's elite troops, up the steep hill past Aberteifi, along the coast road and then to circle back to the River Teifi and cross the bridge by Nghenarth Falls, some half a day from Aberteifi, and the only other crossing in the area.

There was a knock on the main door, and the guard entered. He stood to attention, and stared at a spot over the top of Jon's head. He said nothing.

"Well, Emlyn?"

The young guard looked at the floor, and blew through his lips. "The sergeant's dead, m'Lord."

Jon stared blankly at Emlyn, who had only recently been appointed to the castle guards. The young man was clearly upset.

"Dead?" Jon felt a sense of unreality. This was the man who had bullied him when he first arrived. He was the violent sergeant; the terror of all new recruits and the scourge of older soldiers who wanted to dodge their duties. It had never occurred to Jon that this cornerstone of the castle's security could die. "What did they tell you?" he tried to keep his voice under control.

"They said one minute he were snoring, m'Lord, and the next moment he were silent. They thought he were sleeping, m'Lord, then when they tried to wake him they found he were dead." The young guard looked as though he might burst into tears.

"Thank you, Emlyn, you may go. Return to the barracks and tell them I'm coming." It was going to be a long night.

CHAPTER ELEVEN

E arl William Fitzosbern was studying maps of the east coast of England. He was in a large, two-storey wooden mansion in the centre of the town of Norwich that had once belonged to a Saxon Lord. The room was large and tastefully decorated with thick carpets and comfortable chairs. A carved door opened out onto a balcony overlooking the River Wensum, where his wife, Adeliza de Tosny and her lady companion sat quietly embroidering. At times, there could be heard the angry cries of a baby, and occasionally the loud protests of an older child.

"Go and give Nanny some help, Jennin. She's new and is finding my three children a handful. She has yet to learn to be severe. The baby is just hungry, but Robert is being unpleasant. Deal with him."

Earl William smiled – his wife would make an excellent General. "You're a hard mother," he said.

"Not at all, Will, the servants are seen to be the hard ones. You and I are the welcoming, loving parents." She stood up. "At least, that is how they see us." She stretched carefully, placing her hand across her stomach, and walked slowly into the main room. It was only mid-afternoon, but already she felt tired. "I hope we don't have another child, I don't know if I would survive." She sat on a chair close to the table.

"We need another boy to be certain of the bloodline. Anyway, you're as fit as a horse," he joked. If he had looked up from his map, he would have noticed the flash of anger that crossed her face.

"You forget that daughters can make good leaders of households if they are given a chance," she said.

He did not respond, his mind was trying to work out how long it would take to reach an early Roman settlement called Northallerton. It was just north of Jorvik, and King William had suggested it would make a good staging post for marching to most of the northern and north-eastern areas, where he anticipated there would on-going opposition. Also, the King had shown considerable interest in places that the early Romans had chosen as tactically important areas when they had placated the tribes nearly a thousand years before.

"Besides," Adeliza continued, "I always feel sorry for the second son, whom we know will always be in the shadow of his older brother." She suspected that her husband was not listening. "He will almost certainly be spending his days plotting how to get rid of him."

"Who the elder or the younger?" Fitzosbern asked innocently.

Her taut face changed to a broad grin, and she was about to deliver a suitable response when there was a loud knock at the door and their steward entered. "My Lord, a messenger has arrived."

"Send him up." He looked up from the map table, "Have you checked him?"

"Certainly, my Lord. He isn't happy. He says he has ridden hard and exhausted four horses."

The Earl grunted. "Send him up with two guards."

The steward looked affronted. "Of course, my Lord."

With a guard on each side and the steward ushering them in, the messenger was propelled into the room as though he were a convict. The Earl had taken a position on the far side of the table, and his wife had moved to a seat near the door to the balcony. There had been a time on the Isle of Wight, shortly after the big battle, when a man posing as a messenger had tried to kill him, and since then the Earl had taken no chances.

"Well?"

The messenger bowed. He was a young man with the sallow skin and black hair that indicated Norman descent. He was sweating and his clothes were dusty. "I come from the Bishop of Pons Aelius which the Saxons call Newcastle. I was ordered to put this into your hands, my Lord, and not give it to any lesser man." The steward frowned.

"Quite right." Fitzosbern took the sealed scroll and moved over to where the late afternoon sun was shining through the open window. He quickly read the message, which was written in Latin, and stormed over to the open door onto the balcony.

"There's an uprising in Newcastle, damn it."

"Is that far?" His wife was used to unexpected bad news.

"It will take a week for soldiers to march to Northallerton, and perhaps another two days to reach Newcastle."

"What is so important about Northallerton?" She was a bright woman who took a real interest in her husband's affairs, and if it had not been for her last birth, which had almost killed her, she would have been travelling with him on his lightning trips around this fractious island. It was her slow recovery that had convinced Fitzosbern to set up his temporary headquarters in Norwich, which was less than a hundred miles from London and had usable, established roads leading north and west. It also possessed a useful port on the River Wensum that enabled a relatively speedy exchange of messages between himself and the King while he was back in Normandy. Norwich was a pleasant area, and the house was easy to defend as the Earl's troops could be billeted nearby and the house had a walled garden with a guard post in the front.

"The King has decided that it will become a major encampment for our soldiers, and some are already billeted there. It means my men can take a rest at an established camp before engaging the enemy. He's right to think that Northallerton will become an important staging post – it will be vital to quelling the uprisings that seem certain to arise in that area."

"Why that area?"

"Because the further away from London they are, the more likely the Saxons are to feel that they can oppose us."

"You have taken on a lot as ruler of this country, my husband," she placed her hand gently on his face. "Do not rush into danger. I will remain here until your return."

"With luck, I will be back in three weeks." He turned and gave rapid orders to the steward, who bowed his way out. The messenger looked exhausted, and after a few words of praise the Earl handed him a silver piece.

As the beaming man was escorted out of the room, Fitzosbern stopped one of the soldiers, "Inform the senior officers to meet me for a working supper in two hours."

The soldier snapped to attention and carefully closed the door as he left.

"You will be safe here," Fitzosbern said softly. "I will arrange for Bishop Odo to send soldiers from London to replace the ones I am taking with me." He kissed her, and returned to the map table.

"I will give the orders to the cooks, and prepare Robert for your departure." She looked at him sadly. "We will all miss you, even our daughter Adeliza and baby Emma."

The Earl did not respond, his attention was totally focused on the planning for this new campaign.

As she left the room, Adeliza reflected on her association with this remarkable man. Since their marriage in 1051, he had been the only person she cared for. He was intelligent, witty, loving and loyal. She could not think of any man she had ever known who met these criteria. Unlike most Lords he did not have a mistress, did not get drunk, and took an active interest in their children. She bit her lower lip; if she were honest, he was the better parent.

His most remarkable attribute, from her point of view, was his habit of involving her in everything he did. In contrast, her few women friends revealed that were treated as mere sexual objects whose authority was confined to the managing of the servants and the care of the children. Most Lords only took note of their sons when they had reached an age where they could ride, hunt and learn the martial arts, and girls were often ignored by their fathers until they were of marriageable age, at which time their political worth was measured in their looks, their suddenly appreciated social qualities, and their ability to produce sons.

She knew she was lucky to have been well educated, and to have been born into a family that saw happiness as being more important than political gain. When she first met Fritzosbern it had been a whirlwind romance, and she had known immediately that he was destined to be her life partner. Her father had been delighted to agree to her choice, and had bestowed on her an unexpectedly large dowry.

A sudden pain gripped her, and she paused at the top of the stairs holding her stomach and groaning.

"My Lady?" a guard stepped forward.

"Thank you. I'm fine." She forced herself to walk in a dignified manner down the stairs. She did not wish to be the subject of gossip in the household, especially with her husband about to leave her on his constant travels to quell yet another uprising. It never occurred to Adeliza that he would not succeed – in her mind he was a paragon. Her job was to concentrate on getting back to full health by the time he returned, and to make sure the children remained safe and well.

CHAPTER TWELVE

Angwen's plan to create a small market had proved to be more difficult than expected. Bethan and Angwen had been well received at the small farms they visited; the women were glad to meet them and keen to get any news from the outside world. Many had children to care for, men to feed and little time to themselves, and the apparent freedom of the two visitors was hard for them to comprehend. They were all delighted to see the fine workmanship of the cloth, but when their husbands returned from the fields, tired and hungry, it was soon apparent that money was scarce and there was no spare food or items for barter, especially for cloth and artistic weavings.

"I don't know what I was thinking," Bethan said at the end of a dispiriting day. There had been some vague interest in the creation of a market, but the fact that it was not yet established made some question the value. As one man explained: "Now listen, woman, I'm not going to the trouble of taking my vegetables all that way to find there are no buyers."

After one farmer, a sharp-eyed ferret of a man, asked: "Do ye have permission to start a market?" Bethan had made a quick retreat.

Idris laughed when he heard what they had been up to. Bethan had kept their idea from him, wanting to present him with a success story, and was feeling truculent and argumentative. "So, what's so funny?"

"Bethan, if you had asked me, I would have told you that you can't just start a market. You have to have permission from the local Lord, and he'll send his tax collector to assess what you should pay."

"We only wanted to sell our cloth and our wool and have a way of bartering with the local farms and selling the barter on the market. We weren't going to make a lot of money! Why has everything got to be so complicated?"

Idris nodded in agreement. "Everyone who sells on a market expects to pay a rent. You and I did when we went to Cwm. That money goes to the person who is in charge of the market, and he pays taxes to the local Lord. Did you think you would be different?"

Bethan sulked, while Angwen nodded in agreement. This seemed to be something she knew. Perhaps in her earlier life she had worked on a market?

"However, I have some good news." He waved towards Iago. "We," he stressed the word, "have some good news."

"Well?" Bethan was still smouldering over her failure.

"We had a visit from one of Prince Anarwd's officers and a platoon of mounted soldiers. It would seem that the Prince is raising an army to fight back against the Normans, and he needs new weapons."

"You don't make weapons," Bethan said resentfully.

"Not since I've been here. But, I used to make swords and spears, and even helmets. Now that I have Iago to help me, it could mean a lot of money coming this way." He took hold of Bethan's hand. "I could marry you in style, woman."

Bethan's scowl faded and she looked at him in wonder. "Oh, Idris, you great twpsyn, I don't need a big wedding, just a big man." She leaned over and kissed him. Iago coloured up and cheered loudly to hide his embarrassment; Angwen clapped her hands and wondered, once again, what it must be like to sleep with a man. Even to kiss a man must be pleasant.

. . .

A FEW DAYS LATER, GWRIAD arrived in Caerfyrddin with a small guard of local men who were glad to get away from their normal duties. He had sent a messenger to Prince Maredudd to announce his arrival, and Gwriad was confident in the welcome he would receive.

The Prince lived in a majestic wooden house built on a raised mound and surrounded by a high palisade of strong stakes that formed an imposing fortification. A deep trench surrounded the walls and entry was confined to a single imposing bridge that led to two heavy gates. There were soldiers on the ramparts and a guard post protecting the bridge. Although it was just a fortified home, it was known as Caerfyrddin Castle.

Close by were the remains of an ancient Roman fort, known in the past as Moridunum, that had been built above the River Towy, which with its deep anchorage and its close proximity to the sea, had been strategically important.

Gwriad was always aware when he approached such fortifications that this was the normal form of defence for a manor or palace, and that his stone castle at Aberteifi, built by his famous father and his late uncle, was a rare achievement in Wales. Recently, Dafydd had received a letter from a monk on the Isle of Wight, reporting that the Norman Earl, Fitzosbern, was constructing an imposing stone castle that would deter any further uprisings. Carisbrooke Castle, as it had been named, was to become his permanent home once he had finished subduing the Saxon opposition.

"Earl Fitzosbern, just wait until you meet the Welsh opposition," Gwriad muttered cheerfully as the guards opened the gates. "We'll teach you to stay in your Carisbrooke Castle."

He was warmly greeted by the Prince, a tall, white-haired man with a lean, muscular body. He embraced Gwriad, towering over him, and giving little physical indication that he was at least two decades older. Ignoring protocol, he enthusiastically led the way into his comfortable house.

"Gwriad, my dear boy, I am delighted you have come to visit at last. It's years since we last met. Your uncle was alive then." He laughed, a rich joyful sound. "My, what a man he was with the women!"

Once the wine had been served and the servants had left, the Prince toasted Gwriad's good health, and settled back in his chair. "I imagine you've come to ask me to contribute soldiers for the revenge attack on the Normans?" He noted Gwriad's surprise. "I heard from Prince Anarwd a few days ago. He's a very persuasive man. Now, there's no way at my age that I'm going to lead an army, but I am certain that some of my ambitious, and younger, relatives will be desperate to do so." He looked quizzically at Gwriad, "I also heard that you and Dafydd are willing to help with an initial attack in support of Anarwd and his small army?"

"Yes, my Lord, we are both convinced it's a worthwhile cause." He raised his goblet in a quiet toast. "Also, we both feel we have one more battle in us."

The Prince nodded thoughtfully. "When I was a little older than you, I decided I had tempted fate long enough. I had lost count of the battles and skirmishes I had fought, and I suddenly became aware that I had lost the urge to kill people," he paused. "I've even given up hunting. Do you hunt?"

"Oh, yes. It keeps me fit and provides the castle with much-needed meat." Gwriad gave one of his toothy smiles. "There's plenty of game in the local forests, and even my adopted son killed a huge wild boar," he said. "Single-handed!" he added proudly.

"I had no idea you had adopted a son," the Prince leaned forward. "I'm right in thinking that you and Dafydd have no sons of your own?"

"Dafydd has a daughter." He cleared his throat. "You heard about our wives?"

"I did. The Saxons have a lot to answer for." He sipped his wine. "Tell me about your adopted son?"

Gwriad felt strangely awkward. "He's called Jon, and he was the illegitimate love child of Lord Gomer. I only became aware of him a few years ago, when Angharad was alive."

"He must be a great support to you."

"Indeed," Gwriad finished his wine. "He's a fine young man." As long as he doesn't make any more servants pregnant, he thought to himself.

"As you may know, I have no sons, but I'm blessed with two grown-up daughters. Both are fine women who have given their proud husbands male children. My two brothers also have fecund wives who have each produced a large family with a riot of young boys, now grown up and each ready to test their manhood against our enemies." He frowned. "I have never experienced that obsession with producing male heirs. I understand that my elder brother of the two, or his elder son, will inherit my Princedom, depending on how many more years I survive. But for me, the fact that my children were healthy and happy was always most important. I have no problem with my brother inheriting. To be honest, I am more interested in the wonders of the natural world."

"Ah," Gwriad tried to show interest.

"Would you like to see my collection of such wonders?"

"Indeed, my Lord." Gwriad looked intently at his empty goblet, but Maredudd had stood up and was striding towards a door at the other end of the room. The Prince produced a key, which he kept on a chain around his neck and opened the door, which seemed unusually heavy.

"I don't allow the servants into this room. Ignorant people are quick to think that anything unusual must be a form of devil worship." He tapped the side of his nose in a significant manner.

The room was larger than Gwriad had imagined, and had no windows.

The Prince lit a brazier on the wall and continued around the room lighting others. As the light increased, a wild assortment of animal skeletons, drawings and preserved animal parts were revealed. There were long polished tables around the room, on which were some unusual skeletons of creatures Gwriad did not recognize next to collections of teeth, tusks and antlers. In the centre of the room was a large round table on which was an assortment of thick books with embossed leather covers, and a pile of large sheets of velum, on which detailed sketches – birds, fish and insects had been accurately represented. But the most space had been given to a pile of huge bones that had been arranged on the floor, beyond the round table, unlike anything he had ever seen. The skeletal outline that had been created was of an animal that he was unfamiliar with. He moved towards them, drawn by their strangeness. "What are these?"

"I obtained them recently," Maredudd said. "It is my belief, Gwriad, that these bones come from one enormous creature." He reached down and, moving aside some heavy limb bones, carefully lifted up a large damaged skull. It was roughly the shape of a horse's skull, but three times as big, with deep eye sockets and two terrifying sets of teeth embedded in a strong protruding jaw. "This is the sort of skeleton that gives rise to peasants' nightmares and their ideas about the devil. Don't you think?"

"Indeed," Gwriad felt he was out of his depth. "A beast this size could trouble my sleep as well. You think this was an animal that walked our land?"

"Obviously. I have often wondered where the stories of Welsh dragons came from. What I am certain of is that this monster lived a long time ago, perhaps at the dawn of time."

"You think this was a dragon?"

"Certainly." He placed the heavy skull on the table and picked up one of the huge limb bones and handed it to Gwriad. "Imagine the weight a bone like this might have been able to support. I think, perhaps, it could have been the weight of three cows, and bigger than any creature we have alive today."

"Do you believe they've died out?" Gwriad felt like a novice questioning a bishop, and was acutely aware of his limited experience of life.

The Prince nodded. "Can you understand why I don't allow the servants to come in here?"

"It would scare them?" He realized he had not given the answer the Prince required. "You don't want them spreading rumours?"

"Are you a religious man?"

The unexpected question blindsided Gwriad, and he turned to face Maredudd. "Not really. The local priest is my friend, but we have never discussed religion. Dafydd is more knowledgeable about the Bible than I am, but he's not interested in attending services. Like me, he's not afraid of Hell or damnation or any of the other stories that the Church uses to make people afraid."

"Would it surprise you to know that there is no mention in the Bible of dragons, even though they exist in our ancient stories? The Church would find it difficult to explain where, in God's creation of the world, the dragons fit in. I believe that these creatures existed before us, and that this was, perhaps, one of the last few that walked this earth. It's possible that many were killed by the first people. Believe me, these bones cast doubt on the teachings of the Church, and I dare say I would find myself denounced as a heretic if it became known that I have such a collection. That is why it's only you, my friend, and other nobles of like mind, who are ever invited into this room, especially now that I have these wonderous bones."

"How did you get hold of them?" Gwriad asked politely. He could sense the Prince's excitement but found it hard to share. When it really got down to it, these were just a pile of unusual bones of a creature that had died out. When it was alive, it might have been a challenge to hunt, but now it was of no use to anyone. He ran a finger over one of its teeth.

"I happened to be in the area of St Davids, and visited a tin mine that was getting near the end of its usefulness." The Prince raised his eyebrows in a questioning manner, "Did you know we're rich in tin?"

"No," he was still staring thoughtfully at the teeth.

"Well, we are. Most of it we sell to other countries. When a mine is reaching its end, I travel there to reward the miners who have been paid little for their work, although it has made others very rich. While I was talking to these miners, they mentioned they had uncovered some strange bones. I went into the mine to verify their discovery, and was amazed by these massive examples protruding from the walls. I immediately sent for more troops to guard the mine, and gave the miners extra silver to excavate these bones carefully," he patted the skull, "and wash them and swear on a Bible and on their lives that they would never mention the discovery again. I had the bones brought back in separate journeys and by different soldiers." He slowly replaced the head to the collection on the floor. "This is the pinnacle of my interest, and perhaps the most important find in our history."

"Well, yes, I suppose so." Gwriad was convinced of the Prince's enthusiasm, but was unable to understand the importance.

"I know that there are few, if any, collections such as this," the Prince said. "I have a grandson who I hope will continue my work."

"Your work?" Gwriad queried.

"You will have no idea of the hours I have spent reading and studying the writings of early collectors like myself. I have followed their discoveries, and in some cases added to the limited knowledge we have of the living things around us. A man like you who hunts will have some knowledge about the creatures you kill: where they are to be found, how best to hunt them and which times of the year to leave them to reproduce. When you eat an animal or bird, you know which parts of the creature are best to eat, and which parts are only fit for the dogs."

"Indeed."

"But have you ever wondered why birds are so different, why certain animals live where they do? Why some creatures have lots of offspring, and others raise only a few? That is what I am interested in. You may be surprised that fish and hot-blooded animals share similar bone structures? I could go on," he said, noticing Gwriad's eyes beginning to glaze over. "But that is my work and passion." He walked slowly round the room, gently touching some of the objects. "My only regret is that I wasted so many of my best years fighting for causes that I did not always believe in and encouraging others to do the same."

"But if we didn't fight our enemies, they would destroy us. We would end up in slavery."

"You may be right, Gwriad, but history shows us that wars are wasteful and we end up losing the best and brightest of each generation. It must be better to negotiate with people rather than fight them." He sounded tired, as though he was no longer interested in the discussion.

"If you don't think we should fight, why are you agreeing to send your relatives and the local people to join Prince Anarwd?" Gwriad, in contrast to the Prince, had come alive. This was an area of discussion he was interested in.

"Because we live in an imperfect world, Gwriad. When I was young, I did what my younger relatives want to do. They seek honour and glory on the battlefield and have the firm belief that they will save their country. If they survive to be my age, they might develop different views." He walked over to Gwriad and placed an arm around his shoulders. "But enough, you have endured my obsession and my philosophy, it is time to have some wine, eat and draw up plans for the campaign."

As they walked back into the hall Gwriad reflected on the fact that Dafydd would have been a far more enthusiastic visitor. "I think it's a good job that Dafydd didn't come to visit you, Prince Maredudd. You would never have forced him out of your secret room," he joked.

"When this campaign is over, he must pay me a visit." The Prince smiled, tactfully concealing the thought that he wished Dafydd had come instead.

CHAPTER THIRTEEN

It was the end of May, and the weather had continued hot and windless, and the west coast valleys were full of life. The local trees, mainly broadleaves, were at their most attractive with their cool shade and the vibrant freshness of their leaves. Wildflowers carpeted the edges of ploughed fields and lanes and the sky was alive with amorous birds. The River Teifi had lost its threatening roar, and flowed deep and silent along the valley, except at the Nghenarth Falls where the water surged, white and angry, through deep channels and over dangerous, slippery rocks. Before the completion of the stone bridge, a hundred paces downstream, the falls had, over the years, claimed the life of many a fearless child, usually a boy, who despite warnings, had attempted at this time of the year to cross the abating torrent.

The bridge had been completed during the reign of King Gruffydd, and had enabled travellers from northern Ceredigion to cross the Teifi on their way to the important town of Caerfyddin. Before the bridge's completion, it had been necessary to continue west to Aberteifi, and cross at the bridge below the castle. The previous Lord Gomer had instituted tolls to cross the stone bridge which, although a useful source of income for him and employment for some of the village, had caused great resentment among traders and local people travelling to distant relatives. This toll ended once the bridge at Nghenarth Falls was completed, and Gwriad and Dafydd agreed to use the reduction in travellers as a reason for abandoning their uncle's tax on travellers, which they had intended to do regardless of the effect of the new bridge. Dafydd had pointed out that the income was not worth the hostility it generated.

It had been a trying time before Jon was able to leave the castle to help with the recruiting. He had informed the two Lords that their sergeant had died and, as he had expected, his father had said he was to deal with it.

He had then approached his uncle who had been more helpful, and had suggested that he arrange a short ceremony and a quick burial in the castle's grave plot. Father Williams had been invited and a wagon had been provided to convey him around and, as a popular touch, Jon had asked the older Megan to arrange a small feast for the rest of the castle's soldiers and servants, and had provided ale for the occasion. As a precaution, he had appointed the unperturbable Gavin, who loved hunting, as the new sergeant, and had told him he was to arrange the guard and ensure that none of those drank too much.

Some days later, Jon was riding towards a narrow bridge and leading a small company of officers, mostly local nobility and important landowners. He rode across the bridge at the head of a long, straggling line of men who marched in pairs, and whose sergeants patrolled along each side. The column was followed by a variety of heavily loaded wagons pulled by horses, mules and some unhappy oxen whose protests combined with the noise of the excited voices of the camp followers who trailed behind.

His father and uncle had left a week before with a small but well-equipped cavalry in company with General Maelgwn and his elite force to join Prince Anarwd near the border. Their departure had made a distinct impact on Jon's embryonic army. The professional soldiers' fierce discipline had instilled in the new recruits an example of how to behave as soldiers. Now that they had gone, the marching had become less impressive, and many of the men, who were unused to military discipline, felt it was their right to leave the column to take a rest when they felt like it, or to relieve themselves in the bushes. The sergeants, who wished to establish strict patterns of behaviour while they still could, reacted to this behaviour with heart-stopping rage, causing simmering resentment in some sections of the army, and a cheerful, determined attitude by others who understood the need for order.

"We're not going to reach the gathering point by nightfall, my Lord," a young officer observed. He frowned as he looked back. A casual observer might have thought that the high spirits of some elements of the column were more representative of a summer festival than an army on the march.

"I never thought we would, Rees," Jon said. He was enjoying his leadership role, and had discussed with Dafydd what he should do if things did not occur on time. "My plan is to march to the next village and camp overnight nearby, and if by tomorrow we do not meet up with the other groups, then we will march to the village of Brecon, and make permanent camp by the River Usk until we are joined by General Maelgwn and the others."

"And then we march to the border?" Rees asked, unable to keep the expectation out of his voice. The eldest son of a self-made man who owned a large flock of sheep, Rees had been appointed as Jon's second-in-command. He was the same age as Jon, and determined to make his father proud of him.

Jon nodded and covered his mouth with a gloved hand as though deep in thought. In fact, he was hiding a grin: Rees was displaying the naïve enthusiasm that he had recently shown, before his father, uncle and especially General Maelgwn had shared their experiences of war. "Indeed, Rees, that will be the mustering place where we will gather before we march as a powerful army to rebuff the enemy." He nodded gravely, "But I'm hoping we will have time to train this ragtag army before we fight, as very few of them have ever faced an enemy, and most of them have no idea what life is like outside their village." As he spoke, he was conscious that his entire life experiences had been like theirs. The big difference between himself and Rees was the knowledge he had gleaned from Father Williams and his new family; it was this background that gave him the confidence to lead.

Jon was aware that Rees and the small officer corps, all inexperienced young men and mostly the sons of minor nobility and wealthy landowners, were envious of his appointment, and their ambitions were often clearly apparent. When he thought about it, there was none that he could consider a true friend.

Things appeared to go well until they reached the edge of the village just before sunset. A large untended field near a small stream had been selected and there was just enough light for tents to be erected and fires lit. The men were allowed to eat and sleep in preparation for an early start, and it had been made clear that no soldier was allowed to leave the camp to enter the village or the small pub that was the largest structure among a meagre assortment of hovels.

In reality, however, some of the camp followers and a few unruly soldiers avoided the sergeants and, under the cloak of darkness, slipped into the pub. Their numbers and their association with the army, had given them bragging rights in the small pub, and the locals objected. The result had been a bar fight that had spilled out onto the narrow road and had involved increasing numbers on both sides. Few knew why they were fighting, and it had taken a determined intervention by the sergeants, supported by a strong detachment of experienced soldiers, to bring the fight to an end. The result had been a severely damaged pub, a number of injured villagers and a deep well of resentment among the local families.

Jon was informed of the situation during the night, and knew it was his first test as a commander. He ordered that all those who were associated with the disruption should be placed under arrest and held in a secure area, where any attempt to leave was to be harshly dealt with. At first light, with his junior officers beside him, he questioned the dispirited captives. When it was clear that all of them were protesting their innocence, and were unwilling to admit to their involvement, Jon arranged for them to be lined up with their hands secured behind their backs, and the abused villagers were encouraged to walk the line and identify their assailants.

Those who were not recognized were ordered to do camp duties for breaking the curfew, and those found guilty of violent assault and drunkenness were given three lashes of a horse whip and the promise that any further disobedience would result in twenty lashes and a dishonourable discharge from the army.

"You are Ceredigion people!" Jon bellowed at the assembled bunch of disheartened men, most of whom had never experienced a whipping. "If you're sent home in disgrace, your community will remember you as cowards and ne'er-do-wells." There was a deep rumble of agreement from the rest of the army and the local people who had watched the punishments. "From now on, you will obey orders and march like soldiers, not children going on an outing." There was a ripple of sniggering from the audience. Jon raised his sword above his head and paused until the only sound was the complaining of the oxen.

"We are marching to fight the Normans, and save our country!" He yelled, his voice reaching those on the edge of the crowd. "You can all be

Welsh heroes! Don't let me down! Don't let your friends down! Don't let Wales down!"

He was surprised when a roar of approval and clapping greeted the end of his speech and he glowed with pride as he marched back to his tent, clutching the sword. It was the first time he had ever made a speech, and if it had not been for the applause at the end he would have had no inkling of how he had performed.

"Well done, my Lord," Rees gasped as he tried to keep pace with Jon's long strides. Jon stopped and looked up at a cloudless sky. The sun was almost overhead.

"Tell the officers to give the order to break camp and form up. We have a long march ahead of us if we are to make up for lost time." He disappeared into his tent closing the flap behind him. Resting his head against a tent pole, he took some deep breaths. The experience had drained him, and he realized that he must get used to making decisions. Before Gwriad had left for the border, he said something that Jon had not fully appreciated until now: "Being in command is a lonely business. Always remember to seek advice, but have no doubts about your final decision."

Now, he knew what his father meant. But it did not prevent him giving an ironic laugh, noting that: Having a brother, like Dafydd, must make it easier.

.   .   .

THE RAPID JOURNEY TO MEET up with Prince Anarwd's force was almost complete and had been without incident: the weather had remained fine and warm, the horses were strong and the soldiers cheerful and experienced. Gwriad was energized by the steady easy canter the cavalry maintained as they journeyed through the rugged countryside with its changing and challenging aspects. They crossed numerous valleys, mostly tree-lined, with small, fast-flowing streams of ice cold water that was welcomed by the sweating horses, and steep, stony hills, where the riders were forced to dismount and walk their animals for fear of injury. Bare, majestic mountains surrounded them, mostly empty except for the impressive red kites that hovered in the warm air, and small, distant flocks of sheep that moved like white clouds farther up the steep slopes at their advance. During the hours of riding Gwriad was conscious of how few people scraped a living in this unforgiving country.

"Apart from the impoverished villages near the rivers, and in those few wide valleys where farming is possible, there's little to attract settlers," Dafydd observed.

"True, but the stark beauty of this country takes my breath away, and at times like this I know why I want to defend it against all invaders," Gwriad said expansively.

General Maelgwn rode up alongside them, the sweat rolling down his sunburnt face, and pointed to a flag on a distant hill. "We're almost there!" he exclaimed excitedly. He enjoyed campaigning, especially with soldiers he could trust. "We should be there in time for a good supper and plenty of wine." In his world, campaigning and drinking went hand-in-hand.

"Will the Prince want to break camp tomorrow?" Dafydd asked. Like all of them, he had a great desire to cross the border and come to grips with the enemy. However, he wondered if he would be feeling the same way if Teifryn, his enigmatic wife, were still alive, or if Derryth had agreed to become his wife.

"No, my Lord, I think that is unlikely. He will want to go over his plans with us and be certain that the main army will be in position to cover our retreat. He is convinced that, unlike the Saxons, the Normans will counterattack almost immediately."

"There's no doubt we need a standing army," Dafydd said, looking back at the ordered column behind them. "If we had several hundreds of men such as these, we would not fear the Normans."

"We had such an army when we were a united nation under King Gruffydd," Gwriad observed. "If we could do it then, we can do it again."

"Gwynedd and Powys will never agree," said Dafydd. "Their recently self-appointed Kings and Princes will have to be defeated first, and I am against Welsh men fighting each other."

Maelgwn frowned. "We could take out Prince Bleddyn ap Cynfa quite easily. Most of Powys hates him, especially the way he's cozying up to the Norman Marcher Lords. He's a weak link on our border. There would be very little blood shed if we decided to remove him." He brightened up. "When we've repelled the Norman counterattack, we would be well positioned to make a courtesy call, and with the glory of our victory, we would be sure to have the whole of Powys cheering us."

"Perhaps we should defeat the Normans first," Dafydd replied dryly.

"Oh, there's no stopping us once we get going," Gwriad quipped. "My concern is whether the wine will be worth drinking. Prince Anarwd is not noted for his taste in wines."

Even the dour Maelgwn laughed.

.   .   .

THE RAMBLING STRONGHOLD OF PRINCE Anarwd, which some politely called his palace, was alive with the noise of an army preparing for war. In the building, harassed junior officers were rushing about giving orders; the kitchen was full of cooks and servants producing enough food for the evening's feast, and the Great Hall was being prepared to accommodate the whole squadron of the elite cavalry soldiers and their officers. Outside, the spacious courtyard was cluttered with wagons and carts; the stables were overwhelmed and recent horses were being guarded in the out-lying fields. The forge was in continuous use with a rotation of blacksmiths.

"Now here is what I propose," Prince Anarwd said, as he poured over his map table. Around him Lord Edwin stood on one side and Dafydd on the other, while Gwriad and Maelgwn sat on the opposite side of the table and enjoyed wine that was much better than expected. "We will cross the border at Brycheiniog and ride directly to Hereford which is well garrisoned, but with the advantage of surprise I expect us to achieve a swift victory." There were grunts of assent from the others.

"This will the first attack on Hereford since King Gruffydd ap Llywelyn burnt the town to the ground in 1056," Dafydd said thoughtfully.

"Indeed," Edwin said, "but he was only King of Powys and Gwyneth then, not the whole of Wales."

"Thank you for the history lesson," Anarwd said, irritated by the interruption. "Now, to continue. We are entirely cavalry, so I want us to be able to strike fast and kill as many Norman soldiers and Saxon irregulars as we can, before we return across the border. We will destroy any structures we encounter, but we will not waste time attacking their peasants, unless they try to resist. Our aim is to cause chaos and to defeat their soldiers." He smiled, and took a sip of his wine. "I want the Normans, and especially Fitzosbern, to be outraged. I want them to be convinced that we are a small force that was seeking revenge for their attack on Cwm. I want them to believe that they can follow us with impunity, and that with their larger force of soldiers they will defeat us in the field of battle. Then, we will surprise them and make their defeat such that they will wish to negotiate a peace." He raised his goblet. "To victory!"

When the toasting was over, Anarwd sat down and indicated that they should study the rough map. "Look carefully. Tell me what bothers you, if anything. We must be in total agreement."

"If Hereford is well garrisoned, what happens if they simply stay inside their walls?" Lord Edwin asked. "Cavalry can't take a town by itself. We need siege machines and hundreds of foot soldiers to storm the breach when we break through. What's your plan?"

Anarwd beamed, pleased with the question. "Indeed, Edwin, I do have a plan." He turned over a fresh sheet of vellum on which was a carefully drawn outline of a town. "This is a plan of Hereford. I paid a gifted merchant to put down everything he could remember of the way it is laid out." For the next while Anarwd pointed out the shape of the walls, the gates, the watch towers and an approximate idea of how the main roads in the town had been clearly represented. "We will be travelling fast on horseback, so nobody can give a warning before we get there, and I want to tempt the town's guards to attack us." He looked around the group, waiting for the next obvious question, but was disappointed. His audience waited patiently for him to continue.

"Before we are in sight of the town, we will divide into two sections, the smaller section will go to the right, and approach the main gate facing Wales. The larger group will circle the town and approach this gate," he pointed to the gate that faced east. "I have chosen a handful of old horses that will be ridden by some of my own soldiers, and they will attack the houses and farms on the west side within sight of the walls of the town, and even the structures near their parade ground, which is beyond arrow range from the town's defences. I want the attackers to appear as though they are just a bold gang of Welsh thieves. As soon as the guards ride out to chase them away, the rest of the smaller group on their fine horses will attack the guards from both sides, and should easily outnumber them in numbers and fighting skills.

Meanwhile, at the east gate, that least expects an attack, the main group will operate. If we time this correctly, the guards at this gate will be distracted by the activity at the west gate."

"What if they close all the gates at the first sign of trouble?" Dafydd asked.

"Well, I am fairly certain that the guards at the west gate will find it insufferable to stand and watch a gang of outlaws on flea-bitten horses, make such a blatant day-time attack. The cream of their soldiers will be used to track them down. If I was in charge of the town, that's what I would do."

Nobody raised any disagreement on that point. "But if I was in charge of the east gate, I would secure that gate until there was a general all-clear," Gwriad said.

"Which is why I will have a distraction at that gate as well," Anarwd said excitedly, and emptied his goblet without noticing. "I have some men who speak English and could pass for Saxons. They will drive a single, heavy, open wagon towards the gate, and will be dressed as impoverished peasants. Hidden under a pile of reeds will be two or three more fighters, and most importantly another soldier will be under the wagon."

There was silence as each of them waited for Anarwd to continue. "The merchant tells me that the guards at this gate wait around outside to inspect those who wish to enter. They are more interested in those who look as if they might pay a bribe. Poor peasants are bullied and if they bring anything edible, some of it is stolen. This is why this wagon will carry reeds used for the floors of the wealthy, and will be of little interest to them," he grinned, "especially, if the men stink."

He made a show of refilling their wine, as they looked carefully at the diagram. "The soldier under the wagon will kill the old horse when the wagon is passing through the gates, preventing the guards from closing them. Our soldiers will fight to keep the gates open until the cavalry arrives. Then, we start fires, kill their soldiers and make a speedy retreat. We will cause damage and destruction as we return to the border, leaving a clear indication of the route we've taken. We'll meet up with our main army and wait to ambush their counterattack." He raised his goblet in a silent toast.

Anarwd's enthusiasm was not immediately shared by the others.

"There are too many things that could go wrong," Gwriad said. "I would prefer a simpler plan."

"I agree," Maelgwn said, scratching his beard thoughtfully. "The whole idea of using cavalry is to achieve a surprise attack. A wagon is slow moving, it can't be used across rough country and would have to follow paths. It would have to be in position hours before the cavalry joined it, and it would be seen by local people…" he let his voice trail off.

"I like the idea of attacking both gates at the same time," Dafydd said. "but that requires a careful knowledge of the countryside, and a good deal of luck. I think it would be better to go for a simpler plan that relies on speed and lightning attacks."

Anarwd said nothing. He had to admit to himself that he had got carried away with his ideas. The wagon would have been such a clever idea as a way of keeping the gates open, but it did rely on luck. He knew it was never a good plan to split up an army unless it was to achieve a reserve force for encirclement during a battle, and to have the two forces doing separate attacks was risky. He nodded slowly and sat down, indicating he had accepted their comments.

"My friend," Lord Edwin raised his goblet, "you have always been a leader with ideas. When we attacked Shrewsbury it was you who planned the trickery that enabled us to break through into the town. Then, we had a large army. In this attack, as you said, we want to do some damage, kill soldiers and leave the impression we are just a lightning raid. We do not intend to take the town of Hereford, and I liked your first idea, of enticing some of the garrison soldiers out of the safety of their town, and defeating them. That will be, perhaps, our only major military action. However, the cavalry can then attack everything on our route back to Wales to punish the Normans for their attack on us. Then, we wait for their reaction."

After some further discussion, it was agreed that they would accept the first part of Anarwd's plan and try to create a situation that Earl Fitzosbern would feel unable to ignore. It was accepted that although not personally responsible for the attack on Cwm, he was the newly appointed Earl with overall command of Hereford, and the other border areas. All agreed it was certainly a Lord under his authority who had carried out the previous attack. Such a Lord might expect the Welsh to react, and it was possible he would be expecting them to respond.

Maelgwn banged his fist on the table. "If we could kill the minor bastard Lord responsible, it would certainly cause Fitzosbern to react." He took a long drink, "We might even have a chance of killing Fitzosbern as well!" He gazed about the group in a happy stupor. The others nodded good-naturedly.

"How many horsemen do we have?" Dafydd asked, bringing a sense of realism back to the group. He was always interested in figures.

"With your men, I think we'll have about two hundred," Prince Anarwd replied, and looked to Lord Edwin.

"Yes," Edwin said, "It's the most horsemen we have assembled since the days of King Gruffydd."

CHAPTER FOURTEEN

It was raining. It had been raining continuously since Earl Fitzosbern and his cavalry had reached Northallerton. They had travelled up north on the main road from London to York, which had originally been created by the Romans, and had been their artery to the Scottish border. The road had not been maintained, but as the former King Harold had shown in his lightning attack on his brother Tostig and his Norwegian allies at Stanford Bridge, near York, it was still the best way of moving troops quickly.

Fitzosbern had taken possession of all of the main houses in the centre of the small town, and his troops had quelled all opposition with brutal efficiency. From this central position he set up guard posts and watch towers around the rest of the town, with defensive positions on the important bridge over the nearby River Swale, to the west, and on a number of smaller bridges to the east. All of this was accomplished as he waited for his main army of marching men to arrive. What he had planned as a relatively straightforward operation had been made infinitely more difficult and unpleasant by the seemingly unending rain. The rivers flooded, roofs leaked, supplies were ruined and the soldiers complained that the conditions were impossible.

In spite of this, and because of Fitzosbern's insistence on strict discipline, by the time the soldiers marched into Northallerton, dry barracks were available, food was prepared and the valuable horses were finally stabled. After two days of rest, the soldiers were ready for further marching, and his plans for the attack on Newcastle had been finalized in his mind. The officer corps had developed a grudging respect for their unrelenting general, and began to accept the almost God-like rumours that circulated among those who had previously served with him.

Fitzosbern valued his scouts, many of whom were Saxons who had seen no point in continuing to fight for a lost cause, and who enjoyed their status and the regular silver they were paid. During the short time he had been in Northallerton, he had received numerous reports from them about the size and shape of Newcastle; the importance of the river that the town had been built around; its port facilities and the quality and number of the men who defended it.

The night before their march he feasted his officers but limited the wine and beer consumption so that they would be alert during his final briefing. As the sun set, and the rain finally stopped, he gathered his officers around his map table, which always travelled with his baggage train when he was on manoeuvres. He approached every battle with a plan based on a clear understanding of the terrain. As a child he had been instructed in the history of the Romans and the Greeks and how they fought their wars and won their battles. He had become convinced that armies were invincible if they had soldiers who were well trained, well-armed, with strong armour and good officers. History had shown him that numbers were less important than discipline, and that once the enemy had been outmanoeuvred or its front ranks had been destroyed, those who were without discipline would flee the field or surrender.

"Newcastle is the name we Normans have given this town, formally it was known as Pons Aelius by the Romans who established a fort on the other side of the River Tyne to protect the stone bridge they built." He enjoyed talking about the Romans for whom he had a great respect. "The town has a functioning port, and is the main centre from which to travel north to the land of the Scots or west to reach Carleol, which the Romans called Luguvalio. Newcastle is an important town, and we can't allow it to remain in the hands of our enemy."

There was a deep murmur of agreement from the assembled men. They had been well fed and, although many would have wished for more to drink, there was a warm sense of well-being among the group.

"They will be waiting for us within the strong walls of their town," Fitzosbern said. "We cannot expect them to meet us face-to-face on the battlefield." He shrugged his powerful shoulders. "Why would they give up their advantage? They will be expecting us to bring siege machines, and therefore they will not be expecting us to arrive so soon. If the weather had been more agreeable, I think news of our reaching Northallerton might already have reached them. But I am confident the heavy rain will have lessened any chance of that. We met nobody on our journey here?" He turned and raised his eyebrows enquiringly at a thickset Norman standing next to him.

"No, my Lord. We met no travellers either. It was some of the worst conditions I've experienced in this," he paused, "wet country." There was general laughter, although many of the officers had quietly expressed doubts on the state of their men if they had not had a pre-arranged camp at the end of their long march in such weather.

Fitzosbern returned to the map. "My scouts report that the enemy lacks both numbers and discipline. Once we have breached their defences, we should have little trouble overwhelming them." His face darkened. "Those who have taken up arms against us must be executed. We take no prisoners." There was a hushed silence. "However, I want the town's people to be left unharmed unless they fight against us. There will be no pillage, no rape and no unnecessary setting fire to any buildings. If we are to avoid constant rebellion, we must show that we can rule fairly. Once we have secured the town, I want the majority of the soldiers to be withdrawn. The cavalry will patrol the streets, soldiers will guard the gates and the main squares. All others will encamp on the other side of the river."

He stared round at each officer, "You will each choose a squad of trusted men, and if they survive the fighting, they will be the ones to prevent any outrage to the community by our soldiers. Those caught will be hanged in public the next day. I will show that we mean to maintain the law.

I would like to believe that all of our army will obey my orders. Sadly, that is never true."

For the next hour he explained the stages of the attack, and how attention to detail would ensure a successful assault on the town. "Remember," he said at the end of his briefing, "our reputation as a fighting force will dissuade future uprisings."

.   .   .

IT WAS ANOTHER WARM DAY as Angwen and Bethan walked down to a nearby stream to wash some clothes and collect water. They rarely saw much of Gwenllian as she spent most days and the occasional night at the home of her future husband, and the two women were glad of each other's company. As they turned away from the village, Angwen noticed a man was watching them from behind some thorn bushes. She did not recognize him. He was darkly bearded with a vivid scar down one side of his face, as though he had been slashed by a knife. Thin, matted hair hung like rat tails on either side of his boney face, and his bright, blood-shot eyes stared angrily out from deep sockets. He ran his tongue over the gaps between his few yellowing teeth as he leered at them, and she felt a shudder go through her. She pointed towards him.

"Take no notice," Bethan said, making a rude face at the man. "That's Madog. He's bad news. In the summer he lives rough, and tries to steal things. In the winter he lives in his mother's barn, over the other side of the stream. He has tried to attack women, but since Idris arrived in the village, he hasn't dared come near." She patted the small knife she carried tucked into her waist band. "He's one of the reasons I always carry this. If you're alone always carry a thick stick."

Angwen indicated she had not heard about him. Bethan shook her head, "He's not been around for a long time. Nobody's seen him this year. I'll tell Idris."

They continued to the stream where they filled their buckets and washed their few small clothes. It was a pleasant place, and if Angwen had not felt that Madog was still around, she would have stripped off and washed herself in the stream. It was the first time she had felt any danger since she had arrived many months ago, and she gestured to Bethan that she felt he was hiding in the bushes.

"Oh, don't worry, Angwen. That man's a coward. He would never attack two of us. Anyway, he's afraid of me." She was silent for a while as they walked back. "How do you think he got that scar?" She pulled out her blade and attacked the air in front of her. "That's what I did when he tried to grab me one night. He'll never try that again." They both laughed as Bethan pretended to be Madog and fell over backwards in the grass, covering her face. "Don't worry," she lay her arm around Angwen's shoulders, "I'll tell Idris. He'll pass the word around, and Madog will soon be gone."

That evening, after a small communal gathering and the summertime sharing of food, everyone went back to their homes once the light began to fade. Angwen quickly made her way to her small hovel near the southern end of the hamlet. It was set back a bit from the road, but she had always felt completely safe. In fact, since the time she had fought the Bishop, she had always felt imbued with confidence. But the thought of Madog made her cringe; there was something evil about him.

She carefully opened her door, allowing as much of the dusk light as possible to illuminate the dark interior, and checked within. After satisfying herself that there was nothing unusual inside, she took a deep breath and entered. She had not lit her fire as she had known she would be with Bevan for most of the day, and with only one small window, the light was limited. Angwen grunted with satisfaction, she owned so little, and the place was so small, that nobody, not even a child could hide.

She quickly arranged her bed while she could still see its outline, and went back to close the door. As she did so, she thought she saw a movement near a building thirty paces away. She froze, straining her eyes to penetrate the gathering dark. There were no candle lights to be seen as the hamlet was a poor and frugal community, and there were no dogs nearby to bark a warning if strangers approached.

From behind her door Angwen picked up a stout ash club which she kept in case of wild animals and which she usually used for beating a way through nettles and briars. She stared into the dark. It was a moonless night, with not a whisper of a breeze, and she stood motionless for a long time listening intently and surprised how dark it had suddenly become. She had good eyes, and she was still able to distinguish the faint outline of her doorway. Moving slowly, she retreated to her small table, and felt about until she found the sturdy knife that Idris had given her, and which she used for so many purposes. Unlike Bethan, she had never felt the need to carry it around with her unless she had a specific reason.

A feeling of relief flooded over her as she gripped it. Now, if she had to, she could defend herself. She moved as silently as a cat back towards her door, picking up her single stool, the only furniture she possessed for sitting on, and placing it between her bed and the opening. There was a single piece of thin wood which served as a bar to secure the door at night, but the old woman who had inhabited this shack before had rarely used it, having lived securely in the hamlet all her life. Likewise, Angwen had not seen it as a security, but just as a way of keeping the door shut against wind and bad weather. She was suddenly aware that any determined person could easily break through. Feeling carefully for the bar, she secured it in place.

Her temporary home had one small window set into the wall near the door at shoulder height. It had a single shutter, that when closed was secured by a cracked piece of wood. She rarely closed it. When Iago had stayed with her, he had suggested she have it fixed, but she had not bothered. It was possible that a grown person could climb through, but it would be difficult, and she had dismissed his worry.

Eventually she sat down on her bed, bare-footed but fully clothed, and fitted the knife securely into the rope belt she wore. She held her club in one hand and held a mug of water in the other. It was a humid night, and as she sipped the water, she concentrated on listening.

An owl hooted in the distance; a dog barked briefly and she could hear the faint cry of a baby, for in most homes the walls were so thin that there was little privacy when people were walking close by, and the protesting voices of babies and angry adults were often heard. Yet, there was no way she could call for help.

She stared into the dark and began to think about the strangeness of her life and how lucky she was to have a friend like Bethan. Her eyelids began to close, and she finished her water, shifted her position and instantly fell into a deep sleep. It seemed only moments before she was sitting up straight, and fumbling for her knife. She quietly moved her position and sat like a coiled-up snake, ready to fight back any attack.

Something had awoken her, and she waited slowly controlling her quick breathing. There was nothing, not a sound disturbed the deep tranquility of the night. She was beginning to think it was a night creature that she had heard, when something pressed against the door. There was a slight creaking sound as though the door was being tested, and she heard the soft scrunch as feet repositioned themselves.

Making no sound, Angwen stood up, replaced the knife in her belt and gripped the club with both hands. She moved to a space just behind where she visualized the stool was placed, and prepared for what she was certain was an attack by Madog.

The weak door began to groan as the thin wooden bar tensed. There was a sudden crack, and the door burst open. Faint starlight outlined the hulking shape that rushed into the room. He had worked out where the bed would be, and was counting on his victim to make a sound indicating her exact position. He had not imagined the knee-high stool, that he tripped over, nor the hefty club that smashed into his face.

Madog lay on the ground groaning, and it was this that enabled her to continue her frenzied attack, in total darkness, on his body. She only stopped when he ceased making any sound. Weeping copiously, and shaking with fear, she gradually edged round the body and found her way out into the night. Stars had appeared and provided just enough light for her to make her way to Bethan's house, where she pounded hysterically on the door.

It took no time for Bethan to assess the situation and light candles. "Stay here," she ordered. "I'll get Idris."

Angwen shook her head, and insisted on holding onto her arm as they crossed over to the smithy. The lone courage she had displayed had been replaced by a nervous reaction and a need to be near people.

Idris and Iago carried lamps as they led the way to Angwen's hovel, and Bethan carried a shaded candle, with her other arm around her shuddering friend. They came to the open door and saw the shattered wood. "Wait here," Idris said gruffly. He and Iago went inside to assess the situation, while neighbours gathered around, forming a semi-circle around the two women and offering comfort to Angwen.

"You'd better take her to your place, Bethan," Idris said when he re-emerged. He placed a gentle hand on Angwen, who continued to hiccup and snuffle. "There's nothing you can do here." He smiled at Angwen, "You've been a brave woman. You're in good company with Bethan."

The next day, it was revealed that Madog had died. He was quickly buried in a pit away from the hamlet, and Idris refused to say whether he or Angwen had killed him. "He deserved to die, and it is the bravery of our friend, Angwen, who has allowed the women and mothers of this place to live in peace and free from fear."

But people are curious, and even though grateful, they would like to have known if the strange newcomer, who couldn't speak, had killed Madog, or whether Idris, the powerful blacksmith, had finished him off. When asked, Iago said, "Does it matter? Perhaps it was me. You should all be grateful that a monster has been defeated. There is nothing more to be said," he glared at them, "ever again."

Later, Idris said to Bethan, "Iago has become a man. I'm proud to work with him."

Angwen was consumed with guilt. "Did I kill that man? she signalled to Bethan. "I did not want to kill him, just to stop him hurting me."

"You did well, Angwen. He was a dangerous man. He had no good features. He attacked women and even worse, he attacked young girls. The men should have dealt with him long ago. You did what you had to do. I don't think I would have done so well." Bethan's clear clipped speech was a comfort to Angwen, but it took her some days before she moved back into her own home, and only after Iago and Idris had strengthened her door and her window.

CHAPTER FIFTEEN

The Norman army crossed the River Derwent and camped just out of sight of the town of Newcastle. The soldiers had marched more than forty miles in two days, and Fitzosbern allowed them a short rest before the attack on the town would commence. Scouts were convinced that they had prevented any news of his approach from the south, and the sun was still high when he sent a cohort of his cavalry off to the west, together with a troop of mounted engineers that he always used when he was attacking structures. Following them at a quick march was a full platoon of volunteers; some of his elite warriors.

The cavalry kept out of sight of Newcastle, and attempted to cross the River Tyne at a ford, a mile west of the town. However, the river was swollen by the recent rains, and when the crossing proved impossible they were forced to make use of one of the large rafts that the mounted carpenters and a few engineers were building for the attack on the town.

A young engineer, clad only in trousers and a blouse, rode his horse bareback into the river, with the end of a long coil of thin rope attached around his waist. The horse fought its way bravely across the turbulent water, and eventually landed on the other side, but not before the strong current had taken the frightened animal further down the bank than anticipated. It took a long time for the rider to drag the rope back to a position opposite where the heavy raft had been constructed, and then to pull the thin rope across. A thick rope had been attached to this, together with a pulley and another rope through it. Once the structure was laboriously dragged across by the fast-tiring man, it was carefully secured to a large tree, at which point it was possible to attach another pulley to the raft and begin to ferry the war horses and riders across to the north bank.

It had taken much longer than expected, and a rider was dispatched to report back to Fitzosbern. During the crossing of the river, the other engineers had constructed two more large rafts and a pile of makeshift paddles. The sweating force of elite soldiers had joined them, ready to be transported downstream. They stood silently staring at the edge of the dark waters, with the growl of the river strange to their ears. There were many who had never travelled on a large river, made more unnerving by the semi-darkness. Their voyage over from Normandy had been terrifying, but the boats had been large and well-built, unlike the pitiful rafts they were to be travelling on.

Eventually, enough riders had crossed the river to ensure that they could prevent any local people near the river from raising the alarm, but on two occasions horses had panicked and a number of soldiers had been injured and two had drowned in the dangerous river. However, the officers had maintained a harsh discipline and order had been maintained. In darkness lit only by flaming torches, the soldiers were filed aboard and given paddles, which would only be needed when they started their journey, and to slow down the rafts when they reached their destination.

Each raft was controlled by two soldiers who managed an awkward rudder that directed the heavy platform through the untrustworthy current. Long poles had been suggested, but the unexpected strength of the flow and the increased depth of the flooded river had ruled against that idea.

It had been agreed that the rafts would not proceed downriver until after darkness had fallen. When they were getting close, a horseman on the south side would ride ahead down to the town and alert the waiting soldiers. They would, as quietly as possible, dispose of the inexperienced guards on both sides of the bridge. The soldiers had been in position for a long time, and Fitzosbern, on hearing of the delay upriver, sent them reassurances. Shortly after the Saxon guards had been removed, without any reaction from the walls of the town, the rafts were glimpsed approaching at an unplanned and uncontrollable speed. They bumped heavily into the bridge supports, causing some soldiers to fall into the surging water, and with the weight of their armour they were quickly sucked under. One raft got caught on the up-river side of one of the bridge's piers, and although the soldiers struggled to paddle back against the strong current, they were unable to force the raft away.

The guards on the walls were alerted by the noise, and on getting no reply to their challenges from the guards on the bridge, they rang their warning bell, blew the alarm trumpets and lit torches to see out into the moonless night. Meanwhile, two of the rafts shot past unnoticed. The surviving soldiers paddled furiously and, with the help of their primitive rudders, managed to push themselves over to the north side. Once there, under the high walls of the town, they found the power of the river's current lessen at the same time as the stone wharfs appeared.

A large merchant ship was tied up to the dock, and one of the barely controllable rafts managed to lock itself between the bow of the ship and the stony side of a wharf. The thundering crash of the raft against the front of the ship caused the crew to pour up onto the deck, as the soldiers scrambled frantically up onto the quay. The sailors were poorly armed, and many had been drinking, and they appeared confused, staggering up from the warm cabin below. There was a brief and bloody skirmish and the experienced soldiers quickly took command of the ship, before turning their attention to the gate that connected the port with the town.

The other raft was not as fortunate. It careered past the ship as, just at that moment, the two soldiers who were attempting to control the primitive rudder, lost their balance and almost fell into the dark waters. The raft was in danger of being pulled back into the main current, and the paddlers on right side exerted themselves to regain control of the forward movement of the raft, while the left side, on the urging of their officer, backpaddled to try to turn the craft. All this time, the two exhausted men on the rudder struggled to regain their footing, and finally retook control. They directed the unstable raft towards the bank, unable to see where they were going, but intent on one thing: to get ashore and flee the horror of the raft. They careened into a small backwater choked with reeds, and jumped off into the shallow water, clawing their way up the muddy bank and onto dry land. For many, it was a miracle of deliverance.

Michel, the officer in charge, was a young man from an important family who had little military experience; certainly nothing resembling the nightmare river journey. As he assembled them in the dim light, he was surprised how easy it was to re-establish his control over the small shuddering group of men who had feared they would drown. As none of them knew how to swim, they were all amazed to be alive, and each man felt inviolate and considered the prospect of fighting to be a welcome chance to give thanks to their God for their deliverance. Michel shared their enthusiasm as they raced, with grim determination, across the uneven ground to join up with those from the other raft who had gained control of the stone dock.

The quays could accommodate a number of merchant ships, but the prospect of fighting had caused most of the captains to avoid the port. Many of the warehouses were empty as the imports they normally stored had been moved into the safety of the town, and only bales of wool for export remained. From the docks, a single path led to a sturdy pair of gates into the town. The gate was wide enough to allow a wagon through, but it was well protected. The two heavy wooden doors had been reinforced with iron bars, and guard posts had been established above each side, allowing the defenders to rain down arrows on any enemy who approached.

Fitzosbern had been quite clear in his instructions to his officers: they were to try to breach the door before the town was alerted. However, the noise at the bridge had resulted in the alarm being sounded with every Saxon soldier turning out to man the walls. The senior Norman officer in this diversion attack was a man named Henri, who had been aboard the raft that had made the first successful landing. He was forced to abandon the attack on the dockside gate after two of his small party were struck down by a rain of arrows as they tried to batter down the gate with an improvised ram. He retreated back to a shed just out of range of the archers and waited impatiently for the soldiers from the third raft to appear. Henri was an optimist as well as a realist, and knew he could not do much until he was reinforced. At least, he consoled himself, if the assault on the main gate was successful, he could prevent the enemy from escaping,

On the north side of the town, the small contingent of cavalry were in position, and waited to ambush any who sought to escape. Meanwhile, the unhappy survivors on the trapped raft were finally rescued, but not before the archers on the town walls had killed half of their number.

Fitzosbern's attack began to gain momentum. First, massed Norman archers quickly cleared the parapets of Saxon bowmen, and continued to shower arrows on the area above and around the main gates, preventing the defenders from making use of their superior positions. Then, the soldiers charged across the bridge and holding their shields above their heads, formed a defensive roof for the two teams of strong men who managed the battering rams.

As the first ram thudded against the gates, the Norman archers discharged a fiery hail of flaming arrows over the walls, and onto the dried thatched roofs of the enclosed buildings. It was an eerie sight that discouraged the defenders, as fires broke out on all the buildings close to the main gate. There was immediate chaos as the town's people struggled to get ladders and buckets of water to fight the fires, risking their lives as more fire arrows fell from the dark sky.

The majority of the Saxon soldiers were not local men, but had gathered at the town to establish a headquarters for a general uprising. They had been barely tolerated by the town's civilians, who only wanted to be left in peace, but who, initially, had been delighted when the small Norman garrison had been slaughtered. But now that the Normans were destroying the town, and might soon overrun it, the local men were uncertain whether it was better to fight against the attackers, or hope that by hiding away they might be able to negotiate a surrender. The women were equally anxious for their own safety and that of their children, and with that fear came a hatred for the men who had endangered their homes and families. And now the town was burning.

The Saxon force gathered in front of the main gate, hoping it would hold, but prepared to fight if it were breached. Many brave men continued to risk their lives on the parapets, dropping heavy stones onto the massed soldiers below, and causing death and injury to those manning the rams. But with the burning houses behind them, and their outlines clearly visible on the walls, making them targets for the Norman archers, the morale of the Saxon warriors began to waver.

With a deafening scream one of the gates splintered, and this was immediately followed by the shuddering crash as the gate was forced from its massive hinges and fell sideways down in front of the waiting defenders.

They charged forward and formed a strong shield wall preventing the onrush of the attackers, and for a short while the Saxons held their ground until they began to be attacked from three sides. When the gate fell it diverted the attention of the defenders, and many left their positions to support their friends in the defence of the gate. The Normans took advantage of this, and placing ladders against the outside walls, quickly overwhelmed the few soldiers on the parapets. As the disciplined, armoured men swarmed over the walls, they divided into two groups and made a surprise attack on both sides of the Saxons who were stubbornly defending the gates. It was a massacre, and before their officers could reorganize their defence, the shield wall broke, and the soldiers began a rapid retreat, trying desperately to maintain some semblance of order.

At this point, the main body of the army poured through the gateway, and into the town. Directed by a trumpet call, they stood to the side to allow their cavalry to charge through and turn a semi-organized retreat into a disorganized and panic-driven rout. It was a scene of horror as Norman soldiers raced through the town, bursting into houses looking for the fighting men who had survived. The homes near the main gates burnt furiously, forcing their families out into the path of the invading force, where they were murdered in a mindless blood rage.

A strong force of retreating Saxons rushed towards the dock gate intending to seek refuge on the ship in the harbour. Up until then, Henri had been listening to the sounds of the main attack as it developed in the town, and had watched with satisfaction as fire lit up the sky. At that moment, Michel and his small group arrived, breathing heavily, but keen to play their part.

"We must stop them from reaching the ship!" Henri warned the junior officer. They still did not have many men, but Henri was determined to perform his duty. "Form a shield wall!" he yelled as the enemy soldiers burst out through the gates and charged towards them.

The Saxons were desperate. They had just witnessed their defences overwhelmed by the well-trained Norman army, and saw the ship at the dock as their last chance for survival. Henri and his few men fought well, but were soon out-flanked on both sides, forcing them to conduct a steady retreat back towards the ship.

"Michel!" Henri yelled. "Take one man and set fire to the ship!"

The young officer grabbed the nearest soldier, and they vigorously fought their way out of the diminishing semi-circle they defended. With the unnamed soldier, he sprinted to the ship, and as they ran up the gangplank they were pursued by a handful of Saxons who had slipped past the remains of the shield wall, and were determined to prevent the Normans from occupying the ship, which remained their only hope of escape. Michel ordered the soldier to defend the gangplank, and ran across the deck towards the hatch. He did not know much about ships, but assumed there must be some form of light in the dark interior.

As he climbed down the narrow ladder into the spacious cabin below, he saw a lantern hanging from the ceiling. He grabbed it, and took out the flaming candle and began to rush into the bowels of the ship looking for material he could set alight. Soon he had two fires going, and ran back towards the ladder, in time to see the figure of a Saxon descending. He had never knowingly killed anyone before, but he felt no regrets as he stabbed the man in the back, pushed him away from the steps, and climbed up quickly as smoke began to fill the cabin.

As he reached the top, an enemy soldier lashed out at him with his sword. Michel avoided the stroke and was able to injure the man, who fell back with his sword arm hanging loose. Michel saw instantly that the soldier who had defended the gangplank was dead and more Saxons were charging aboard. He was tempted to retreat down the stairs, but the smoke was billowing up from below, and he could hardly breathe. Knowing it would be impossible for the Saxons to fight the fire, he rushed to the river side of the boat, avoiding the confused Saxons, who suddenly had no plan.

Thick smoke made it hard to see or breathe, and the Saxons were soon fleeing back down the gangplank, paying no attention to him. He stripped off his leather breastplate and his helmet, and dived into the cold river, grateful for his childhood swimming training, and determined to survive. Above him, flames began to appear in the smoke, and he felt he had completed the order he had been given. He had yet to find out that Henri and the rest of the brave soldiers he had commanded were dead.

Later, when Fitzosbern was celebrating with his officers in his large tent, there was no mention of the atrocities his men had committed. He was a realist, and having laid out clear orders, he expected them to be carried out to the best of his officers' abilities. After the event, there was never anything to be gained by an investigation. He had been a soldier long enough to know that battle-weary men did not become model human beings immediately. Tomorrow, he would punish those who were not back in camp. As the dawn broke, he raised a cup of wine: "To another victory!"

In the port the sinking hulk continued to burn.

CHAPTER SIXTEEN

"When are you delivering the swords, Iago?" Bethan's voice could be heard above the noise of hammering.

The hammering stopped. "Um. I think Idris intends to deliver them tomorrow." The young man sounded embarrassed.

"Where is he now?"

"He's um, out the back somewhere."

There was a silence, and even without seeing what was going on, Angwen could feel the tension. She had been walking from her small home down the centre of the hamlet to barter two small trout for some eggs, when she saw Bethan cross from her house and enter the front of the smithy without looking either way. There was something about the frown on her friend's face and her jerky body movements that were so unlike her usual carefree self, that Angwen felt driven to stop outside and listen to the conversation.

"Right. Then I'll look out the back."

"No, no, Bethan!" Iago sounded anxious. "He, um, he went out."

"Where?" Bethan's voice had become icy.

"Where?" Iago could not conceal his embarrassment. "He didn't say, exactly."

"I'll look out the back then." There was the sound of bodies moving quickly.

"I don't think he…" Iago sounded desperate.

A door crashed as it was flung open, and this was followed by a roar of anger from Bethan.

Unable to contain her curiosity, Angwen peered around the corner of the open front, where the two anvils and a hot fire were situated. On the far side, Iago was standing, biting his lower lip, his large gloved hands still clasping a hammer and a piece of metal. Beyond was the door leading to the back of the work area, where spare metal, fuel and completed work was kept. Bethan stood just inside the open door and to one side, facing Idris who stood awkwardly, dressed in armour. He was wearing a metal breastplate, a round pot-shaped helmet with a face guard, and gloves that had metal pieces attached to the top. He had a thick leather belt with a long sword on one side, and a dagger on the other. He looked threatening, quite different to the usual relaxed Idris.

"All dressed up for a fight, are we?" Bethan had placed her hands on her hips, and was looking very aggressive.

"Just trying them on," Idris said.

"Why? Why do you need armour? You're too old to fight, you stupid man. Did you think I didn't know what you both were up to? You're too old, and you should not be encouraging Iago."

"We're going to Prince Anarwd's assembly camp to deliver the swords, and it seems a good idea to offer our services while we're there." Idris removed his helmet and although he looked sheepish in front of the angry Bethan, there was a determination in his voice.

"But why? You're too old and Iago is totally inexperienced."

"Idris has been teaching me how to fight," Iago said, determined to be included in the argument.

"But you both—."

"We're going, Bethan. We've made up our minds." This was a voice Angwen had never heard before. The easy-going side of Idris had been replaced by a cold, unemotional voice. The finality in his tone took the air out of Bethan's anger, and she stood very still, staring at him. Then, with a loud sound that resembled a cow's fart, she turned and stormed out of the smithy. Again, she did not notice Angwen.

"Bloody men!" she roared. But as she crossed towards her house, Angwen saw her taught body relax like a punctured bladder, as her whole frame shuddered with grief. She reached her house, pushed open the door and collapsed on her floor, leaving the door ajar.

Angwen followed her and slipped inside, closing the door quietly behind her. Bethan was crying with an intensity that shocked Angwen, who had always admired her strong, independent friend, who seemed happy to take on the problems of the world. She knelt down, placing her two fish on the floor beside her, and embraced the older woman in her arms.

After a while, Bethan composed herself. She sat up and put her arm around Angwen. "Thank you, my friend. I really lost it, didn't I?"

Angwen shook her head, and rested her head on Bethan's shoulder.

"I love Idris, and I don't want to lose him. We were going to get married at mid-summer. I just can't understand why he has to fight. It's not as though he's important. Nobody will miss him if he does not join Anarwd's army." She took a deep breath. "I began to suspect he was going to do something stupid, when he started to act in a shifty manner. That's not like Idris. I've known him a long time and he's a sweet man. But when he stopped work every time I called in unexpectedly at his smithy, and when Iago kept saying they were just trying out new ways of shaping metal, when even I could see they were making armour, I knew what he was up to."

The women stood up and, after a long hug, Angwen left and continued on her journey to a woman who kept chickens. She walked along the dusty track, away from the hamlet and towards a small enclosed field on a gentle slope. The chickens were reared by an elderly woman whose husband carved plates and bowls and mugs from the local hardwoods. Over time Angwen had become a regular customer, and a mutual liking had developed.

After the customary greetings, Angwen shared some broth with them, and she went through her usual mixture of mime and drawings in the dust as they conversed.

"I hear Idris and Iago are going to fight for Prince Anarwd," the husband said. His eyes flashed, "If I was a bit younger I would have joined them."

His wife raised her eyebrows expressively at Angwen. "I don't imagine Bethan was very pleased?"

Angwen gave an impression of Bethan erupting.

"I don't know what gets into men," the wife continued, ignoring her husband's grunts. "However, I think Idris is used to being his own man and, now that he's agreed to marry Bethan, he wants to have one more adventure before he becomes a married man. I hope he doesn't regret it." Her husband pretended not to hear.

On her way back, Angwen thought about the idea of a husband. She liked the idea of someone sharing her bed and her meals. If she had a husband, she would never have to worry about being attacked by people like Madog. She passed some children playing happily and smiled at their laughter, wondering if she had ever had children. It made her sad to think about it, and her mind turned back to marriage. She frowned: she had not met any man in the area that she had been attracted to, except perhaps the laughing man on the horse. There had been something about him that had interested her, and she had looked forward to meeting him again. But it had never happened. She had tried to ask Bethan about the rider, but although her friend had paid rapt attention to her attempts to describe the man, she had not come up with any suggestions.

Back at the smithy, Idris handed a metal helmet to Iago. "I think we should leave now before Bethan comes back for a second round." He coughed self-consciously. "Women don't understand these things, you know, Iago. They don't understand that we have to defend our homes and our women folk; it's our job. Now's a good time if we're going to get our own back on the Normans for what they did at Cwm, and Prince Anarwd needs support from people like us who don't produce food. The farmers' job is to produce our food. It's no good winning a war if we starve afterwards."

Iago stared at the helmet. Unlike Idris's which was a pot helmet with a visor, his was shaped like a cylinder with a narrow visor. It fitted comfortably, though he suspected it would get very hot in direct sunlight. What pleased him most was the helmet looked evil, and he imagined any enemy would think twice before fighting him.

"What do you think?" Idris grinned.

"Do I look frightening?

"Oh, yes, boy. It would give old women nightmares," he erupted into a roar of laughter, and helped Iago get the heavy helmet off his head. "You're getting taller every day, I think I'm feeding you too well."

"So, we'll take the wagon?" Iago queried. It seemed a long way to travel in the wagon.

"Yes. It's better than marching, and we have the swords to deliver." He removed his breastplate, and weighed it in his hand. "This is a heavy thing to march with. Most soldiers who wear metal armour ride horses. But it's worth the effort if it saves your life." He grinned in a boyish way. "There won't be many foot soldiers as well-protected as we are. They'll all think we're gentry!" He looked appreciatively at Iago who was now taller than he was, and had quickly developed strong shoulders since working with the heavy metal. "I wouldn't want to face you on the battlefield. You look a really mean fellow!" He guffawed and patted Iago's muscular arm. "We'll teach those foreigners a lesson, then we'll come back as heroes. Oh, Iago, the women will be fighting for your attention!"

Iago flushed. He worshipped Idris, and was always delighted to receive such rare compliments. He couldn't wait to prove himself on the battlefield defending his country, and coming back a hero. His father had only thought in terms of making money and, until he met Idris, Iago had never considered the importance of being Welsh and fighting for something more important than money. "Will Bethan forgive you?" he asked.

"Oh, yes, boy. Women are like that, you know. One moment they're mad at you, and the next they're like honey."

"Honey?"

"Yes," Idris laughed. "All sweet and sticky!"

Iago felt his face grow hot. He wasn't too sure what Idris meant, but he thought he could imagine.

"Better hurry now. I'll get the wagon hitched, you bring out the armour. Then we'll eat something, take extra food and leave quietly. We'll meet the rest of the army at a gathering near the River Usk. It'll take about two days, maybe a bit more."

It all sounded so easy.

CHAPTER SEVENTEEN

It was a hot morning, and the continuing dry weather provided firm conditions for the horses as they travelled towards the border. A few older horses were being led to ensure they were able to make it to Hereford without becoming tired, and the scouts who were patrolling ahead and on both flanks of the cavalry had reported no sign of any military activity. Gwriad and Dafydd had volunteered to lead the feint attack with about thirty men. Prince Anarwd had taken charge of half of the remainder that would be in place on the north side of the valley through which the brothers would retreat. Maelgwn took command of those on the south.

They travelled at a fast trot, easily fording a small river and continuing through hilly country. They kept to the valleys and passed through occasional small communities where the occupants hid themselves, and only barking dogs marked their progress.

By mid-afternoon, they rested within a mile of Hereford. The scouts had been reinforced as farms became more numerous and traffic began to be encountered on the road. Anyone on horseback who tried to flee had been cut down, but those who surrendered were allowed to survive after parting with their weapons and their horse.

"There's no need to kill peasants unnecessarily," Anarwd had ordered. "Once we've returned over the border, they can tell whoever they like!"

After a short wait to water their horses, the two main bodies moved off to left and right, leaving the small remainder under Gwriad and Dafydd to prepare themselves for their frontal attack. They wore their armour under their smocks, and some removed their helmets, replacing them with coloured scarfs. It was agreed that those on the old horses would lead, leaving their warhorses in the care of two scouts. When the theatrical costuming had been completed amid much laughter, Gwriad spoke to them.

"We've had our laughs, boys, now for the serious stuff. If you don't fight well and be alert, you could be dead by the end of today." The smiles left the faces of the men, many of whom had never been in a battle. "Now, the scouts report that there is a mess of poor houses and hovels near the town, with a few small farms close by. It's almost certain the inhabitants have heard about the attack on our village and I imagine they have thought we might seek revenge. However, that was months ago, and I doubt if they are expecting us today."

The men all listened with keen attention.

"The scouts have said that if we continue along this road we will see the town as we come over a ridge. We will not take any notice of any farms or houses until we are in sight of the town. Then, we will attack on both sides, and set light to houses, straw stacks, anything that will burn. Kill those who try to stop us, ignore the rest unless they have bows. I will lead the older horses and attack those places nearest the town, but do not ride too close. Keep out of arrow range. Remember, we want to draw them out. As soon as they open the gates, those of us on the old horses must retreat, and it is up to the rest of you to cover us."

He smiled. "As soon as their soldiers follow us over the ridge, our forces will hit them from both sides. You will have done your part! Just keep riding for home! You will be the heroes!"

They all cheered, and Dafydd clapped. He knew he could not have rallied the men in such a way.

Gwriad waited until a scout returned to confirm the rest of the Welsh cavalry were in position, and led the way with the older horses, while Dafydd took charge of the rest. Soon, they came over the ridge and saw the large town, with its high wooden walls, spread out ahead of them. From the higher ground they could see the town's imposing gates were open, and a crowd of people were gathered around a large space outside the walls. Gwriad brought them to a sudden halt.

"This changes things a bit," he muttered to Dafydd. "The townsfolk are all watching their soldiers on the parade ground. There must be over a hundred of them in armour, all well-armed and ready for a fight." He groaned. "There are too many of them for us to attack. We only have a few men on good horses. Bloody hell! If we had all two hundred of us, we could have charged down and slaughtered them. There are no horsemen down there, and it would have been a victory unlike any other!"

"We'll have to go back and alert the rest!" Dafydd said, turning his horse and waving to the other riders. "You move back out of sight, and keep watch. I'll bring up our main force, and the good horses to replace your old nags. We can still make something out of this."

"Too late!" Gwriad roared. "They've seen us!"

From their exposed place on the low hill, they could see the townsfolk suddenly streaming towards the main gates, and the soldiers were quickly forming a shield wall and were moving back towards the town in an organized retreat. Trumpets were sounding a warning and more men appeared on the walls.

"Alright. So they're expecting us," Dafydd said between clenched teeth. "They'll have the gates tightly closed, and they will be ready for an attack. But unless they come out to fight us, they will have to watch as we lay waste to the habitations and structures outside their town. This will be no different to how it was before. Even with the original plan, we could never be certain they would have the cavalry to follow us. We will carry out our side of the plan." He turned to the waiting riders. "Light up the torches! Set fire to everything."

Gwriad agreed, but with a definite lack of enthusiasm. He realized they had squandered an opportunity that, with better planning and up to the moment intelligence, would have enabled them to demonstrate their military power. Instead, they were reduced to a small raid on undefended homes and could be seen as just a rabble. He hoped the result would be that the Normans would retaliate in force, but he doubted they would see the need for an instant response. Keeping their Welsh army waiting in camp would be a problem, when most would be wanting to get back to their farms.

"Alright!" he yelled. "Follow me. We've got a job to do."

.   .   .

JON WAS WORRIED AS HE marched his small army towards Brecon. They were already a day later than he had planned with Daffydd, and the hot weather showed no signs of letting up. Eventually, he had been forced to agree to short breaks when they crossed streams in order for the exhausted volunteers, who were not used to marching, to refill their water flasks and rest their legs. The animals pulling the wagons had been equally affected by the heat and their task was made worse by the uneven roads. It was not until Rees pointed out that the army had lost its compactness, and was stretching out along the narrow road, that Jon had agreed to a slower pace and longer periods of rest.

"The professional soldiers and those with experience have no bother marching most of the day, my Lord, but the new recruits are struggling, and the sergeants are under pressure."

Jon nodded. They were not the only ones who were inexperienced. "We must start earlier in the day while it's still cool, Rees. Spread it around that we will break camp at first light from now on and have a longer break midday."

He and his men were expected to have reached Brecon by tomorrow, but the scouts had assured him he would not arrive until the next day. Even if he increased the pace, which he now realized was impossible, he would still be late. His nightmare was that he would arrive at the assembly point to find that the main force had left, leaving him unaware of Prince Anarwd's intentions. He knew they were going to position themselves near the border, waiting to ambush the Norman army as it advanced into Wales, but he worried he might miss the action, or worse still end up confronting the enemy in a place where he and his local men would have to fight alone. How would he cope being in command of an army of mainly inexperienced soldiers?

That night, as he lay in his tent, he reviewed his lack of experience. It seemed so unlikely that by a series of lucky chances he had been elevated from scullery boy, the lowest in the kitchen, to Lord Jon, adopted son of Gwriad and heir to the Castle. If Lord Gwriad had not taken a liking to him after he killed the wild boar, he would never have gained the attention of Lady Angharad and become her servant. It was the teaching and friendship of Father Williams, Lord Dafydd and Lady Angharad that had educated him in time for the revelation of the Wise Woman that he was the bastard child of the late Lord Gomer ap Griffith. Some Lords would have ignored him, unwilling to acknowledge the mistakes of their uncles, but Gwriad had immediately adopted him and completed his training in riding and the use of weapons. But until now, he had never been in charge of anything other than the few soldiers in the Castle. He was determined not to fail those who believed in him.

On the last day of their march to the gathering, he came over a ridge and could see the village of Brecon in the distance. Beyond, along the banks of the River Usk, was a huge array of tents, men and horses. The smoke from a host of campfires drifted in the air, and even from this distance he could hear the call of trumpets. A sense of accomplishment flooded over him. "Thank God, we're in time."

He turned in his saddle and grinned at Rees, "Bring the column to halt. Allow the men to refresh themselves, and let the sergeants know we will march into the camp like an army, not like a summer gathering."

"Oh yes, my Lord! What a relief to get here. The men will be pleased."

He rode back along the column, gathering the other officers with him.

Jon stared down at the large camp. "Not nearly as pleased I am," he murmured. He dismounted, and stretched, allowing his horse to chomp the sparse greenery at the side of the trail. His father would understand why he was late, and Father Williams had often mentioned that campaigns rarely went to plan. Jon looked forward to leading his small army into the camp, where he would be in the company of experienced men and where he could look forward to fighting the enemy under the guidance of officers who knew how to fight.

It was past midday as he rode into the huge camp. A trumpet had announced his coming, and he was aware of immense activity. Columns of men were being drilled, horsemen were coming and going, smoke drifted from dozens of fires, and guards were patrolling the outskirts of the encampment. A crowd of camp followers cheered and clapped his laughing men, and as they moved through the organized lines of tents the aromas changed from the mouth-watering smell of roasting sheep carcasses to the stench of the distant pit latrines. In the still air, the heat, noise and smells were an assault on the senses of the tired soldiers, for most of whom this was a new experience. Jon handed over the responsibility of his men to Rees and the junior officers, who had already been met by the camp adjutant and his sergeants.

As he dismounted, a big man with a full black beard and dressed in bright armour approached Jon, and indicated for a soldier to take the horse. "Lord Jon, I'm Sir Medwin, Lord Edwin's aide-de-camp. Welcome to our," he paused, "to our gathering." His eyes sparkled, "I'm to take you immediately to Prince Anarwd's tent, where they're having a planning meeting."

"Thank you, Sir Medwin." Jon took an immediate liking to the man. "Did the attack on Hereford go well?"

"About as well as catching fish in the desert," he replied ambiguously. They had reached a large tent with guards outside. "I'll let the generals explain." He smiled, "I hope you haven't come a long distance for nothing." He entered the tent and announced Jon's arrival. As he left the tent, he winked.

"Well done, my boy," Gwriad boomed with what sounded like false jocularity. He strode over to his adopted son and put an arm around his shoulders, ushering him to a bench where they both sat on either side of Dafydd. Prince Anarwd was sitting on the only chair, with Lord Edwin, General Maelgwn and a third man on a bench facing Jon. There was a palpable feeling of gloom, and Jon looked expectantly at Prince Anarwd.

"Welcome, Lord Jon," Anarwd nodded his head. "This is Prince Eoin of Deheubarth, the first cousin of the current ruler Prince Maredudd."

The Prince, a man in his middle age, gave Jon a quick appraisal, and after a brief nod stared straight ahead, giving the impression he was not impressed.

"For the benefit of Prince Eoin and Lord Jon, I will give a brief summary of our attack on Hereford, and then you can suggest what we do next." Anarwd looked around the group of unemotional faces. "At that time, you may wish to suggest some new ideas." He cleared his throat, and slowly described what happened and what should have happened. "I agree that if we had known what was going on, we would have launched a lightning attack with our full force and achieved an important victory that would definitely have caused an immediate response from the Marcher Lords and particularly Earl Fitzosbern. As it is, our attack, if we can call it that, will be seen as a petty, uncoordinated raid by a few Welsh outlaws. I doubt if this will be seen by the Normans as worthy of an immediate response." None of the listeners responded.

"However," he continued, "for the first time for ages, we have a sizeable army ready to fight the Normans when they invade. However, if the Normans don't bring their soldiers over the border, what will we do with our army? Most of them want plunder or they want to return to their farms." He stared around the group, "Who would like to start?"

General Maelgwn raised his arm. "I'll start." He looked fiercely around the group. "I agree that for the first time since our revenge attack on Earl Harold, we have assembled a large army of men, although many of them don't know how to use a weapon or how to obey orders. We have started to train them, and after two weeks we should have created some semblance of an army of soldiers. So, I am happy if the Normans give us some time."

"And what then?" Gwriad said. "Suppose they don't respond? Our army, like any army, wants to fight, and they want to pillage, and without loot they want to be paid. If none of this happens, then we are going to have a very discontented lot of soldiers who could desert and cause mayhem on their way back to their farms."

"My men will do as I ask them and for as long as I ask them."

All faces turned to look at Prince Eoin. He sat bolt upright, with a sanctimonious sneer on his thin face. He was an unknown entity to most of them, other than Prince Anarwd.

"How many men did you bring, my Lord?" Jon asked. His question was merely to understand how he had such certainty.

The Prince stared at him as though he was a naughty child. "Why do you ask?"

"Because I've brought in an army of over two hundred, many of them without military experience, and I couldn't be certain how they would behave if they were kept here with nothing to do." He caught his father grinning and was encouraged to proceed. "I wondered if you had brought in a small elite force that was employed by you."

The Prince breathed out loudly in a long-suffering manner. "I also brought two hundred men. They are proud to serve me, and will always obey orders. If we are not needed, I will march them back."

"Did you say two hundred men?" General Maelgwn queried.

"Yes, and forty cavalry."

"I ordered all men to be counted on their entry into the camp. I have you down as bringing only one hundred and three soldiers, twenty-two cavalry and a large wagon train with many camp followers."

There was an awkward silence as the Prince stared coldly at Maelgwn. "I know how many men I brought, and I don't intend to discuss the matter further."

"Indeed," Prince Anarwd quickly interjected. "To answer your question, Lord Gwriad, I think we are left with no option but to ensure that the Normans will respond. We'll cross the border again, and this time in force. We will use the cavalry and I will be giving new orders to our scouts. Any objections?" He rose to his feet before anyone could respond, "That's good then. Now, it's time to get something to drink."

The meeting broke up awkwardly, after Prince Eoin stormed out of the tent, and everyone was uncertain how to react until Gwriad told a humorous tale about a man trying to milk a bull. Everyone laughed, more loudly than they might have done in normal circumstances.

"What a fart!" Maelgwn observed, and pretended to fan the air. Gwriad let out a whoop and they reached for more wine.

Later, when alcohol had relaxed them and they had eaten well, they continued the formal part of their meeting. Prince Eoin returned and casually conceded that one of his officers had made an error in his calculations. With a certain improvement in the atmosphere, Prince Anarwd discussed his proposed raid on settlements to the south of Hereford. This area was under the control of the Marcher Lord Reginal de Braose, who it was reported had been responsible for the attack on Cwm.

"If we attack as a regular army, we will certainly get a response from Reginal de Braose and this could upset Fitzosbern, who I understand is up north on the other side of England. I believe this de Braose will be keen to show how well he can control his domain, and if we defeat him, it will almost certainly bring Fitzosbern into the picture, and then it will be the time to test our resolve. As far as I am concerned, the time has come when we have to prove that we can defend ourselves. We have to have a major victory, or we are facing an invasion!"

Everyone enthusiastically banged the table, even Prince Eoin, and they left the meeting in good spirits to prepare for the raid.

.   .   .

IDRIS LEFT THE HAMLET BY a back trail to avoid upsetting Bethan. The old horse seemed happy to pull the ornate wagon full with the swords, their armour, personal weapons and their supplies.

"Do you think this is a good idea, Idris? Bethan will be cross when she finds you have left without saying goodbye."

'You will find, Iago, that women worry too much. If they had their way, we would never leave their beds!" There was a slight pause as Iago thought about this, then Idris gave a whoop of laughter and Iago smiled self-consciously. Most of the time he could only guess at the meaning of Idris's sexual jokes. As the old horse lumbered along the lane, they saw a woman coming towards them.

"Oh hell!" Idris exclaimed. "It's Angwen. She'll tell Bethan, and before you know it, they'll both be wanting to come with us."

"Too late," Iago muttered. "She's waving at us."

They pulled up before her, and both stared down at Angwen's smiling face. She seemed to be in good spirits.

"Hello, Angwen. Fancy meeting you here." Idris cleared his throat.

She pointed to her basket of eggs, and indicated her question as to where they were going.

"We're taking swords to Prince Anarwd," Idris said. Then, lost for words, he patted Iago on his shoulder like a proud father. "He's learning to be a good blacksmith. It was lucky you brought him back to health."

Angwen smiled and made a dismissive gesture, and Iago, feeling decidedly uncomfortable, said, "I think we have to get a move on, Idris." He turned to the unusual woman smiling up at him, "Enjoy your eggs."

She stood to the side and waved as the wagon moved forward. She knew what they were up to. They're just like naughty boys, she thought. Bethan would be furious. Perhaps she should pretend she had not seen them. With that thought, she left the path and cut through the forest to approach the hamlet from a different direction. Their leaving was none of her business.

"We should get a move on," Iago repeated, glancing behind as Angwen turned into the forest. "I think she's taking a short cut."

"No, I don't think so. More likely she's pretending she hasn't seen us."

"Oh?" Iago was surprised by the older man's conviction, and wondered how long it would be before he felt as confident with women as Idris did. "Where are we going?"

"To a large village named Brecon, on the River Usk. That's what the officer said, so we should be there in two days or so."

The weather remained warm and dry, and it was a pleasure to sleep in the open air. Idris took great care of his old horse, and as the weather continued hot, he stopped in the shade whenever the animal showed signs of exhaustion. "Poor old fellow," he sighed as he patted its wet neck. "You've not been on a long trip like this for a long time." He fed and watered the horse, and sometimes would stand close to it talking quietly.

Iago would watch, and would remember his family's old horse. It had not been well treated, and his father was in the habit of whipping it whenever he had a loaded wagon to get to market. It was simply a beast of burden. He had known the animal for most of his life, but he had never formed a close relationship with it as Idris had with his horse, and until recently he never thought about it. It was another example of how different his life was becoming

It was the end of the day when they finally reached the huge camp where hundreds of men were marching, and where trumpet calls and the screams of red-faced sergeants' rent the air. They had donned their personal armour and, as Idris had predicted, the guards were impressed. Idris had announced that they had brought weapons for Prince Anarwd, and he was taken to see Lord Gwriad, who was delighted to meet these two well armoured soldiers and particularly impressed with the weapons they had created.

"I understood from the officer who visited my forge that I would be paid when I arrived, my Lord?"

Gwriad smiled, "Yes, indeed. The Prince Anarwd is off on a raid. He'll settle such things when he returns." He took an immediate liking to the tall smith, and was fascinated by the intricate design of the large, clean wagon which he understood had been made by Idris. "Have you travelled far?"

"Not really, my Lord. It took us two days, but only because the old horse travelled slower than we could walk. We live close to Cwm, which you may have heard of?"

"Indeed. A sad business." He stared admiringly at the wagon. "Would you be prepared to sell this? We might need it to carry our injured officers.

We have other wagons, but they are really for soldiers who are used to lying on farm manure."

Idris stood to attention, staring ahead and avoiding Gwriad's penetrating stare. "I'm sorry, my Lord, my wagon is not for sale."

Gwriad admired the man, but was not used to being defied. "I was offering to buy it, soldier. In time of war the army can requisition anything it wants. Now, what do you want to charge?"

Idris stood like a statue. The colour had drained from his face. His hands clenched and unclenched by his sides. Idris had never liked officers, and was disappointed in Lord Gwriad, whom he had thought might be an exception to his previous experiences. A long, tense pause ensued.

Unable to believe how quickly the situation was deteriorating, Iago suddenly spoke out. "M'Lord, the old horse is only used to Idris, and wouldn't allow anyone else to control him."

"Really?" Gwriad tried to prevent a mocking laugh. To him, animals did as they were told. He glared at Idris and felt strangely uncomfortable with this proud, stubborn man for whom he had an irritating respect.

"Yes, m'Lord. Perhaps Idris and I could ride the wagon and move the injured officers for you? We might look like soldiers but we're only blacksmiths. We wouldn't be missed in a fight, and the horse would be happy."

Gwriad turned to look at the tall, young man whom he had barely noticed. Iago had a strong, muscular frame, and clearly adored Idris. "How long have you been a blacksmith?"

"Not long, m'Lord. Idris took me in after the Normans killed all my family at the time they attacked Cwm. He's training me." Iago looked respectfully at his hero. "He's taught me everything. I even helped with making the weapons."

Gwriad relaxed. "Go and see General Maelgwn's staff and tell them I have put you two in charge of the transportation of injured officers, and responsible for the horse and especially the cart." He watched the tension fade out of the Idris's body and turned to Iago, "Let me try on your helmet."

With awkward speed Iago did as he was told and handed it over to this unusual Lord. Gwriad tried it on, just as Sir Maelgwn appeared. "You look quite fearsome!" Maelgwn jested. His expression changed, "The scouts have reported back. I'm calling a planning meeting."

"Good." Gwriad removed the helmet, and spoke to Idris. "I like it. Make me one."

Before the startled blacksmith could respond, Iago spoke up: "You keep it, m'Lord. Idris will help me make another one."

Gwriad looked gravely at both men. "Thank you, but for this battle I won't be on a horse. Make me one like that and I will see you get paid for the weapons and the armour." He marched off towards the waiting Maelgwn and they both disappeared into the main tent.

Idris turned and looked approvingly at his apprentice, "You saved the situation there, boy." He shook his head, and then frowned. "However, that helmet wasn't yours to give away, even though you claimed you were a blacksmith!" he tried to keep a straight face. "However, I believe we might actually get paid for our work, thanks to you!"

"And you'll keep your horse and wagon," Iago grinned. "I thought he was going to take them from you."

Idris flexed his back, "Over my dead body."

CHAPTER EIGHTEEN

The training of the soldiers had continued from dawn to dusk, so they never had time to cause trouble or sneak away. At the meeting, Gwriad and Maelgwn agreed to oversee the army, while Dafydd and Jon joined Prince Anarwd and Lord Edwin to lead the cavalry. In spite of the fact that Prince Eoin had only brought a handful of mounted soldiers, Anarwd had thought it best to include the testy Prince in the raid.

A small base camp was to be established in the Black Mountains, just north of the River Usk and close to the border, to allow the men and their horses to rest after their journey from Brecon, and where they could reform after the raid. It had been reported that Reginal de Braose had returned to Hereford since the abortive Welsh attack, with a strong retinue of cavalry, and Anarwd was confident the Marcher Lord would respond as soon as he received news of further attacks.

It was agreed that they would divide into two units with Dafydd and Jon leading one and Anarwd and Edwin the other. Prince Eoin had been placed with Edwin, and in charge of the scouts. Edwin was not happy about the appointment, but Anarwd was confident he could do no harm, and it did prevent the Prince from taking offence. He had been offered the chance of being in charge of the training, but Eoin dismissed the idea. "I'm not a mere weapons instructor," he said, "I'm a Prince, and I fight on a horse." Luckily, Gwriad was not present at the time.

Over the next few days their strategy was planned in detail. It was agreed that with the Norman build-up at Hereford, it would have to be a short campaign to avoid the chance of the enemy cutting off their retreat. "We don't want to be the ones to be ambushed," Anarwd insisted. He had garrisoned the base camp, and scouts had been scouring the Welsh side of the immediate border to ensure that the camp's existence remained unknown to the Normans.

"As soon as we leave the main camp at Brecon, the army will remain in a state of readiness, with the opportunity for the sergeants to knock some military skills into our farmers and would-be heroes. I want every soldier to be training throughout the day, and a section of the cavalry will remain to provide constant scouting. We will not allow them to make a surprise attack on us." He pointed to a rough map showing the River Usk and the Black Mountains. "We will leave the base camp, and approach Hereford from the south-west, and seek to devastate this area here," he waved his hand over a general area between the border and the town. "After that, we come back this way," he pointed to the dotted border, "and we will reform and hopefully rest at the base camp."

"Then we return to Brecon?" Jon could hardly control his excitement.

"As soon as we have reorganized ourselves," the Prince nodded. "We could have injured and dead soldiers to transport, and we want to make sure that we leave enough men to stage a final retreat when we get news of the Norman advance." His eyes flashed, "We must treat them like a beehive and give them a resounding kick if we want to make certain they attack us when we want them to."

The cavalry left at midday and made an unhurried journey to the base camp. The weather was oppressive, the bugs were everywhere and the sun beat mercilessly on the heavily armed soldiers. At times the long line of horsemen was shaded by deep forest, but mostly they were passing through rocky passes below low peaks where the small streams had dried up, and where human habitation was infrequent.

The base camp was nicknamed Paradise, spelled 'Paradwys'. It was well named, as it was situated in a flat area on one side of a large stream which was still flowing strongly and carried ice-cold water from the nearby mountains. Their horses were allowed to drink first, and having given them horse bags to feed on, the men stripped off and bathed in the refreshing water. The camp was manned by a team of thirty experienced soldiers who had set up the tents, prepared the food and carried out the guard duties. They were under the command of Prince Anarwd's son, Alun. "You high-living horse-lovers had better do a good job this time," the young commander joked, "or you'll have to clean up the camp yourselves and watch us as we go swimming instead!"

"These men are worth their weight in gold," Anarwd said proudly to his officers. "They're all expert archers who can also fight with a sword.

Most of them have been with Alun for some time, and he's fantastic with a sword." He suddenly looked embarrassed, "Although I say it myself."

The others nodded in agreement. It was clear Prince Alun was a natural leader and had the loyalty of his men. "If we had an army of such men," the Prince continued, "we could beat the Normans, no matter how many they sent to fight us."

Dafydd laughed. "Oh, Anarwd, that has been the cry ever since we lost King Gruffyd."

They all muttered their agreement.

After the evening meal, some of Alun's men gave a display of archery that impressed even the most hardened cavalry soldiers.

"So, if we see you all being chased back over the border by the blood-thirsty Normans, we'll come to your rescue, boys," Alun quipped. "We know you let your horses do all the fighting, but we'll look after you, don't worry, we promised your mothers!" The friendly mockery from both sides continued until the change of guard signalled an end to the social.

At first light the riders left the camp and crossed into England, south of Hereford. When the scouts confirmed they were within a few miles of the town, they cut further south and divided into two squadrons, each of approximately one hundred cavalry. Both squadrons carried flags bearing the red dragon of Wales, to clearly identify that this was a serious challenge.

The scouts had identified a number of partially fortified villages, but the cavalry was able to force the gates before the guards had realized what was happening. In some areas the inhabitants fought back, but mostly it was the speed of the attack that led to panic and a rush for cover. In all places the cavalry set fire to the structures, killed or released the animals and burnt hay and straw stacks or any crops that had begun to grow. Prince Anarwd had ordered his men to kill only those who fought back and to avoid attacks on women and children whenever possible.

Soon, the sky was dark with black smoke, and with the loss of only a handful of men Anarwd ordered his squadron to return to the border. They turned their horses, and with the excitement of battle draining away, each man felt relieved to be leaving. It had been agreed that the two squadrons would return independently and reform at Paradwys. By keeping in two squadrons it was hoped that any information that reached the Normans would underestimate their numbers. In spite of the almost non-stop action, their tired horses still moved swiftly through the damaged land. Soon the scouts reported that they were passing to the south and west of Hereford.

The terrain allowed each squadron to bunch up, and Anarwd continued to set a fast pace until a scout appeared from a treed area to their south, and galloped towards them. Anarwd stopped the squadron as the man approached, and felt a thrill go through him as the scout arrived, dripping with sweat and barely able to speak. "My Lord, there's a strong force of Normans just ahead, over the high ground in front."

"Do they have cavalry?"

The scout shook his head, "No, my Lord, but they're marching for the border in a tight column. They're carrying spears, and some have bows, and they're wearing light armour."

"Well done, soldier. Take a rest at the back of the column."

The Prince's immediate thought was to overtake them and with the advantage of surprise he was confident he could defeat them. But when he rethought the matter, he realized that his men had been active all day, their horses were tired and more importantly, he could not afford the loss of the only trained cavalry he possessed.

"We will hold back," he told his officers. "When the other squadron joins us, we will review the situation."

They remained out of sight from the Norman marching column, and Anarwd wondered where their cavalry was situated. "We're close to the border," he said to Edwin. "Do you think their cavalry have gone ahead to clear the way, or are they likely to come from behind when we attack their troops?"

"My scouts have seen no sign of them behind us," Eoin said. "I would have known if there were any reports." He rode slightly in front of the other officers, as though he was in overall charge.

Edwin gave Anarwn an old-fashioned look, "If they were behind us, they might find themselves between our two cavalry columns." He paused. "Perhaps we should remain where we are, and send out more scouts to clarify the situation."

"That is unnecessary," Eoin protested. "My scouts would have seen such an enemy formation. We must attack the Normans in front of us. After all, that is why we are here," he glared at the two Generals. "We did not come all this way to burn the houses of a few peasants." He spoke in a pedantic, clipped manner.

"The scout says they're well-armed. If we attack this large column, they'll form a shield wall," Edwin frowned. "We'll be forced to use the horses to batter them down, and if they're a really large force we could find ourselves boxed in. I suggest we wait for the rest of our cavalry."

"We have come to fight!" Eoin snarled. "I am a Prince of Wales. I am prepared to lead the men."

Edwin rode up to the side of the Prince's horse. "Have you led a charge before, Prince Eoin?" There was a dangerous tone in his voice.

"Of course I have!" the Prince turned pale with anger.

"I've served in all the major battles and raids over the past twenty years, Prince Eoin. You were not involved in any of them."

"Right then," Anarwd intervened. "We'll send out more scouts to check the area, and hopefully they'll locate our second squadron. Our mission was to encourage the Norman cavalry to react, to ambush and destroy them, and to provoke a major reaction by Earl Fitzosbern. I had not anticipated that they would react by sending foot soldiers, and I suspect that this could be a trick."

Prince Eoin stared ahead, his lips tightly compressed. "So, we wait, and lose the advantage of surprise. We wait, because we are afraid of losing some of our cavalry?" He cast a haughty glance at Anarwd. "If there had been a sighting of any other Norman forces, my scouts would have reported them."

"The scouts are not yours," Edwin corrected him. "I will remind you that you came with a mere handful of cavalry. These scouts are ours. Also, since when have our scouts become saints? They sometimes make mistakes, like they did the first time we tried to tempt the Normans out of Hereford. You have a lot to learn, Prince Eoin."

"How dare you speak to me like that! You are a mere Lord, I am a Prince. You should remember your place!"

Anarwd found himself in a difficult position. As leader of the campaign, he agreed with Lord Edwin, but as a Prince he felt that he should support Prince Eoin. All his life he had believed that the survival of the Welsh culture depended on the leadership of its Princes, and being one, he had never considered that his decisions might be challenged. For this reason he felt that although he disliked this unpleasant, vain man who had no experience of fighting, Anarwd found himself unable to speak against him.

"I think Prince Eoin has a good point," he said, giving his friend a warning frown. "As the scouts have not located any other Norman forces in this area, and as it appears that we can attack these soldiers with the advantage of surprise, I agree that Lord Eoin can lead the charge."

Edwin stared at Anarwd, as though he was looking at a lunatic. He took notice of the Prince's warning frown, and decided this was not a discussion that he could be involved with.

Eoin relaxed and bestowed on both men the benefice of his rare smile.

"Thank you, Prince Anarwd. Now, you are speaking like a true leader." He walked his horse back to the waiting squadron, and gave brief orders to the officers. "We attack immediately in two columns. No trumpets. Make sure the Normans are unable to form a shield wall." He stared proudly down the squadron. "We fight for Wales!" He waved his sword arm in the air in what he assumed was a dramatic manner, and prepared to lead the charge. "I will take command of those on the right. You," he pointed to Edwin, "will lead the left." Without further discussion he trotted into a waiting position, while the horsemen formed up. Then, without checking if the left column was ready, he signalled to the officers and waved his sword. "Charge!"

The wave of Welsh horsemen surged over a rise. Before them was a patchwork of small, partially-cleared fields with dense forests on both sides. The area was suitable for a cavalry charge, although not ideal, with trees and bushes scattered about. A small stream curved its way down the centre, and the terrain on both sides looked boggy. They were within two hundred paces of the soldiers, when the Normans became aware of them, and within moments the rear of the column began frantically forming a solid shield wall, urged on by their officers. This part of the column was able to form two lines, the front crouching down behind their shields, holding their spears ready, the back pointing their swords over the tops and to the sides of their defence. However, the front of the column was the last to realize the danger, and the soldiers were still running back to seek shelter behind the rapidly forming the shield wall when they were overrun by the two lines of cavalry, which ignored the shield wall and sought easier prey among those who were yet to form up. The column's vanguard of Normans and their Saxon mercenaries were decimated, with little loss to the Welsh.

The first charge proved a success only because Eoin's troops copied the example of Lord Edwin and Prince Anarwd, and instead of charging into the front of the enemy's shield wall, as Eoin was directing, formed instead a pincer movement that surged past the Norman wall, and separated at least a fifth of the running soldiers from their column. Prince Eoin had found himself alone as he raced towards the bristling wall of armour, and in spite of his futile screams of "Follow me!" he was forced to swerve to the right at the last moment, thus avoiding certain death.

The next moment, he was among the running enemy soldiers, and succeeded in chopping down the first man he had ever killed. This event was of such importance to him that when the riders reassembled for their next charge he had forgotten that his cavalry had disobeyed him, and by doing so had saved his life.

"We will charge them again!" he bellowed, gasping for breath. He felt the Gods were on his side, and he could achieve anything. He pulled too hard on his horse's bite, and the animal reared up, almost throwing him off his saddle. But, somehow, he remained on his terrified mount and, believing he had cut an image of utmost bravery, led the next assault using all of his cavalry to charge directly at the reforming shield wall.

"Oh God! What's he doing?" Edwin moaned.

"Hold back!" Anarwd said. "Let him have the glory, or achieve his own death. Either way, we can't prevent it now."

"Amen," Edwin said fervently. "But we have to win this. Regardless."

"Of course. But I'm hoping my men will pull away if he tries another sacrificial move."

They both galloped down towards the fight, in time to see Prince Eoin complete his charge. He suddenly realized that the Normans in front of him had not retreated in fear, as he had imagined they would at the sight of the power of the cavalry but, unwilling to lose face, he urged his horse into the solid wall of shields and weapons that had hastily reformed. As his brave animal died under him, its momentum broke the wall, and Eoin had a fleeting moment of satisfaction as he killed the soldier whose spear had ended his horse's life. He crashed to the ground, losing his sword and narrowly avoiding being crushed by his mount. His head was spinning and there was a ringing in his ears. He tried to focus and saw, above him, an enemy soldier about to plunge a sword into his unprotected body. He closed his eyes, momentarily wondering if it would hurt, but nothing happened. He stared up in disbelief as his attacker was decapitated by a flashing sword, and he became drenched in Norman blood. He fought to get to his feet. In the melee he was pushed aside by a passing horse and knocked unconscious as he fell in front of the thundering hooves of yet another cavalry animal.

The ferocious battle was over once the shield wall was destroyed, and the surviving Normans and their Saxon mercenaries ran in disorder towards the forest, hoping to reach the trees before they were cut down. The cavalry regrouped and were on the point of a last charge to mop up their disheartened enemy, when the trumpets of Prince Anarwd called a halt.

"I want some of them to survive, to spread the word that we are a force to be reckoned with," he said to Edwin. "This is what we wanted, a victory against their soldiers. Now, their Earl Fitzosbern will be compelled to retaliate, especially as he is supposed to be in charge of England." He stared at Edwin. "Was the flag they were carrying that of Earl Reginal de Braose?"

"Yes," Edwin's lined face formed a smile. "It was a double victory, my friend, in that it was almost certainly his men who attacked the village of Cwm. That will teach him a lesson."

Edwin quickly arranged for the junior officers to organize a make-shift medical area, where wounds were bandaged and where the corpses were laid in preparation for their return to camp for a formal burial. He returned to Anarwd, to find him looking grim.

"And so, Prince Eoin is dead?" Anarwd sniffed. He had not liked the man, but he was a Prince of Wales, and that mattered. "I suppose it was inevitable?"

"Oh, Hell, no. You can't kill a stupid fart like that. He was found unconscious, and covered in someone else's blood. He didn't even have a scratch, just a big lump on his stupid head!" Edwin bellowed with mirth. "And yet he broke their shield wall, and won us the victory!"

Anarwd stared, his mouth gaping. "He's alive?"

"Oh, yes!" Edwin composed himself. "That type have the luck of the devil." He blew out his cheeks. "He's going to be bloody insufferable from now on. He's even complaining about a strained sword arm, so he can tell you how he cut down the soldier who killed his horse. A real hero after all!"

CHAPTER NINETEEN

D afydd and Jon had led their squadron on a fast and effective raid to the west of where Prince Anarwd was leading his forces. During four hours of almost continuous engagements, their men had wreaked havoc on the small communities in the area. Only once had they been engaged by a small army of local men who had decided to fight, but the result, from the start, had been clear to both sides.

"We have shown them!" Jon yelled, as they began their return to the border. It was his first experience of warfare, and the ease with which they had defeated any opposition had given him an idealistic view of war. "Let's hope we get the chance to defeat their real soldiers."

"'We have done nothing but terrorize a few untrained, poorly armed people," Dafydd cautioned. He had begun to be irritated by Jon's youthful enthusiasm. "If we meet the professional Norman soldiers, it will be a different matter. As you have no previous experience, Jon, you will follow my orders without question. Is that understood?"

"Well, yes, of course, Uncle," Jon felt his cheeks burning. He hoped that the officers who were close by had not heard Lord Dafydd's outburst, and decided not to comment any further on their military success. It was at this point that he noticed one of their scouts returning quickly towards them. Four scouts in total had been sent out ahead of the squadron at regular intervals, and each wore a coloured scarf around his neck to provide instant identification of how far they had travelled: red, blue, yellow and green in that order. This man was wearing red, indicating he had been out the longest. Jon, hesitantly, pointed this out to Dafydd, as they watched the scout approach.

"Good," his uncle murmured, and brought the squadron to a halt.

"My Lord," the man gasped as he reined in his frothing horse, "our other squadron has attacked a large and heavily armed force of foot soldiers. No sign of any enemy cavalry."

"How far away?"

"South-west of Hereford, my Lord, near where we crossed the border."

"How soon could we reach Prince Anarwd?"

The man looked confused. "It's hard to say, my Lord. It depends on how much energy your horses have left. My horse is nearly done. It's a hard ride."

"Yes, indeed." Dafydd extended his hand and patted the man on the arm. "You've done well." The man nodded his head, delighted with the recognition. "One more question. What was the state of the battle when you left it?"

"I first heard our trumpets sounding the charge. I rushed towards the sound, and saw the Normans still forming a shield wall. Our men had bypassed the wall and were attacking the enemy vanguard as it was running back to join the main force." His face lost its animation. "I thought it best to report back immediately?"

"Yes. Good work." Dafydd dismissed the man and turned to Jon. "He makes a good point, if we travel at the speed he did, our horses will not be fit for battle." He addressed the junior officers. "The other squadron has engaged a heavy force of enemy foot soldiers. It's a difficult ride, but we will travel as fast as the terrain will safely allow. Remind the men: the horses must be ready for battle at any time. Keep a tight formation."

They reached the scene of the battle as the heat of the sun began to lessen. A large murder of crows took off at their approach, their raucous cries adding to the gloom of the scene. Dozens of Norman and Saxon corpses were scattered around the ground and concentrated in what must have been the area of their shield wall. There were no Welsh bodies, but a number of dead horses gave silent testament to the ferocity of the battle.

"This is clear evidence that our cavalry won the battle, although I'm surprised there are so few enemy corpses between here and the forest," Dafydd said.

"Can we assume they've taken prisoners?" Jon said as he looked around.

"No. Prisoners would slow down their retreat. Almost certainly our men are rushing back to Paradwys, probably expecting us to be there already." He turned to the junior officers, "Give the men permission to collect any weapons they wish, while we rest the horses."

A short while later, as they approached the border, a scout returned to confirm that the other squadron had reached Paradwys, and a general feeling of contentment settled over the riders. It had been a long day, and they had achieved their aim to get revenge on the Normans. They all looked forward to a warm meal, a flagon or two of ale and a well-earned rest. The orange sun was beginning to set in a sky of blues and greens when a scout brought a warning of a strong force of Norman cavalry that was approaching from the east.

Dafydd frowned and drank quickly from his water flask. He had to decide whether to race for the border and the chance of support, or to use this opportunity to prepare for the oncoming enemy. "Jon!" he yelled, "take half of the men into that wooded area. I will form up here to face the enemy. When they attack, charge down behind them." He frowned at the keen young man, "Make sure you don't arrive too soon!" His face relaxed, "Or too late! Go! Go!"

Jon quickly led his half of the squadron into the protection of the trees. Long shadows were forming as the hot sun began to sink below the western mountains. "Form up behind the trees!" he yelled. "Keep silent. Wait for my order. Rees, sound the trumpet for charge as soon as I give the order, and keep sounding it." He positioned himself behind a large oak, his junior officers immediately behind him, and tried to calm his pounding heart. He knew that the result of the upcoming battle was in his hands, and he was determined to prove to his uncle that he was capable of leading men into a fight.

Dafydd waited at the front of his riders who were formed up in rows of ten, each line with its own officer. He knew they would be wanting to charge towards their enemy, but he was determined to save the energy of the tired horses and it was his hope that he could turn the direction of the enemy's charge in order to give Jon the advantage of a surprise attack. He stared towards the direction the scout had indicated with the setting sun behind him, and realized the Normans would be charging into the sunset, made more intense in a cloudless sky.

A line of horsemen, bathed in reddish light, appeared over the raised ground in the distance, and immediately halted. An officer rode to the front with two troopers, each carrying a limp flag. There was some distant yelling and trumpets sounded before a host of cavalry, spread out in a disorganized wave, charged towards the silent Welsh lines. The Norman officer in charge had apparently decided that they would easily overwhelm the smaller opposition, who appeared not to understand that it was about to lose any advantage its horses provided.

Dafydd watched carefully as the ragged line of cavalry, with their commander in the centre, approached at breakneck speed, each trooper determined to be among the first to engage the Welsh. The terrain was scattered with small trees and bushes, and already some of the enemy horsemen were riding into each other as they tried to avoid the obstacles.

"Now!" Dafydd yelled, and broke into an immediate gallop, as the trumpets sounded, his men drew their swords and followed in tight formation. Once they were all riding at maximum speed, Dafydd began to peel away to his right, aiming at the left wing of the advancing forces. With the sun in their eyes, the Normans were slow to see what had happened, and their right wing, on the other flank, was suddenly forced to come around in a wide circle, causing a number of collisions and the loss of horses and riders.

Dafydd now straightened up and met the disorganized fringe of the enemy's left wing with his tight formation that cut through them with lethal ferocity. All of his Welsh soldiers were involved as they cut a wedge into the enemy who, in contrast, were only able to bring fewer than half of their troopers into the fray. The Welsh kept going at full gallop, passing through the opposing forces like a sharp knife through butter. They pulled away, turned, and immediately formed up and charged again at what was now their enemy's damaged right wing.

The Norman Lord, having learned his lesson, tried to get some semblance of order into his men. He was the cousin of the Marcher Lord Reginal de Braose, and a victory in this battle would secure his future with his dominant older cousin. A triumphant smile crossed his plump face as he realized the Welsh were going to be boxed in this time, and their small triumph was at an end. As he signalled the charge, he heard trumpets from behind him and to his left and, glancing back, and he saw, to his alarm, a powerful squadron of fresh Welsh cavalry approaching his wing at speed. He turned back to see the original enemy formation forcing another wedge through his troops, but was now unable to bring his unused cavalry from his left into what should have been his winning move. The leader's moment of indecision proved fatal, as he finally decided to order his second-in-command to take on the new threat.

Jon had led his men out of the forest and towards the unsuspecting enemy in a spearhead formation, only sounding his trumpets when it was clear that some of the enemy had become aware of them. He knew the trumpets would give support to Dafydd and empower his outnumbered men, and he hoped he had not held back for too long.

The unused Norman wing had turned and was gathering speed preparing to box in the outnumbered Welsh forces, when they realized the threat to their rear. They came to a sudden halt, tried to turn in some order, but were barely starting to resemble a cavalry formation when the Welsh surged into their midst. A short, static battle followed with the Normans outnumbered and becoming quickly discouraged when their officer, who was trying to regain control, was killed by a well-aimed spear.

The fighting was intense until Dafydd sounded a recall to allow his tired men to regroup. The Norman Lord took the opportunity to leave the field with as many troopers as were able to ride. His trumpets sounded the retreat. He estimated he had lost more than half of his men and their loose horses, crazed with fear, added to the chaos. He knew if he stayed that his losses would increase, and his cousin would be unforgiving, having trusted him with what the Marcher Lord considered his elite cavalry. As he galloped away, his remaining forces gathered around him, forming a strong retreating body.

In the last moments of the fighting, Jon received a deep wound to his sword arm from a Norman who had attacked from behind. Suddenly the elation of the charge paled and he felt faint and light-headed. It was at that moment that he heard Dafydd's trumpets, followed by the Norman trumpets, and was relieved to see the enemy horsemen quickly disengage. Moments before he would have urged his men to increase the bloodshed of the enemy's retreat, but now he sat very still in his saddle, clutching his damaged arm, and staring with dulled eyes at the blood that seeped through his fingers. An officer noticed his condition and organized his removal from his saddle and the application of a tight temporary bandage. Jon fainted as it was being applied.

Dafydd decided against pursuing the retreating Normans. He had won a decisive victory in spite of having fewer numbers, and his men, and especially their horses, were exhausted. The decision was reinforced as the final line of the sun sank below the distant hills.

A sense of peace descended with the darkness, and gathered over the bloody landscape like a soft blanket, replacing the angry sounds of battle with the muted tones of exhausted voices and the groans of the wounded. He breathed out and dismounted. Coupled with the scout's report of Prince Anarwd's victory they had achieved more than they could have hoped for, and he was suddenly aware that this was the first time he had ever fought without having Gwriad by his side. He smiled: perhaps he had finally reached adulthood. The thought was so profound that he failed to notice an officer appear at his shoulder.

"My Lord, I'm sorry to report that Lord Jon has been badly injured."

His tired mind sparked into life: he ordered torches to be lit, sentries to be posted and, giving the care of his horse to the officer, he ran to where the wounded were being treated. He noted that Jon was unconscious and that everything necessary was being done by his second-in-command.

"Rees, isn't it?" The man stood to attention and saluted. "You've done well, Rees. Stay with Lord Jon on the return journey. Tell me immediately if his condition changes in any way."

"Yes, my Lord," Rees glowed. He had never spoken to Lord Dafydd, yet the commander knew his name, and had praised him. Perhaps he'd get promotion.

Dafydd approached his sergeant. "Make sure all our injured are moved to this area and treated, and have our dead troopers conveyed back to camp on the spare horses."

"Yes, my Lord." He paused, "Should we take care of the enemy injured as well?" He stared straight-faced at a point in the distance.

Dafydd turned away. He would have preferred not to have to answer. He knew he was being asked to give permission for his troops to murder any enemy soldiers who showed signs of life. But the alternative was to leave these wounded men for many hours, most in great suffering, before the wild animals, the crows and the local crones attacked them. He nodded, "Thank you, Sergeant." He walked back to check on the readiness of the injured, and mused that war was a two-edged sword: even the victors suffered.

A cruel smile replaced the sergeant's previously impassive face. He hated the Saxons and the Normans; it would be good to see them suffer. "You boys," he indicated a small group of tired troopers who were sitting in a group, chewing dried meat strips, "I've got you a job that you all deserve." He laughed, "Work in two's, and each pair carry a torch. We're the cleaning-up squad, boys! Take anything you fancy."

It was three hours of careful riding, guided by their diligent scouts, before the squadron reached Paradwys. As they moved through the darkness, slowly traversing the undulating landscape, they were entranced by the star-encrusted sky and each man felt a strong sense of camaraderie, and the bonding of a shared experience. When they approached the flickering lights of campfires dotted along the moon-lit river, trumpets sounded, sentries challenged them and cheers rang out as the tired horsemen returned. The men were quickly dismissed, and as soon as they had cared for their horses, they sank down around the fires, ate, drank and were hailed as heroes.

In the main tent, Anarwd and Edwin and his top officers were enjoying the company of those who had returned later. Dafydd had finally joined them, having checked on the care and wellbeing of Jon, who remained unconscious, and was suffering from a fever. His wound had been carefully cleaned and rebandaged and it was expected that, being a strong, young man, he would recover. However, Dafydd was conscious of an unusually strong emotion regarding the possible mortality of this young man who, other than Gwriad, was his nearest male relative.

"Today, he proved himself," Dafydd said, "but I think he's discovered that war is not a glorious adventure, but is a necessary evil that brings out the worst in people." Dafydd raised his cup to toast Jon's recovery. "To Jon! May he quickly recover." The others raised their cups. At this time of the night after a day of action and danger, most were just grateful to be alive.

In an attempt to lighten the atmosphere, Edwin stood up and said, with an attempt at looking sorrowful: "I'm sorry Prince Eoin is unable to be with us tonight." There were broad grins around the flickering light. "It would appear," he paused, "that his sword arm is unused to killing so many Normans, and he's exhausted." There was some spluttering. He forced a frown. "I think we may have to allow him to make his way back to Deheubarth, especially with that awful bump on his head." He gazed into his cup of wine, "His generous contribution of horsemen might also be missed, although I understand that their lack of experience did prove a slight problem." He sat down amid a ripple of laughter.

"It's been a remarkable day," Anarwd said loudly, changing the subject. He spoke slowly, taking care with each slurred word. He was bone-tired and aware of his age. "Although we have lost some fine soldiers, we have killed many more of the enemy." He took a long drink. "We have taught them to take us more seriously, and when they seek revenge, which I know they will, we will teach them a real lesson, which I hope will give us years of peace!" Everyone cheered, emptied their mugs, and slumped down, happily drunk.

At first light, Dafydd found the situation with Jon was unchanged. In fact, to his inexperienced eye, it seemed that the fever was worse, and blood had seeped through the bandage.

"The wound needs to be stitched, my Lord," Rees said. He had just returned to duty having taken a few hours of sleep. "We have nobody here who is experienced in dealing with wounds this bad," he explained. "Prince Anarwd sent out an urgent call to the main camp for wagons to be sent to get Lord Jon and soldiers back as soon as possible."

"When are they expected to arrive?"

"Any time from now on, my Lord. The Prince ordered them to be sent immediately." Rees stifled a yawn. "I will remain with him."

Dafydd nodded his thanks, and wondered what he could do. What if there was no capable doctor in the camp? Feeling light-headed, and in need of food, he wandered over to the kitchens which were already distributing bread and soup with cuts of cold meat, and weak beer for those who had brought their own cups. He took a hunk of stale bread, dug out the middle with his knife, and had the centre filled with the soup. With the other hand, he used his knife to spear a thick chunk of meat, and wandered off to an open spot near the river, where he sat on a log and concentrated on his meal. He could have ordered an auxiliary to bring his breakfast to his tent, but he needed to think.

He had never given much thought to the medical needs of the soldiers after a battle. Normally the sergeants had taken responsibility, and had used men they knew who had some experience in bandaging wounds. After the slaughter of battle, the army that won had always provided limited care to those who could still walk and piled the seriously injured into the wagons where they had to survive until they reached the nearest camp or fortification. There was never any care given to the wounded enemy, who were most often treated with a single slash of a sword. Sometimes, even those who surrendered faced the same fate. By custom, only captured officers and nobility would be spared – their release could bring a handsome ransom to the victor.

When Gwriad had been seriously injured some years ago in the last phase of their retreat after attacking Earl Harold's palace, there had been little anyone could do for him. He had received a powerful blow to the front of his head and face from a Saxon shield, that would have been less damaging if he had not lost his helmet only moments before. Dafydd remembered stumbling exhausted from his war horse as the Saxons' attack crumbled, and trying to understand what injuries his brother had sustained. He lay unconscious on the rocky ground, his face covered in blood, and Dafydd had just watched, slowly undoing his sweaty armour as junior officers had gently wiped Gwriad's damaged face with rags and water. It was clear that Gwriad's nose was badly broken, and the area around his eyes was a complex pattern of blues, blacks and yellows; he might never look the same again.

He chewed on his cold meat. It had not occurred to him at that time that Gwriad could die. He had survived the battle and there was nothing to be done but to get him back to the security of his home. If he had needed immediate treatment, he would have died, yet Dafydd realized he had blocked this from his mind. Perhaps it was the lack of alternatives that was why soldiers did not dwell on these things. Now Jon was badly injured, and although there was the opportunity to get him back to camp and get his wound dealt with, he needed the type of help none of the soldiers could provide.

Dafydd finished his meal and was pleased when the wagon train arrived almost immediately; he was particularly delighted when he saw Idris's wagon. He walked over to examine it, and Idris glowed as this Lord, whom he had never met, showered him with praise. Iago was sent to get some food for them both, while Idris supervised the loading of Jon's body. After a short break Idris approached Lord Dafydd.

"We're ready to move off, my Lord. Do you want me to take the direct route which is faster, but it's rougher?"

Dafydd looked at the silent body in the wagon. Great care had been taken to pad the wooden interior and keep Jon's blood-stained bandaged arm from further damage. It was a dilemma: Dafydd was anxious to get the wound treated as soon as possible, but it might be safer if he ordered the wagon to take the longer route along the valley floor. He wished that Derryth were with him; she would have known what to do. In fact, she would already have treated the wound. His logical mind fought with his emotional response, it was not something he was used to. "Take the lower road. Get to the camp as fast as you can."

Anarwd decided to leave a small guard of archers at Camp Paradwys under the command of his son, Alun. The idea was for them to withdraw into the forest and launch a series of ambushes when the Normans tried to invade. A small detachment of scouts also remained to maintain a constant flow of information. It was not expected that the Normans would launch an immediate attack after their recent mauling, and Anarwd agreed to allow the main body of the cavalry to return to Brecon and have a well-earned rest before returning to Camp Paradwys. "A number of these boys have small wounds and strained muscles, you know," he explained to the other officers. "You don't fight battles without some form of injury, and we need to look after our cavalry, they're the best soldiers we have."

After what seemed an interminable journey to Brecon, Dafydd directed the wagon to Gwriad's tent, where Jon was carefully unloaded and laid out on a table. Gwriad was out supervising training when they reached the camp, but returned as soon as he received news of their arrival.

After some brief exchanges, the two brothers watched in silence as a team of medics changed the bandages on the unconscious Lord. The area of the wound was washed and quick, but basic, action was taken to staunch the blood loss. A medic applied some rough stitches and carefully rebandaged the wound, washed Jon's face and applied cold pads to his fevered brow. They tried unsuccessfully to get him to drink.

"What next?" Gwriad asked the sergeant in charge.

"There's nothing more we can do, m'Lord," the soldier avoided eye contact. "None of us are surgeons. Lord Jon must be taken somewhere where his arm can be sewn up properly, and where something can be used to lower his fever."

A tense silence descended, like walking into an impenetrable fog. The soldiers bowed out, leaving Gwriad and Dafydd staring fixedly at the unconscious Jon. His pale face was covered in sweat, and already blood was beginning to seep out of the fresh bandaging. Occasionally, a tremor pulsated through him, as though he was sending out a message.

"Now what?" Gwriad said, and cleared his throat. Like Dafydd, he was surprised at how concerned he was. Since the loss of his wife he had slowly shut himself away from feeling emotion. He often showed anger and impatience, on rare occasions kindness, but love and tenderness had been blocked out. Yet, here he was finding himself choking-up as he looked at his adopted son.

"He can't stay here. I had assumed that we had doctors with us, or at least wise women, but we have nobody other than medics who are basically untrained."

"It's always been the same." Gwriad walked slowly round the table, examining his adopted son from different angles. "When you were planning, did you consider how we would get our injured treated? Of course not. We think only in terms of the battle, the number of soldiers we have and how we might retreat if we have to. We let the men sort themselves out, and if they get injured we assume they will recover."

"Anarwd's fortress is the nearest place I can think of, and that might have healers and surgeons. I'll go and find him."

After Dafydd had left, Gwriad sat on a stool and contemplated the situation. If Jon died, he realized that he would be deeply affected. He noticed that Dafydd also had shown a level of concern, quite different to his usual reserved and unemotional behaviour. He smiled grimly to himself, it would seem that their uncle's mistake had been to their benefit.

Hurried arrangements were made, and Anarwd agreed that Jon should be taken to his fortress, where the best local medical help in the area could be found. He suggested that they leave immediately if they were to arrive before Jon's fever became fatal. In order to keep a watch on his beloved wagon, Idris agreed to drive, even though he and Iago had already spent two days driving to Paradwys and back.

"We could be hanging around here for weeks while we wait for the Normans to attack," he said to Iago. "It will give us a chance to stop in at the smithy on the way back."

"Why do I have to come?" Iago moaned. "I'm learning to be a soldier. I want to fight the Normans."

"Of course you do," Idris said consolingly. "There's no doubt you're a brave man. But I need you to drive the wagon while I have a sleep, and I don't trust anyone else with my old horse."

"But we'll have to look after that dying Lord all the time," Iago muttered. He had had enough of death and dying, and it had not occurred to him that there would be a lot of that when they fought the Normans.

"'Course not, boy. Our job is driving the wagon; they'll have medics in the back with Lord Jon."

After further argument, Iago reluctantly agreed to help drive the wagon. Anarwd sent messengers to prepare for the arrival of Jon, ordered two medics to travel in the wagon, and agreed that travelling through Cwm and, by chance, through Idris's hamlet was the most direct and least difficult route.

"You could do it in under a day and a half if you keep up a steady speed," Anarwd said, looking doubtfully at the old horse.

"No bother, m'Lord," Idris patted his beloved animal. "This old girl is made of strong stuff."

In the big tent, Gwriad and Dafydd gazed helplessly at the suffering Jon. Gwriad picked up a damp cloth and carefully wiped his son's face, spending some time patting his hot forehead.

"I'm going to travel with him to Anarwd's house," Dafydd suddenly declared.

"What for? There's nothing you can do that the medics can't do. Also you're needed here, Brother. You can't just go."

"I'm not needed here. You and Maelgwn will control the army and Anarwd and Edwin control the cavalry. I'm not needed. Also, Brother, has it occurred to you that Jon is our nearest relative? Suppose he died on the journey. Do you want him to die alone?"

Gwriad flushed up, and his expression changed from anger to embarrassment. "Alright. You go," he said after a long pause. He paced slowly around. "One of us has to stay, and it had better be me."

Dafydd poured them both a cup of wine. "I doubt if the Normans will attack in the next week, and I'll be back in about three days. I will ride escort, and as soon as Jon is in the care of the healers, I will return with the two medics.

"Alright then." Gwriad sat in silence, slowly sipping his wine. He recognized that things had changed, and he had to change with them. It would never have occurred to him to accompany Jon to Anarwd's fortress, and he was still rethinking his reaction to that fact.

"I am determined not to let anyone down, be it you, Jon or Anarwd," Dafydd said as he bustled about, making his preparations for the journey. "I suppose I could use one of the medics to act as a messenger if Jon had a dramatic recovery?"

Gwriad said nothing. He hoped it would not be to give news of Jon's death.

CHAPTER TWENTY

Following the victory at Newcastle, Fitzosbern began to reinforce the defences of the town and make necessary changes to the harbour. He gave directions to establish permanent forts along both sides of the river, with a strong gate across the bridge, and a central barracks within the town.

"I will do what the Romans did," he explained to his officers. "I will establish strong fortified centres around England, especially here in the North, from which we will control these areas. I do not intend to spend my time constantly putting down small uprisings that are almost certain to happen if the local tribes feel our forces are elsewhere."

His next military excursion, he determined, was to take the main body of his forces across the northern end of England to the important town of Carlisle. Although, as yet, there had been no uprising in this important centre, he was determined to settle the whole area before he left to deal with the Welsh problem. He had worked out, in his usual methodical manner, how many men he needed to leave to guard Newcastle, and was already planning the movement of hundreds of men, when bad news came from the South.

"My Lord, your wife is dying." The messenger did not know how else to deliver the awful news, and stood shaking with fear as he watched the effect of his words on England's most powerful man.

Fitzosbern's face went pale and without speaking he turned away, waved his hand for the terrified messenger to go and walked down to the river to sit and think. After a while, when he had composed himself, he summoned his officers and, in a series of precise orders, he arranged for an experienced friend, with whom he had campaigned since being in England, to lead the expedition to Carlisle. Another friend, a Norman

Lord, was chosen to govern Newcastle and to be responsible for the North-East, up to Hadrian's wall, the Roman edifice that separated Scotland from Northumberland.

On the same day, he left with a small contingent of cavalry. After frequent brief stops to change his tired horses, he arrived in Norwich three days later and found, to his intense relief, that Adeliza had rallied slightly, and was still able to recognize him when he staggered into her darkened room.

He sat with her for a long time, holding her hand and exchanging short conversations when she was awake. She had been drugged to help with the pain, and slept a lot with only brief moments of clarity. He sent for the doctor, and discovered that she had collapsed on the day he had left for Newcastle. The doctor revealed that she had never fully recovered from the birth of the last child, and in recent days had lost a lot of blood and had been in great pain.

Fitzosbern returned to sit by her side, and stared at her once beautiful face now ravaged by illness. She had been his greatest friend and a constant support, and he blamed himself for having been so unaware of her changing health. He realized that she must have been suffering on the day he had left for Newcastle, but had refused to allow him to know. She had always put his career ahead of her own needs, and had shared his triumphs and his rise to power with an enthusiasm that had made it all so much more exciting and worthwhile.

The doctor had been unable to say how long she might live, but had ruled out any real hope for her recovery. Fitzosbern sat gazing at her as she slept peacefully, and decided that he would stay with her to the end, regardless of any bad news from around the country.

As if fate was testing him, a small detachment of Norman cavalry arrived the next day, bringing news of the Welsh incursions and the failure of the local Norman defence.

"Tell me what happened," Fitzosbern said quietly. He was cold, direct and resented having to leave his wife's bedroom.

The messenger was an officer who had fought alongside the cousin of the Marcher Lord Earl Reginal de Braose, and had been sent by the Marcher Lord to explain the situation.

"So, the Welsh defeated a strong marching column and then defeated a well-armed cavalry squadron?"

"Yes, my Lord. I was part of the squadron under the command of the cousin of Earl Reginal de Braose."

"Why did Earl Reginal not command this himself?"

The officer paused for a moment, but realizing this was no time for half-truths, stared fixedly over Fitosbern's shoulder, and spoke without further hesitation. "My Lord Reginal de Braose received reports that this was a small marauding group, and decided to send his cousin."

"Did you have enough men?"

"Yes, my Lord. The idea was that we would engage the Welsh with our soldiers and that the cavalry would outflank them. What happened was that the Welsh had divided into two squadrons. The first broke the shield wall of our soldiers, and having defeated them, the Welsh retreated. Then, when our cavalry attacked, we were facing a fresh squadron."

"Give me your opinion as to why our forces were defeated. I want your honest appraisal. Remember your first duty is to me."

"Yes, my Lord." The officer swallowed and tried to keep the fear out of his voice. "The Welsh were well armed and well led. We outnumbered them, but they were able to take advantage of the landscape, the time of day and they dominated the field."

"Were you well led?"

The officer shuffled. "No, my Lord."

"Return to Hereford. Tell Earl Reginal that I am ordering him to lead an army into Wales and to devastate the area from which the enemy may have originated. He is to raise his army quickly, and I want to hear that this situation is under control by the end of this month. Is that clear?

"Yes, my Lord. I will leave immediately."

England's most powerful man nodded curtly and returned to his wife's bedroom. The officer breathed out. He did not look forward to delivering the blunt message, and suspected there were difficult times ahead. He knew that Earl Reginal had expected Earl Fitzosbern to bring his army over to assist in the defeat of the Welsh, and would be unhappy to be ordered to take on this task unassisted and to complete it immediately. As he left the building he was told of the reason for the Earl's decision, and decided to keep that piece of information to himself.

CHAPTER TWENTY-ONE

A wagon pulled by an old horse will not make fast progress on a journey, no matter how urgent it is to get a wounded man to a recovery centre. But when the only alternative is to strap the unconscious patient to a horse for untold hours, there is no debate.

Although they travelled at walking pace, Idris kept going, only stopping for short breaks for the men to stretch and for the animals to rest. They continued throughout the night with Idris and Iago sharing the driving and the medics taking it in turns to sleep. Throughout the travelling, Jon remained mostly unconscious, sometimes going through short bouts of thrashing about, when the medics had to restrain him, and when he would cry out and yell gibberish. His fever remained unbroken, and Dafydd worried that his kinsman was weakening.

At first light, Idris declared a halt, and while he and the drowsy Iago cooked breakfast, Dafydd gave the two medics, Morgan and Brin, a chance to take some time off and suggested they freshen up in a nearby stream. He climbed up into the wagon and carefully changed Jon's blood-soaked bandages, trying to limit the bleeding in any way he could. Finally, he replaced the urine-soaked hay on which Jon lay, and realized the unpleasant conditions that the two medics were confined to. He began to wash Jon's face, and decided he needed to collect more water. He climbed down with a jug in his hand, waved it at Idris and turned towards the sound of the running water.

He reached the stream, but found no sign of the two medics, and knew immediately what had happened: they had deserted. Dafydd paused in thought, then whistled for his horse which was cropping the grass near the wagon. It came immediately and, as he had taken the saddle off the animal, he was forced to vault onto its bare back. It was not something he had done in recent years, and he let out a gasp of satisfaction that he was still able to mount that way.

"Which way would they go?" he said to the horse. "They would most likely retrace their journey and go north, knowing that I am desperate to go south." Without another thought he crossed the stream and noticed where they had left wet footprints on the other side. The prints soon faded but his sharp eyes noticed the occasional broken twigs and bent bushes. It was an old forest with no indication that woodchoppers had ever worked there, and there was a multitude of tall trees and fallen branches. Some large trees had collapsed or become uprooted in a storm, leaving wide open areas in the canopy and allowing segments of the forest floor to be bathed in light.

He was beginning to think he had lost their trail, and that he would have a problem finding his way back when he came on a deer trail, and looking ahead he glimpsed the medics in the distance. They had slowed down, perhaps confident that they had escaped.

Dafydd drew his sword, and quietly urged his horse into a fast trot down the trail. In moments, he was upon them, and with cries of alarm they threw themselves off the path and tried to scrabble through the bushes, each choosing a different side. John ran down the man on his left, named Morgan, and with the blade of his sword forced him back onto the path, where he ordered him to call back Brin. Dafydd yelled that if he had to chase him he would kill him, but his life would be spared if he returned. In moments the miserable man reappeared.

Both men stood with heads bowed, knowing that Dafydd had the right to kill them for desertion, and uncertain what he would do. His promise of sparing them was their only hope. They did not know this Lord, apart from the past day's travelling, when he had seemed distant, and concerned only for the young wounded Lord they were trying to keep alive. Both had wondered what would happen to them if their patient died under their care, and they waited, their chests heaving, for his decision.

"I want you boys to finish the job you agreed to do." They looked up hopefully. "I now realize you have had a difficult job, and it's not going to get easier." He reached into a pocket and tossed two small silver pieces at their feet. "This is to seal a bond. You pick up the coins and you are sworn to stay with me until we get Lord Jon to the healers." The two medics were amazed, this was not the way their local Lords behaved. "Pick up the coins."

They quickly retrieved the silver, nodding their thanks and unable to believe that this was happening, when they had expected dire punishment.

Dafydd turned his horse, replaced his sword in its scabbard. "Lead the way, and hurry or you'll miss Idris's breakfast."

The men smiled weakly and took off on a loping trot with Dafydd following behind. He mused as he followed: if they had fought back he would have to have killed them, but by saving their lives, it might mean saving Jon's.

.   .   .

BETHAN WAS SITTING ALONE IN her house spinning. Her face was grim, unlike the usual relaxed expression that suffused her face when she was sitting and letting her nimble fingers carry on automatically. She was thinking of her friend, and how the atmosphere in the hamlet had changed since Idris had left.

When Angwen killed the murderous Madog, the hamlet had treated her like a hero, but slowly a whispering campaign had started among the women, many of whom distrusted her, and the word witch had once again been used. Some believed their husbands were attracted to her good looks and her unmarried status; others could not come to terms with the livid gash across her throat, and her refined way of behaving. "It's a devil's mark," one unhappy woman was heard to say.

Bethan believed the woman wanted Angwen to suffer, to compensate for her own brutal marriage. The belief in devils and witches was always just below the surface in small communities, where life was hard, and those who were different were victimized. When animals died, when children perished at birth and when some people seemed to suffer more than their neighbours, it was an outlet for their own frustrations to go on a witch hunt.

Later, when Angwen called to deliver eggs, Bethan offered her a mug of beer and they sat in the doorway together. "I want you to come and sleep here with me, until Idris returns from his stupid adventure."

Angwen mimed the question.

"Because it's not safe. There are a few silly women who are muttering that you're a witch, and you used your satanic powers to kill Madog."

Anwen laughed, making a strange breathy noise in her throat, and made a dismissive gesture with her hands.

"You must take it seriously. If these women really stir up their husbands, you could be in danger."

With a shrug of her shoulders, Angwen embraced her friend and mimed her agreement to stay, but insisted on going back to get some things.

"Alright then," Bethan said, "let's face the dregs of this hamlet."

They made their way down to where Angwen's small hovel was located, and saw a woman sidling out of the door. She looked frightened when Bethan blocked her way. "What were you doing in there, Marged?"

"Nothing." The woman tried to push past, but Bethan gripped her arm like a vice. She was a thin, poorly dressed woman, with long, dirty hair that hung like rats' tails. There was a mean, hungry look about her, and it was easy to see why she envied Angwen.

"You're the one that's been whipping up hatred towards my friend," Bethan spoke with an edge to her voice that hinted at violence. "You're the one that has called her a witch, aren't you?

"She is!" the woman said in a cracked voice. "I know she is."

"So, what were you doing in her house? And if you say nothing, I am going to hurt you," Bethan growled.

"I was looking for witch's signs," the woman gasped. But it was clear she regretted saying it the moment she had spoken.

"And did you find any?" Bethan said, looking at the women's empty hands. "Or did you really go in there to plant something that you hoped others would find?" She shook the woman with her powerful hands.

"You're hurting me," she whined.

"Now, we're going back into the house, and you're going to show us what you have planted, and if you miss anything I might kill you."

The woman looked terrified, and Angwen had to control herself from laughing. She could never imagine her friend killing anyone, especially this pathetic woman who whimpered before her.

They went into the house, and reluctantly Marged showed them a cross hanging upside down in one corner of the small room, and some chicken heads that she had hidden under Angwen's straw paillasse.

"Is this all?" Bethan yelled, her face up close to the frightened woman. "No black cats? No murdered children? You stupid woman! Do you realize that I could accuse you of being a witch? I could tell the others what I found you doing, and they might burn you at the stake!"

"Oh no! Please. I didn't mean any real harm." She turned to Angwen. "I'm sorry. I won't do it again. I'm sorry." She was shaking with fear, and her eyes were spurting tears. It was like catching a hungry child stealing food.

"Now, Marged, you listen to me very carefully." The woman rubbed her eyes and nodded furiously. "You're going to tell your friends that Angwen is not a witch, but a good woman who has had a hard life. You will make sure I never hear anyone call her a witch ever again, because if I do, I will get you burnt alive." She spoke slowly and with great emphasis.

Marged stared at her like a rabbit at a stoat, and continued to whimper and nod her head.

"I will keep these just in case you should ever break your word. Now go and tell everyone you made a big mistake."

The woman rushed out of the open door and fled to her house on the other side of the path.

Bethan closed the door and blew out her cheeks. Angwen clapped her hands, and bowed to Bethan, who stretched to get the tension out of her body. "Most of the women in this place are totally uneducated. They're beaten and abused by their fathers and sometimes their brothers, they marry unsuitable men, raise unhappy children. For Marged to call you a witch was perhaps the only bit of excitement she has had in her whole boring, violent life."

Angwen nodded and pointed to her bed with a questioning rise of her eyebrows.

"Why not? We enjoy each other's company. Why should the men have all the fun?" She looked out of the door. "Don't worry about her. She really believes I could get her burnt alive, silly cow." She laughed, "You should be safe now."

While Angwen collected her few things, Bethan removed the cross, roughly made of plaited straw, and the chicken heads. "Silly cow," she said as they went out of the door. When they reached her house Betha gave the chicken heads to a marauding dog and put the cross on the fire.

That evening, as the light was beginning to fade, Idris and the small company reached the hamlet. He stopped the wagon outside his smithy, and with a sigh of contentment stood up and stretched. "This is where I live, m'Lord. I'll get us something to drink." Iago woke up with a start, and the two medics climbed slowly out of the wagon, glad to be able to stretch their legs and get away from the sickly smell of urine. Jon lay still, as though dead.

"How is he?" Dafydd demanded.

"He's quiet for a moment, m'Lord," Brin answered. Morgan nodded encouragingly. There was a noticeable increase in their enthusiasm.

Dafydd would like to have pushed on, but recognized it was time for a short break, and this seemed an ideal place. As he dismounted, a woman appeared, yelling Idris's name and flinging herself into his arms, weeping with joy.

Idris nodded at Dafydd, "I'll just get us some refreshment, m'Lord," and amid mixed sounds of merriment and sobbing, he disappeared into his smithy with Iago trailing behind.

At this moment, Jon began to flay around in the wagon, and Dafydd climbed up and gently restrained him, instantly aware of the overwhelming odor, and the dampness of the straw. The two medics stood a short distance behind the wagon, grateful for the chance to breath fresh air, and Dafydd noticed a small group of peasants had appeared, curious to know what was happening. One was feeding the old horse some hay, but most were just watching like an audience around a market performer.

Idris appeared with cups of ale and, while they drank, the dominant woman began to argue with Idris, and point furiously at the wagon.

"M'Lord, this is Bethan, my future wife," he paused as though unwilling to go on. "She insists that we should allow her and her friend to wash Lord Jon, and leave us to clean up the wagon. She says he will die of disease if we don't clean him up."

Dafydd was surprised and suddenly guilty. It had not occurred to him that they could do anything other than get his nephew to the healers as quickly as possible. In his mind that would be where they would clean him up. It was a woman's job. Unwillingly, he agreed, and watched anxiously as the two medics and Iago carefully removed Jon from the wagon and with Idris's help carried him inside, where they laid him on a table. Bethan ordered the men outside to clean and wash the inside of Idris's fine wagon, and to replace the straw with clean hay, while she and her friend began to slowly undress the battered body, recruiting Iago to fetch water, and find clean rags and soap.

When Iago finally returned outside, the wagon had been washed and dried and the sweet smell of hay had replaced the smell of a castle jakes. The men were relaxing, drinking more ale and chewing on dried meat. When asked by Lord Dafydd how the clean-up had gone, Iago seemed embarrassed when he answered, as the sight of a naked male body being washed carefully by two women had reminded him that both these women had done the same to him.

Dafydd was anxious to reach Prince Anarwd's fortress, and told Idris that they should be moving. By the light of torches, Jon was carefully lifted back into the wagon, and the two medics beamed when they climbed in beside him. As he waited for the passionate farewells to be concluded, he noticed Bethan's friend embracing the old horse, and for a brief moment he wondered about her. She was tall, with long black hair that hung on either side of her face, and by the flickering light he noticed she had a vivid scar across her throat. She never spoke or looked up at him, and his eyes moved on to the collection of old and young peasants who had gathered at a respectful distance. Some seemed as much interested in the woman and the horse as they were with looking at the activities around the rest of the wagon.

At last, Idris and Iago climbed into the front, and the wagon moved off. Bethan was calling out advice, and her friend was standing by her side watching but saying nothing. There was something about her that seemed unlike the rest of the peasants.

The next day the tired group arrived at the fortress. The garrison had been warned of their coming, and a party of women healers had been recruited. In a remarkably short time it seemed to Dafydd, Lord Jon was rushed into the main building, the old horse was led to a stables, food and drink were provided and beds had been set up in the barracks for the four men. Dafydd was taken straight to a sparse, but spacious room where a hot bath awaited him, and where his meal and wine were served. Nobody awoke until the following morn.

Dafydd instructed Idris to take his time, and to return to the Brecon camp when he and Iago were able. He gave orders to the two medics to remain with Jon until he was able to travel, when they were to escort him back to Aberteifi. He gave each man some money and said there would be more when they reached his castle. He checked on Jon and found him changed. His fever had broken, and a natural colour had returned to his hollow face. The chief healer explained he had been drugged, and his arm had been repaired. "We are looking at a long recovery, m'Lord," she said.

So, it was with a sense of accomplishment and relief that Dafydd prepared for his return journey. "Your wife-to-be is a very determined woman," he joked with Idris. "But she knew what was needed."

Oh, yes, m'Lord, she's a real catch," Idris smiled broadly. "That's why I want to marry her."

"Who was the unusual woman with her?"

"Ah, you mean Angwen, m'Lord? Yes, that's not her real name, that's what we named her." He explained how she had come into their lives, and how she couldn't speak or remember anything of her early life. He mentioned some of her earliest memories.

"She attacked a Bishop?" Dafydd queried. It was unheard of for a peasant to lay a finger on a senior member of the Church.

"Oh, yes, m'Lord, she's a very unusual woman." He went on to recount how Angwen killed Madog, "and he was a nasty piece of work, m'Lord, and attacked women."

"She's quite an enigma," Dafydd said.

Idris nodded solemnly, unsure what the Lord meant.

Dafydd was prepared to start the long journey, when he noticed the two medics dozing in the sun, and realized that he also needed more rest.

"Morgan! Brin!" They awoke with a start. "I'll leave tomorrow at first light. Work with the healers when needed. You might learn something."

They stood to attention as he walked back into the house. He arranged for another hot bath to be set up in his room, and for food and wine, checked on his horse, and set off for a short walk to the river, feeling his muscles relax and the tension fade.

The next day, he passed through Idris's hamlet without stopping and as he moved past the smithy, Dafydd caught a glimpse of Bevan and the woman called Angwen waving from a doorway. It was not until he had left the hamlet behind that he recalled seeing her before, hiding behind a tree, when he and Gwriad had passed nearby travelling up from Caerdydd, almost two years ago.

CHAPTER TWENTY-TWO

When the Marcher Lord Earl Reginal de Braose received the abrupt message from Earl Fitzosbern, he knew he had no alternative but to achieve a quick and successful campaign against the Welsh. Fitzosbern had a reputation for generously rewarding success, but for being ruthless in his demotion of anyone who failed him.

Reginal was a large, unassuming man, who liked to live well and was both ambitious and proud of his modest achievements. He often misunderstood other people's jokes and was unsure of his authority, and this manifested itself in the way he would shout at junior officers, especially those he suspected of mocking him. After performing well against the Saxons at the crucial battle near Hastings, he had been rapidly advanced by King William and Earl Fitzosbern. Becoming a Marcher Lord had been the pinnacle of his career.

When the Welsh raided around Hereford, he assumed it was a small and insignificant incident and, unwilling to leave his newly-acquired courtly life, he had sent his cousin, recently arrived from Nantes, to deal with this minor problem. The defeat of the sizeable army that Reginal had entrusted to his cousin, compounded by the more serious vanquishing of his cavalry, had shocked him and, coupled with the order from Earl Fitzosbern, had convinced him that he had no option but to lead a major attack on Wales. His cousin had been demoted to being an officer with the army.

Reginal quickly recruited an army drawn from all the local regions. It was an army of men who had never fought together, had been trained under different leaders and, in some cases, were mainly Saxon mercenaries. He did not care. Numbers were what counted, and he was convinced that the Welsh would have gone back to their farms, gloating over their victories, and that he would be able to sweep into the border areas and ravage the country with minimal opposition.

He had received numerous reassuring reports from people who had studied the Welsh, and he had learned that they had very few centres of population. They were predominantly farmers, fishermen and miners, but were also a warlike people who were proud of their country and would fight to the death when provoked. He had been assured that the attacks near Hereford were in revenge for his men attacking the border areas in the first place, and that by now, they would have returned to their small villages to attend to the harvest of their crops. It was a satisfying thought that he would be able to teach them that Norman authority was not to be challenged.

The weather was slowly changing and the long weeks of seemingly unending clear skies and heat were at an end. From the south-west, a line of dark clouds began to accumulate, like visual prophesies of doom. These were noted by those soldiers who had fought in all conditions, and knew how to read the signs. "It's going to be a big storm when the weather breaks," one declared.

"But this will be a short campaign," another added, "and with luck we'll be back over the border before it hits."

On the first day of the invasion, the one person who did not take any notice of the impending weather was Earl Reginal, for whom the campaign was not turning out as he had planned, especially after what had promised to be a good start. To begin with, his scouts had identified a base camp that was occupied by only a small company of Welsh soldiers, who did not appear to have any guards posted, and who were spending their time drinking singing and sleeping.

"I'll teach them a new song," Reginal joked with his officers. "Send in our cavalry, wipe them out and destroy the camp."

But, as he led the main body of his marching soldiers into Welsh territory, he received the unpleasant news that the Welsh had set a trap, and that far from being unprepared, the Norman horsemen had met a barrage of arrows that had devastated the front line of the attack. The sleeping soldiers were found to be stuffed sacks, and when the cavalry had stormed their positions, the archers had just melted away.

"What were the losses?" Reginal roared.

"Four officers and at least twenty men, m'Lord."

"And their losses?"

"Unknown, m'Lord. But we did not find any bodies."

Reginal called a halt, and had an emergency meeting with his top officers. "How was it that the scouts were so wrong?" he bellowed, deeply aware that his leadership was under scrutiny. Before anyone came up with an answer, he had moved on. "Now listen, as the scouts come in, I want them carefully questioned. Do not let them report half-truths. We rely on them, and we must have accurate information!" He continued to lecture the silent officers, until the meeting was interrupted.

"My Lord, I have important news," a junior officer bowed, and gritted his teeth. He knew he was in a dangerous position with the recent bad news having preceded what he had to report. He took a breath, "My Lord, none of our scouts have returned."

"Which scouts?" he yelled. "Which scouts?"

"All of the scouts, my Lord. Those that were sent ahead to discover if the Welsh were able to produce any opposition to our advance."

Reginal stood like a statue, his mouth open, unable to process the information. Finally, taking a firm grip of the panic that had seized him, he turned away and stared grimly at the officer who was in overall charge of the intelligence section, and who had sent out the scouts. "Explain what this means," he growled, waving away the relieved messenger.

The officer, known as Clovis, was an experienced and trusted friend who was used to Reginal's inability to quickly grasp situations. "It would appear that the Welsh have been spying on us, and have been ambushing our scouts when they leave camp." He glanced around the table and noted the silent nodding of heads. "I suggest we change our plans and send out riders in small groups, starting tonight." Reginal grunted his approval. "This is a good place to camp. We're well inside the Welsh border, and if we rise at first light, we will be ready for the scouts' reports, and can move quickly when we know where they are massed."

"Of course, Clovis. My thoughts entirely." He poured himself some wine, and was suddenly aware that everyone was waiting for him. "Oh, dismiss. Get it all arranged." He hated this part of being in charge.

As the officers stood up, the expectation of joining battle with the Welsh gave him fresh energy. "Tomorrow, we'll destroy their petty army.

They've been attacking us like the bugs of summer, and we will slap them down like the annoying insects they are!" It was an unusual image and the officers stayed silent. "Tomorrow, we'll show them that Normans are to be feared! We will cut through their forces like avenging angels. We will destroy them!" It was not a good speech but, led by Clovis, the men cheered and clapped as they left.

At dawn, the Norman soldiers broke camp and were ready for the order to march. After a short wait a small squadron of scouts returned, and the commanding officer reported immediately to Lord Reginal and his intelligence officer, Clovis.

"We have come across the enemy forces about two hours away, m'Lord. They are prepared for battle and have established a strong shield wall set up in a broad valley. They are blocking a road with some flat land on either side, giving way to dense trees. It would be difficult to out-flank them."

Reginal flared his nostrils and glared, he did not like to be told what he could and could not do. "How many?"

"About two hundred men, m'Lord. They looked well-armed."

"Keep to the question," he said impatiently. "How many cavalry?"

"We saw none, m'Lord." The junior officer did not add that the soft ground showed evidence of many cavalry. He was learning not to say more than he was asked.

"Any comment?" he turned to Clovis.

"We know they have a small, but efficient cavalry, and I can't believe they have left the area." Clovis turned to the reporting officer and smiled, "For how long did you observe them?"

"That was the strange thing, m'Lord. They seemed to notice us, and nothing happened at first, and then they began blowing trumpets. We knew no other scouts had got through, so we withdrew immediately, rather than risk engaging their scouts."

"You did well," Clovis said. "Did you see where their camp was situated?"

"No, m'Lord. There was no sign of it."

"That might indicate that they are some distance from their supplies. Maybe we should call their bluff, and not attack? They won't stay there for long."

Once again Reginal was feeling undermined. This was his army and he would decide when they would attack. What was the matter with Clovis? "The Welsh only have a few fighters, most will have gone back to their farms. If we attack this remnant of their army, we will easily defeat them. We outnumber their soldiers at least three to one, and their cavalry, if they have any, at least two to one, maybe more. We will attack immediately." He felt quite overcome with importance. This would be his victory. He would become the most famous of the Marcher Lords. "Give the order to march!"

.   .   .

"WE THINK THEY HAVE FALLEN for the trap!" Prince Anarwd announced to his senior officers. "Thanks to Alun and his archers," he paused to compose himself, "we have managed, as far as we know, to kill all their scouts, with the exception of one group we have allowed to return to report our position. I have told the men at our battle line to stand down, and we have a host of scouts reporting back on the enemy's movements, and more stationed to ambush any of their scouts who dare to cross our lines."

"How do you see this unfolding?" Gwriad asked. He did not mind the old Prince being in overall charge, but he was in charge of the soldiers, and intended to have the last say.

"With luck," Anarwd smiled, "they will think we have only been able to muster two hundred men, and our aggressive posture at the front will convince them that we are small in number but prepared to fight to the death. I imagine it will develop like this," he pointed to a rough map. You, Lord Gwriad, as commander of the army, will position the rest of our solders, well hidden, on either side of the path, and about five hundred paces in front of our position. You will not sound the trumpets until they have engaged us, and then you will attack from both sides. I am holding the cavalry in reserve, in case the Normans use theirs to threaten the battle. As soon as we have established ourselves as victors and they are engaged in an organized retreat, I will bring in the cavalry to ensure a complete rout. Any questions?"

It was agreed that Prince Anarwd and Lord Edwin would lead the cavalry, that Gwriad and Dafydd would organize the soldiers who would be hidden deep in the forests on both sides, and General Maelgwn would be in charge of the two hundred soldiers who would pretend to be the only local troops to face the Norman invasion. The absence of Prince Eoin was not mentioned, but among those officers who led the cavalry there was a sense of relief.

"Well then, good luck to you all!" Anarwd shook each man's hand with his usual intensity. "Get our main forces hidden now, Gwriad, and Maelgwn, let those men of yours take a short rest and get something to eat."

He was still giving random orders as the officers went about their duties, but he was known for his passion, and his officers saw him as the embodiment of what a Welsh Prince should be, and loved him for it.

CHAPTER TWENTY-THREE

"So, you're staying?" Bethan screamed with joy, and rushed across the smithy to embrace Idris in a bear hug. "There's a clever man! I knew you'd get some sense before the Normans stuck something in you." She kissed him with unrestrained passion.

"Well, I've delivered my armour," Idris said, fighting for air. "They'll have had their big battle before I get back there, and Iago and I won't be missed." He winked at Iago, who was standing awkwardly, waiting for Bethan to notice him. He felt like a peeping tom.

"Oh, Iago, you lovely boy!" she rushed at him and gave him a big, soft kiss on his lips. It was the first time anyone outside his family had kissed him, and he felt his cheeks burning with embarrassment, although he had to admit he liked it. "Thank you for bringing my silly man back to me in one piece."

Iago nodded, not sure what he should say.

"I know you wanted to fight the enemy, my love, but you don't have to kill people to prove you're a man." She paused, "You saw what had happened to that young Lord. You don't want to end up like that, he might lose his arm. Imagine the rest of your life with only one arm."

At that moment Angwen entered and ran towards Idris and gave him a warm hug, then turned towards Iago and embraced him in her strong arms, resting her cheek against his. She stood back with a broad smile and raised her arms in celebration.

"See, Iago, we women can be much nicer than going to war!"

Idris had been watching the scene with interest and a certain sympathy for Iago. "Well, I'm sorry, ladies, but Iago and I have to unload the wagon and attend to the poor old horse, who's done more work in the last two weeks than she has in her entire lifetime. Also, we have some serious beer drinking to do."

"Not without us you're not!" Bethan said forcefully. "If I have to wait for you to take me to bed, then at least Angwen and I are going to join you two for the beer." She turned to Angwen, "We might even cook you a decent meal."

The next day, when Idris had satisfied Bethan's more basic needs, he suggested to Iago that they clean up the smithy. Once Bethan had gone back to her house, they began the heavy and tedious job of moving the metal bars, and sorting out the stuff that he had saved from the destroyed forge at Cwm.

"Have you met Wynny?" Idris asked innocently.

"Who?" Iago nearly dropped the metal he was carrying. How did Idris know about Wynny?

"She's that girl we noticed when we were on our way to Prince Anarwd's place. You remember, she and a dog were driving some sheep. We passed her on the road. Lovely looking girl, about your age. She's the daughter of Gwynn the shepherd. You'd like her.

"I didn't see her," he pretended to busy himself .

"Really? I suppose the reason you nearly fell off the wagon was your interest in sheep?" Idris placed a fatherly hand on his shoulder. "Now listen, I know Gwynn, he's not a bad fellow. I'd forgotten about his daughter though. The last time I saw her she was a child. She's certainly not a child now!"

Iago shuffled his feet.

"I remember when I was your age, I could never think of a reason to talk to girls, although I thought of nothing else." He chuckled. "Now, I'm going to help you out." Iago groaned. "I promised to make Gwynn a knife, and I did, and then somehow with everything else happening, I forgot. I think he has too. Anyway, I have decided to visit him tomorrow, and you'll come with me."

Iago nodded dumbly. He wanted this more than anything, but he was also terrified by the prospect.

"You might get a chance to speak to Wynny. You never know your luck."

Iago hardly slept that night, and was up at first light pretending to do small jobs about the house while he waited for Idris to appear from Bethan's house. The old horse seemed to have recovered from its long journey, and after he and Idris had restored the wagon to its former glory, they finally prepared to leave. That was when Bethan and Angwen appeared.

"Angwen would like to come with you. Unlike me, she has not had the excitement of some sexy man coming back from the war." She raised her eyebrows meaningfully.

"You're welcome, Angwen, it's good for us mere males to have an attractive woman with us!"

She laughed, and Bethan waved a finger at Idris.

"She wants to buy some more wool for both of us, but I have work I must get done."

Angwen sat on the front bench between the two men, and waved happily at Bethan as they moved slowly out of the village. Marged stood outside her poor hovel and waved cautiously. She still felt the silent woman was unnatural, but she dared not say so. Deep down she was jealous of Angwen's good looks and the way the menfolk seemed to ignore the unsightly scar that she never attempted to cover. Marged envied her independence and the way she had just appeared in the village and had become friends with the most influential people in their community. It was not fair.

The journey to the Gwynn farm was pleasant, but before they arrived, Idris pointed out the gathering clouds beyond the mountains to the west. "I think we could be in for one of those violent storms that often come after a long period of good weather. I hope we can get back before it hits, or you're going to get as wet as a fish and wish you hadn't come."

Angwen signed that he was not to worry, and that the storm would come later. She gave a big smile that lit up her face, and put her strong arms around the men's shoulders, and made her strange happy sound.

They turned off the track, and along a slowly rising path, through a dense forest that gradually thinned until they moved out onto a wide, grass-covered plateau. The view was sudden and spectacular, for laid out before them was the treed valley through which they had passed, and beyond they could see low hills and to the west the bare mountains with the darkening sky beyond.

After a few miles they reached a large wooden house with barns and a well-fenced yard, and it was clear that Gwynn's farm was one of the more prosperous in the area. During the summer his sheep grazed on the rugged high ground, and in winter he brought them back to the safety of his fenced fields and paddocks. He was a short, thick-set man in his middle age, who had a happy marriage and three older sons and a single daughter, who he adored, but also kept a very close eye on. He knew she was attractive, but he had no time for young men who thought the same. His wife, Morgana, worried that Wynny would be an old woman before her husband relaxed his control.

"She's a young woman. It's healthy for her to meet young men. My father was very easy going, and I never suffered from having lots of friends."

"She can have as many girl friends as she likes," Gwynn always replied, "but I'm not having some local ne'er-do-well lifting her dress."

He refused to discuss the matter. He well remembered how he behaved when he was in his late teens.

The wagon stopped, as a powerfully built young man with piercing blue eyes opened the gate into the yard. "Idris!" he bellowed. "Where have you been hiding yourself?" Iago understood that they were visiting long-time friends.

Gwynn appeared from a barn with his other two sons, who all looked remarkably alike, and very warm greetings were exchanged. Iago helped Angwen off the high wagon, and an attractive, motherly woman with long hair joined them. The introductions were soon completed, and Idris was bustled off by Gwynn towards the big barn, followed by his three sons and a pack of sheep dogs. Morgana took Angwen into the house, and the shy Iago was left patting the horse.

"What's your name?" a melodic voice with a hint of amusement caused Iago to turn around quickly. Behind him was a girl of about his age with long glossy black hair, bright blue eyes and the most attractive mouth he had ever seen. Although if he was honest, he had little experience of girls' mouths.

He swallowed, and tried to speak casually. "Iago. What's yours?" he already knew her name, but he wanted her to confirm it.

"Wynny," she said, "like the sound of a horse." She giggled. "I already know your name, and I know you're training to be a blacksmith?"

He stared in disbelief. "How did you know that?"

"Idris and my father are great friends. I've been waiting to meet you."

"You have?" Iago felt his knees go weak.

"Now, I want you to come with me. I know a place where we will not have my irritating brothers interrupting us." She smiled, "It's not far, and when we hear them looking for us we can reappear as though we have been here all the time." She had a roughish smile, and he felt he was unable to reply. He nodded, and took a deep breath when she took his hand.

She led the way behind a small hut which contained sheering scissors, small stools, and an array of pails and nets. "You should be here when we shear the sheep in spring, it's a long job." Past the hut was a dense clump of aspen, its leaves gently shaking in a slight breeze. Wynny led the way through a gap, and on the other side was rough plank of wood on two flat stones forming a useful seat. It was positioned on the edge of a small cliff, and beyond was a breath-taking vista of mountains and tree-clad valleys.

Iago gasped at the unexpected view. "That's something," he murmured.

"It's more than something!" Wynny laughed. "It's magnificent and utterly beautiful. It's why I love living here. I never want to live anywhere else." She sat down, and patted the space next to her. "Do you know, my brothers never come here? I suppose they did when they were boys, but I think they've forgotten. Now it's all mine." She smiled at him, "And yours too, now that you know about it."

Iago was affected by the view, the closeness of her body, and an overwhelming desire to impress her. "Thanks." There was so much he wanted to say, but he knew he could never express himself in the lively, confident way that she did. "I, um," he cleared his throat. "I'm really happy to meet you."

She looked steadily into his eyes. "You're shy, aren't you, Iago?"

"Not really. I just haven't met many girls since my family was killed."

"Oh! How terrible." She grabbed his hand. "You must tell me all about it, and I mean everything."

He had no idea of time as he recounted the murder of his family. He left out the detail about his sisters, but described how his father fought bravely, and how later he found his younger brother, his uncle and aunt and their baby, butchered by the roadside. He spoke with such feeling that she was gripped by his story, and her large eyes filled with tears as he told her how Idris, Bethan and Angwen found him and gave him a new home and a new life.

"Oh, you poor man," Wynny squeezed his hand, and suddenly she had thrown her arms around his neck and was kissing him. It was like Bethan's kiss, but much, much better. He felt his body responding, and was about to shift his position to hide the fact, when they heard a voice calling them.

"Quick! It's Dad." She jumped to her feet and led the way back through the aspen. "He probably thinks you've had my skirt up by now." Iago, who was silently trying to rearrange his lower area, almost lost control at this unbelievable suggestion.

They moved quickly behind the shearing shed, and were standing by the wagon when Gwynn appeared with Idris and her brothers in tow. "Oh, there you are!" he exclaimed. There was an element of relief in his voice. "Come in the house, were going to eat." He looked past Iago and his forced smile vanished. "God almighty! I don't like the look of that sky."

Iago looked behind and was amazed how he had not noticed the black clouds racing towards them or the change in the air.

"We must get the sheep off the mountain!" Gwynn yelled. He gave his sons a stream of orders, and they ran off with the dogs behind them. "What can we do?" Idris said.

"Help me with the big paddock, I was in the process of replacing the fencing, I had no idea we might need to hurry the job. The boys and the dogs will bring in the sheep." He pointed at his disappearing sons and their dogs. "Each dog is worth a handful of men. You wait and see."

He led the way into the enormous paddock, where on one side the fence had been dismantled. Along the empty space was a large pile of fence posts and close by the fence rails that were needed to form the barricade. "I had this all prepared," Gwynn said proudly. He looked at the threatening sky. "This storm will hit soon, and my boys could have problems with the panicking sheep, in spite of the dogs. The tools we need are here," he pointed to a covered pile. "I want you, Iago, to help me dig the fence holes, and we will get the posts in, and I want you, Idris, to fit the rails. It's going to be a hard job, boys. I'm so glad you came."

Iago could not believe how things were working out. He had met the most wonderful girl and now her possessive father was giving him the chance to prove himself.

Time passed in a blur of hard work with occasional breaks as Morgana, Wynny and Angwen came with food and refreshments. The first sheep arrived as the storm hit, and the animals began to panic, surging up against the restraining bars of the fence. The three tired men completed the fence as rain came down like a waterfall. Cold, hard, wind-driven rain that felt like a physical presence, obscured everything around them, and the wind threatened to blow them off their feet. Lighting revealed the immense flock of sheep that had been gathered into the newly completed pen, and the thunder almost deafened the men as they fought to keep together.

"Well done, boys!" Gwynn shouted trying to be heard above the din of the storm. "I think we've saved most of my sheep. I couldn't have done it without you!"

They staggered like a group of drunkards towards the house, where they entered to the gasps and cheers of the women. "You must get out of those clothes. I have arranged dry ones for all of you through there," Morgana ordered, and they walked like obedient servants to a back room where they stripped off, dried themselves on towels and in an exhausted state, climbed awkwardly into the first loose clothes they picked up.

When the three of them returned to the hot, bright main room, they were greeted with cheers and clapping. The three sons had returned earlier and had received the same treatment. They collapsed into chairs and couches and the women plied them with much needed beer and food, while outside the dangerous storm pounded against the house, and deafening thunderclaps and vivid lightning continued to terrify the huddled sheep.

There was a powerful sense of comradery and satisfaction in the room, and after Gwynn had consumed a number of cups of beer, he gave a drunken toast to his friends and particularly to Iago, with whom he had worked ceaselessly for the past hours. "You're lucky to have such an apprentice, Idris," he said, waving his cup of beer. "He's got the strength of an ox, and the sort of quality that you don't find in many young men."

He raised his cup, "To Iago!" He sat down heavily, spilling most of his cup, and was asleep in moments.

Iago was sitting on a couch with Wynny and, once her father closed his eyes, she clutched his hand. He sat there in a glow of happiness, and tried to ignore Idris when he winked at him. The brothers were discussing the merits of certain dogs, and Morgana was agreeing a wool transaction with Angwen, with whom she had adopted a way of communicating similar to that used by Bethan. "I think my father likes you," Wynny whispered. "That's important. Do you like me?"

"Oh, I love you," Iago murmured drunkenly. He could never have dreamed of saying such a thing if he had been sober and not physically exhausted.

"That's good," Wynny grinned and squeeze his hand, "because I want you to keep coming here. I've always wanted a man who's big and strong." She glanced approvingly at Iago's trousers. "Yes, indeed."

CHAPTER TWENTY-FOUR

Regardless of the impending weather, Earl Reginal marched his forces to within sight of the Welsh army. Looking down from a slight rise, he was satisfied that, although they occupied a strategically well-defended position, the Welsh were limited in numbers, and there had been no reports of any cavalry movements. However, although vain, he was not a stupid man, and would, reluctantly, listen to the advice of those he respected. Clovis had repeated the warning that the Welsh had demonstrated that they possessed a small but efficient cavalry, and it was likely they were holding them in reserve. Reginal had to agree that this was possible, but it was equally possible that their limited cavalry, which was almost certainly composed mainly of their nobility and landowners, would have returned to their homes to manage their affairs.

From his vantage point, at least two hundred feet above the valley that stretched away in front of him, he could see the tight formation of the Welsh, and how their shield wall barely reached the sides of the valley, where thick forest would prevent any of their cavalry, if they had any, from being used effectively. But, he mused, it would be possible to breach their defences on both sides with the use of his cavalry.

He decided, therefore, that the cavalry would advance on both wings, when his trumpet sounded, and his large army of soldiers would march up towards the Welsh shield wall and prepare for a running charge. With an army that was three times the size of the Welsh, and with superior armour, he was confident he would push the enemy aside in the first charge. Then, when his cavalry attacked their wings, he would quickly reduce this band of savages to a retreating rabble. The image pleased him, and he took no notice of the wind that was beginning to flap the flags and pennants of his cavalry, as overhead black clouds gathered.

"I will remain here and send orders as the battle develops," he said to his senior officers. "I will have the trumpets sound from here when you are to charge." He sat proudly on his war horse, his armour gleaming, and with a personal bodyguard drawn up behind. He would not have felt so pleased if he had seen the expressions on the faces of his officers as they trotted down to take charge of their squadrons.

"I would prefer my aged grandma to be in charge," one of the officers remarked. It produced a rare laugh from the others.

The army marched forward to within forty paces of the jeering Welsh, who rattled their shields, and beat on them with their swords and spears. Behind them their archers began to fire wave after wave of arrows that dropped out of the sky like a deadly shower, causing multiple deaths and injuries among the waiting Normans, who raised their shields and waited impatiently for the order to come and their stolid suffering to end.

At last, Earl Reginal decided that his forces were in place to his satisfaction and gave the order. The bugles sounded out across the tense valley, releasing the pent-up emotions of his suffering soldiers.

"Charge!" the sergeants yelled. "Charge!" and the long-awaited battle began.

Earl Reginal sat like a statue on his placid horse up on the hill from where he would conduct his battle plans; earlier in the day, Prince Anarwd and Lord Edwin had surveyed the valley from the same hill. They had decided where their forces would form their shield wall, where their reserves would hide on each side of the valley, and how their cavalry could best be placed.

"Once the Norman Earl sees where we have our small shield wall, he will almost certainly plan his attack from here. It's the most obvious place."

"Indeed," Edwin nodded, "which means we can almost predict his battle plan. He knows we don't have a standing army, and when he sees the small number of our men, he will almost certainly throw all his soldiers into a mass charge. If I was him I would place my cavalry on both wings, and expect them to roll back our men while their soldiers achieve a breakthrough in the centre." He gave a grim laugh. "If all goes well this could be the victory we need."

Anarwd nodded thoughtfully, "Warn all the officers that when the

Normans sound their trumpets, that will be the signal for a fast attack by our reserves, and will be the sign for our cavalry to sound their trumpets and confuse the enemy." He looked around the small hill. "When our cavalry gets involved, and when the outcome of the battle is beyond doubt, you might want to take a squadron back up here. It could be interesting." He raised his ragged eyebrows in a suggestive way.

Edwin chuckled, "We'll see how things work out." He stared towards the west, "I reckon we're in for a big storm."

"That might be in our favour." Anarwd rubbed his beard. "We're used to these early summer storms raging around our mountains. I doubt if the Normans are."

As the sun reached its highest point, the massed ranks of the Norman and Saxon soldiers marched into the valley, with their cavalry on both flanks, and the Welsh shield wall shuffled into its final position. General Maelgwyn gave his soldiers an uplifting speech in which he warned them that they were the bait, and that they would be taking the brunt of the battle for a short time. "But, when the Normans are suddenly attacked on both sides, that will be the time to get your revenge. So, no individual heroism boys, you have to keep the shield wall intact. Later, you can be brave individuals when you chase them off the field. Archers, when their front rows are in range keep up a constant barrage, but as soon as their attack starts, your role is to reinforce the wall. Remember, boys, this is our big chance to show the Normans what we're made of!"

They had all heard this before, but they cheered anyway, and now they banged their shields with their weapons and ran their tongues over their dry lips as they watched the enemy form up in solid ranks in front of them.

When the trumpets sounded, the Welsh archers released their last feathered shafts, dropped their bows and grabbing their heavy shields, rushed forwards. Over the heads of their friends, each threw a spear that could not fail to find a victim in the massed ranks of the advancing enemy whose shields were in position for their solid shield wall, not guarding against aerial missiles. The Norman unrestrained charge resulted in those at the front being hemmed in from both sides and pushed forwards from behind, and it was difficult for them to find room to use their shields as battering rams and also be able to swing their swords to beat back the jeering Welsh.

The Norman cavalry galloped down on both sides, intending to smash the thinly manned ends of the extended shield wall. The Welsh, who had expected this, quickly drew back, rounding the end of their wall and forming a double rank of shields with their iron-headed spears pointing out like a large hedgehog. As the cavalry charged towards them, the front fighters buried the heels of the wooden shafts into the earth to give maximum resistance and the second row prepared to throw their spears when the charging horses were within range.

The Welsh right wing were preparing for the imminent attack, as the first, heavy raindrops began to fall, and watched with relief as a flurry of arrows was fired from the cover of the trees. The cavalry charge slackened as riders and horses were hit, and in moments the attacking squadron became aware of the ambush on their left, and many ceased their attack on the Welsh wing and turned to fight off what they assumed to be a small group of vulnerable archers. As they rode into the trees they were confounded to see an unexpected wall of rapidly advancing soldiers.

Gwriad led the charge through the trees as soon as he heard the distant trumpets. Behind him were more than two hundred men, many of whom had never fought in a battle, but all of whom had reached the point where they needed to prove themselves. Reaching the edge of the tree line, he saw the Norman cavalry galloping towards the right wing of the Welsh shield wall. He bellowed for the archers to rush forward, and tried to get some order into the excited mob of men. "Archers! Fire once and then retreat!" He watched as the arrows disrupted the continuity of the Norman charge and, as he expected, many of the riders turned to get revenge on what they assumed were vulnerable archers, only to find they had vanished and had been replaced by a mass of sword-waving peasants racing towards them.

A well-armoured cavalryman on a war horse was considered to be the ultimate fighting machine in a battle, especially against foot soldiers. He was vulnerable only if attacked on both sides, and even from behind, at the same time. The weakest areas of an armoured rider were under the arms and, if the rider could be pulled off his horse, then the space between his helmet and his breastplate allowed his adversaries to cut his throat.

The horsemen in the front line attacked the charging foot soldiers, and using their long, deadly swords and wielding their heavy maces, they were almost invincible as long as each rider could keep the foot soldiers in front. But, the sheer numbers of determined Welshman overpowered those cavalrymen who advanced too far into the trees where they found themselves limited in movement and attacked from all sides. The horsemen at the back, seeing the danger, retreated to the field, intending to reform and return to their attack on the right wing of the Welsh shield wall. They were shocked to find that in so short a time the bad weather had intensified, and the density of the rain augmented by the power of the wind made it almost impossible for them to see what was happening.

In the centre of the battle, the sheer weight of hundreds of Normans and Saxon mercenaries threatened to push back the undermanned Welsh lines, and if a momentum was achieved, those soldiers knew they would be forced back, would lose their defensive posture, and slip and fall and be trodden under foot. It was a frantic battle for the quickly tiring Welsh soldiers who knew they had to hold their line just a bit longer, even though their reserves were being rapidly depleted as they replaced injured and dying men in the front line.

From both sides of the valley, lines of screaming Welsh soldiers appeared, as if by magic, and attacked the rear columns of their enemy. They appeared like avenging spirits in the dim light, with the wind and the deluge adding to the confusion. Their sudden appearance and their fresh energy immediately lessened the pressure on the Welsh shield wall as the rear lines of Normans slowly realized they were surrounded. The forward motion of the dominating Norman attack faltered under the bludgeoning from the new Welsh forces that attacked just in time to prevent a general massacre of their outnumbered countrymen. However, at that moment, and under the most intense weight of the attack, the centre of the Welsh defence gave way, and the front lines of their battle-crazed enemy rushed into the gap, convinced that the battle was theirs.

Overhead, the black clouds erupted in spectacular forks of silver lightning. The deafening drumbeats of thunder drowned out the urgent Norman trumpets, and the rain fell like a waterfall: cold, confusing and turning parts of the battlefield into an immediate quagmire. The most affected area was in the middle of the valley, where a natural stream flowed in wet months along the side of the path, but which had dried up in the recent drought. It was here, where both shield walls struggled, that the ground transformed to mud within moments.

General Maelgwn, never a man to hold back, was reinforcing his right wing when he heard the triumphant roar of the enemy to his left. In spite of the unreal light and the difficulty of seeing through the obscuring rain, he was aware of a sudden change of movement by the attacking forces. At the same moment, he heard the comforting calls of the Welsh trumpets: the reserves had arrived. He raced down behind his faltering troops, yelling encouragement and looking for a place where the retreating shield wall had been breached. He was knocked sideways by a line of Welsh soldiers as they retreated, still fighting bravely against a mud-clad surge of Normans who were remorselessly beating the Welsh back on themselves.

"Form shields!" he bellowed, struggling to regain his balance. It was like no battle he had ever fought in. The unnatural sky was like an omen from Hell, and the blinding flashes gave momentary bright glimpses of the chaos all around him. Both sides were struggling in the deepening mud, and it was difficult to differentiate his soldiers from the enemy.

"Hold together! Our cavalry is coming!" As he was yelling in Welsh, the Normans and Saxons had no idea why the soldiers they were fighting suddenly began to yell and cheer, and why they seemed to revive themselves.

Maelgwn heard Prince Anarwd's trumpets getting closer, and feeling a fresh burst of energy, he charged into a knot of suddenly retreating enemy soldiers. "Behind me!" he roared to his men, and lashed out with a last burst of energy at an enemy that had just killed so many of his soldiers. He advanced with big strides, but unexpectedly felt his feet trip on a fallen body that was immersed in the sludge. He struggled, but was unable to extract his legs from the sucking mud, and instantly felt vulnerable. The soldiers he was chasing sensed a change and, turning, they understood they had regained the advantage. Three of them attacked him. He tried desperately to pull his legs free as two of the enemy rushed at him and the third tried to move to his right side. He raised his shield and felt a sword crash down on it, and with a defensive movement of his body managed to bring his sword up under the soldier's arm. As the man fell away, Maelgwn felt his body tremble as something very heavy smashed against his armoured sword arm. He turned to see a giant of a man preparing once again to swing his fearsome mace. Unable to move, the General tried to defend himself, but found his sword arm was numbed. In a frantic act of self-preservation, he brought his shield up to defend himself, only to have it knocked aside by a ferocious blow of the mace that shattered its framework. In vain, he tried to raise his sword and was knocked senseless by the next blow of the mace.

In the fluctuating outcomes of the battle, the giant warrior's triumph was short-lived by a spear to his throat, and with his death the Norman soldiers became confused and dispirited. The loud trumpets made them aware of the advancing cavalry, and each man broke ranks and tried to fight his way out of a suddenly developing trap.

"Maelgwn's down!" an officer cried out. "Defend the General!"

Tired soldiers mouthing Welsh swear words staggered through the gripping mud and formed a defiant wall around their fallen leader. The officer bent down and raised the General's head and shoulders out of the slime in which he lay face down. It took only a glance to know that one of Wales's greatest soldiers was dead; the terrible power of the mace had crushed his helmet and caused fatal injury.

Gwriad led his men into a widening attack on the rear columns of the enemy, but his rapid advance faltered and soon became a slog through the increasing mud. He felt befuddled by the wind and the unrelenting rain beating into his face whenever he looked west, and all around him men were fighting, while others were pushing forward to get to their enemy. At times, he heard faint trumpets, and then his ears would ring as the next thunderclap crashed and eye-searing lightning ripped the black sky. The wind eased for a moment and by the lightning's glow he saw the centre of the Welsh shield wall had been breached.

Near him were two of his officers, and he grabbed them and shouted in their ears that they were to direct their men to the breach. "We must stop them!" he yelled, pointing in the approximate direction.

They nodded their drenched faces, and staggered off to pass the command. After looking for any enemy soldier who might be near, Gwriad lurched towards the gap that he had clearly seen during the brief flash of lightning. He waved his sword and bellowed at any nearby soldiers that they were to follow him. He realized he was gasping with the effort, and made a note in his mind that he was getting too old for this type of fighting. "I'll stay on a bloody horse next time," he gasped.

A hundred paces away Dafydd was leading an organized assault on the rear of the enemy near the centre of their line. He heard the cheer go up as the Welsh centre buckled, and saw the enemy soldiers rushing away from the stalemate of the two opposing shield walls and struggling to get to a place where they seemed to be sucked into an expanding hole. He visualized how they would be attacking the crumbling defences of the disheartened Welsh soldiers as their vital shield wall disintegrated. "Charge!" he yelled, trying to get himself heard above the chaos of the storm. "Charge!" he waved his sword, and taking long, ponderous strides through the mud, he led his fresh fighters into the rear of the attacking enemy, many of whom died without realizing that their opponents were behind them.

Up on the hill, Earl Reginal raged at his officers, swore loudly at the weather and worried as to how a battle that he could no longer follow was developing. It had been only a relatively short time ago when the battle had been going entirely as he had planned, and he had watched in disbelief as his valued cavalry had been ambushed, and had failed to destroy the undermanned wings of the enemy. His massed army had charged in a spectacular display of power, and just as victory had seemed inevitable, hundreds of Welsh soldiers had suddenly poured out of the forest on both sides. Then the rain had fallen like a massive waterfall from a rapidly darkening sky, and as the wind howled and the thunderclaps ricocheted around the valley he had been unable to get his trumpets to convey his orders. He had sent members of his unhappy officer corps to take messages to the field officers, but in the chaos of battle and storm, they had been unable to find any cohesive leadership. Some had galloped into Welsh bands of soldiers and met a sudden end, others had roamed around in a fog of rain and gloom and had given up trying.

Prince Anarwd had always realized that his plan had one main weakness, and that was the situation of the two hundred brave soldiers who had acted as the bait. They had to be few enough to tempt the Normans to commit their complete army, but they needed to be reinforced as soon as the bait had been taken. He had hoped the hidden armies on both sides of the valleys would reach them in time, but failing that, he had divided his cavalry into two sections: one that he led and was hidden in the forest behind the Welsh shield wall, and the other, led by Lord Edwin, was hidden in a valley behind the Norman lines, and would be used to destroy the fleeing enemy at the end of the battle.

He had not imagined that the storm would become so intense, and as he galloped towards the battle he found it hard to control his terrified animal when the deafening thunder crashed down like a physical blow, and the lighting seared the dark sky. It was as though the natural world was fighting its own war. Amid the pulsating rain and the huge wind gusts, he could barely make out the situation as he aimed for the centre of the Welsh line and prayed he was in time.

Ahead the Prince could just discern that there was intensive fighting, and realized that a part of the shield wall must have collapsed. He soon realized that the centre of the wall, always the most vulnerable, was occupied by a powerful wedge of Normans who were forcing the exhausted and dispirited Welsh to retreat back on themselves. He paused, pleased that there was still some Welsh opposition to the enemy, which contained the enemy wedge in a solid mass. He paused for a moment to allow his cavalry to catch up, then signalled for the trumpets to sound and immediately led a ferocious charge across land that was still firm.

When his struggling soldiers heard the trumpets so near, they made a final effort, forcing their once confident enemy back into the path of the oncoming cavalry. In the confusion, the Normans realized they were no longer winning, but had become the victims of a murderous trap. The cavalry cut though them, and the Welsh war horses trampled the enemy under their iron-clad hooves. The invigorated Welsh soldiers counterattacked from both sides, and soon there were no survivors of the wedge of the once seemingly invincible Normans.

Across the field, the enemy soldiers realized there was no chance of winning and, reluctant to lose their lives in a lost cause, they turned and ran. The remains of their much-vaunted cavalry that had been overwhelmed by the unexpected numbers of ferocious Welsh soldiers joined the route, unaware as they fled, that an important drama was occurring above them.

Earl Reginal was unable to believe how the battle had changed and as he could no longer get his orders out to his officers, he decided to leave the field and return to a safer position. "Take charge!" he bellowed at his senior officer, barely able to make himself heard. "Report back to me when our army has regained control of the battle." Without further interest in a situation he could neither see or control, he left the hill with a small bodyguard.

As he began to descend, he became aware of the approaching sound of trumpets and, for a moment, wondered if it was his cavalry coming to his rescue. It would explain their disastrous performance in the battle if there had only been a limited number in action. His hopes were dashed as he witnessed, in the valley below, his retreating soldiers being slaughtered by a powerful column of Welsh cavalry.

Amid the confusion caused by the deafening wind and pounding rain, he signalled to his bodyguard to fall back. A level of panic gripped him as he returned to his storm-battered hill and realized there was only one way off the hill. Clovis, the intelligence officer in charge of his safety, pointed to a line of Welsh cavalry that had broken away from the fighting and was making its way up the side of the hill, along the path that he had just taken.

"Do we fight, my Lord?" Clovis had drawn his sword, as though there could be only one answer.

Reginal nodded mechanically; he knew he had no choice. He had to fight or be seen to flee like a broken leader, and if he did not fight to the end, reports were sure to get back to Earl Fitzosbern. Better to die now than risk total humiliation. "Charge them down!" he cried.

For a brief moment, as lightning lit the sky, he felt immortal. He would surely survive and live to fight another day. He did not fear death because he was not going to die. With this self-made assurance he led his small force against another small force, and the battering storm increased the sense of unreality.

Lord Edwin led his own select column of elite troops up the bare hill, where he was convinced the Norman Earl was cornered. He slowed and allowed his riders to catch up, and drew his sword, determined to end the life of the man he blamed for the recent troubles. When they were about two hundred paces from the charging Normans, Edwin indicated they should approach in a tight spearhead formation. He raised his small shield and, setting his eyes on the well-armoured leader of the approaching horsemen, led the charge.

Edwin understood that the Normans had a tactical advantage in attacking from above, but he also saw they were charging as a loose band and did not have the military structure of his elite cavalry. In a tight spearhead he drove through the loose band of Normans, and rode directly for the man whose bright armour indicated he was the leader. It was clear he had not been involved in the battle. "Like me, boy. Like me!" Edwin taunted. "But I think you don't want to fight, whereas I do!"

Both men had chosen swords and shields, and as they came closer Edwin noticed his adversary was right-handed, as he was. Their lines of attack were such that both men would pass with their sword arm nearest to each other. He grinned with excitement, and when their horses were closing fast, Edwin suddenly altered his approach, pulling his horse to the right, so that their shield arms were nearest. This unexpected move confused Reginal who, although a strong man, had little imagination. He was in the process of shifting his position when they clashed with their shields taking the shock.

Edwin used his shield as a weapon, not merely as a defensive piece of armour, and having absorbed the initial contact he did an upwards movement, ramming it hard at the Norman's visor. Reginal was knocked sideways, and as they passed Edwin swung round delivering a resounding blow with his longsword to the back of Reginal's sword arm. Although well-armoured, the Welsh blade broke through the Norman's defence, numbing his arm, and causing the Earl to drop his sword as he fell off the other side of his horse.

"Got you, boy!" Edwin crowed as he pulled back on his horse.

He did not see Clovis ride up on his blind side, and it is arguable that he never felt the Norman sword bite deep into his neck. When his body was found a short time later, there was a smile on his face.

The battle disintegrated into an uncontained rout, with Norman soldiers seeking safety in the nearby forests, or risking detection as they fled in numbers down the road that led to the border.

The storm had passed over when Prince Anarwd received news of the death of his two closest friends. He sat stony-faced on his huge horse, silently staring around at the carnage of war, but saw nothing. "Bastards!" he bellowed and waved a clenched fist at the brightening sky. His eyes slowly refocused and he sent out orders for all of his victorious cavalry to gather around his flag.

"Today, you have all fought like heroes, and we have gained a victory that the Normans will remember," he paused. "But, we have lost Lord Edwin and General Lord Maelgwn," a gasp went up around the tight circle of mounted men, "and I want a total victory to make their loss bearable!" He stood up in his saddle and raised his sword above his head. "I want those retreating bastards to suffer! I want their blood!" A roar went up from the cavalry, and all tiredness forgotten, they followed him off the field and towards the border.

He had transferred command, in his absence, to Gwriad who slowly assembled his surviving officers and the sergeants. "You take charge of the injured," he said to Dafydd, after giving him a bear-hug of relief that he had survived, "and I'll deal with the dead." They shared drinks before getting up and facing their grim tasks. Across the battlefield Welsh soldiers were searching the corpses of the Normans and quickly dispatching the injured. It was a ritual followed by victorious soldiers throughout the world.

While this continued, two valleys away, Prince Anarwd and his cavalry were descending like avenging angels of death on the remnants of the enemy army that had thought they had escaped, and were retreating in a disorganized rabble, more like refugees than soldiers.

When the massacre was over, Anarwd's only disappointment was that he had failed to capture Earl Reginal, who had been rescued by Clovis and spirited away with his bodyguard through a minor pass back to the border.

"It's time to go home, boys," Anarwd said quietly. "You've done what needed doing. You all deserve a rest," a tired smile crossed his lined face, "and a good woman!"

The men yelled and banged their shields.

CHAPTER TWENTY-FIVE

"News is that we've won a great victory!" Iago said, bursting into the smithy, where Idris was sorting out some metal.

"Good," he replied. "I wonder if Lord Gwriad will still want me to make him a helmet?"

"It's wonderful news!"

"Yes, indeed," Idris said.

"You don't sound very excited."

"No, not really. It won't be long before the other side want their revenge, and then we're back to where we started."

Iago rubbed the new beard he was growing. "You were the one who was keen to join the army at the beginning, Idris. You created all that armour. Why the change?"

"I was trying to relive my early days, boy. Stupid. When we got to the camp, it all came back to me: the boredom, the useless training, the bloody officers. At the end of it all you march off and hope the ones in command have not made a mistake that will lead you into a disaster. Even if you win, many of your friends will be dead, and you'll be lucky not to have some injury that will change your life for ever. And for what? We kill more of them than they kill us, and we are the winners. Very occasionally, the victory is so big that the winning side can make sure they have killed the enemy leaders, and destroyed so much of their towns and people that they will never rise up again for a generation." He threw down the metal. "That is not the case this time. We have punished the Normans for attacking us, but we have only won a battle, not the war. We were trying to defend our land, but their land remained safe, and they will soon be attacking us again in greater numbers and with better officers, and where will our army be? Back on the farms and trying to feed our families. Oh, Iago, we are on a hiding to nothing."

"Oh. I didn't see it that way." He stared out at some children who were happily splashing in puddles in the lane, delighting in their new experiences after the long drought. "The soldiers I met were pleased with themselves: they were riding Norman horses, and carrying Norman armour. They said the Normans and their Saxon mercenaries were slaughtered. They said it was a great victory."

"Ah," Idris nodded. "No doubt they won the battle single-handed?"

Iago did not respond. "Oh yes," he said after a long pause, "they said two of our top generals were killed, and that Prince Anarwd was very upset."

"Well at least it wasn't Prince Anarwd. Now he would have been a great loss. Who died? Do you remember?"

"Yes, there was a short stocky general, with grey hair. He was in charge of the border in this area. We saw him at the camp."

"General Sir Maelgwn?"

"Yes. The other was Prince Anarwd's best friend. They'd fought together for years."

"Lord Edwin ap Tewdwr?"

"Yes. Their bodies have been taken to Prince Anarwd's home for a big burial service.

"They were good leaders," Idris frowned. "Wales can't afford to lose men like those, and I doubt if Anarwd will lead another battle, he's not a young man." He poured two mugs of beer, and they sat together outside, where a weak sun was barely penetrating the clouds. "What about that Lord Dafydd, who came with us when we transported his injured nephew?

"I heard he and Lord Gwriad, his brother, weren't injured."

"That's good news then," the smith gave a humourless laugh. "I've made the visor he ordered."

They drank in silence, until their thoughts were interrupted by Bethan and Angwen, who seemed in high spirits. "We've heard some wonderful news," Bethan said. Angwen clapped her hands. "I won't tell you, lovely man, unless you pour us some beer." She put an arm around Idris's neck. "You'll really want to know about this," she said blowing in his ear.

"We've won a great victory," Idris said in a deadpan voice.

"Oh shit! You knew! Well you could at least be happy about it, both of you."

"Idris has just explained to me why we should not be too happy," Iago said apologetically.

"Oh, for God's sake," Bethan erupted. "You get us some beer and mister down-in-the-mouth can tell us why good news is in fact bad news!"

Later, when Idris had reluctantly explained his lack of enthusiasm, and Bethan had pointed out that they would be far worse off if they had lost the battle, they took to making music and singing. Idris produced his drums, Bethan went home to get her harp, Angwen played a flute which she had quickly mastered in the past few months, and Iago sang. It was only recently after getting to know Wynny that Iago had shown the confidence to reveal he had a fine tenor voice. They were enjoying themselves, and a number of their neighbours had come out to listen, when two strangers on tired old hacks galloped up to their group.

"We've got some very good news for you all!" one of the men announced grandly, and after nearly falling off his horse, he advanced with a slight stagger. The other man followed, giggling and repeating, "Very good news. Oh yes." He hiccupped and continued to giggle.

"You've come to tell us that we've defeated the Normans," Bethan said, and glared at them.

"Oh? So, you've heard, then?" He looked obviously at the beer in Idris's hand. "Well, all that way to bring the good news. It's hot work," he smiled knowingly at the two men. "We wouldn't say no to a beer."

"Well, I'm sorry, boys, you're too late for beer, just as your news is too late," Idris stood up. "But I notice you've already had a few? And you don't want to get lost getting home, do you?"

The smile vanished from the faces of the two drunks. The first man laid his hand on the knife in his belt, but changed his mind when Iago stood up, a head taller, and reached for a metal pole. There was a moment of indecision before the men clambered back on their old horses. They looked back as though they were going to yell something, but Iago had moved up close to them, swinging his iron bar from side to side.

"Bastards!" one of them yelled back as they hurried off.

"That's an old game that drunks play whenever there's good or bad news," Idris said as he sat down. "Now, where were we?"

IT WAS A GOOD DAY for travelling. The summer heat had not returned since the storm, and low cloud and a light breeze was pleasant for riders and their horses. Gwriad and Dafydd led a small party of local Ceredigion horsemen, some riding their own horses and a few on captured mounts. The brothers had stayed on, after the departure of Prince Anarwd, to organize the distribution of captured items and the loading of wagons. There had been a subdued mood among the soldiers that had stayed to help dismantle the camp, partly because of the deaths of their two generals, but mainly because it had gradually become clear that, although the death toll among the enemy had been worth boasting about, many of their friends had been killed or severely injured, and there were going to be hard times on some farms.

"Why are we coming this way, Dafydd?" Gwriad asked. He didn't really mind, it was a pleasant journey and they had no particular reason for hurrying back to Aberteifi. "We could have travelled directly west from the camp."

"This was the way I travelled when I took Jon down to Prince Anarwd's home. On the way we'll be able to stop at the small hamlet where Idris lives. I have something to show you."

Gwriad looked askance.

"You remember? He's the blacksmith with the remarkable wagon that you tried to impound?"

"Oh, yes." He suddenly looked interested. "Yes, of course. I ordered a helmet like the one he was wearing."

"I want to thank the women there for washing Jon, and redoing his bandages. I think it was their nursing that saved his life. It was a long journey, and he was barely alive when we reached the healers at Anarwd's place."

"Yes, I remember you telling me before the battle. It all seems so long ago." Gwriad shifted in his saddle. "But you said he was able to travel?"

"Yes. The two medics stayed with him, and as soon as he was fit enough for the journey, they accompanied him back to Aberteifi." He paused, and a pained look crossed his face, "He'll be nursed by Derryth."

Gwriad glanced across at him, "Lucky fellow. She'll soon have him back on his feet." He waved at an urchin child who waved back. She was wearing a grubby shift and was bare-footed. She had a joyful, saucy smile, and Gwriad found himself grinning back. He reached into a purse attached to his belt, and threw her a coin.

"Thank you, Sir!" She caught the coin in one hand, and gave a graceful little curtsy.

"What's your name?"

"Afanen, Sir."

"Well, Afanen, you can tell your family that you met a real Lord."

"Yes, Lord." She waved until they were out of sight.

"I must be getting soft in my old age," Gwriad muttered. "There are times when I think I would have liked a daughter."

Dafydd had pulled back and watched the interaction with interest. It was not like Gwriad to act in this way. But his last statement, as he rode a few paces ahead, caused Dafydd to flush with guilt. He was reminded that he never gave his daughter a second thought, leaving Tegwen's upbringing entirely to Alys, her nurse, and to the rest of the castle's servants. He had employed a scribe to teach her how to read and write, but he had never checked up on the man, relying on regular reports from Alys. It was natural that she reminded him of her mother, but when he looked at his daughter he was reminded of the fact that at the time Teifryn died he was having an affair with Derryth. He knew the time had come when he had to behave like a father and not blame Tegwen for his mistakes.

They reached the hamlet the following day, arriving before the midday meal. "There it is," Dafydd pointed at the smithy. "Idris brews a good mug of beer."

"Well then, we will definitely stop!" Gwriad joked. He turned to the handful of soldiers, "I'll pay for you all to have a mug of beer!"

A cheer went up from the riders, which attracted Iago's attention.

"My Lord Dafydd," he said giving a slight bow. He had admired the way this Lord had conducted himself on the long journey to Prince Anarwd's fortress. "M'Lord," he bowed to Gwriad. "Idris is around the back," he was somewhat overwhelmed by the occasion. "Um. Please come in." He bowed his way out, and fled to find Idris.

"He's a useful looking fellow," Gwriad observed. He was still feeling mellow from his meeting with the smiling child. "He's taller than you are, Dafydd, and did you see those arm muscles! That's what being a blacksmith does for you."

"Perhaps I should have been a smith, and then Derryth would have found me more acceptable," Dafydd said, trying to make a joke of it.

Gwriad gave him a quizzical look, but said nothing.

Idris appeared and after bowing to both Lords, smiled at Gwriad. "I've made your helmet, Lord Gwriad."

"I would like to see it. But first I understand you brew a good beer. I will pay for my men."

"Indeed, m'Lord, beer first." He indicated to Iago to get it organized.

They dismounted and went through the usual stretching that men did when they left a saddle they had been encased in for some hours. Idris appeared with a jug and a number of mugs, and Iago handed the beer around. They were just downing their first mug, when Bethan appeared and, recognizing Lord Dafydd, immediately enquired after Lord Jon.

"It's one of the reasons we are here," Dafydd said. "I wanted to thank you for the wonderful care you gave to my nephew. I truly believe it was your timely intervention that saved his life. He is recovering." He turned to Gwriad, "This is the woman who, with her friend, insisted on bathing him and replacing his bandages...."

Gwriad nodded, "Yes, you told me." He smiled at Bethan, "Jon's my adopted son, but very dear to me." He took a drink of his beer to cover his confusion: why was he explaining himself in this way?

"Perhaps you would like to come and see the helmet, m'Lord?" Idris said, noting this might be a good time.

"Good." Gwriad moved quickly towards Idris and disappeared inside the smithy, just as Angwen appeared. She smiled at Lord Dafydd, who was suddenly lost for words. It had been dark the last time he had seen her, and his attention had been fixed on Jon's care and condition. But deep down, he knew he had been motivated to bring Gwriad here to see this woman who in spite of her unsightly wound, her tangled long hair, her tattered clothes and her total lack of memory was, he was now certain, the long-lost Angharad. He bowed slightly and turned to attend to his horse to cover his emotion.

Gwriad strutted proudly out of the smithy, looking like a demon from a nightmare. The polished helmet was in the shape of a cube with a wide eye-slit visor that could be raised. He staggered slightly as he tripped on a piece of wood.

"This is designed for you on a horse, m'Lord, when all you need to see is the armoured horsemen coming towards you. It's always awkward walking with it."

Gwriad made a rude noise from inside and raised the visor. The first person he saw was Angwen, who was finding the whole performance quite disturbing. She smiled nervously as the man in the helmet suddenly stopped moving and fixed his blue eyes on her in an unwavering stare.

"Oh my God!" he yelled, his hands wrestling with the helmet. "Get this bloody thing off me!"

Idris and Iago rushed forward to ease it off his head, and no sooner had they managed this, but Lord Gwriad rushed forward and sank to his knees in front of Angen.

"Angharad! Is it really you?" He was almost crying. "I thought you were dead, my love." He stood up and advanced on the amazed Angwen. "My wife! I've found you."

Bethan rushed forward and, realizing that this could explain so many things about her friend, placed a protective arm around her. "M'Lord, this is a woman who came to us one night, unable to speak and with no memory beyond her time at a local nunnery. We have named her Angwen, but if she is your long-lost wife, it would explain so much."

Angwen stood gazing in amazement at the man before her. This was the jovial man she had seen a long time ago from behind a tree, when he and another rider rode past. She glanced at Dafydd, who was staring as though cast in stone. Yes, he was the red-haired man who had seemed so thin at that time. She had felt something for this stocky man then, and now the same person was saying he was her husband. She turned to Bethan for help.

"M'Lord," Bethan said, coming between them, "we have a bench at the back of this building where you might like to talk." She gave a nervous giggle, "Well, you can talk and," she paused, "this woman will write words in the dust."

Gwriad gently took her arm, and he and the woman he believed to be Angharad walked slowly to the back of the building.

Idris smiled at Bethan, and nodded at the men. "I think it's time for more beer." He bowed towards the immobile Dafydd, "A lot more beer!"

CHAPTER TWENTY-SIX

Earl Fitzosbern stayed with his wife for more than three long weeks as she slowly slipped away, dying in the early hours of a sunny day in July. Adeliza de Tosny was the love of his life and had born him three healthy children, whom he had not seen since his return to his sick wife. Somehow, he could not bring himself to see them while Adeliza had been suffering, and now he felt like an empty vessel, drained of emotion and lacking empathy.

After sleeping for a few hours, he awoke to find a messenger had arrived with the grim news that the Welsh had gained a huge victory, and had routed the Norman-led army under the command of Earl Reginal. The battle had taken place well inside Wales, and the Earl had survived and retreated back across the border.

He sent the messenger back with a demand to know how the defeat had happened, the size of the Norman losses and what the Earl intended to do. When the man had gone Fitzosbern called a servant and ordered a bath tub to be brought to his balcony and for hot water to fill it. Later, when everything was to his liking, he soaked in the hot water while staring out at the forest beyond his house, and thought about Adeliza. He had never believed that she would die, and for the past weeks he had persuaded himself she was slowly recovering. When he had tried to encourage her, she had pretended to share his conviction, but behind her weak smile she must have known she was fading away. He screwed up his eyes in frustration; he should have been more aware.

His thoughts went to her burial. Although he liked the town where they had briefly lived, he did not want to have her buried here. She deserved to be buried in a place where she would be remembered. If it had been practical, he would have had her buried in her family plot in Calvados.

Still pondering the issue, he put on a robe and called for his servant, who reported that a messenger had arrived from the King. The messenger, accompanied by a small detachment of the Royal Guard, announced that the King had returned from Normandy, and required his immediate return to the capital, which explained the Royal Guard. Fitzosbern sent back a message informing the King of the sad news of his wife's death, and asking for permission to bury her in sacred ground within the city of London.

A hand-written message from William arrived a few days later, giving Fitzosbern the honour of burying his wife in the grounds of Westminster Abbey and of having a public procession in her honour. The Earl immediately prepared to travel from Norwich to London; his wife had already been prepared for burial and after sweet smelling herbs had been scattered around her body, the coffin was nailed down and placed in a decorated wagon with a full honour guard. When he left Norwich the town's people gathered in a silent crowd to see him off. It was a town where he had expected to live with his wife and family for many years, and he lowered his visor to hide his emotions.

His return to London was both an honour and an emotional trial. He had agreed with the King the time when he and his retinue would reach the city, and found the street to the Abbey lined with soldiers and crowds of silent people. He led the procession in front of the decorated wagon, wearing armour and surrounded by his friends and officers. Ranks of armoured soldiers marched behind the cortege, and it occurred to the Earl that William was also sending a message to the townspeople that their Norman King was back in command.

The King met the procession at the door of the Abbey, and after a short ceremony the coffin of Adeliza de Tosny was laid to rest with solemn grandeur. After the Bishop had said the final words and the traditional flowers had been tossed onto the open grave, William led his friend back to the palace where, after a short toast to Fitzosbern's late wife and some words of comfort, he indicated two ornate chairs and a small table with wine and cold meats. It was time to move on.

"You must be hungry?" William gave him a friendly pat on the shoulders.

Fitzosbern nodded, "Yes, I have not thought about eating for a while."

After further general enquiries on both sides, the subject turned to a review of the time when the King had been in Normandy. "I understand that the uprising in the North-East was quickly put down, and that Newcastle is now secure?"

Fitzosbern nodded, chewing furiously. He felt he had not eaten for days. "I've followed your plans based on those of the early Romans, and I've made Newcastle the most secure fortress in the North-East. It is from where we can launch lightning attacks on any invasion either from abroad or from the Scots. It is also a most valuable port from which we can quickly reinforce our military might. I have also sent a strong force to take charge of Carlisle so that our western domains are secure."

William smiled, "Always my right-hand man." He raised his glass and drank deeply. "Now tell me about the Welsh problem."

Fitzosbern explained his reasons for allowing Earl Reginal to take responsibility for the defeat of the Welsh. "He had initiated an attack on Wales that had killed many people and reduced a border village to burnt embers. As expected, the Welsh launched a revenge attack, and chose to harass Hereford and the surrounding area. Reginal thought he was dealing with a small band of local Welsh insurgents. So, he decided to send a relative of his to command the Norman forces. Apparently, the man had little campaign experience."

"I understand that the Welsh defeated a superior force?"

"That is true, my Lord, which is why I ordered the Earl to raise a large army, devastate the border country and defeat the army that I was sure the Welsh would assemble. As you know, they do not have a real standing army. They are predominately farmers, fishermen and miners and they come together to defend their country. They are, however, ferocious fighters and will fight bravely against invaders." He paused, "My wife was dying, and I was convinced that this was a matter the Marcher Lord could and should deal with."

"It was why I appointed Marcher Lords," William said. "You acted correctly, my friend." He refilled both glasses. "Now, tell me what your assessment of the situation is?"

Fitzosbern sat back in his chair and admired the Italian glass as he slowly swirled the dark wine. The pressure of the past weeks and the emotion of the last few days had left him fatigued beyond his experience. He took a slow sip of his wine, feeling his body start to unwind.

"Take your time," William murmured, although he was gripped by his usual desire to move on, and follow through with the ambitious plans he had for his new kingdom.

"I have demanded from Reginald a full report of how our well-equipped army, superior in numbers, came to be defeated. I want to know the losses we sustained, which I have heard were large, and I want to know what he intends to do." He reached for a chicken leg and took a bite. "As you know, my Lord, the Welsh are not a united nation. The North has its own Kings and the South have Princes.

"Yes, I have heard of how their great King Gruffydd was murdered by the present King of Gwynedd," William said. "How does that effect the present time?"

"It is my belief that because they have a complex system of local Kings and Princes with total power in their immediate areas, they believe that the Marcher Lords are the same. So, now that they have effectively punished Earl Reginal for making war on them, I believe they will be happy to leave it at that and go back to their pastoral lives. In other words, I do not think we are looking at an invasion from Wales." He stifled a yawn.

"Good, I agree." William finished his wine, and raised the glass decanter towards Fitzosbern.

"No. Thank you, my Lord. It's been a difficult day, so with your permission I will retire to my bed. I will be better company tomorrow."

"You've done well as joint ruler of this country while I have been away. I have had a detailed report from Bishop Odo, who believes the country has been very well run in my absence." He rose to his feet, and Fitzosbern forced himself out of his chair. "Well done. Well talk again tomorrow," the King said. He embraced his loyal cousin. "Also, I imagine you will want to return to your lands in Normandy and pay a visit to the family home of Adeliza to give them the sad news?"

Fitzosbern nodded, bowed and left William to study his maps. If Wales remained quiet, William could concentrate on the problems in Cornwall.

CHAPTER TWENTY-SEVEN

Jon stood on the castle walls above the gatehouse, and watched the silent movement of the River Teifi as it surged around the stone structures of the bridge below. It was a tranquil, summer evening, and although his bandaged arm throbbed and he chaffed at the insistence of the Wise Woman's strict instructions on his limited movement, he was constantly aware of how lucky he was to be alive. He had dim moments of recollection after the battle, and often pondered those images.

He remembered his sword arm being forced aside by a powerful Norman soldier, and the pain that had made him drop his sword. Jon had only a brief recollection of being catapulted off his horse. He grimaced at the memory; if it had not been for the intensity of the final stages of the battle, he was certain he would not have been caught off guard. He must have passed out, for the next thing he remembered was Dafydd arranging for him to be carried back to camp. He had faint memories of being loaded onto a wagon, and then brief, vivid moments of reality when he was aware of the smell of urine, of the constant bumping of the wagon and a conviction he had lost his arm. He recalled feeling intense heat, as though he were burning up and of slowly acknowledging he was dying.

It was the warm water on his skin, the soft hands working on his body and the encouraging smell of soap, that had briefly revived him. His last memory of that time was of a woman with blue eyes, long black hair and a strange mark across her throat. He knew her, and his tired brain made the conclusion that he was in Heaven, because he was certain she was dead.

"Ye feeling a bit better, m'Lord?" Gavin, the newly appointed sergeant, was standing next to him, and felt the need to make some small talk.

Jon rubbed his brow with his left hand and forced a smile. "I'm getting better each day, Sergeant. Thank you for asking."

Gavin bowed. "Glad to hear that, m'Lord." He smiled contentedly. He was delighted to have been made up to sergeant, certain that Lord Jon had been responsible, even though Lord Gwriad was the one who valued his hunting skills. "When d'ye expect the Lords Gwriad and Dafydd to return, m'Lord?"

Jon shrugged a shoulder. "I have no idea, Sergeant, but I hope they will return in the next few days." He had been back a week, and after two days to recover from the journey and with Derryth in constant attendance, he had slowly begun to feel stronger. He had rewarded the two medics and sent them back to their homes in northern Ceredigion, and now he waited anxiously for the return of his two relatives.

As is sometimes the case, possibilities are discussed just before they happen, as though there is some predestination in human activities of which some folk get the occasional glimpse. It was at that moment that the warning trumpet sounded and the gate was closed with a thunderous crash.

"Riders approaching!" the guard yelled, and Sergeant Gavin rushed down to check the security of the gate. Soldiers tumbled out of the barracks and from the kitchen, some fumbling awkwardly with their belts and weapons, all adjusting their helmets as they ran to man the walls.

It was soon possible to identify Lord Dafydd leading a small detachment of horsemen, with Lord Gwriad and a veiled woman rider on a pony at the back of the column. The arrivals were clearly tired after a long ride. Jon called down to Gavin to open the gate, and arrange an honour guard for the Lords' arrival. With a smile on his face he carefully descended into the courtyard.

Dafydd rode slowly through the gate and up to Jon who was standing at the end of the two lines of soldiers. He climbed down from his war horse with obvious stiffness. "You're looking well, Jon." He stretched and rested a hand gently on Jon's left shoulder.

"I am, and I have you to thank, Uncle." He turned to greet Gwriad, his father, who gave him a careful embrace.

"I am eternally grateful to see you, Jon. You've made a good recovery." He turned and helped the veiled woman from her horse. As she descended her veil lifted and revealed a lurid gash across her throat.

"This is the lady who helped to save my life!" Jon exclaimed. "Lady,

I have a vivid memory of you…" he paused as she raised her veil. "Lady Angharad?" he gasped. It seemed too good to be true. He realized he was standing with his mouth open.

Gwriad placed a supporting arm around her. "If you had not been injured, Jon, it is likely I would never have been reunited with my wife." She gave everyone a beaming smile, and stared lovingly at Jon, before moving forward and kissing him on his cheek.

Everyone stared, and from some of the servants and soldiers came a burst of excited chatter. Some cheered and others just stared in amazement, their interest focused on her wound.

"Angharad lost her voice when she was injured," Gwriad explained to Jon, "and sadly she has also lost her memory of anything that happened before she almost died. She has no memory of me or Dafydd or you, apart from helping to nurse you." He turned to Angharad, "But, she has come to understand and believe that we were part of the life she has forgotten."

Angharad nodded and looked slowly about her, amazed by the size of the castle. She pointed to Gwriad and Dafydd and waved her hand encompassing the walls and the buildings and especially the bailey.

"Yes, Angharad," Dafydd said eagerly, "this is our castle and all these people work for us. You lived here for many years."

Angharad, for that is what she accepted as her name, could only smile; she felt this was like a rainbow: wonderful, exciting but likely to fade away at any moment. She wished Bethan was with her.

Gwriad signalled to Emrys and gave orders for a hot bath to be arranged for Lady Angharad in his bedroom, and for a hot meal to be served for the four of them in Dafydd's room. He knew that, with the level of interest among the servants, they would constantly be finding reasons to be coming and going if the meal had been served in the hall.

Angharad could not remember ever taking a heated bath, and when the male servants had filled the copper tub with hot water, she was surprised when her female servant insisted on helping her disrobe and giving her assistance as she climbed hesitantly into hot water that was rapidly cooling. It was an exquisite experience, and she felt the weariness of the long journey gradually fade away as she immersed herself. After a while, the servant suggested she might like to have her back washed with soap, and Angharad found herself enjoying another sensation she could not recall but was assured had happened regularly before she disappeared.

The servant helped her out of the bath, and Angharad indicated she could dry herself. The servant, who had been instructed by Dafydd and knew her mistress could not speak or remember being in the castle, explained that all the dresses on the wide bed were originally hers. It was for her to choose which one she wanted to wear. Angharad stared at the numerous dresses and chose a flowing one of pale blue with freshwater pearls adorning the deep cut neckline. When she put it on, she found there was spare room around her hips, but that her ample breasts threatened to break out of the narrow confines of her neckline.

"You look beautiful, m'Lady," the servant said admiringly. "Let me brush your hair."

Angharad was trying her best to be accepting of everything that was happening to her, for she realized that everyone from the Lords to the servants wanted to make her feel welcome and at ease. She forced a smile as her hair was well brushed by the servant, who then checked the blue dress and showed her the jewellery she owned, but she did not feel comfortable having this woman do things for her that she was quite able to do by herself. For as long as she could remember, she had owned only one dress, and while it was a delight to have a second one, she felt it troubling and wrong that she should own so many beautiful clothes. The jewellery was another problem; she dimly remembered her two gold rings that were in the care of the Prioress, and understood they were valuable, but she had never tried to regain them as they had never seemed important. Now, she was looking at a range of jewellery that the servant explained were rings, necklaces, bracelets and broaches that had either been passed down in her family or bought for her by Lord Gwriad. Unwilling to try to give them importance, she directed her amazed servant to choose for her.

After the servant had left and the tub had been taken away, she stood by the open window and stared down at the castle walls and the river beyond. She tried to grasp the fact that if she was Gwyriad's wife she must have seen this view countless times. During the journey, he had told her stories about their life together, and how Dafydd's wife, Teifryn, had been murdered by the Saxons at the same time as she had disappeared, and how everyone had believed her murdered or abducted.

She had indicated her memory of the priory and her coming to the small hamlet where Bethan and Idris lived, a place so small that it did not have a name, but she had not the faintest clue as to how her life had been before that gradual awakening in the priory. Gwriad and Dafydd had both confirmed that her scar was most likely caused by a sword, and how she must have been amazingly strong to have survived. She thought the help of the abbess and of Bethan had been important in her recovery, but the concepts of strength, age and belonging were not real to her, and she gave them little thought.

There was a knock on her door, and after a moment Gwriad entered.

"Can I come in?" he asked awkwardly.

She smiled and gave a small bow, indicating with her hand that the room was his.

"You look good in that dress, I remember when you first wore it." He moved towards the bed and stared down at the other dresses. "I could never bring myself to get rid of these. Do you remember any of them?"

She shook her head, and flirtatiously held out the spare material around her hips, and then pointed to her tightly-clad breasts.

Gwriad stared, unsure how to respond. After a moment he realized that she was trying to tell him the dress only just fitted her, not making an invitation for sex. "Ah," he said, aware he might be looking confused. "Yes, I understand. I'll send a dress-maker to you and you can have these altered."

Angharad looked closely at him and wondered how they had behaved together before she lost all memory. He seemed a powerful man, with laughing eyes and seemed keen to make sure she was happy, yet she had not even the slightest glimmer of their former relationship, except for the fact that she had always been attracted to him, from the time she had watched him ride by her hiding place in the trees.

"Let me show you around the castle, while the servants put your clothes away." He held out his arm to her. She was uncertain how to respond, and Gwriad gently took her hand and rested it on his sleeve. She gave her breathy laugh, and smiled, nodding her head in amusement at him. In this manner they explored the upper landing, the lower areas of the bailey and the Great Hall, and eventually the kitchen and the other sections off the courtyard. Throughout this time, Gwriad kept up a constant stream of information, as though he feared walking in silence.

Dafydd was in the stables, and greeted Angharad in a relaxed and friendly way, as though her appearance with Gwriad was a normal, everyday occurrence. "This was your horse, Angharad, you named it Rhiannon," he said indicating a fine chestnut mare. "We all take turns in riding her, but somehow she has always remained your horse…" his voice trailed away, and he covered his confusion by leading Angharad to the animal, which immediately responded when she rested her hand on its glossy coat. It was a large animal, but Angharad showed no fear of it although she could not recall ever having ridden such a powerful creature. Her only memory of riding had been on the elderly pony Gwriad had chosen for her to ride back from the hamlet. She showed such joy in being recognized by Rhiannon that the two men went outside, where they met up with Jon, who was just returning from the barracks.

"How is Lady Angharad settling in?" Jon asked, uncertain how to refer to her.

"Very well," Dafydd said.

"Yes, indeed, very well." Gwriad seemed uncertain. "It's just… I can't get used to the fact that she doesn't remember me." He looked apologetic. "I know she will take a while to settle in. She's doing very well. I try to imagine how I would react to everyone who I don't know recognizing me and remembering things they take for granted and that are new to me." He blew out his cheeks and looked about him, not seeing anything. "She has no memory of the dresses I gave her, or the jewellery. Her servant says she has little interest in either." He looked bewildered.

"You have to remember she has spent a long time living in a hovel and with only one dress and no jewellery," Dafydd said. "These expensive things are new to her."

"She must be a remarkable woman to have survived," Jon said, admiringly, altering the direction of the conversation.

"Did you notice how excited she became when her horse recognized her?" Dafydd asked. "I think, in her mind, she might have thought that we had all ganged up together to pretend we knew her. Her horse was important, we could not have arranged that."

Gwriad nodded abruptly, "Jon, I want you to stay with Angharad and escort her back to the Great Hall. We'll meet you there."

He took Dafydd's arm and directed him towards the back of the castle. They walked in silence for a while, and then Gwriad spoke in a rush. "I need your advice, Brother." He looked quickly around to make sure nobody was near. "Angharad is my wife, but she has no idea of how we lived together. I remember clearly, the way we were in bed and our love making, but she is like a stranger: my wife, but not my wife. Should we sleep in the same bed or should I wait until she gets to know me? She's wants to please me... all of us, but how do I act towards her?"

Dafydd frowned. His experience of life, unlike Gwriad's, was confined to getting to know Teifryn, who had been a reserved, innocent girl who had been heavily influenced by Angharad, and who had no idea of what a real sexual relationship might be. Both she and Dafydd had seen sex as a frontier that neither of them had been able to fully explore. Teifryn's baby, Tegwen, had come as a surprise to both of them, and after her birth their sexual activity had become very intermittent. Before Teifryn's death, Dafydd had discovered how wonderous and enjoyable sex could be with Derryth. Following Teifryn's death Dafydd had been reminded by Derryth that he lacked an understanding of the meaning of a free sexual relationship. He cleared his throat, he knew he was the wrong man to give his brother any realistic advice.

"Well?" Gwriad demanded.

"What I suggest is that you discuss this with Father Williams," Dafydd said, trying to sound assured. "Although he is a celibate priest, he has a lifetime of advising people in such matters."

Gwriad looked at him as though he were mad. "I don't need to spread this around the area! I was just asking you for some advice, for God's sake! The last thing I want is having some ancient, sexless priest telling me how to conduct my marital sex life!"

"He will be more help than I can be!" Dafydd exploded. "My marital life was a failure. You need to discuss this unusual situation with someone who can discuss it with you dispassionately, and I am not that man!"

"But... Williams is just an old celibate priest!"

"Brother, the reason you don't want to talk to the most intelligent man in this area is because you feel guilty that you have been nowhere near him for a long time!"

There was a long silence as both men stared anywhere but at each other. "All right, I'll discuss it with him," Gwriad said at last. "But you'll arrange it." He marched off, leaving Dafydd to wonder why he should be the one that arranged the interview.

That night, Angharad enjoyed a family meal, conversing by writing down questions and answers with chalk on a piece of slate and with mime. She relived her experience with the Bishop, and had the men roaring with laughter when she gave a demonstration of how she had dealt with him. Because of the lively atmosphere, nobody noticed how Gwriad kept ordering more jugs of wine, and it came as a surprise when he suddenly passed out as he tried to give a toast to his wife, slipping back into his chair and instantly beginning to snore.

Angharad supervised the servants as they carried their heavy Lord across to his bed, then nodded happily to a relieved Dafydd and an amused Jon, and closed the door.

It was mid-morning when Gwriad staggered downstairs. His head hurt, his stomach was complaining and he had no recollection of how he had come to find himself naked in the large bed with fresh clothes laid out for him, and clear evidence of the fact that he had not slept alone. There seemed to be no sign of the others.

"Lord Jon and Lady Angharad are visiting Aberteifi village, m'Lord," a servant informed him, "and Lord Dafydd is passing judgement on a land ownership dispute."

He went down to the stables and asked if Lord Dafydd had sent a messenger to Father Williams. A stable lad came forward. "The Lord Dafydd sent me, m'Lord," the boy bowed.

"When was this?"

"At first light, m'Lord."

Gwriad looked amazed. "Was Father Williams up at that time?"

"Oh, yes, m'Lord. He were pleased to see me."

"When are we meeting?"

"Before lunch, m'Lord. Lord Dafydd sent me back to tell the Priest."

Gwriad groaned. He walked out of the stables and stared up at a cloudless sky. "Get my horse saddled up, I will need it when Lord Dafydd returns." He walked towards the well, pulled up the small bucket and drank deeply. The water was icy cold, and with the castle so close to the river, it never ran dry. He was in the act of pouring the water over his head when he was aware of a figure standing close to him. He shook his head like a dog, ran his fingers though his thick hair and rubbed his eyes.

Before him stood a tall, self-possessed young girl with jet black hair and vivid blue eyes that marked her out as unusual. "Hello, Tegwen, you've grown since I last saw you," he said kindly.

She smiled, revealing a gap in her white teeth. "I'm losing my baby teeth, Uncle," she said proudly.

He smiled, and wondered why he saw so little of her. "Has your father given you a horse yet?"

"Oh, yes, Uncle, I've been riding for ages." She moved a bit closer. "Uncle, can I come with you to Llanduduch? I asked Father, and he said I should ask you."

"Did he?" Gwriad smiled, his head was clearing. "You could come with us, Tegwen... Or I have something else you might do for me...."

Her face dropped. "What's that?"

"You know that your Aunt Angharad came back with us yesterday?" She nodded. "And have you heard that she is unable to talk, and unable to remember her life here? In fact she doesn't know me although we have been married for a long time?"

"Alys told me, Uncle. She said I was not to mention it as I am too young."

Gwriad laughed. "Alys is right in one way, Tegwen, you are young, but you're not a typical child. I hear you can read and write?"

"Yes, Uncle," she blushed with pride.

"Well, what I have to ask you, I could not ask of any other child of your age." Tegwen gave a small gasp. "I think you will be able to make her feel more accepted than I or your father can do. When Lady Angharad returns with Lord Jon from the village, I will introduce you. I want you to show your aunt those parts of the castle that only you know about. You can tell your nurse that I have given you the morning off your studies."

As they were talking, the gates opened and Jon and Angharad rode over to where Gwriad and his niece were standing. Angharad dismounted and was delighted to meet Tegwen, and hugged her warmly. Dafydd came out from the stables and watched with an uncertain look on his face.

"Angharad," Gwriad said, "Dafydd and I have some business to attend to, and while we're away Tegwen wants to show you around the castle in a way I am unable to do." He gave a small bow, and watched as Tegwen took her aunt's hand and walked towards the kitchens, explaining and pointing to places as they walked. Angharad turned and gave a small wave to Gwriad. He wondered what she was thinking.

He called for his horse, and he and Dafydd rode out of the castle and were soon across the bridge.

"I imagine old Williams must be confined to his chair by now," Gwriad joked as they trotted down the river trail.

"You're in for a surprise," Dafydd grinned.

"Why so? I know he's a good sight older than me…."

"And you can hardly get into a saddle," Dafydd quipped.

"After our recent fighting and travels, I have never been so fit!"

"Jon has been treated by the Wise Woman," Dafydd said, avoiding her name, "and she has been visiting the old priest. She told Jon that Williams has lost weight, drinks less and has regained the ability to travel down to Llanduduch and climb back up again. I gather he's once more insisting that the villagers attend his church."

"Let's get it over with," Gwriad said, pushing his horse into a canter.

Dafydd smiled, he felt his brother was in for a shock.

·   ·   ·

A HUGE CHANGE HAD OCCURRED in Bethan's life. Her high-spirited daughter had finally married her mysterious farmer boyfriend, whom Bethan had only met once, on the day they married. They had set up home an hour's walk away, and with a mother's mixed emotions she had bid her daughter farewell and welcomed Idris into her home, which was considerably more comfortable than the "man's dump" that she called Idris's shack, which he had bequeathed to Iago.

"I think it won't be long before Iago marries Wynny," Idris said sadly. "Her possessive father likes Iago, which is a miracle when you think that for years Gwynn has chased every young man off his land. My worry is that Iago might be tempted to become a farmer, and give up working for me."

"Don't be silly," Bethan laughed. "I don't think Iago would give up being a blacksmith, he's a natural."

"His father was a miller. Iago's closer to the land than to the life of a smith. If Gwynn offers him the prospect of his farm as a wedding gift, Iago will be greatly tempted, especially if his wife wants him to accept."

"My feeling is that Wynny would like to get away from her controlling father," Bethan said looking about her house. "However, if you want Iago to stay, you'll have to help him to build a comfortable house, like mine. Your old place is a disgrace."

"It suited me."

Bethan tweaked his nose. "I wouldn't have taken up with you if that shack was all you had to offer. Luckily for you, I came with a house. If I was Wynny, I wouldn't agree to move from the comfort of her farmhouse to live in a dump. Can you imagine Wynny's mother when she sees that the forge is better built than the living area?"

Idris was about to protest, but thought better of it. "Alright," he said thoughtfully, "I'll pretend that I have plans for the back of the forge, and that I want to help him build a bigger place behind it. He's not daft, he might tell me he doesn't intend to stay, but I bet he hasn't really thought much about marriage. He's not very worldly."

"Says the man who knows about these things!"

"Which reminds me," he gave a lascivious smile, "Iago is looking after the forge, and you and I have some serious business to attend to."

"Oh, I don't think it will be serious," Bethan said as she led him towards the sleeping area. "I think I'm in the mood for fun."

CHAPTER TWENTY-EIGHT

In his palace in London, Willliam the Conqueror, as he enjoyed being called, was studying a map of the South-West of England.

His cousin, Fitzosbern, was staring out of a window overlooking a manicured garden, and noticing that the roses were blooming in a profusion of colours. "When will you launch the attack on Cornwall?" Since the death of his wife he yearned for action, and was unable to focus on the attractions of London.

"As soon as I receive news that the forces from the Marcher Earls have assembled in Bristol under the command of Baron Martyn de Tours," William replied. "We will travel to Exeter with our army on the lower road via Salisbury, while he will be approaching down on the higher road. In Exeter we will meet up with the forces of the Earl of Cornwall, Count Mortain. As you know, he has been ambushed on a growing number of occasions and that is the reason for this major attack. Our armies will be a warning to any others who are thinking of rebelling in the areas that we pass through, and if we experience any resistance, so much the better. Finally we will move into Cornwell and destroy their uprising."

"Good," Fitzosbern murmured, "I feel the need for action."

William raised his eyes from the map table. "When we have restored our rule of law in the South-West, it will be time for you to return to Normandy to visit your late wife's family," he paused, "if only for a short while."

"Yes, my Lord," Fitzosbern replied with heavy sarcasm.

The King laughed. "You are my most loyal friend, so it falls to me to remind you of your duties."

"I would prefer to fight and continue to complete your kingdom rather than spend awkward days with my in-laws."

"If you take your children with you, I'm sure you will find your mother-in-law less accusatory." He handed a goblet to Fitzosbern who sniffed the wine, and nodded in a gesture of appreciation. "When we have subdued the Celts in Cornwell, I am happy to concentrate on ruling this country, and establishing the laws and the structure for peaceful governance."

"And the Welsh?"

"They have achieved their revenge on Earl Reginal, and I am confident they will be content to avoid further fighting this year. The fact that I have moved the incompetent Earl Reginal up north to take charge of Newcastle will not be lost on Prince Anarwd."

"I agree. That will be seen as a peace offering, to which he'll be happy to respond." He sipped his wine. "I understand that the Prince lost his two best Generals, which is another reason that he'll be unwilling to declare war unless he's forced to."

"My spies tell me that the Welsh lost many of their trained soldiers in that battle, and unlike us they do not have the money to hire mercenaries. I will leave them alone, until they seek further conflict." He joined Fitzosbern by the window. "It will be interesting to see how the Northern Princes – or Kings as they call themselves – behave. I hear that they avoided supporting Prince Anarwd in his attacks."

"If we leave them alone, they will almost certainly end up fighting each other," Fitzosbern jested. "If they were united as a kingdom, as they were under King Gruffydd, they would be a more dangerous enemy."

In the following weeks the two Norman armies advanced across the South-West of England, spreading fear and an acknowledgement of Norman power. In the settlements they passed through only the small children waved at the marching columns of armoured soldiers with their flags and squadrons of cavalry. The adults either hid in their hovels or stopped work in the fields and stared with muted hatred. As the armies marched through their land, the soldiers caused only minor problems for the peaceful Saxon peasants, but it was not the same for those areas where they set up camp at the end of each day's march. Once the camps were established, the soldiers went out to scavenge for food. Although threatened with death if they assaulted women or children, they were encouraged to take farm animals and any other food they could find, including the sacking of any ale houses they discovered.

By the time the King and Fitzosbern reached Exeter, the word had spread, and the Celtic warriors of Cornwall had retreated into the wild areas of their land, prepared to fight a war of ambushing and retreating, and avoiding any major battles which they knew they would lose. However, they had not expected the Normans and their mercenaries to invade in such numbers, or to adopt the ruthless reprisals that they initiated wherever they were attacked.

Following each ambush, the Normans destroyed everything in the immediate area: burning the buildings and the crops and slaughtering the animals. Any man captured was executed, and the earlier restrictions on rape and brutality towards women and children were loosened. After two weeks the support for the uprising collapsed, and many of the leaders fled to Wales and Ireland. Soldiers were garrisoned in the larger villages around Cornwall, as a temporary show of strength, and after the public hanging of men known to be involved in the resistance and turned in by their communities, King William and Fitzosbern returned to London.

A few weeks later the Earl made his delayed visit to Normandy with his children. He visited his mother-in-law, Francesca de Tosny, leaving his children with her and her family, while he re-established personal control over his lands in Normandy. As he had joked to the King, "The peasants will play when their master's away."

"Take your time, my friend," William had said. "Your children will enjoy meeting their grandmother."

However, neither had imagined that Fitzosbern's visit would last more than three months after he picked up the sweating fever and was seriously ill for a long time.

.   .   .

WHEN THEY REACHED LLANDUDUCH, THE tide was in, and from the mountain above the village they could see in the distance the small fishing boats bobbing in a choppy sea in the bay and, in contrast, the calm lake-like quality of the river estuary at full tide.

"One could grow old here, and never get tired of the view," Dafydd said. He leaned forward on his horse which was cropping the thick grass. To their left was the priest's house, and beyond was the old church.

"I'm ready," Gwriad said impatiently.

"My Lords!" Father Williams shouted in welcome.

Gwriad dismounted and walked towards him, unable to believe what he was seeing. He was the first to admit he had not visited the priest for a while, but the last time he had seen him Williams had been an elderly looking, very rotund man with a full face and pronounced jowls. The person he was looking at seemed younger; he had lost so much weight that his robe hung loose about him, and the flushed, flabby face had been replaced with an angular jaw, hollow cheeks and a thin neck.

"Father Williams! I would not have recognized you if I had seen you in another place."

"Lord Gwriad, our God works in remarkable ways. He has shown me that I have more to do on this Earth before he accepts me into his Heaven."

Gwriad always felt awkward talking about God and Heaven. "How did you achieve this remarkable transition, Father Williams?"

"It's thanks to a young fisherman named Deri." The priest glowed with pleasure as both Lords bowed to him. He walked towards his house and continued: "I made him and his proposed wife realize that they were not suited to each other. She has since found another man, and he has become my student." He laughed happily. "Every day he comes for lessons and in return he has helped me around the house and has encouraged me to take more exercise. I eat less, drink less and I have never slept better!" Pointing to a horse in a nearby enclosure, he proudly stated, "I have even started riding again!"

He led the way into his bright, tidy house and asked them to sit. There was a jug of wine and cups on a small table, and smoked salmon with chunks of bread. "Please, my Lords, help yourselves. I have already indulged."

They sat for a short while, talking about general matters, and then Dafydd stood up and said he would leave them to talk, as he wanted to meet the horse and enjoy the view.

He had no sooner closed the door, than the priest leaned forward. "I understand Angharad is back?" he said excitedly. He knew Gwriad well enough to know that the Lord hated those close to him using titles.

Gwriad nodded as he chewed with a full mouth.

"It is a miracle. I have heard she is unable to speak due to a sword wound and that she remembers nothing of her life prior to the assault?"

"Indeed," Gwriad grunted, taking a long swig of wine.

"It must be very strange for you both." The priest reached across the small table and laid a reassuring hand on Gwriad's arm.

Gwriad took a deep breath, emptied his cup and placed it carefully on the table. "That's why Dafydd has persuaded me to come and see you." He took a deep breath. "You see, I don't know how to treat her. She's my wife, but not the wife she was."

Father Williams leaned back in his chair. "I remember you as a much younger man, when you and Lord Dafydd became the wards of your uncle. I seem to recall you had quite a reputation with the women?" He laughed and refilled Gwriad's cup, pouring a smaller amount in his own.

"My youthful days," Gwriad grinned. "Then, I met Angharad and we had a colourful life in the court of King Gruffydd. We returned to Aberteifi after his death, and in spite of the huge changes in our lives we remained very close to each other." He sipped his wine and gazed vacantly at his cup. "As you know, a while later I was seriously injured in battle and suffered a long recovery, but through all that time Angharad and I were…" he cleared his throat, "we remained very much in love." He found it difficult to say the words, even though he knew the priest often dealt with delicate matters.

"When Angharad disappeared, I lost interest in women." He drank deeply and raised the cup in a toast. "I even cut right back on my drinking, until recently!" He cleared his throat. "The thing is, Father, I am unsure if I would be taking advantage of her if we made love…." There was a long pause, "or whether I am still able to."

The older man stared unblinking at him, and nodded slowly. "I know you think that, as a celibate priest, I have no knowledge of women, but I was not always a priest." He rose and walked over to a large wooden box, and took out a bulky object wrapped in cloth, which he carefully unwound to reveal a magnificent long sword. It was clearly a weapon of some value with a pommel, inlaid with gems, at the end of a long, two-handed hilt made of tooled leather, that was protected by a strong, engraved guard. The two-sided blade had a thin fuller groove running down both sides, and the sharp edges gleamed in the light of the window.

Gwriad let out a gasp of admiration and jumped to his feet. "May I?" He held out both hands.

"Of course. That is why I'm showing it to you."

Gwriad held it carefully in both hands and moving away, practised some slow movements. He examined it intently. "Where was this made?"

"In the Holy Land." Father Williams took back the weapon and silently wrapped it up and placed it back in the box. "The last occasion I carried that weapon was when the Picts attacked the village. I realized then that it would be the last time."

"Yes, Angharad told me about it. It seems a long time ago."

"Indeed," the priest returned to his chair, and Gwriad helped himself to more wine. "The reason I showed you that weapon, was not to demonstrate its beauty or its value, but to demonstrate that our lives change. When I captured that sword, the idea that I might one day become a priest was laughable. But all things are in constant change, as are our habits and beliefs, and the most noticeable changes are in our physical abilities. You have passed the time when you or Angharad can take up your lives as they were a few years ago." He sat quietly and let his words sink in.

"How do I cope with my own problem?"

"First, you may not have a problem; you have turned off that part of your brain, but perhaps when you and Angharad get to know each other again you will return to sexuality. You're still a relatively active man. And remember, this will be as strange for her as it is for you. My advice is to treat her gently, move slowly and let her rediscover for herself what it is to have a husband. Also, don't treat your bedroom as a place for worry and hesitation; enjoy the funny things of life, and laugh with her."

Gwriad sat still, thinking deeply about the words the priest had said, then he stood up, grasped Father Williams's arms in a warm embrace and walked towards the door. "Thank you. You make good sense. I will travel down to see you more often. Next time, I'll bring Angharad." He strode out of the house with a sense of determination.

"How did it go?" Dafydd asked on the way back. He was trying not to smile as his brother urged his horse along the narrow path.

"Fine. His wine was good."

"What about his priestly advice?"

"Fine. I'll race you back to the castle."

From years of experience, Dafydd knew his brother would have been cursing all the way back to the castle if things had not gone well. 'Fine' seemed an excellent result, and Dafydd sat back on his saddle and let his brother disappear in a cloud of dust. He wished old Williams could soften-up Derryth – that would most certainly be 'fine'.

When Dafydd returned to the castle, he found Gwriad and Angharad sitting together in the Great Hall listening to Tegwen strumming a lute and singing a ballad with a confident, clear voice. He felt himself flushing with embarrassment, as he had no idea she could sing or play. Without interrupting, he quietly pulled up a stool and stared at his daughter, realizing he was looking at a stranger.

CHAPTER TWENTY-NINE

"**P**rince Maredudd has invited me to visit him now that the fighting is over," Dafydd said, as he read a message inscribed on vellum. "You went there when we were gathering our forces."

The brothers were meeting in the Great Hall, and both were, for different reasons, in good spirits.

"Ah yes! Prince Maredudd is an interesting person, you'll like him." Gwriad was feeling in an outrageous mood, having spent some happy hours exploring the boundaries of sexual behaviour with the lively Angharad. "He's an unusual man who's only interested in strange animals! You will remember that we ended up with his nephew the odious Prince Eoin because Maredudd claimed he was too old to lead an army?"

"Yes," Dafydd smiled as he rolled up the message. "I was quite envious that you were the one to negotiate with him. I'm thinking I'll pay him a visit; he is a renowned scholar. Can I leave Tegwen with you?"

Gwriad nodded absent-mindedly, his thoughts focused on how he had become overwhelmed with the awakened Anharad. He did not remember that their love-making had ever been so intense. "Sorry?"

"I was wondering if you and Angharad could look after Tegwen when I visited Prince Maredudd?"

"No. Take her with you. It will be a wonderful experience for her, and it's about time you spent more time with your daughter."

"Well, I thought..." he wondered what he really thought. "Yes, you're right. She's old enough."

They set out early the next day with a small guard, arriving at Caerfyrddin Castle at the end of the afternoon. Tegwen had impressed Dafydd with her riding skills and, even though it had been a long ride, she had not uttered a single complaint. In fact, he had to admit that she was good company and took a great interest in the countryside and in the birds and animals they encountered.

"Oh, look at that, Father! What a beautiful river."

"It's the Towy. It's a good salmon river, like the Teifi." Dafydd sat unmoving on his tired horse, closely observing the scene and sharing Tegwen's happiness. The river was wide and deep and curved around a raised stone area on which was the wooden fortress of Caerfyrddin, and close by were the stone ruins of a Roman fort. There was a romantic beauty about the peacefulness of the scene: swans glided along the still water; two men were slowly pulling in a net, and beyond them wisps of smoke from the village's many roofs floated lazily into the windless sky. He realized that the last time he had come he had been focused only on the castle, and other than knowing it sat in a commanding place above the river, he had taken little notice of the surrounding area. "You're right, Daughter, it's worth spending time noticing the beauty of things."

As they crossed a sturdy wooden bridge, the castle gates opened, and there to greet them was the tall, white-haired Prince Maredudd, who seemed over-joyed to see Dafydd. "My Lord Dafydd and Lady Tegwen!"

Tegwen blushed, she was never addressed as Lady Tegwen; she glowed with delight. "Thank you, Prince Maredudd! You are the first Prince I have ever met."

The Prince laughed, "And you are the first young lady of beauty that has graced my meager palace for a long time!"

Dafydd looked on in amazement, suddenly aware of the fact that his daughter was developing into a beautiful person. In recent years he had left her education and up-bringing in the hands of a woman he had thought of as a mere wet nurse who had not only become Tegwen's companion, but had arranged for her to become proficient in the things that Teifryn would have educated her in. It was becoming a day of revelations, to which he seemed suddenly to have come aware, and he was uncertain of how to react.

The Prince showed Tegwen around his fortress, or palace as he liked to call it, finally ending up in a hall with a locked door at the end of the room. "That is something I want to show you tomorrow," he said. He glanced meaningfully at Dafydd. "You must both be tired after your long journey. My servant will show you to your room, and we will eat as soon as you have rested."

Over a modest, but nutritious meal, in a fine wood-paneled room overlooking the river, the Prince entertained Tegwen to some stories about his interactions with wildlife, and she told him the story about how her cousin, Lord Jon, had killed a giant wild boar single-handed. The Prince showed great interest, although he had heard the story from Gwriad. When she had retired to the room she was sharing with Dafydd, the men moved outside onto the battlements to drink wine and discuss the outcome of the recent war.

"You and Prince Anarwd did well. I was delighted with your remarkable victory. I would like to think we had settled the border issues, but what I fear the most, is that the Normans will attack in force when it suits them," Maredudd said. "Attacking the North is more difficult than the South; they have the high mountain ranges around Ya Wyddfa and many difficult valleys and rivers that have always made life awkward for an invading army. They have never been invaded with the exception of the unstoppable Romans, who conquered the South before finally working their way into the heartland of the North, eventually occupying even the holy isle of Ynys Mon. I have noticed that the Norman King tends to follow their example, and builds stone forts as he extends his control. If, therefore, the Normans were to attack through Gwent, the terrain is relatively easy for them, and although that is one of our strongest areas in military terms, Prince Anarwd would certainly be outnumbered unless he had time to raise a national army. The Normans could sweep through Morgannwg, and I could find them outside my walls, and soon they could be outside yours. We must have good spies in England, or we will not survive."

"Yes, I agree," Dafydd said thoughtfully. "Gwriad said you were not much interested in military matters, yet here we are in deep discussion."

The Prince stared out at the fading landscape. "He's right in the sense that I no longer have any interest in fighting or leading armies, but I am passionate about the future of our country." He laughed, "I have become an old man who has the answer for everything, and one who knows how best to rewrite history!"

Dafydd raised his cup in mock salute. "It is a valued role in our society, where the old get wiser while the young relive all our mistakes! So, speaks the middle-aged man."

The Prince let out a joyful laugh and patted him on his shoulder. "I like you, Dafydd. I know you will enjoy what I am going to show you tomorrow. Sadly, I thought your brother was not as enthusiastic as I feel you and your daughter will be."

The next day, after an early breakfast, Prince Maredudd led them into the hall with the locked door. Tegwen was intensely excited and doing her best to control herself.

Her keen expectation had not escaped the Prince. "Stand next to me, Lady Tegwen, and when I have unlocked the door, I want you to be the first to enter. And after you have looked around I want you to stand by the exhibit that most interests you."

The room had not changed much from the time Gwriad had been allowed to enter: there were still numerous skulls, bones and teeth on display around the room, as well as drawings and maps on the wall. But the heavy main table with its display of the more unusual items had been shifted to one side to allow the skeleton of the dragon to be assembled in its almost complete form along the floor. Some minor bones were missing, but the massive head with its neck bones leading down to its huge ribs, and gargantuan leg bones were intact.

Tegwen stood in front of the skeleton, her mouth open, unable to say anything.

"Well, Tegwen, what do you think?"

"Is it a dragon?" she gasped.

"I think it was a creature that walked this country long, long ago," the Prince said proudly. "Long before we humans lived on this land, this huge creature was hunting for something to eat. You could call it a dragon. I don't know what to call it, but I do know that very few have ever been discovered."

Dafydd had remained quiet, intrigued by the detail and originality of the bones and diagrams that ornamented the walls, and only now had he focused on the huge skeleton. "This is a discovery that could change the thinking of the world," he said quietly. "The Church would not be pleased."

"Indeed, Dafydd. This is, truly, the sort of discovery that puts the teachings of the Church into question. Where in the Bible does it mention dragons?" The Prince stood behind Tegwen who was tentatively touching the long teeth. "What do these teeth tell you?"

"That this dragon killed things to eat?" she answered cautiously, enjoying the attention. "The animals it ate must have been large."

"Good. What does the size of the leg bones tell you?"

"It must have been very heavy to need such big bones. Perhaps it was bigger than any other animal?"

"I agree," he smiled. "There are many people who see things but never ask why. Sadly, most people are like that. You notice things, my dear, and I want to encourage you to be like me and your father."

"My father?" she looked at Dafydd. "You never ask me 'why', Father."

"Until recently, I never thought you were old enough." Dafydd noticed the Prince looking at him curiously. "But now I know that you are, we will play the 'why' game." He tried to make a joke out of it and crossed the room to study a map.

They spent the rest of the morning exploring the wonders of the Prince's collection, and during the afternoon they rode slowly around his immense estate. He showed them the way he had preserved the badger sets and protected a small herd of red deer, and before returning he took them to a cave where a bear always hibernated in the winter. "My family thinks I am more concerned with the animals on my lands than I am with the people," he made a dismissive sound, then laughed. "Certainly, the animals are more interesting!"

They set off for home on the fourth day on Dafydd's insistence, in spite of intense pressure by both Prince Maredudd and Tegwen, who had formed a strong bond. "You must persuade your father to bring you here before too long," he said looking solemnly at Dafydd, "and if your father is too busy then persuade your cousin Jon to bring you. I would like to meet him."

It was an uneventful journey back, and when they reached the castle at Aberteifi, Gwriad greeted them at the gate, and Angharad made a great show of affection towards Tegwen. "I bet you're glad to be back after all that time with a room full of bones!" Gwriad bellowed with laughter.

"Oh no, Uncle! It was the best time of my life." Tegwen said earnestly. "Next time, I might go with Jon if Father will let me."

The two brothers made eye contact, and Gwriad pushed his tongue into his cheek.

.   .   .

PRINCE ANARWD ARRIVED AT ABERTEIFI with a strong retinue, having sent messengers ahead to warn the brothers of his arrival. It was late afternoon on a wet October day, and the Prince and his soldiers were cold and tired, and were quickly taken care of. Later, after the Prince had had time to take a hot bath and had eaten some warming food, he reappeared in the Great Hall like a guest who had rested for days.

"Prince Anarwd!" Gwriad embraced him. "You honour our castle with your visit. Welcome. You certainly make a fast recovery!"

"Nothing like a hot bath to restore the body!" He greeted Dafydd as a fellow general, and smiled at Jon, remarking on his obvious return to good health. Angharad had stayed back, unable to share the mutual affection of the men for this older man who reminded her of an old oak tree. "My Lady Angharad! You won't remember me, but I remember you," he bowed and grasped her hands. "You were always a beautiful woman, and you have remained so. I'm delighted you have been able to return to your family!"

Angharad glowed with pleasure, and gently pushed Tegwen to meet the great man. "Your daughter?" the Prince gasped.

"No. My daughter, my Lord," Dafydd said. "This is Tegwen."

Tegwen curtsied and took the Prince's hand in a firm grip. "I have heard so much about you, Prince Anarwd. May I sit next to you?"

They ate a basic hot meal around a table set for five, and once the impromptu meal was eaten, they sat around the great fire, drinking mulled wine while Tegwen was given a warm cordial. The conversation covered the recent war, Dafydd's and Tegwen's visit to Prince Maredudd, the discovery of Angharad and the hardships of the Prince's journey from his fortress in Morgannwg.

"Did you meet wolves, Prince Anarwd?" Tegwen asked, her eyes wide with excitement. This was the first time she had been allowed to sit with adults at night.

"No, my dear, but we did see a bear!"

After a while Gwriad looked meaningfully at Angharad, who rose to her feet and curtsied to the Prince, nodded to Dafydd and Jon and placed a hand on Tegwen's shoulder. The smiling girl reluctantly took her leave of everyone, kissing her father on his cheek, and taking Angharad's hand, before leaving the warm hall for the cool of the bedrooms.

"It must seem a miracle to you to have your wife reappear in your life?" the Prince said.

"It is indeed a miraculous story, my Lord, and every day is a new page."

Dafydd looked with interest at his brother, unused to him expressing himself in this way.

"And you, Dafydd, in spite of your great loss, you have a fine daughter who seems unusually bright and thoughtful."

"Indeed, my Lord, she never ceases to surprise me," Dafydd said, staring into the fire.

"Lord Jon, I was pleased to get to know you. You acquitted yourself bravely in the fighting and I am delighted you have made such a good recovery." He leaned over and patted Jon's arm, "Wales is going to need leaders like you in the next few years."

Jon was overwhelmed with the compliment and could only bow his head and thank Prince Anarwd, whom he considered to be a national icon.

Gwriad signalled to the servant to refill the cups, and leave the hall.

Once they were settled, Gwriad spoke: "My Lord, we're delighted with your unexpected visit, especially at this time of the year, but we know this is not just a friendly visit?"

"No, I wish it were. I came myself, rather than send a messenger, because I no longer have Lord Edwin or Sir Maelgwn to act for me, and because I need to get your reaction to my news, face to face." He stood up and stretched. "You may have heard of the famous Roman town known as Eboracum?"

They all nodded, although Gwriad had no idea where it was situated.

"As you know it is about halfway up the east coast of England, and since Roman times has always been an essential military and commercial centre. It is also a religious centre and is now known as the City of York. So, it was no small thing when there was an uprising. I understand the Normans wanted to build a second castle in York, and to make space for it they laid waste to one of the seven areas of the city. The local people were outraged and attacked the two castles, and were supported by a large army led by the King of Denmark. And with the help of local Anglo-Saxon Lords, they captured both castles, burnt them to the ground, and massacred all the Normans. In the fighting, most of the buildings in the city were also set alight."

The Prince was a good story-teller, and his audience listened attentively. "This happened in August, and King William immediately raised a large army and laid siege to the city. He paid the King of Denmark a rich bounty for opening the city's gates and sailing away with his fleet. He then began the rebuilding of the two castles and using them as his base, he defeated all local opposition. Since then he has systematically destroyed the whole area, massacring everyone regardless of age or sex. He's burnt all the buildings and crops and killed all the animals; he's killed thousands, and the survivors are dying of hunger. It is the most terrible thing that has happened since he invaded the country, and they are calling it the 'Harrying of the North'." He looked gloomily into his cup, which Gwriad promptly renewed.

"Well, I'm glad he's not getting upset with Wales!" Gwriad roared. "I'm always pleased when our enemies are killing each other." He looked around for support.

"My worry is that our Northern Princes will cause trouble and with his army gathered in one place, King William could use their nuisance as a pretence for a full-scale invasion. Anyway, he's returned to London and has left Earl Fitzosbern to continue the rape of the country."

"His cousin," Dafydd added.

"Indeed," the Prince agreed with a hint of annoyance at being interrupted.

"And if the snake shall strike at me, I will destroy it and all its family," Gwriad quoted, and poured himself more wine.

The men stared at him, surprised at his unusual speech. Dafydd recognized the quotation as coming from a book he had loaned to Angharad, and remembered he had come across her listening attentively as Gwriad read to her. It all made sense. Angharad was having a profound effect.

"What are you thinking we should do, my Lord?" Jon asked.

"I think we must form a standing army," the Prince said. "It must be an army stationed in Gwent, with men drawn from all of the areas of South and West Wales, and paid for by all the Princes and landowners whose lands will be protected by this army."

"That won't go down well," Gwriad said gruffly. "We're short of young men as it is, and nobody likes paying taxes."

"Are you saying we should do nothing?" The Prince glared at Gwriad. "Or do you have a better idea?"

"Prince Maredudd thinks as you do, my Lord," Dafydd said quietly. "He is convinced that when the Normans attempt to invade Wales, they will attack through Gwent, press on through Morgannwg and take the whole of Deheubarth. This was the way the Romans invaded us, all those centuries ago, and the Norman King has been following their example in his conquest of England."

"Suppose the Normans attack the North?" Jon asked. He wanted to be taken seriously. "Do we send our army up to help them? They haven't helped us recently, although they must be aware that our actions have relieved the pressure on them."

"Good point," the Prince said, keen to encourage Jon. "It is our great weakness. If we are to survive the power of the Normans, we must present a united front. But the self-appointed King of Gwynedd, Cynan ap Iago, sees us as the enemy. We supported King Gruffydd whom Cynan murdered for killing his father. He remains the strongest power in the North, with the most powerful army, and has a strong influence on the Princes of Powys. It is very unlikely that he or the lesser Princes will support us if we are invaded. If they are invaded, which I think is unlikely, we will see if they ask for our help."

There was a long silence following this speech, as each of the Griffith family thought about their options. "So, you think the only thing we can do is to send our young men to Gwent?" Gwriad muttered.

"With the money to pay them and provide for their equipment," the Prince added.

"For how long?"

"Perhaps for as long as our enemies want to invade us."

"If we trained them, we could replace them each year, and slowly build up a reserve army," Dafydd said thoughtfully.

"And where are we going to get all this money from?" Gwriad was beginning to sound bullish.

"Under the reign of King Gruffydd, we made a lot of money through trade. You were one of the first to establish that, Father, when you captured two trading vessels from the Bretons," Jon said, keen to show his knowledge.

"The event you refer to was not for trade. I used the boats to attack the Saxons up the Severn River." Gwriad smiled, "You will remember that, Prince Anarwd?"

The Prince nodded.

"It was Prince Rhodri ap Williams who took over the creation of a fleet and developed the trade with the mainland." Gwriad looked at Jon, "Well done though, if we can re-establish our trade, it would help us avoid too many taxes. People hate taxes."

The wine flowed and all four talked well into the night, but without reaching any formal agreement. The next morning, the Prince informed them that he would have to return the next day at first light, but would welcome some time by the sea, which he had not seen in recent years. Dafydd made arrangements for the four of them to ride to the long beach past Llanduduch, where they could finish their discussions.

"We'll see you this afternoon, Lady Tegwen," the Prince promised in a firm voice, and Tegwen knew it was no use protesting.

They left their horses in a grassy dip among the sand dunes, and a moment later were descending from a high mound onto the soft sand where the tide rarely reached. On the wind-blown beach, the Prince stood staring out at the unsettled sea in the bay, where waves crashed against the jagged rocks with the high cliffs to the right, and with the barren island beyond. He walked slowly along the sandy beach, enjoying the lash of the salty breeze. Slowly turning his head, he watched the masses of gulls that patrolled the shallow waters of the retreating tide, and noticed the small fishing boats coming through the gap from the estuary to the sea, the fragile crafts bobbing dangerously in the gathering sea.

"This is a beautiful place," he observed.

"This where our uncle used to train us in the use of weapons and where we learned how to control a horse in battle," Gwriad said.

"It is one of my most favourite places," Dafydd added, watching a large crab retreat back into the waves. "I've often come here when I needed to think about a problem."

240

Jon said nothing. He remembered his childhood on the other side of the river estuary, and how he had always been hungry and badly treated in the small, damp hut that he had formally known as home.

"My Lords, I need your support at this dangerous time!" The Prince spoke abruptly. He stared out at the darkening sky. "If we are to defend our beautiful country and be able to provide our children with a safe future, then we will have to make an effort now, no matter how difficult or painful that may be."

"I will support you, Prince Anarwd," Dafydd said immediately, looking questionably at Gwriad, "I will promise to create an overall plan for our area. It will show how many men we could realistically contribute to your standing army. I will work out the costs and the possible ways of raising the money to pay them, and how we can train, arm and feed them. The idea of replacing them on a yearly basis might involve offering promotion to those who agree to do a second year." It was clear that his mind was racing with ideas.

"I would like to volunteer to work with you, Prince Anarwd, now that you have lost your two generals," Jon said, finding himself breathing heavily, and being aware that his father was frowning at him.

"My Lords! That is good news!" the Prince embraced them both, while Gwriad stood like a rock, a grim expression on his face. "And you, Lord Gwriad, can I rely on your support?"

"Prince Anarwd, you know my military history since the time of King Gruffydd. Of course, I will support you, but on my own terms. I will not agree to leave my castle for long periods of time; I will not spend my days training men on the borders and I will not become a tax collector extracting money from the poor, who are the majority of the people on my lands." His face relaxed after he had said what he would not do. "What I will do, is to draw up a set of plans with you, that we can improve with time, and that will allow us to prepare for an invasion from whatever direction it comes, and I will help Dafydd organize our home-based training, and the defence of our own lands. But, I repeat, I will not leave my castle for long periods of time."

He looked out to sea. "I'm getting older. I have rediscovered my wife and I do not intend to waste the life I have left to me." He turned to Jon and with great emphasis spoke directly at him. "I will grant my permission for you to join Prince Anarwd's officer corps, even though you did not ask me." He cleared his throat. "However, my agreement is dependent on you making regular visits back to Aberteifi."

Jon was amazed when his unpredictable father embraced him in a bear hug.

When the Prince left the next day, he thought deeply about the way the outcome of the visit had changed from the prospect of no realistic agreement to a result that was better than he could have hoped for. As his horse consumed the miles, he reflected on how the Griffith Lords were a valuable ally, and how they should never be underestimated.

CHAPTER THIRTY

K ing William was angry, and when he raged the Lords kept quiet. He paced the wide floor of the main hall of his London palace, his voice thundering with rage. His cousin, and invaluable supporter, Earl Fitzosbern, stood like a statue looking into space, and made no reaction as William swore what he would do to Eadric the Wild, the latest Saxon Lord to rise up against the Norman rule.

"No sooner do I lay waste to the North, but the Western Midlands rise up!" He showered spittle around as he stormed about the hall. "Do they learn nothing? Surely this Eadric can understand that my army far exceeds his in numbers and training! What does he hope to achieve except the destruction of his lands? He must know how stupid this is?" He stared wildly around at his silent Lords. "Does anyone have the answer? I would have thought that my harrying of the North would have served as a warning to prevent any further uprising in England. For blood's sake, what drives this fool?"

There was total silence in the hall, as the Lords pretended they were not there.

"It's the Welsh, my Lord," Fitzosbern said quietly. "I have just received news that the Princes of North Wales have decided to join forces with this Saxon Lord. We have no idea of their numbers."

"Why was I not told of this?" William said, his voice dangerously low.

"I have only just received this news, my Lord," Fitzosbern stared at William's glowering face. "I would be honoured if I could have your permission to lead our forces against this rag-tag army of dissenters. I think the army in the North-East has ensured there will be no further uprisings there, and they would be useful soldiers with their recent experience."

The King's face relaxed. He wiped the spittle off his mouth, and took a deep breath. "You may all go, my Lords," he said waving a bejewelled hand.

As they silently filed out of the hall, the King put his arm around Fitzosbern's shoulders. "What would I do without you?" His roar of laughter caused raised eyebrows among the departing Lords.

"Come, my friend, let's study the map and see how soon we can engage these fools!" As they walked to his library, he grinned at William Fitzosbern, "We must remember that these Welsh Princes were fighting each other and their new allies before we came to bring them peace."

"They have difficulty understanding that obvious fact, my Lord," he laughed. Fitzosbern was used to the moods of his quixotic friend. It had ever been so.

They spent a while considering the campaign, and eventually settled on an area a day's march from the town of Shrewsbury which the rebel army had occupied. "We also have strong forces in Chester, and could march into this area from the North in a pincer attack," the King said. A dangerous smile crossed his face. "I could also send some hundreds of my personal guard from London as well. I want you to do more than defeat Eadric the Wild, I want you to punish the Welsh."

He poured two cups of wine, and made a silent toast. "I was prepared to allow them their little victory, but as they can't be trusted, I think this will be the time to show them that their mountains won't save them. After the certain defeat of this Shropshire rabble, I want you to march south and into Gwent, and bring the war to their precious country."

Fitzosbern studied the map thoughtfully. Although the Welsh tended to see themselves as two nations, he understood the King was going to treat them as one. "I'm sure I will have enough Northern forces to defeat Eadric's forces even if the Welsh show up in numbers. It would be helpful, my Lord, if your London army with fresh soldiers and equipment could meet me at Hereford. From there, with battle-hardened soldiers I will be able to plan a lightning attack into Gwent."

"Good," the King felt a wave of optimism. "There will come a time when I shall rule all of Britain, and when peace will be established throughout this contentious island." The King emptied his cup. "Whether they like it or not."

Within two weeks, the separate Norman forces were being assembled, in York, Chester and London. Fitzosbern traveled up to York to assemble the main army, while the Marcher Lord of Chester prepared his men for a lightning attack in support of this army, when it arrived. It was assumed that the recapturing of Shrewsbury would be easily accomplished and that they would then march quickly down to Hereford. Fitzosbern's main concern was to convince the Welsh that he was merely reinforcing this town and was not preparing for a wider offensive. The King gave orders for his personal guard to prepare to travel to Hereford, and for the supply wagons to be provisioned. The weather had become cold and wet, and his hope was that the campaign could be completed before snow closed the passes.

William assembled some officers. "I want you to go on ahead and make it known that the King is coming to supervise a complete reinforcement of Hereford's defences, so that there will be no further threat to the town. The area is rife with Welsh informants, and I want them to believe that this is a defensive action, not an offensive one. It will calm their worries when my army arrives." He stared out of his palace and watched the leaves being blown off the trees in his grounds. "Take enough troops to clear one section of the town in preparation for my arrival. My men will need barracks and stables." He walked back to look at his map. "Do it firmly, but without causing a general uprising. The Saxons in the town hate the Welsh, and most will be pleased to have their lives and property protected. Assure those who are inconvenienced that they will receive payment when I arrive."

"Should I mention how much, my Lord?" a young Lord asked.

"Tell them whatever you wish! This is a short-term occupation. When we've beaten the Welsh, they can have their wretched hovels back." His eyes flashed. "People have to learn to do as they're told!"

CHAPTER THIRTY-ONE

Aberteifi was basking in an unexpected warm spell and Gwriad, true to his promise, was assisting Dafydd in drawing up a list of the possible fighting men throughout Ceredigion. While his younger brother worked out the structure needed to assist Prince Anarwd on the border, Gwriad sent out orders for men to attend short meetings in all the villages. This involved getting the word out to the isolated farms and hamlets, and as an encouragement, he offered each man money for giving up a day's work.

For most, this was like a holiday. It gave them the chance to meet neighbours, set up deals and many took the opportunity for a rare visit to the village pubs. With this in mind, Gwriad had insisted that all meetings would be before mid-day to ensure that the men were sober. Wales was a matriarchal society, where women tended to run the homes and advise their husbands, and although the men did the fighting, it was not uncommon for women to take up arms to defend their families. Consequently, the villages where the meetings were to be held became an unexpected celebration for women and their families.

At each meeting there were some men who had served with Lord Gwriad when he commanded the Central Army at the time of King Gruffyd, a number had served with him when Prince Anarwd had attacked Earl Harold's palace, and a few had been involved in the recent battle with the Normans. However, many had never travelled and had never seen the man on whose land they lived and to whom they paid an annual tithe. Curiosity and excitement gripped each event, and Gwriad would appear with a well-armed cohort of soldiers, both to impress the peasants that something serious was to be discussed, and to keep order if necessary.

It was the right time of the year to call these meetings: the crops had been harvested, the animals were still being fattened in the fields, and people were beginning to prepare for winter. The warm weather was a rare bonus, and it was a good time to hunt and fish, and for social events. Gwriad sensed this as he explained the dangers of a Norman invasion and the plan that Prince Anarwd had for defending the country. He was not a man of great imagination or spontaneity, and having worked out his speech, he delivered the same one wherever he went.

"Nothing is easy in this life," he said, his voice carrying clear over each assembled gathering. "Even Lords get injured and die in battle!" A mutter of agreement always greeted this statement. "But we all, you and me, have no choice but to fight to defend our beloved country against these foreign invaders! We must look after our families and those we love. We are Welshmen and we will fight!" There was always a roar of agreement, and people waved their arms and embraced each other.

It was a much more thoughtful reaction when he explained how they would be needed to help defend the border. He promised they would be given training; that they would be paid during their year of service; and how it would be possible for those who volunteered for a second year to become sergeants. He explained that eventually the area would have plenty of experienced soldiers to help defend the communities from the foreigners if they launched an invasion.

"I am planning for the future, and all the other Lords are doing the same. Now listen, boys, you must give your name and age to this clerk here. As this is a year's commitment, we will not leave until the snow melts, but by then you must be ready to march to the border. I will let you know which of you has been chosen for the first year, and the rest of you will be given the chance in the years to come." He took out his sword and held it up above his head. "I've killed Saxons and Normans with this bloody sword, and I will be proud to have you in the army that I will send to Prince Anarwd!"

Everyone cheered.

"So! Give the clerk your name, and you will receive beer money!"

There was typically an unruly rush to form a line, which was when his soldiers became involved.

As Gwriad toured his lands, Dafydd worked on the numbers, and tried to bring some sense to the plan.

"We have a lot to consider, Gwriad. The time for invasion is past for this year, but we need to be ready as soon as winter is over," he stared into the fire. "Neither of us wants to lead the local army to the border, and we no longer have Jon to fall back on. We might have to take on that responsibility, whether we want to or not."

Gwriad scowled.

"Well, just in the first stage, anyway," Dafydd shrugged, "we have no choice. It is vital that the first year is a success, and once we get the men to Prince Anarwd, his sergeants will take over and get our men to face the fact that this is for a year, not for a quick fight and the chance to get home with some plunder. This is going to be a shock for many of them when this sinks in. We must lead them there, or they will desert on the way."

"Jon can take over once our men arrive at the border camp," Gwriad suggested. "A fort will have to be constructed, like the one our father built at the battle of Rhyd-y-Groes." His eyes glazed over.

"We will have to think of new ways of raising money," Dafydd nodded, as though agreeing with himself. "Our system works at the moment, but there will be outrage if we put a new tax on the people, no matter how logical it might appear to us." He sipped his wine. "We could build some large boats and re-establish the trading we used to have with Ireland."

"We won't have time to run a trading business and organize the creation of a standing army," Gwriad said dismissively. He was unwilling to take on anything more, and once the identification of the fighting men had been established, he had hoped to step back.

"I agree," Dafydd said. His eyes had suddenly brightened. "We could ask Angharad if she would like to take it on."

"Have you lost your mind?"

"Not at all. You may not have noticed, but since she has been here, she has reorganized the way the kitchens are run. She has insisted on some obvious improvements to the running of the jakes, which is why they no longer smell so badly. You must have noticed more children in the castle? Angharad thought it was wrong that Tegwen rarely met other children, and she has arranged for the local nobility and landowners to send their daughters to meet here for dancing, and singing. Once Angharad has identified a problem, she is determined to solve it."

Gwriad stared at his brother as though he was talking about some unknown creature. "Angharad?"

"You have been living in your own little world, Brother," Dafydd chided. "There is more to your wife than what happens in your bed." He laughed to see his brother so shocked. In the past, the roles had been reversed.

When asked, Angharad was happy to agree, and immediately spent much of her time writing long lists of what to sell and how to encourage trade, and then making Gwriad read her plans. Contacts with Irish traders that had been made during the reign of King Gruffydd were renewed, the local boatbuilding yard was enlarged and new apprentices were taken on, while local fishermen were encouraged to become short-term mariners. Gwriad's concern was that they should make some money before he went broke.

Meanwhile, Jon had settled in at Prince Anarwd's fortress in Morgannwg, and had become a close friend of the Prince's son, Alun, whose personal detachment of archers had made such an impact on the massed forces of the enemy during the last battle. The two young Lords had slipped naturally into the role of providing the support that Prince Anarwd needed, and had already begun to direct the expansion and fortification of the support camp they had previously used for their attacks on Hereford. Gwriad would be impressed.

"We are moving towards a time of greatness again!" the Prince spoke with a passion that his son recognized as a cornerstone of his father's personality, especially when it was enhanced with wine after a long day's work. "When the Lords of Aberteifi bring their men, and Prince Maredudd finally sorts out his dysfunctional family," he laughed good-naturedly, "we will have an army large enough to stop any incursions, which will allow us time to bring up our reserves, and defeat them."

"How are we paying for this, Father?" Alun did not wish to spoil the optimism of the evening, but it worried him as his father spoke of hundreds of men, all of whom would need feeding, training and arming, as well as paying.

"Oh, don't you worry about that, my boy. I've arranged a large loan from an Italian bank."

Alun stared at him in amazement. "But what did you offer as security?" His mind was frantically searching the possibilities.

"You might not know, my son, but I own several gold mines in Cornwall, and they are in safe hands. If we are invaded, they will remain untouched. That is the security I was able to offer. I am also in touch with Prince Rhodri ap Williams who was, during the reign of King Gruffydd, the Admiral of our small Southern fleet. He disappeared after the King was murdered, and his fleet fell apart without the necessary organization, but he's back and willing to use his knowledge to rebuild a trading fleet... if I provide the money." Anarwd gave them a toothy smile, and poured himself some more wine.

The two young Lords stared. This was the answer to their dreams. If a loan provided the ability to pay their soldiers, and if the loan could be paid off through the re-establishment of trade, then they could see a future for their defence of Wales. "I'm proud of you, Father," Alun said raising his mug.

"I've been in regular communication with Lord Dafydd, and he tells me that they are also intending to renew their trading as a way of paying for their soldiers. If only we could start meaningful talks with the Northern Princes, then we would really be in a position to be confident."

"I heard that some of the Princes are preparing to attack Chester," Alun said.

"Oh? That's not a good idea, unless they're able to double their forces." Anarwd scratched his beard thoughtfully. "They must know that Chester is well defended." He sat silently for a while staring at the fire. "I understand their Marcher Lord has increased his soldiers with help from King William." He sat back in his chair, deep in thought, "Have you heard of a Saxon Lord called Eadric the Wild?"

They both shook their heads.

"Is he important?" Alun asked.

"I hope not. The Saxons have never been good news for us. I heard Eadric was planning an uprising in a part of England close to northern Powis." Anarwd scowled. "He thinks because winter's approaching, that he can clear the area of Normans, and establish himself as a beacon to attract the local Saxon Lords in a general uprising. Who knows? Perhaps he's offering the Northern Welsh Princes a chance to retake some of their traditional lands, in exchange for their support?"

"Why is this bad news, my Lord?" Jon asked.

"Those Welsh Princes have always been a contentious lot. They can't agree among themselves, let alone working with the Saxons who have been their traditional enemies for generations. Unless they can muster a large army to make up for their lack of coordination, any contribution they make to Eadric the Wild's uprising will be minimal."

"Well, it keeps the Normans busy," Alun joked. "If the Northern Princes want to support a Saxon, then it's not our affair if they get a bloody nose. It might even remind them of what they lost when they murdered our King."

"I hope you're right. But, I don't think King William sees us as two separate areas. He might decide to teach the Welsh a lesson, and historically Powis, Brycheiniog and Mogannwg have always been seen as easier for invading armies than North Wales.

"Wasn't the great battle of Rhyd-y-Groes fought in Powys?" Jon asked innocently.

The Prince sniffed. "It was, indeed." He rubbed his beard thoughtfully. "Perhaps you're right. Perhaps I'm worrying too much. When the snow comes in a few weeks, I'll be quite relieved." His mood changed, "Let's get back to talking about this new army of ours. As soon as spring arrives, I want the soldiers from the west to assemble here, and for that to happen, we must be ready."

.   .   .

EADRIC THE WILD, ON HEARING that the expected Norman army from York was close by, took up a defensive position on a hill some miles north-east of Shrewsbury. It was not his choice. He would have preferred to fight the Normans from the security of the walls of Shrewsbury, and watch them suffer during a winter siege. He had tried to prevail on his new allies to hold back and to attack the Normans at the first sign of spring, when the enemy would be caught between their two forces, but the Welsh insisted on fighting while they had their army ready for battle.

"Once we have decided to fight, and have assembled our men, it is not a question of waiting out the winter in warm, well-supplied barracks," a

Prince explained. "We don't have that sort of supply line. We do not have the population that you and the Normans have, but we are prepared to fight for what we believe is ours. If we do not fight now, we will have to disband and return to our villages. Our personal guards are few in number, and when spring comes around it takes a long time to raise a large army. At this moment, we are offering you our support, and we must fight in the open. If you stay inside Shrewsbury when the Normans come, you have dreams of our arriving and breaking the siege: the enemy caught between our two forces. But it will not work out like that. You will remain bottled-up in the town, and we will have to face the Normans by ourselves. If you want our support, we must meet their army at a place that is agreeable to both of us. We have brave fighters and good archers, but we lack the powerful cavalry that the Normans possess."

"We have some cavalry but few archers. Like you we have a majority of foot soldiers." Eadric the Wild was a large man with an unruly mass of blond hair, hence his name, which most strangers misunderstood. Those who did not know him expected him to be a violent, unpredictable man, whereas in reality he was thoughtful and strong-minded. He hated the Normans, and was prepared to compromise his own plans for the sake of a much-needed alliance with the Welsh.

At first light their forces took up positions on a gently rolling hill on a cool, cloudy day that threatened rain. The Welsh and Saxon archers were formed up behind two lines of shields and swords, with the soldiers protected by sharpened stakes set in the ground in front of them to disrupt a cavalry charge. On both sides of the archers were blocks of soldiers armed with an array of shields, swords, axes and spears. The Welsh formed up on the left, the Saxons on the right, with their cavalry formed up behind them.

The Welsh Princes insisted on being on the brow of the hill from where they could survey the area. Eadric the Wild and his officers were to the right and further down the hill to control their large army of foot soldiers. There was wave after wave of chants and the banging of shields as the men geared themselves up for the expected battle, but as the day wore on the scouts reported that the Norman army had ceased to advance and had formed up a thousand paces away, behind another small hill.

There followed a heated argument. The Saxons wanting to advance and the Welsh unwilling to forsake their hill, fearing for the safety of their archers. In the early afternoon the scouts reported that the Normans were advancing in battle order, and the disgruntled soldiers began to chant and bang their shields to restore their morale.

The Normans marched into view and immediately attacked the Saxon and Welsh front lines, using their shields to protect themselves from the hail of arrows, and soon hand-to-hand fighting developed. The Saxons attacked on the right wing and were engaged by a heavy cavalry charge. Meanwhile the Welsh stormed down on the left wing, causing a Norman retreat until their cavalry became involved.

When the battle seemed to be moving in favour of the Saxon/Welsh alliance, trumpets from behind their lines announced the arrival of the Norman forces from Chester, led by a strong cavalry charge. The Welsh Princes fearing defeat, and not wanting to waste their soldiers, ordered a retreat, fighting their way through the Chester Normans, and leaving the main battle to the Saxons. The result was the bloody defeat of Eadric the Wild's forces and his death in a dispirited retreat.

Later that day, the Welsh Princes took up defensive positions on the high grounds of their beloved Wales, but the expected attack by the Normans never materialized, and eventually they retreated into the mountains to reassess their situation.

CHAPTER THIRTY-TWO

Jon was in Anarwd's stables carefully brushing down his horse, which he refused to leave to a stable boy. It had been a good day, and the planning for a permanent army was slowly becoming a reality. He looked forward to building a sense of pride in each of their centuries, formations of one hundred men built on the structure of the Roman armies.

"Jon!" Alun yelled as he rushed into the gloom of the huge stables. "My father wants us immediately!"

"What's happened?"

Alun glanced at the assembled stable boys. "I'll tell you as we run back. Family problems!" he yelled for the benefit of the curious crowd.

"Is this bad news?"

"The Normans have defeated the combined Welsh and Saxon armies near a place called Shrewsbury, near the Powis border," Alun gasped as he ran towards Anarwd's hall. As they entered, the Prince was bent over a map table.

"Here, boys!" He looked up at Jon, "Has Alun told you the news?"

Jon nodded, "The Normans won the battle?"

"Indeed. The Welsh Princes have retreated, safe behind their mountains, and the latest news is that the Normans are marching down south. Yesterday, I heard that King William's cavalry had reinforced Hereford, and that it was to defend it from further Welsh attack." He stared at them, his eyes wide and his chin thrust forward. "I'm thinking this could be reinforcements for an invasion of Gwent."

They spent the evening discussing the possibilities of a Norman attack; the various defences they could adopt; whether mobilization was possible; and, most importantly, how much time they might have if an invasion was going to happen.

"Jon, tomorrow I want you to travel back to your father and uncle and warn them. If they can get some of their men here as soon as possible, that would make me feel a lot more secure." The Prince attempted a smile, but it merely emphasized the worry that he was feeling. "Meanwhile, Alun, you and I will get our troops prepared for action."

He stood up and stretched. "We'd be so much better off without those bloody Northern Princes causing trouble!"

.   .   .

JON LEFT AT FIRST LIGHT with a small guard of local soldiers who had accompanied him when he'd recently left Aberteifi, and after three days of hard riding he reached the castle as darkness gathered. His unexpected arrival was seen by Angharad and Tegwen as a welcome surprise, and Jon gently excused himself from their embraces, pleading the need for a bath following his long journey. After a hurried supper, the men gathered around the fire in the Great Hall, while Angharad helped Alys prepare Tegwen for bed.

"That sounds bad," Gwriad said when he heard Prince Anarwd's news.

"Things are changing. In the past, if the Welsh lost a battle to the Saxons, we withdrew to lick our wounds and the Saxons went back to their side of the border. But I fear, as Anarwd does, that this Norman King wants to put an end to our independence. What we had not imagined is that we might be threatened at this time of the year." He emptied his cup of wine. "Those rabid Northern Princes! They couldn't even be trusted to fart together! It's all their fault."

He went off into a rant about how useless they were. Dafydd and Jon waited patiently for him to calm down.

"It won't be easy to raise our local army at this time of the year," Dafydd said thoughtfully.

"Too damn right!" Gwriad exploded. "When I recruited the local men, they were all thinking they would not be needed until next year. They're all preparing for winter now. They're making decisions on which animals to kill, and which will survive, depending on the feed in their barns. It's a busy time for them. They'll want to put the security of their families first, not march off to a possible invasion on the border. For most of them, the border could be the other side of the world. They will not want to endanger their families for some vague threat, especially as we might get early snow, and then they could be hanging around for weeks if the passes become blocked."

"If the Normans invade Gwent, which is most likely if they wanted to launch a full invasion, then there is only Prince Anarwd and his small army that could put up some reasonable opposition," Dafydd said. "The other areas will fight, but they will lack both the numbers and the organization of the Normans, and with their defeat, the security of all the families in the South-West will be threatened. Our local men must be made aware of this, and if we are determined to defend our borders, we must leave with our army in a week's time at the latest."

"It can't be done," Gwriad said with a dismissive flick of his hand. "When we turn up at the individual villages, it will be possible to alert the men to the danger and get them agreeing to a plan to gather at certain local points if we have to defend this area. But, to raise an army to march to the border at this time of the year will take some weeks to arrange, and don't forget the supplies, the wagons and the hundred-and-one things that are so much easier to arrange in the warm months."

"King Gruffydd was defeated in the winter," Jon said brightly.

"Thank you for reminding us," Gwriad said, giving him a withering glare.

"You're right, of course," Dafydd said absent-mindedly staring at the old hound asleep in front of the fire, "but if we start tomorrow, and aim to raise an army as soon as possible, we'll be in a better position to defend ourselves if they invade before we can march to the border."

"I must return tomorrow," Jon said, avoiding Gwriad's eyes. "I hope to help Prince Anarwd fight off the Normans until you arrive with our army."

Dafydd raised an eyebrow at his brother. "Of course you must, Jon, and we will do everything we can to gather at least some of our men to support you."

At that moment Angharad brought Tegwen into the hall for the ritual bedtime hugs and jokes, and while she was spending extra time with Jon, whom she had begun to hero-worship, Gwriad mentioned to Angharad that she should hand Tegwen over to Alys and return immediately. She raised her eyebrows, and gave him a knowing smile.

When she returned, Gwriad explained the situation and she immediately indicated she would like to help. "If the Normans invade, they might reach this far and we might have to withstand a siege," Dafydd said. Angharad nodded, her eyes alight with excitement. "We two, starting tomorrow, will try to raise an army, and I wondered if you would take on the job of getting the castle prepared for a siege?" She nodded vigorously. "Food, medical supplies and sleeping quarters for the villagers are your areas. Also, how to keep the castle from smelling like an open sewer?"

"This castle has never had a siege, and I believe will be difficult for the enemy to capture, especially if we get prepared," Dafydd said. "I'll get the sergeant to bring in piles of heavy stones, arrange buckets of oil and have plenty of long poles to push away scaling ladders."

"You'll need more fences to contain extra animals, and lots of buckets of water to deal with fire arrows," Jon said, determined to be part of the conversation, "and you'll need to stockpile arrows."

"Well, at least we'll be prepared and have plenty of notice if the Normans attack," Dafydd said. "Tomorrow, I'll call meetings at our village and at Llanduduch and have the men alerted to the fact that they may have to march or at least take refuge in our castle. The people can't bring all their animals and possessions if there is likely to be a siege, we won't have the space, and they will need time to get used to the idea." He turned to Angharad, "You might like to come with me. You might not remember the local people, but they will remember you, and after hearing you've returned, they will be keen to see you." He paused, "I'll introduce you to Derryth, our local Wise Woman. She'll be very helpful in preparing our medical supplies." He cleared his throat, "You'll like Derryth."

Angharad nodded, and understood in that moment that Derryth might be someone who was important to Dafydd. She turned to Jon, and formed a question with her hands.

"I'm leaving at first light, my Lady. I am needed by Prince Anarwd." He found it difficult to call her mother.

Angharad placed her hands on either side of his face and kissed his forehead. Then she sat back and smiled at him, and patted her heart.

Gwriad stood up and cleared his throat. He was unwilling to agree to Jon's departure, yet realized that his adopted son was a man, and was determined to do what he, Gwriad, would have done if the roles were reversed. He felt great pride in Jon, but was desperate not to lose him. As a way of changing the subject he began to pace about the hall.

"Thank God we've done all the grunt work. At least we have some idea of the numbers we can raise. I will concentrate on the North and alert the villages. If we have time to form an army to march east, all well and good, but at least we will get them prepared to fight to defend this area. I will send out Sergeant Gavin, and bring back those local men who have fought with me in the past, and I will send messengers to the others."

His earlier reluctance had been replaced by an enthusiasm that Dafydd suspected had a lot to do with Angharad's involvement, and a realization that if Jon had stayed he would be undertaking some of this work.

"How long do you think we have before they invade?" Jon asked.

"If they invade," Gwriad cautioned, moving strongly towards a more optimistic standpoint.

"But if we assume that they do intend to attack, it will take them at least a week or two to get organized," Dafydd said thoughtfully. "Then, they will have to defeat Prince Anarwd and his small but efficient army to which we should be able to add some hundreds of men. With us all working together we should be ready in time to give the Normans another beating!"

Jon stood up and raised his mug. "Here's to family! As the most recent family member, I feel we are more united now than we have ever been."

Everyone stood up and raised their cups; there was a warm optimistic feeling in the group, and they felt emboldened by each other. Gwriad drank deeply, and wiped his eyes.

At first light Jon left with his small guard. Gwriad and Angharad, warmly clad in the night robes, were at the gate to see him off, and Gwriad said a few words of encouragement while Angharad hugged him with tears in her eyes.

From the battlements, Dafydd and Tegwen watched Jon ride away. "Will Cousin Jon be alright?" she asked as she waved her small hand.

"Oh, yes," Dafydd said cheerfully, "I'm sure he'll be fine." He gave her a forced smile.

Tegwen looked up at him thoughtfully. "Yes. I think so too."

.   .   .

BETHAN WAS SHOWING WYNNY HOW she created the intense colours in her weavings, and the younger woman was keen to know, with the intention of eventually becoming a skilled weaver. Wynny was now a married woman and living in the 'man's dump' as Bethan called it. Her father had reluctantly agreed to her short engagement and a no-frills wedding, after his wife had pointed out that this was what Wynny wanted and it would save him a lot of money. "Your Wynny is like you," his wife said, "if you don't agree, she'll do it anyway, and you know you've got a good son-in-law in Iago, and even if he's not wanting to be a farmer he'll always be ready to help you."

At the back of the smithy, Iago was working on his new house, a permanent smile on his face. Whenever he was not needed in the forge, he was working to create a rural palace for his lusty wife. It was a good day for getting things done, as Idris had gone down south with his old horse and the wagon to collect a load of charcoal, and was not expected back until the evening.

Iago stopped at midday, and was just crossing the path to Bethan's house to share some soup and bread, when he saw Idris approaching, driving his old horse as though he was in a race.

"Get the women!" Idris yelled. He pulled up outside the forge, jumped down from the wagon, and led the old and exhausted horse to the trough. Bethan ran over with Wynny close behind and after a brief hug, Idris led them into his smithy. Outside a small group of curious neighbours waited to discover what had happened.

"The Normans have invaded Gwent," he said accepting a mug of beer. The others gasped and stared at each other as he downed the mug. "Prince Anarwd is gathering an army and he hopes to stop them before they reach Caerdydd."

"Why is he not fighting them in Gwent?" Iago asked.

"Because the Normans have a big army, and the Prince needs to gather his men. The messenger I spoke to said the enemy seems to be following the coastline, and unless the Prince can stop them, they could invade the whole of Southern Wales."

"Do you think they'll come up to our area?" Bethan chewed her thumb nail.

"Who knows?" Idris rubbed his face. "If they do, it means that the

Prince has failed to stop them. Nobody expected them to attack at this time of the year. You remember Lord Dafydd?" They all nodded. "He said when he was last here that he hoped the victory we had in the summer would make the Normans think twice before attacking us again."

"What do we do?" Bethan placed her arm around Wynny who was staring wide-eyed at Iago.

"Do we join Prince Anarwd and fight them?" He sounded excited by the prospect.

"I don't think so," Idris said forcefully. There was a noticeable sigh of relief from the women. "The messenger said things were moving fast, and Prince Anarwd will almost certainly have joined battle with them by now. We need to prepare ourselves for two events," he was speaking fast, his mind racing. "Either he has beaten them, and that will be the time to reinforce his army as he retakes Gwent, or he's been defeated, and we will have to pray the Normans don't come this way."

"If they come this way, do we fight them?" Iago wanted to appear a husband capable of defending his wife, but at the same time he was painfully aware that he had no fighting experience.

There was a moment of silence, and everyone looked at Idris. "If they come here in large numbers, it would be useless to oppose them. I understand that they are unlikely to cause trouble if they are just passing through. But if we attack them, they will destroy everything and everybody." He took in a deep breath, "That is what they did in Cornwall, according to the messenger."

"You mean we just let them take our country?" Iago sounded shocked.

"With luck, we will beat them. We can join up when we have something to join." Idris looked around the small room, his eyes resting on the weapons on the walls. "There are few, if any, of our neighbours who have any fighting experience, and you and I could do little to stop an invasion by ourselves."

"And if they come this way, what do we do?" Wynny sounded surprisingly composed.

"We build a hiding place in the forest, and we stock it with food and drink and our weapons. If we hear they're coming we will hide and see if they are going to attack us or just pass through. If we show no sign of fighting them, we may survive. Then, we will have to see how things develop. We can only fight back when we know the situation. Agreed?"

There was a long silence, and Iago realized they were waiting for him to speak. In his imagination he had thought of being a hero and fighting the Normans and impressing Wynny, but the cold reality of Idris' words had shattered his dream, and he realized how limited were their options. "Idris is right," he said forcefully, "we must prepare for the worst and only fight them if we have to."

Wynny fixed her blue eyes on Idris. "Are we going to stay here?"

"Where else would we go?" Idris raised his eyebrows.

"We could go west." It was such an unexpected statement, that they all stared at her.

"We could go where Angwen's gone!" Bethan exclaimed. "I mean where Angharad's gone." She turned to Wynny, "That's Lady Angharad now. My best friend." She faced Idris who seemed struck dumb. "We saved Lord Jon's life, Idris. You sold his father a helmet! They live in a castle!" She seemed lit up, her face suddenly alive. "You and Iago are valuable people. I know they'll want blacksmiths. That's where we must go!

Iago smiled at Wynny. "I think that's a good idea," he said. He was not given to long speeches, but since becoming a married man he had gained more confidence. "I think we should leave immediately. I don't want to live a life of constant fear. I want to take my wife to a safer place, away from the threat of the Normans. I don't want to live like a coward constantly fleeing into the forest in the hope we will be left alone. Let's go west."

Idris ran his hand down his ragged beard. He looked at Bethan who was smiling in a very enticing way. "Well done, Wynny," he said thoughtfully, "I think that's a fine idea. I'll be sad to leave this forge, but you're right, Iago, we have no future here." A smile developed on his face, "I have some money," he avoided Bethan's enquiring look, "and with that and some trading we'll get three horses, and put only the most important stuff in the wagon," he looked slightly embarrassed. "My horse is getting older, and I'm not leaving her."

They hugged each other, ate a quick meal and began to gather their few things. As darkness fell, Idris appeared with three horses which he had traded for his forge, and for Bethan's house. "They're no use to us anymore," he said to an amazed Bethan. "We'll leave when the last candle is out. We don't want people to find out too soon." He gathered them in a tight circle. "Tonight, we start a new life," he said. He was feeling emotional. "We are four strong people, and we're going west!"

CHAPTER THIRTY-THREE

It was two days later, on a cool blustery morning, when an exhausted sergeant from Prince Anarwd's personal guard, accompanied by a small detachment of soldiers, brought the unwelcome news that the Normans had invaded Gwent in an early morning attack.

Gwriad was away recruiting soldiers, and Dafydd and Angharad were at Llanduduch. The messenger and his troops were made comfortable by the servants and, unable to believe that he had almost killed himself getting to Aberteifi in record time, the disappointed sergeant drank beer with his men. Shortly after, the soldiers found a comfortable place in the stables and, helped by the steward, he climbed the stairs and collapsed on Dafydd's bed, and was immediately in a deep sleep.

When he awoke, it was getting dark and he gingerly made his way down to the Great Hall, where he met Gwriad coming through the door. Feeling considerably awkward, the officer quickly explained his presence and gave his message from Prince Anarwd.

"Prince Anarwd and his son have gathered their small army and intend to ambush the Normans before they advance too far into Wales," Gwriad explained later to the family. "He's asking for everyone to march immediately to Morgannwg so that he will have enough soldiers to be able to stand and fight these vermin. At the moment they greatly outnumber his army, and he can't risk a battle."

"So, Gwent is lost?" Dafydd tried to control the emotion in his voice.

"Yes, it would seem so, until we beat them back. Most likely they intend to attack along the coastline," Gwriad said quietly. "They seem to be making for Caerdydd, so that is where we should make a stand."

Gwriad called for his steward. "Make sure the messenger and his men are well fed, and then send him to me. Quick as you can." The steward bowed and left with a smile; he liked giving orders.

By the next morning the messenger and his detachment had left; the castle's sergeant was organizing for a siege, while Dafydd and Gwriad were arranging for an immediate muster. "Whatever our numbers, I will march tomorrow," Gwriad said. "Dafydd, you will follow in two days with the rest who have responded to the call, and with the supply train." He turned to Angharad and gave her a hug. "You, my love, will be in charge of the castle until we return." He did not say "if", and Angharad nodded, determined not to show any emotion.

Throughout the day everyone concentrated on the job they had been allotted, and it was a tired group that sat for supper around the big table. Gwriad had said he wanted the meal to be memorable, and Megan, the cook, had driven her kitchen staff to produce such a meal. Everyone dressed for the occasion, and Tegwen, although delighted to sit between Angharad and Dafydd, missed Jon.

Gwriad had ordered his best wine, and his face was flushed when he reported that he expected more than three hundred soldiers to gather outside the castle by mid-morning of the following day. He tried to sound up-beat in his presentation. Dafydd also gave a positive list of those villages that were further away, but had still promised a large response. He indicated that he should be able to follow with the wagon train within two days. Angharad included Tegwen when she passed around a written report of the castle's preparedness.

"Is Prince Maredudd going to help?" Tegwen asked innocently. "I like him. He's a nice man."

Gwriad gave her one of his big-eyed simpleton expressions, which made everyone laugh. "He most certainly will, my little lovely. I think he intends to frighten the enemy with his collection of bones." Tegwen chuckled, and everyone joined in.

"He discovered the dragon of Wales, Uncle," she said importantly. "I think he discovered the dragon in your flag."

It was at this moment of relaxed family fun, that the steward entered and whispered in Gwriad's ear. There was a moment of anticipation as everyone watched, knowing something important had happened. The steward disappeared, and Gwriad stood up. For a moment he seemed lost for words. "We have some new reports from Morgannwg," he blew out his cheeks. "Angharad, I would be grateful if you would take Tegwen to bed."

He blew Tegwen a kiss, and Dafydd gave her a hug and, understanding that something important had happened, she quietly took Angharad's hand and went up the stairs without a backwards glance.

When Angharad returned, Gwriad and Dafydd were sitting around the fire with an officer from Prince Anarwd's personal guard. The man looked hollow-eyed with exhaustion, and his uniform was grubby and exhibited patches of blood. Dafydd was refilling his cup.

"This is Lord Iestyn ap Llywarch who has taken over from the late Lord Edwin," said Gwriad doing the introductions. The stranger made a move to rise.

"Please don't get up, my Lord," Dafydd said, giving him a bow. "I have heard of you from Prince Anarwd's son, Prince Alun, who is a close friend of Jon's." He noticed the man's face twitch slightly, as though he had been bitten by a bug.

"Lord Iestyn wanted to wait until we were all gathered," Gwriad announced gravely. It was clear it was not good news.

Lord Iestyn gave his message in a flat monotone, that indicated his controlled emotion. He announced that Prince Anarwd and his son Alun were both killed in a disastrous battle. "We had set up an ambush on what the scouts had said was an isolated regiment of Norman foot soldiers that seemed to be taking a short cut towards Caerdydd. We attacked, and after an initial success the Normans formed a shield wall that forced us to regroup. At that point in the battle we had superior numbers, and committed all our cavalry in an attempt to break their unity. No sooner had the cavalry been committed, but the Normans unexpectedly attacked from behind us with a huge cavalry charge that decimated our formations. Suddenly, we were outnumbered, and unable to form any unified defence. It was a massacre. We lost the core of our army."

He sat back in his chair, barely able to control the emotions that racked him. Gwriad handed him a full cup of wine, and the others waited silently, while he composed himself. "I was leading our cavalry, and we were soon fragmented and fighting for our survival. After a brave stand, our army began to retreat and then to scatter. It was a rout." He took a deep breath, and clutched his arm, trying to cover the blood that was seeping through his uniform. Nobody had noticed how he had used only his right arm.

"My Lord!" Dafydd rushed to Iestyn as he collapsed back in his chair. "Emrys! Fetch the Wise Woman!" he yelled.

Gwriad called for the servants and gave a hailstorm of orders.

Angharad appeared and had the officer laid carefully on the main table, where she and Alys gently removed his uniform to reveal a gruesome wound across his muscular arm, partly covered by a make-shift bandage that was soaked in blood.

She had begun to wash the wound when Derryth appeared clutching a large basket. Angharad immediately indicated that she should take over, and she and Alys dismissed the servants and acted as Derryth's helpers. The brothers withdrew to their chairs around the fire, and discussed the situation.

"He didn't mention Jon," Gwriad said in a hoarse whisper.

"That must be a good sign," Dafydd muttered, encouragingly. "He would know Jon, who was close to Alun and to Anarwd, and he must know we are his family." He cleared his throat. "If Jon had been killed he would have told us."

"Yes. Yes, I'm sure your right, Dafydd," he took a deep breath.

"Indeed." He reached over and squeezed Dafydd's arm. "The death of Alun and his father are a great loss. Prince Anarwd was our leader, our uncrowned King of South Wales. In a short while we have lost our three most experienced generals, and Alun was becoming a fine image of his father. This news is as bad as I could imagine it." He tossed more wood on the fire. "I think we can hope that Jon is still alive. We must hold on to that hope."

"I agree. He's strong and resilient, and I'm sure he will get back to us as soon as he can," Dafydd was conscious of the fact that it was a weak speech, and sat staring into the fire. There was a long pause as both men stared into the hot flames and watched as the thick logs were gradually consumed. It seemed symbolic. "If only we had acted sooner."

"I imagine the Normans intend to capture Caerdydd, and then spend some days behind its walls, while they rest their army and take care of their injured and their horses," Gwriad said. The others nodded.

"We should hear from Prince Maredudd tomorrow," Dafydd said, "that is, if he's heard the news. I'll arrange for a messenger to be sent at first light, just in case."

"Do we intend to fight the Normans before they get here, or wait to see if they lay siege to our castle?"

"Good question," Gwriad said. "My gut reaction is that we will not have enough soldiers to fight them on the battlefield. I think our best approach will be to maintain constant ambushes on their columns. We will use our knowledge of our mountains, rivers and forests to keep up an unending war on them until they retreat back to England."

"That might work as they push into Wales, but once they have captured an area, they will threaten the local population with reprisals if there are any further attacks. They used this very successfully in stamping out all opposition in Cornwall," Dafydd said and continued to stare into the fire. "I agree with you that well-planned ambushes might slow them down, and may eventually force them to retire, but if that plan does not work, then we must stop them crossing the Teifi. That must be our final retreat."

The discussion went on until Angharad indicated that her work with Derryth was done. Gwriad called some servants and arranged for the injured man to be placed on a pallet in a storage room, and Derryth explained what she had done and how she thought he would recover. When she left, Gwriad noticed that Dafydd went with her.

At first light Dafydd dispatched a messenger to Prince Maredudd, and others were sent to spread word of the disaster around the area. It was agreed that there would be a general muster at Aberteifi, and that the Aberteifi bridge and the one at Nghenarth Falls would be fortified. It was hoped that they could join forces with other local Lords, but as Dafydd pointed out, "They have always been unwilling to lose their personal control of their areas, and without an overall King or warlord we have never managed to agree to any unified plan. They have never believed that an enemy would ever reach them, and always left most of the defence to those who controlled the border. Even under King Gruffydd, they always put their own local power before general unity."

They spent the day fortifying the castle, and arranging for the local accommodation of a constant stream of men from the outlying villages. Sergeant Gavin had never been so busy or so happy. For him it was the culmination of his ambition: to be a man of importance and authority.

Derryth agreed to move into the castle to nurse the injured Lord Iestyn, who showed no signs of recovery.

Over the next few days, the pace of activity did not slacken, and soon there were more than two hundred men who had answered the call, providing a sense of security for the area, but also providing a host of unexpected problems. As Dafydd explained, "Idle men cause trouble. We must appoint more sergeants and insist that some of the local Nobles take on some of the responsibility for their training and discipline."

It was on the fourth day that messengers from Morgannwg confirmed that Caerdydd had fallen, and that the Normans were pushing along the coastal paths through southern Deheubarth and seemed to be making for St. Davids. Local Lords along the coast had put up a fruitless resistance, and the Normans were making great use of their fast-moving cavalry to create panic.

"If they aren't stopped then they will eventually threaten Llanduduch," Gwriad pointed out, "and we will face them with only the Teifi Bridge preventing them from reaching our castle."

"Unless they cross the river on the tidal plain when the tide is out," Dafydd said quietly. "Anyone can walk across at low tide." There was a long silence as the two men considered the options.

Finally, Dafydd interrupted their thoughts. "Father Williams will guide Llanduduch. The Normans respect priests, and if he counsels non-resistance among the men, the Normans may leave them alone."

It was later in the day that a messenger from Prince Maredudd arrived with further bad news. The Prince reported that his vainglorious relative, the obnoxious Prince Eoin, had led the local Deheubarth forces into a foolhardy attack on Norman forces that were well prepared for battle. The subsequent defeat had been devastating with huge loss of life, including Prince Eoin, who died leading a vainglorious charge on a shield wall.

"The death of that idiot is the only bit of good news!" Gwriad ranted. "I had proposed we join forces, but no, that imbecile wanted the glory of an historic victory. Thank the Gods that Prince Maredudd is still alive and is prepared to defend his castle. If the Normans reach the Towy, then they will almost certainly besiege Caerfyrddin Castle. If that happens, we have to discuss whether we leave this side of the river and try to break the siege, or whether we sit tight and prepare our defences." Gwriad looked expectantly at Dafydd.

"Breaking a siege is, historically, only successful if you have a bigger army than the one doing the besieging, and it's rare that the forces inside are able to add much to the result of the eventual battle. I think we should stay put and conserve our forces. I discussed this situation once with Father Willams. He said that armies liked big battles, after which the victor was able to go home or settle down in the area they had won. He said that a gradual invasion with ambushes and no final battle, made it difficult for the invading army to keep going, as they were constantly losing soldiers to both death and injury, and because they had to station troops in the areas they captured. Perhaps the Normans will be satisfied with this latest victory, and run out of steam?"

"Indeed," Gwriad said enthusiastically. "That is the best thought we've had today. Good for Father Williams."

At that moment, the warning bell began to toll, and the relative quiet of the castle was replaced by the thunder of running feet, the yelling of orders and the frightened cry of "Normans?" Gwriad raced to the battlements with Dafydd close behind, in time to see a small detachment of horsemen facing the local soldiers at the guard post on the bridge. It was quickly apparent that no fighting was taking place and that the horsemen were being allowed through.

"Open the gates!" Gwriad yelled.

As the horsemen crossed the bridge and turned to file up towards the castle, an excited voice screamed out: "It's Jon, it's Cousin Jon!" Tegwen ran past the soldiers manning the walls until she reached her father and Gwriad. "It's Jon! I knew he would come back!"

That evening, as the light faded, they gathered on the castle walls overlooking the swelling river and the bridge. Gwriad had his arm around Angharad, Jon held Tegwen's hand and Dafydd, with a big smile on his face, had his arm around Derryth's waist. Nobody spoke, but all felt their dream of a future was still possible.

HISTORICAL NOTE: It took the Normans more than 200 years to finally conquer all of Wales, although most parts of the country were subject to random Norman attacks by the year 1099. There is evidence to indicate that only the southern part of Deheubarth was attacked in the first wave of the invasion, and that the Aberteifi area remained unaffected for many years, partly due to the topography of the area and the spirited opposition of the Welsh people.

ABOUT THE AUTHOR
BARRY MATHIAS B.ED M.A.

A writer of historical fiction and short stories, Barry emigrated from England with his wife and two daughters in 1990 and moved to Pender Island in 1995. He taught English at Camosun College in Victoria and later opened the bookstore on Pender Island. He created the unique Southern Gulf Islands Car Stops program, is a keen supporter of community and is involved in theatre and Island transportation initiatives. *The Final Dream* is his sixth novel, the third and final in the Celtic Dreams Trilogy.

OTHER NOVELS

The Ancient Bloodlines Trilogy

Book 1: *Power in the Dark*

Book 2: *Shadow of the Swords*

Book 3: *Keeper of the Grail*

Website: **www.barrymathias.net**

Made in the USA
Monee, IL
30 November 2020